*NEW YORK TIMES* BESTSELLER

# Zorro

## Isabel Allende

D0050467

## ALSO BY ISABEL ALLENDE

*The House of the Spirits*

*Of Love and Shadows*

*Eva Luna*

*The Stories of Eva Luna*

*The Infinite Plan*

*Paula*

*Aphrodite: A Memoir of the Senses*

*Daughter of Fortune*

*Portrait in Sepia*

*My Invented Country*

## For Young Adults

*City of the Beasts*

*Kingdom of the Golden Dragon*

*Forest of the Pygmies*

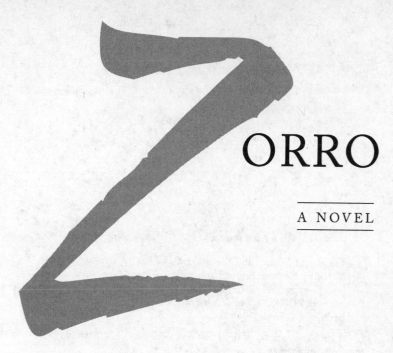

# ZORRO

## A NOVEL

## Isabel Allende

Translated from the Spanish
by Margaret Sayers Peden

HARPER ● PERENNIAL

NEW YORK ● LONDON ● TORONTO ● SYDNEY

HARPER ● PERENNIAL

A hardcover edition of this book was published in 2005 by Harper-Collins Publishers.

P.S.™ is a trademark of HarperCollins Publishers.

HarperCollins books may be purchased for educational, business, or sales promotional use. For information please write: Special Markets Department, HarperCollins Publishers, 10 East 53rd Street, New York, NY 10022.

FIRST HARPER PERENNIAL EDITION PUBLISHED 2006.

Map © 2005 by Jan Adkins

Designed by Nancy Singer Olaguera

Library of Congress Cataloging-in-Publication Data is available upon request.

ISBN-10: 0-06-077900-4 (pbk.)
ISBN-13: 978-0-06-077900-9 (pbk.)

06 07 08 09 10 ❖/RRD 10 9 8 7 6 5 4 3 2 1

# ZORRO

Franciscan
Missions
*established in*
Spanish
California
*along the*
*Camino Real*

Sonoma, 1823
San Rafael, 1817
Dolores, 1776
Santa Clara, 1777
San Jose, 1797
Santa Cruz, 1791
San Juan Batísta, 1797
Carmel, 1790
Soledad, 1791
San Antonio, 1771
San Miguel, 1797
San Luis Obispo, 1772
Santa Ines, 1804
La Purisima, 1787
Santa Barbara, 1786
San Fernando, 1797
San Buenaventura, 1782
San Gabriel, 1777
San Juan Capistrano, 1776
San Luis Rey, 1798
San Diego, 1769

*El Camino Real*

*the*
CALIFORNIA
MISSION
SYSTEM

*the Baja Peninsula*

Pueblo los Angeles

New Orleans
BARRATARIA
GULF
*of*
MEXICO

Mexico City

CARIBBEAN OC

PACIFIC OCEAN

*Isthmus of Panama*

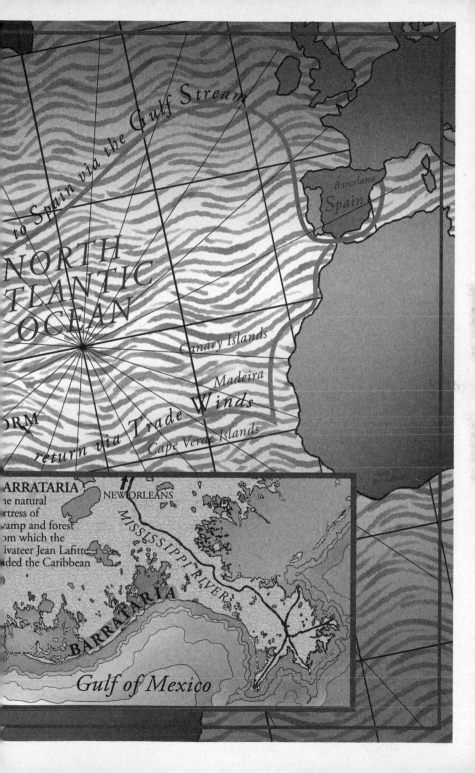

to Spain via the Gulf Stream

NORTH
ATLANTIC
OCEAN

Barcelona
*Spain*

*Canary Islands*

*Madeira*

*Trade Winds*

*Cape Verde Islands*

STORM

*return via Trade Winds*

BARRATARIA
the natural
fortress of
swamp and forest
from which the
privateer Jean Lafitte
raided the Caribbean

NEW ORLEANS

MISSISSIPPI RIVER

BARRATARIA

Gulf of Mexico

This is the story of Diego de la Vega and of how he became the legendary Zorro. At last I am able to reveal his identity, which for so many years we kept secret, though I do so with some unease, since a blank page is more intimidating to me than the naked swords of Moncada's men. With this document I intend to set the record straight before the slanderers who are determined to defame Zorro have their say. Our enemies are many, as is often the case with those who defend the weak, rescue damsels in distress, and humiliate the powerful. Naturally, every idealist attracts enemies, but we prefer to count our friends, who are much greater in number. I am compelled to recount these adventures because it serves little purpose for Diego to risk his life for the sake of justice if no one knows of it. Heroism is a badly remunerated occupation, and often it leads to an early end, which is why it appeals to fanatics or persons with an unhealthy fascination with death. There are all too few heroes with a romantic heart and a fun-loving nature. Let me say it straight out: there is no one like Zorro.

PART ONE

## California, 1790–1810

et us begin at the beginning, at an event without which Diego de la Vega would not have been born. It happened in Alta California, in the San Gabriel mission in the year 1790 of Our Lord. At that time the mission was under the charge of Padre Mendoza, a Franciscan who had the shoulders of a woodcutter and a much younger appearance than his forty well-lived years warranted. He was energetic and commanding, and the most difficult part of his ministry was to emulate the humility and sweet nature of Saint Francis of Assisi. There were other Franciscan friars in the region supervising the twenty-three missions and preaching the word of Christ among a multitude of Indians from the Chumash, Shoshone, and other tribes who were not always overly cordial in welcoming them. The natives of the coast of California had a network of trade and commerce that had functioned for thousands of years. Their surroundings were very rich in natural resources, and the tribes developed different specialties. The Spanish were impressed with the Chumash economy, so complex that it could be compared to that of China. The Indians had a monetary system based on shells, and they regularly organized fairs that served as an opportunity to exchange goods as well as contract marriages.

Those native peoples were confounded by the mystery of the crucified man the whites worshipped, and they could not understand the advantage of living contrary to their inclinations in this world in order to enjoy a hypothetical well-being in another. In the paradise of the Christians, they might take their ease on a cloud and strum a harp with the angels, but the truth was that in the afterworld most would rather hunt bears with their ancestors in the land of the Great Spirit. Another thing they could not understand was why the foreigners planted a flag in the ground, marked off imaginary lines, claimed that area as theirs, and then took offense if anyone came onto it in pursuit of a deer. The concept that you could possess land was as unfathomable to them as that of dividing up the sea. When Padre Mendoza received news that several tribes led by a warrior wearing a wolf's head had risen up against the whites, he sent up prayers for the victims, but he was not overly worried; he was sure that San Gabriel would be safe. Being a communicant of his mission was a privilege, as demonstrated by the number of native families that sought his protection in exchange for being baptized, and who happily stayed on beneath his roof. The padre had never had to call on soldiers to "recruit" converts. He attributed the recent insurrection, the first in Alta California, to abuses inflicted by Spanish troops and to the severity of his fellow missionaries. The many small local tribes had different customs and communicated using a system of signing. They had never banded together for any reason other than trade, and certainly not in a common war. According to Padre Mendoza, those poor creatures were innocent lambs of God who sinned out of ignorance, not vice. If they were rebelling against the colonizers, they must have good reason.

Father Mendoza worked tirelessly, elbow to elbow with the Indians, in the fields, tanning hides, and grinding corn. In the evenings, when everyone else was resting, he treated injuries from minor accidents or pulled a rotted tooth. In addition, he taught the catechism classes and arithmetic, to enable the neophytes, as the baptized Indians were called, to count hides, candles, corn, and cows, but no reading or writing, which was learning that had no practical application in that place. At night he made wine, kept accounts, wrote in his notebooks, and prayed. By dawn he was ringing the church bell to call people to mass, and after morning rites he supervised breakfast with a watchful eye, so no one would go without food. For these reasons—and not an excess of self-confidence or vanity—he was convinced that the rebelling tribes would not attack his mission. However, when the bad news continued to arrive for several weeks, he finally paid attention. He sent a pair of his most loyal scouts to find out what was happening in other parts of the region; in no time at all they had located the warring Indians and gathered a full report, owing to the fact that they were received as brothers by the very Indians they were sent to spy on. They returned and told the missionary that a hero who had emerged from the depths of the forest and was possessed by the spirit of a wolf had succeeded in uniting several tribes; their goal was to drive the Spanish from the lands of their Indian ancestors, where they had always been free to hunt. The rebels lacked a clear strategy; they simply attacked missions and towns on the impulse of the moment, burning whatever lay in their path, and then disappearing as quickly as they had come. They filled out their ranks by recruiting neophytes who had not gone soft from the prolonged humiliation of serving whites. The scouts added that this Chief Gray Wolf had his eye on San Gabriel, not because of any particular quarrel with Padre Mendoza, whom he had nothing against, but because of the location of the good father's mission. In view of this information, the missionary had to take measures. He was not disposed to lose the fruit of his labor of years, and even less disposed to have his neophytes spirited away. Once they left the mission, his Indians would fall prey to sin and return to living like savages, he wrote in a message he sent to Captain Alejandro de la Vega, asking for immediate aid. He feared the worst, he added, because the rebels were very near by; they could attack at any moment, and he could not defend himself without adequate military reinforcements. He sent identical missives to the Presidio in San Diego, entrusted to two swift horsemen using different routes, so if one were intercepted the other would reach the fort.

A few days later Captain Alejandro de la Vega galloped into the mission. He leaped from his horse, tore off his heavy uniform jacket, his neckerchief, and his hat, and thrust his head into the trough where women were rinsing their wash. His horse was covered with foam; it had carried its rider many leagues, along with all the gear of the Spanish dragoon: lance, sword, heavy leather shield, and carbine, plus saddle. De la Vega was accompanied by a couple of men and several packhorses loaded with supplies. Padre Mendoza rushed out to welcome the captain with open arms, but when he saw that he had brought only two trail-weary soldiers as depleted as their mounts, he could not disguise his frustration.

"I am sorry, Padre. I have no available soldiers other than these two good men," the captain apologized as he wiped his face on his shirtsleeve. "The rest of the detachment stayed behind in Pueblo de los Angeles, which is also threatened by the uprisings."

"May God come to our aid, since Spain does not," the priest grumbled.

"Do you know how many Indians will attack?"

"Not many here know how to count accurately, Captain, but according to my scouts it might be as many as five hundred."

"That means no more than a hundred and fifty, Padre. We can defend ourselves. Who can we count on?" asked Alejandro de la Vega.

"On me, for one—I was a soldier before I was a priest—and on two other missionaries, who are young and brave. We have three soldiers who live here, assigned to the mission. We also have a few muskets and carbines, ammunition, two swords, and the gunpowder we use in the quarry."

"How many converts?"

"My son, let us be realistic. Most of the Indians will not fight against their own kind," the missionary explained. "At most, I can count on a half dozen who were brought up here, and a few women who can help us load our weapons. I do not want to risk the lives of my neophytes, Captain—they're like children. I look after them as if they were my own."

"Very well, Padre. Shoulders to the wheel, and may God help us. From what I see, the church is the strongest building in the mission. We will defend ourselves there," said the captain.

For the next few days, no one rested in San Gabriel; even small children were set to work. Padre Mendoza, who was expert in reading the human soul, knew he could not trust the loyalty of the neophytes once they saw themselves surrounded by free Indians. He was disquieted when he caught a glimpse of a savage gleam in a worker's eye and witnessed the unwilling compliance with his orders: the neophytes dropped stones, burst bags of sand, got tangled in the ropes, and overturned tubs of tar. Forced by circumstances, Padre Mendoza violated his own rule of compassion and, without a twinge of doubt, as punishment sentenced two Indians to the stocks and dealt out ten lashes to a third. Then he had the door to the single women's lodge reinforced with heavy planks; it was sound as a prison, constructed so that the most daring could not get out to wander in the moonlight with their lovers. A solid, windowless building of thick adobe, it had the additional advantage that it could be bolted from outside with an iron bar and padlocks. That was where they locked up most of the male neophytes, shackled at the ankles to prevent them from collaborating with the enemy at the hour of battle.

"The Indians are afraid of us, Padre Mendoza. They think our magic is very powerful," said Captain de la Vega, patting the butt of his carbine.

"Believe me, Captain, these people know what firearms are, all right, though as yet they haven't discovered how they function. What the Indians truly fear is the cross of Christ," the missionary replied, pointing to the altar.

"Well, then, we will give them a demonstration of the power of cross and gunpowder." The captain laughed, and laid out his plan.

The mission defenders gathered in the church, where they barricaded the doors with sacks of sand and stationed nests containing firearms at strategic points. It was Captain de la Vega's opinion that as long as they kept the attackers at a distance, so they could reload the carbines and muskets, the scales would be tipped in their favor, but in hand-to-hand fighting they would be at a tremendous disadvantage since the Indians far surpassed them in numbers and ferocity.

Padre Mendoza had nothing but admiration for this captain's boldness. De la Vega was about thirty and already a veteran soldier, seasoned in the Italian wars, from which he bore proud scars. He was the third son of a family of hidalgos whose lineage could be traced back to El Cid. His ancestors had fought the Moors beneath the Catholic standards of Isabel and Ferdinand; for all the high praise of their courage, however, and all the blood shed for Spain, they received no fortune, only honor. Upon the death of their father, Alejandro's eldest brother inherited the family home, a hundred-year-old stone building towering over a piece of arid land in Castille. The church claimed the second brother, and so it fell to de la Vega to be a soldier; there was no other destiny for a young man of his breeding. In payment for bravery exhibited in Italy, he was given a pouchful of gold doubloons and authorization to go to the New World to better his fortunes. That was how he ended up in Alta California, to which he traveled in the company of Doña Eulalia de Callís, the wife of the governor, Pedro Fages, known as The Bear because of his bad temper and the number of those beasts brought down by his own hand. Padre Mendoza had heard the gossip about the epic voyage of Doña Eulalia, a lady with a temperament as fiery as that of her husband. Her caravan took six months to cover the distance between Mexico City, where she lived like a princess, and Monterey, the inhospitable military fortress where her husband awaited. It traveled at a turtle's pace, dragging along a train of oxcarts and an endless line of mules laden with luggage. Every place the party stopped, they organized a courtly diversion that tended to last several days. It was said that the governor's wife was an eccentric, that she bathed her body in jenny's milk and colored her hair—which fell to her heels—with the red salves of Venetian courtesans, and that from pure excess, not Christian virtue, she gave away her silk and brocade gowns to cover the naked Indians she came across along the road. And last, most scandalous of all, were tales of how she had clung to the handsome Captain Alejandro de la Vega. "But who am I, a poor Franciscan, to judge this lady?" Padre Mendoza mused, glancing out of the corner of his eye at de la Vega and wondering, with irrepressible curiosity, how much truth there was in the rumors.

In their letters to the director of missions in Mexico, the friars complained, "The Indians prefer to live unclothed, in straw huts, armed with bow and arrow, with no education, government, religion, or respect for authority, and dedicated entirely to satisfying their shameless appetites, as if the miraculous waters of baptism had never washed away their sins." The Indians' insistence on clinging to their customs had to be the work of Satan—there was no other explanation—which is why the friars went out to hunt down and lasso the deserters and then whipped their doctrine of love and forgiveness into them.

Padre Mendoza had lived a rather dissolute youth before he became a missionary. The idea of satisfying shameless appetites was not new to him, and for that reason he sympathized with the neophytes. He had, besides, a secret admiration for his rivals the Jesuits because they had progressive ideas; they were not like other religious groups, including the majority of his Franciscan brothers, who made a virtue of ignorance. Some years earlier, when he was preparing to assume responsibility for the San Gabriel mission, he had read with great interest the report of a Jean François de La Pérouse, a traveler who described the neophytes in the California missions as sad beings bereft of personality and robbed of spirit, who reminded him of the traumatized black slaves on the plantations of the Caribbean. The Spanish authorities attributed La Pérouse's opinions to the regrettable fact that the man was French, but his writings made a profound impression on Padre Mendoza. Deep in his heart, he had almost as much faith in science as he did in God, which is why he decided to transform the mission into a model of prosperity and justice. He proposed to win followers among the Indians through persuasion, rather than lassos, and to retain them with good works rather than lashings. He achieved that goal in spectacular fashion. Under his direction, the neophytes' existence improved to such a degree that had La Pérouse passed through, he would have been astounded. Padre Mendoza could have boasted—though he never did—that the number of baptized at San Gabriel had tripled, and that runaway converts never stayed away long; the fugitives always returned, repentant. Despite the hard work and sexual restrictions, the Indians came back because the padre showed them mercy and because they had never before had three meals a day and a solid roof to shelter them from storms. The mission attracted travelers from the Americas and Spain who came to this remote territory to learn the secret of Padre Mendoza's success. They were impressed with the fields of grains and vegetables; with the vine-yards producing good wine; with the irrigation system, inspired by Roman aqueducts; with the stables and corrals; with the flocks grazing on hills as far as the eye could see; with the storehouses filled with tanned hides and *botas* of tallow. They marveled at the peaceful pass-ing of the days and the meekness of the converts, whose fame as bas-ket weavers and leather workers was spreading beyond the borders of the province. "Full belly, happy heart," was the favorite saying of Padre Mendoza, who had been obsessed with good nutrition ever since he'd heard of sailors suffering from scurvy when a lemon could have pre-vented their agony. He believed that it is easier to save the soul if the body is healthy, and therefore the first thing he did when he came to the mission was replace the eternal corn mush that was the basic diet of the neophytes with meat stew, vegetables, and lard for tortillas. He provided milk for the children only with Herculean effort, because every pail of foaming liquid came at the cost of wrestling a wild range cow. It took three husky men to milk one of them, and often the cow won. The missionary fought the children's distaste for milk with the same method he used to purge them once a month for intestinal worms: he tied them up, pinched their nostrils together, and thrust a funnel into their mouths. Such determination had to yield results; thanks to the funnel, the children grew up strong and with resilient characters. The population of San Gabriel was worm-free, and it was the only colony spared the deadly epidemics that decimated others, although sometimes a cold or an attack of common diarrhea dis-patched a neophyte to the other world.

Wednesday at noon the Indians attacked. In spite of their silent approach, when they reached the environs of the mission the defend-ers were waiting. The first impression the fiery warriors had was that the mission was deserted: there was nothing in the courtyard but a pair of bone-thin dogs and a distraught hen. They did not see a soul anywhere and they heard no voices and saw no smoke coming from the huts. Some of the attacking Indians were on horseback and clad in animal hides, but most were naked and on foot. All were armed with bows and arrows, clubs, and spears. In the lead galloped the mysterious chief, wearing red and black war paint; a wolf's pelt served as a kind of tunic, and a complete wolf's head topped a flowing mane of black hair. The rider's face was barely visible through its maws.

Within a few minutes' time the raiders had raced through the mission, setting fire to the straw huts and destroying clay vessels, casks, tools, looms . . . anything within reach, all without encountering the least resistance. Their chilling war yells and the speed at which they moved drowned out the calls of the male neophytes locked in the women's lodge. Heady with success, they charged the church, loosing a rain of arrows that bounced uselessly off the strong adobe walls. At the order of Chief Gray Wolf they attempted to ram the heavy wood doors, which trembled with the impact but did not yield. The noise and war whoops rose in volume with each thwarted attempt to breach the door, while some of the more athletic and emboldened warriors looked for a way to climb up to the narrow window slits and bell tower.

Inside the church the tension became more unbearable with each echoing crash upon the door. The defenders—four missionaries, five soldiers, and eight neophytes—were in place along the sides of the nave, protected behind sacks of sand and backed up by Indian girls ready to reload their weapons. De la Vega had trained them the best he could, but not too much could be expected of a few terrified girls who had never seen a musket at close range. Their task consisted of a series of actions that any soldier performed without thinking but which had taken the captain hours to explain to them. Once the weapon was ready, the girl handed it to the man responsible for firing it, and prepared another. When the trigger was pulled, a spark lit the powder in the pan, which in turn ignited the main charge in the barrel. Damp powder, flint residue, and blocked touch-holes often caused misfires; it was not unusual, in addition, to forget to remove the rammer from the barrel before firing.

"Don't be discouraged, that's how it goes in war. Noise and commotion. If one weapon fails to work, the next one should soon be ready, so you can keep right on killing," Alejandro de la Vega instructed.

The remaining females and all the children of the mission were secured in a room behind the altar. Padre Mendoza had sworn to protect them with his life. The valiant defenders, with fingers on the trigger and half their faces protected by kerchiefs soaked in vinegar and water, silently awaited the order from the captain, the one person unfazed by the Indians' yelling and the slamming of bodies against the door. Coldly, de la Vega calculated how long the wood door would resist; the success of his plan depended on acting at the precise moment and in perfect coordination. He had not had occasion to fight since the campaigns in Italy several years before, but he was lucid and calm. The only sign that betrayed apprehension was the tickling in his hands that he always felt before firing.

Eventually the Indians tired of crashing against the door and fell back to catch their breath and receive instructions from their chief. A terrifying silence replaced the former hullabaloo. That was the moment de la Vega chose to give the signal. The church bell began to ring furiously as four neophytes lighted rags dipped in tar, producing a thick, stinking cloud. Two others lifted the heavy crossbar bolting the door. The peals aroused the Indians, who regrouped to attack again. This time the door unexpectedly yielded at the first contact; they tumbled into the church, fell over each other, and collided with the barrier of sacks of sand and rocks. Coming from the brilliant light outdoors, they were blind in the darkness and smoke of the interior. From the sides of the nave, ten muskets fired in unison, wounding several Indians who fell in their tracks, screaming. The captain lighted a fuse and within a few seconds the flame had reached the sacks filled with a mixture of gunpowder, tallow, and lead that had been set up in front of the barricade. The explosion rocked the foundations of the church, set off a hail of metal particles and pebbles, and shook the large wood cross over the altar right off the wall. Protected behind their parapets, the defenders were able to reload their weapons and get off a second round before the first arrows flew through the air. Several Indians lay sprawled on the floor, and those who were still on their feet were coughing and tearing from the smoke, making an easy target for the defenders' musket balls.

De la Vega's crew reloaded three times before Chief Gray Wolf, followed by the most courageous warriors, swarmed over the barricade and surged into the nave of the church. In the chaos of battle, Captain Alejandro de la Vega never took his eyes off the Indian chief; soon he broke free of the braves surrounding him and leapt toward the chief, roaring like a wild beast, sword in hand. He brought down his blade with all his strength, but it slashed through empty air because Chief Gray Wolf's instinct had warned him, and he had dodged to the side, avoiding the blow. The momentum of the swing threw the captain off balance; he lunged forward, tripped, and fell to his knees as his sword struck the ground and snapped in two. With a howl of triumph, the Indian lifted his lance to run the captain through, but the gesture was never completed. A blow to the nape of the neck felled the chief, who dropped facedown on the floor, where he lay motionless.

"May God forgive me!" exclaimed Padre Mendoza, who was wielding a musket by the muzzle, landing blows right and left with ferocious pleasure.

To the surprise of Captain de la Vega, who had thought he was a dead man, a dark pool was rapidly forming around the chief, and the proud wolf's head was turning red. Padre Mendoza crowned his inappropriate jubilation with a stout kick to the inert body of the fallen chief. All he had to do was smell the gunpowder and he had reverted to the bloodthirsty soldier he had been in his youth. Almost instantly, the word spread among the Indians that their chief was down; they began to fall back, at first hesitantly and then at top speed, vanishing into the distance. The victors, dripping with sweat and half suffocated, waited until the dust of the attacker's retreat had settled before they went outside to draw a breath of fresh air. A salvo of shots fired into the air was added to the crazed ringing of the church bell; that and the boisterous hurrahs of men and women with a new lease on life drowned out the moans of the wounded and the hysterical weeping of the women and children still locked behind the altar, swooning in the smoke.

Padre Mendoza rolled up the sleeves of his blood-soaked cassock and set about restoring his mission to normal, unaware that he had lost an ear and that the blood was not his enemies' but his own. He totted up the mission's minimal losses and sent two prayers up to heaven, giving thanks for their triumph but also asking forgiveness for having lost all trace of Christian compassion in the heat of the battle. Two of his soldiers had suffered minor wounds, and an arrow had pierced the arm of one of the missionaries. They had one death to mourn, that of a fifteen-year-old Indian girl who had helped load the weapons. She had fallen faceup, her clubbed skull cracked open, her large, dark eyes wide with surprise. While Padre Mendoza was organizing his band to put out the fires, bind up the wounded, and bury the dead, Captain Alejandro de la Vega, with another sword in hand, was searching the nave of the church, looking for the body of the Indian chief, with the idea of impaling his head on a pike and planting it at the entrance of the mission to discourage anyone who might cherish the idea of following his example. He found Chief Gray Wolf where he had fallen, barely a pathetic bundle in the puddle of his own blood. With one sweep of his hand the captain jerked off the wolf's head and with the toe of his boot turned over the body, which seemed much smaller than it had while flourishing a spear. Still blind with rage and panting from the exertion of the battle, de la Vega grabbed the chief by his black hair and lifted his sword to decapitate him with a single stroke, but just before he swung, the Indian opened his eyes and looked at the captain with an unexpected expression of curiosity.

"Blessed Virgin Mary, he's alive!" exclaimed de la Vega, stepping back.

Even more than the fact that his enemy was still breathing, he was surprised by the beauty of his elongated, caramel-colored, thick-lashed eyes, the limpid eyes of a deer set in a face covered with blood and war paint. De la Vega dropped his sword, knelt, and put his hand beneath the chief's neck, carefully pulling him up to a sitting position. The deer eyes closed and a long moan escaped the parted lips. The captain looked around and found that they were alone in this part of the church, very near the altar. On an impulse, he lifted the wounded Indian, meaning to throw him over his shoulder, but the chief was much lighter than de la Vega had expected. He carried him in his arms as he would a child, threading his way among sacks of sand and rock, weapons, and the bodies of the dead, which still had not been removed by the missionaries, and stepped outside the church into the light of that autumn day, which he would remember for the rest of his life.

"He's alive, Padre," he announced, laying the wounded chief on the ground.

"Too bad, Captain, because we will still have to execute him," replied Padre Mendoza, who by now had a shirt rolled around his head like a turban to stanch the blood flowing from his lopped-off ear.

Alejandro de la Vega could never explain why instead of seizing the moment to decapitate his enemy, he hurried off to look for water and rags to sponge his injuries. Helped by a young female neophyte, he parted the heavy black hair and rinsed the long wound, which began to bleed again at contact with the water. He palpated the skull, verifying that there was an angry wound but that the bone was intact. He had seen worse in war. He took up a curved needle used for making mattresses and a length of horsehair that Padre Mendoza had put to soak in brandy, and stitched up the scalp. Then he washed off the chief's face, noting the light skin and delicate features. With his dagger he slit the bloody wolf-skin tunic to see whether there were other wounds, and as he did so he grunted with shock.

"He's a woman!" he shouted, horrified.

Padre Mendoza and the others came running up, only to stand and stare, mute with amazement, at the virginal breasts of the warrior.

"It's going to be much more difficult to kill him now," Padre Mendoza sighed finally.

†

Her name was Toypurnia, and she was barely twenty years old. She had been able to convince the warriors of several tribes to follow her because she was preceded by a legend. Her mother was White Owl, a shaman and healer from the Gabrieleno tribe, and her father was a sailor, a deserter from a Spanish ship. He had lived for years in hiding among the Indians, until he was carried off by a bout with pneumonia; his daughter was an adolescent at the time. Toypurnia learned the basics of the Spanish language from her father, and from her mother, the use of medicinal plants and the traditions of her people. Her extraordinary destiny was manifest only a few months after birth, on an afternoon when her mother left her sleeping beneath a tree while she bathed in the river. A wolf had approached the bundle wrapped in skins, picked it up in its jaws, and dragged it off into the woods. A desperate White Owl followed the animal's tracks for several days, but found no trace of the baby girl. During that summer the mother's hair turned white, and the tribe continued to search, until the last hope of finding the child had evaporated. At that point a ceremony was performed to guide her to the vast plains of the Great Spirit. White Owl refused to participate in the rites and never stopped scanning the horizon; she felt in her bones that her daughter was still alive. One early morning at the beginning of winter a filthy little creature emerged from the mist; she was naked and covered with dirt, and she was crawling with her nose to the ground. It was the lost child, growling like a dog and smelling like a wild animal. They named her Toypurnia, which in the language of her tribe means Daughter-of-Wolf, and they raised her as if she were a boy, with a spear and a bow and arrow, because she had come out of the forest with a fearless heart.

Alejandro de la Vega learned these things in the days following the battle, straight from the mouths of the Indian prisoners who were locked in the lodge, moaning over their wounds and humiliation. Padre Mendoza had decided to free them as they mended, since he could not hold them captive indefinitely, and without their chief they seemed to have returned to their former docile and indifferent state.

He did not want to whip them, as he was certain they deserved, because punishing them would merely provoke more resentment, and neither did he mean to convert them to his faith, because it seemed to him that none of them had the makings of a Christian; they would be rotten apples spoiling the purity of his flock. It did not escape the padre's attention that young Toypurnia exercised a strong fascination over Captain de la Vega, who looked for any excuse to keep going down to the underground wine cellar where they held the captive. The missionary had two good reasons for choosing the cellar for her prison: first, he could keep it locked, and second, the darkness would give Toypurnia opportunity to meditate on her actions. Since the Indians assured him that their chief could turn into a wolf and escape from any confinement, he took the additional precaution of tying her with leather thongs to the rough planks that served as her cot. The young woman hovered for several days between unconsciousness and nightmares, bathed in feverish sweat, and fed spoonfuls of milk, wine, and honey by Captain de la Vega's own hand. From time to time she waked in total darkness and feared that she had been blinded, but other times she opened her eyes in the trembling light of a candle and saw the face of a stranger calling her name.

One week later, Toypurnia took her first secret steps on the arm of the handsome captain, who had decided to ignore Padre Mendoza's orders to keep her bound and in the dark. By then, the two were able to communicate, since she remembered the fragmentary Spanish her father had taught her and he made the effort to learn words in her tongue. When Padre Mendoza surprised them holding hands, he decided it was time to consider that his prisoner was well, and proceed with her sentencing. There was nothing further from his nature than to execute anyone—in truth, he didn't even know how to do it—but he was responsible for the safety of the mission, and of his neophytes, and willingly or not this woman had caused several deaths. Sadly, he reminded the captain that in Spain the penalty for crimes of rebellion and banditry, like Toypurnia's, was death by garrote, with the iron collar slowly choking off her life.

"We are not in Spain," the captain replied, shuddering.

"I assume that you agree with me, Captain, that for as long as this woman is alive we are all in danger; she will rally the tribes again. There will be no garrote—that is too cruel—but with pain in my heart, I say that she will have to be hanged. There is no alternative."

"This woman is a mestiza, Padre, half Spanish by blood. You have jurisdiction over the Indians in your charge, but not over her. Only the governor of Alta California can set her sentence," the captain argued.

Padre Mendoza, for whom the idea of being the cause of another human's death was too heavy a burden, immediately seized upon that logic. De la Vega offered personally to go to Monterey and ask Pedro Fages to decide Toypurnia's fate, and the missionary accepted with a deep sigh of release.

Alejandro de la Vega reached Monterey in less time than was normally required for a rider to cover that distance; he was in a hurry to carry out his project, and he wanted to avoid the raiding Indians. He traveled alone, and at a gallop, stopping at missions along the road to change his horse and sleep a few hours. He had followed that trail before, and he knew it well, but he was always awed by the magnificence of nature: endless forests, a thousand varieties of animals and birds, streams and gentle slopes, the white sands of the beaches of the Pacific. He had no unpleasant encounters with Indians: they were wandering around in the hills without a chief and without a purpose, demoralized. If Padre Mendoza's predictions were correct, their enthusiasm had been punctured completely, and it would take years for them to reorganize. The Presidio, built on an isolated promontory seven hundred leagues from Mexico City and half the world away from Madrid, was as gloomy as a dungeon, a monstrosity of stone and mortar that served as headquarters for a small contingent of soldiers, the only company of the governor and his family. That day a thick fog amplified the cries of the seagulls and the crashing of waves upon the rocks.

Pedro Fages received the captain in a nearly bare room in which small windows admitted very little light but failed, on the other hand, to keep out the icy wind off the sea. The walls were covered with mounted bear heads, swords, pistols, and Doña Eulalia de Callís's coat of arms, embroidered in gold but worn now, and almost humble. In the way of furniture, there were a dozen bare wood chairs, an enormous armoire, and a military table. The ceiling was black with soot and the floor was tamped-down earth, the same as in the rudest barracks. The governor was a corpulent man with a colossal voice and the rare virtue of being immune to flattery and corruption. He wielded power with a quiet conviction that it was his accursed fate to lead Alta California out of barbarism, whatever the price. He compared himself to the first Spanish conquistadors, who had added a great part of the world to the empire, and he carried out his obligation with a sense of history, although if truth be known, he would have preferred to enjoy his wife's fortune in Barcelona, as she asked him daily to do. An orderly served them red wine in crystal goblets from Bohemia carried thousands of miles in the trunks of Eulalia de Callís, a refinement in strong contrast to the rude furnishings of the fort. The two men toasted the far-off homeland and their friendship, commenting on the revolution in France, in which the people had taken up arms against the king. That had happened more than a year before, but the news had just reached Monterey. They agreed that there was no reason to be alarmed; surely by this time order would have been restored, and King Louis XVI would be back on the throne, though they thought he was a poor specimen of a man and not worthy of their sympathy. Deep down, they were happy that the French were killing each other, but good manners prevented them from expressing that aloud. Somewhere in the distance they could hear the muted sound of voices and yelling, which gradually grew so loud that it was impossible to ignore.

"Forgive me, Captain. These women . . . ," said Pedro Fages, with a gesture of impatience.

"And is Her Excellency, Doña Eulalia, well?" inquired Alejandro de la Vega, blushing to his ear tips.

Pedro Fages pierced him with a steely glance, trying to make out his intentions. He was up to date on what people were saying about this handsome captain and *his* wife; he wasn't deaf. No one could understand, he least of all, why it should take Doña Eulalia six months to reach Monterey when the trip could be made in much less time. It was said that the journey was drawn out on purpose because the two wanted to be together. Added to that was the exaggerated version of an assault by bandits in which supposedly de la Vega had risked his life to save hers. That was not the real story, but Pedro Fages never learned that. The attackers were a half dozen Indians, fired up by alcohol, who went tearing off the moment they heard the first shots; nothing more. And as far as the injury to de la Vega's leg went, that had not come about in defending Doña Eulalia de Callís, as rumor had it, but from a minor goring from a wild cow. Pedro Fages prided himself on being a good judge of human nature—he had not been exercising power for many years for nothing—and after studying Alejandro de la Vega, he decided that it was pointless to waste suspicions on this man; he was sure that the captain had delivered his wife to him with her virtue intact. He knew his wife very well. If those two had really fallen in love, no human or divine power would have persuaded Eulalia to leave her lover and go back to her husband. Perhaps there had been a kind of platonic affinity between them, but nothing that would cause him to lose sleep, the governor concluded.

In the meantime, the uproar of servants running through the corridors, doors slamming, and shouting continued. Alejandro de la Vega, like the whole world, knew of the couple's fights, as epic as their reconciliations. He had heard that in their fits the Fages threw crockery at each other's heads, and that on more than one occasion Don Pedro had drawn his sword against her, but also that afterward they locked themselves in their room for several days to make love. The robust governor thumped the table, making the cups dance, and confessed to his guest that Eulalia had been in her room for five days in a white-hot rage.

"She misses the refinement she is used to," he said, just as a maniacal howl shook the walls.

"Perhaps she feels a little lonely, Excellency," muttered de la Vega, just to fill the awkward silence.

"I have promised her that in three years we will return to either Mexico City or Spain, but she doesn't want to hear that. My patience has run out, Captain de la Vega. I am going to send her to the nearest mission so the friars can put her to work with the Indians. We'll see then whether she learns to respect me!" Fages roared.

"Will you allow me to have a few words with your lady, Excellency?" the captain inquired.

During those five stormy days the governor's wife had refused to see anyone, including her three-year-old son. The teary-eyed child was sniveling, curled up on the floor outside her door, so frightened that he wet himself every time his father beat on the door with his cane. The only person allowed to cross the threshold was the Indian girl who carried in food and carried out the chamber pot. However, when Eulalia learned that Alejandro de la Vega had come to visit and wanted to see her, her hysteria disappeared in a minute. She washed her face, put up her long braid, and dressed in a mauve-colored gown, with all her pearls. Pedro Fages watched her enter, as splendid and smiling as on her best days, and he entertained a hope for a steamy reconciliation, even though he was not ready to forgive her too quickly; the woman deserved some punishment. That night during the austere dinner, in a dining room as gloomy as the hall of weapons, Eulalia de Callís and Pedro Fages, casting their guest in the role of witness, threw recriminations in each other's faces that would curdle the soul. Alejandro de la Vega took refuge in an uncomfortable silence until the moment dessert was served. By then the wine had taken effect, and the wrath of husband and wife was beginning to cool, so the captain set forth the reason for his visit. He explained that Toypurnia had Spanish blood. He described her bravery and intelligence, although he avoided mention of her beauty, and he begged the governor to be indulgent, praising his reputation for being compassionate and asking for clemency in the name of their mutual friendship. Pedro Fages did not need further pleading; the rosy glow of Eulalia's décolletage had begun to distract him, and he consented to change the death penalty to a sentence of twenty years in prison.

"In prison that woman will become a martyr for the Indians," Eulalia interrupted. "Simply saying her name will be enough to cause them to rebel again. I have a better solution. First of all, she must be baptized, as God wills. Then you bring her to me and I will take charge of the problem. I wager that in a year's time I will have converted this Toypurnia, Daughter-of-Wolf, wild Indian, into a Christian Spanish lady. In that way we will destroy her influence over the Indians once and for all."

"And in doing so, you will have something to do, and someone to keep you company," her husband added good-naturedly.

And so it was done. It was left to Alejandro de la Vega himself to go to San Gabriel to collect the prisoner and bring her back to Monterey—to the relief of Padre Mendoza, who could not be rid of her too quickly. She was a volcano waiting to explode in the mission, where the neophytes still had not recovered from the tumult of war. Toypurnia was baptized under the name of Regina María de la Inmaculada Concepción, but she immediately forgot most of it and went only by Regina. Padre Mendoza dressed her in the rough cloth robe the neophytes wore, strung a medal of the Virgin around her neck, helped her onto her horse, since her hands were tied, and gave her his blessing. As soon as they had left the low buildings of the mission behind, Captain de la Vega untied the captive's hands and, with a sweeping gesture indicating the immensity of the horizon, invited her to escape. Regina thought it over for a few minutes, and must have calculated that if she were captured a second time there would be no mercy, for she shook her head no. Or perhaps it was not merely fear but the same burning emotion that clouded the mind of the Spaniard. In any case, without a trace of rebellion, she followed him throughout the trip, which he strung out as long as possible because he imagined he would never see her again. Alejandro de la Vega savored every step they took along the Camino Real, every night they slept under the stars without touching, every time that they waded together in the ocean, all the while waging stubborn combat against desire and imagination. He knew that a de la Vega, an hidalgo, a man of honor and lineage, could never dream of living his life with a mestiza woman. If he had hoped that those days on horseback with Regina, traveling through the solitudes of California, would cool his ardor, he was in for a disappointment; when, inevitably, they reached the Presidio at Monterey, he was as wildly in love as a teenager. He had to call upon his long discipline as a soldier to be able to say good-bye to the woman, and silently swear by all that was holy that he would never try to communicate with her again.

Three years later, Pedro Fages kept the promise he had made to his wife and resigned his post as governor of Alta California so that he could return to civilization. At heart, he was happy with that decision because exercising power had always seemed a thankless task. The couple loaded up mule teams and oxcarts with their trunks, gathered together their small court, and began the march to Mexico City, where Eulalia de Callís had furnished a baroque palace with all the grandeur befitting her rank. Of necessity, they stopped at every town and mission along the road to rest and to be feted by the colonists. Despite their mercurial natures, the Fages were loved, because he had governed with justice and she had a reputation for being wildly generous. In Pueblo de los Angeles, the Spanish colonists pooled their resources with those of the nearby San Gabriel mission, the most prosperous in the province and only a few leagues from the town, and gave the travelers a reception worthy of their station. The town, built in the style of colonial Spanish cities, was a large square with a central plaza, well planned for growth and prosperity, although at that moment it had only four principal streets and a hundred or so houses of cane and mud. There was also a tavern—its back room served as a general store—a church, a jail, and a half dozen adobe, stone, and tile-roofed buildings where the authorities lived. Despite the small number of inhabitants and the scarcity of ready cash, the colonists were famous for their hospitality and for the continuous cycle of parties they offered throughout the year. Guitars, trumpets, violins, and pianos enlivened the nights on Saturdays, and every Sunday they gathered to dance the fandango. The visit of the governor and his wife was the best excuse to celebrate they'd had since the town was founded. They placed arches covered with flags and paper flowers around the plaza, they set long tables with white cloths, and everyone capable of playing an instrument was recruited for the soirée, including a couple of prisoners who were freed from the stocks when it was learned that they could strum a guitar. Padre Mendoza brought his neophytes, several casks of his best wine, two cows, and an assortment of pigs, hens, and ducks to be sacrificed for the occasion. The preparations took several months, and during that time people talked about nothing else. The women stitched gowns for the gala, the men polished their silver buttons and buckles, the musicians practiced the dance music in vogue in Mexico City, the cooks worked like slaves to prepare the most sumptuous banquet ever seen in their town.

Captain Alejandro de la Vega had been put in charge of public order and safety during the visitors' stay. From the moment he learned they would be coming, the image of Regina tormented him day and night. He wondered what had become of her during those three centuries of separation, how she had survived in the dark Presidio in Monterey, and whether she would remember him. His doubts evaporated the night of the fiesta, when amid the light of the torches and sound of the orchestra he saw a dazzling girl dressed and coiffed in the European mode, and instantly recognized those burnt-sugar-colored eyes. She picked him out of the crowd and without missing a beat walked toward him, stopping before him with the most serious expression in the world. The captain, his heart within an ace of shattering, intended to hold out his hand to invite her to dance. Instead, out gushed a proposal of marriage. It was not an impromptu impulse; he had been thinking about her for three years and had reached the conclusion that a stain on his impeccable lineage would be far better than living without her. He realized that he would never be able to present her to his family or to society in Spain, but he didn't care. For her, he was ready to put down roots in California and never leave the New World. Regina accepted him;

she had loved him secretly since those days when he nursed her back to life in Padre Mendoza's wine cellar.

And that is how the governor's festive visit in Pueblo de los Angeles came to be crowned with the wedding of the captain and the mysterious lady-in-waiting to Eulalia de Callís. Padre Mendoza, who had let his hair grow to his shoulders to mask the horrible scar left by his severed ear, performed the ceremony, even though he tried up to the last moment to talk the captain out of marrying. He was not overly concerned that the bride was a mestiza—many Spaniards married Indian girls—it was the suspicion that beneath Regina's perfect European lady's looks lurked Toypurnia, Daughter-of-Wolf. Pedro Fages personally escorted the bride to the altar; he was convinced that she had saved his marriage, for in Eulalia's eagerness to educate the girl, her nature had sweetened slightly, and she had stopped tormenting her husband with her fits. Considering that he also owed his wife's life to Alejandro de la Vega, if the gossip was to be believed, he decided that this was a good occasion to be generous. With a flourish of his pen he signed over the title for a ranch and several thousand head of cattle to the brand-new couple, since it was in his power to distribute land among the colonists. He drew the perimeters on a map, following the caprice of the pencil, and later, when the real borders of the ranch were verified, it turned out that they enclosed a vast territory of pasturelands, hills, forests, rivers, and beach. It took several days to ride across the property on horseback: it was the largest and best-located spread in the region. Without having solicited it, Alejandro de la Vega found himself a wealthy man. Some weeks later, when people began to call him Don Alejandro, he resigned from the king's army in order to devote himself entirely to prospering in this new land. One year later, he was elected alcalde of Pueblo de los Angeles.

De la Vega built a large, solid, and unpretentious home of adobe, with a red tile roof and floors of rough clay tiles. He decorated his house with heavy furniture built by a Galician carpenter in the town, with no consideration for aesthetics, only for durability. The location of the house was enviable: close to the beach and a short distance from both Pueblo de los Angeles and the mission of San Gabriel. The large Mexican hacienda-style house stood on a hill, and its orientation offered a panoramic view of coast and sea. Nearby were the sinister natural tar deposits where no one came willingly because the souls of the dead trapped in the pitch wandered there. Between the beach and the hacienda lay a labyrinth of caves, a sacred place to the Indians, as feared as the tar pits. Indians did not go there, out of respect for their ancestors, nor did the Spanish because of frequent landslides, and because it was easy to get lost in that maze.

Alejandro de la Vega installed several Indian families and mestizo vaqueros on his property, branded his herd, and began to raise purebred horses, using breeding stock he had imported from Mexico. In his spare time he set up a small soap factory and devoted himself to experiments in the kitchen, trying to find the perfect formula for smoking meat seasoned with chili peppers. He was trying to produce a dry but savory meat that would last months without going bad. This experiment consumed all his time and filled the sky with volcanic smoke the wind carried far out to sea, altering the behavior of the whales. He calculated that if he found the precise balance between flavor and resistance to spoiling, he could sell the product to the army and to the ships. He felt that it was a tremendous waste to strip the hide and fat off the cattle and lose mountains of good meat. While her husband multiplied the number of cattle, sheep, and horses on the ranch, directed the politics of the town, and did business with the merchant ships, Regina busied herself by looking after the Indians on the hacienda. She had no interest at all in the social life of the colony, and with Olympian indifference ignored the gossip circulating about her. Behind her back, everyone commented on her unsociable and arrogant nature, her more than doubtful origins, her escapades on horseback, her naked bathing in the sea. However, since she had arrived as a protégée of the Fages, the minuscule social set of Pueblo de los Angeles was at first prepared to take her to their collective bosom without asking questions, but Regina herself bowed out. Soon the dresses that had been made for her under Eulalia de Callís's guidance hung abandoned in the armoires, devoured by moths. She felt more comfortable going barefoot and wearing the rough clothing of the neophytes. And so her day went by. In the evening, when she anticipated that Alejandro would soon be home, she bathed, coiled her hair into a casual bun, and put on a simple dress that gave her the innocent appearance of a novitiate. Her husband, blind with love and occupied in his business affairs, shrugged off the betraying signs of Regina's state of mind. He wanted to see her happy and never asked her if she was, for fear that she would tell him the truth. He attributed his wife's strange behavior to inexperience in life as a newlywed, and to her closed nature. He preferred not to think that the well-behaved lady sitting with him at the dinner table was the same ferociously painted warrior who had attacked the San Gabriel mission several years before. He believed that motherhood would cure his wife of her last bad habits, but despite the long, frequent tumbles in the four-pillared bed they shared, the wished-for child did not arrive until 1795.

During the months of her pregnancy, Regina became even more silent and untamed. Using the pretext of comfort, she stopped dressing and combing her hair in the European style. She went down to the ocean to swim with the dolphins that came long distances to mate near the beach, accompanied by a sweet neophyte named Ana, whom Padre Mendoza had sent from the mission. She, too, was pregnant, but she had no husband and had tenaciously refused to confess the identity of the man who had seduced her. The missionary did not want to keep this bad example among his neophytes, but neither could he find it in his heart to banish her from the mission, so he ended up sending her to be a servant in the de la Vega family. It turned out to be a good idea; a quiet complicity between Regina and Ana blossomed immediately, something good for them both, for the former gained a companion and the second won protection. It had been Ana's idea to swim with the dolphins, sacred creatures that swim in circles to keep the world safe and in good order. Those huge, velvety mammals knew that the two women were pregnant, and lightly brushed past them to give them strength and courage at the moment of giving birth.

In the third week of May, Ana and Regina had their babies. The births coincided with the famous week of the fires, recorded in the annals of Pueblo de los Angeles as the most catastrophic since the founding of the city. Every summer the residents had to resign themselves to watching some of the forest go up in flames because a spark had touched off dry pastureland, but they had never seen anything like the fires that May. Normally the fires were welcome, because they cleared out debris and created space for tender growth the following spring, but that year, according to Padre Mendoza, they were God's punishment for so much unrepentant sin in the colony. The flames burned down several ranches as they passed, destroying both dwellings and cattle that had nowhere to escape to. On Sunday the winds changed and the fire stopped one mile away from the de la Vega hacienda, which was interpreted by the Indians as an excellent augury for the two newborns in the house. The spirit of the dolphins helped Ana during her delivery, but not Regina. While the former had her baby in four hours, kneeling on the ground and with a young kitchen girl as her only help, Regina was in labor for fifty hours, a torment that she bore stoically as she clamped down on the stick between her teeth. Alejandro de la Vega, desperate, summoned the one midwife in Pueblo de los Angeles, but she admitted defeat when she realized that the baby was crosswise in the womb and that Regina lacked the strength to keep fighting. So Alejandro called for Padre Mendoza, the closest thing to a doctor around. The missionary started all the servants praying the rosary, sprinkled Regina with holy water, and prepared to extract the baby. Thanks to pure determination, he succeeded in grasping its feet; he tugged it toward the light, worried only that time was running out. The cord was wrapped around the baby's neck, and he was turning blue, but with prayers and well-delivered slaps Padre Mendoza forced him to breathe.

"What name shall we give him?" he asked when he placed the baby in his father's arms.

"Alejandro, like me, my father, and my grandfather," he replied.

"He will be called Diego," Regina interrupted, drained by fever and by the steady trickle of blood soaking the sheets.

"Why Diego? No one in the de la Vega family is named Diego."

"Because that is his name," she replied.

Alejandro had suffered with her through the long hours of labor, and more than anything in the world he feared losing her. He saw that she was losing blood and he could not bring himself to argue with her. He concluded that if on her deathbed she had chosen that name for her firstborn, she must have good reason, so he authorized Padre Mendoza to baptize the boy on the spot; he seemed as weak as his mother and he ran the risk of ending up in limbo if he died before receiving the sacrament.

It took Regina several weeks to recover from the battering of the birth, and then it was only because her mother, White Owl, arrived, barefoot and carrying her bundle of medicinal plants over her shoulder, just as candles were being set out for Regina's funeral. This medicine woman had not seen her daughter for seven years—that is, since the day she went off into the forest to round up warriors from other tribes. Alejandro attributed the timely appearance of his mother-in-law to the Indians' communication system, a mystery the whites could never unravel. A message sent from the Presidio in Monterey took two weeks to reach Baja California, with horses dropping beneath their riders, but when it arrived it was already old news to the Indians, who had received it ten days before through some magical means. There was no other explanation for how that woman could have appeared out of nowhere without being summoned, just when she was needed most. White Owl took over without saying a word. She was little more than forty, tall, strong, beautiful, weathered by sun and hard work. Her young face, with honey-colored eyes like her daughter's, was framed by an untamed mop of smoke-colored hair, to which she owed her name. She came in without asking permission, pushed Alejandro de la Vega aside when he attempted to find out who she was, walked straight through the complicated layout of the mansion, and stopped at her daughter's bed. She called her by her true name, Toypurnia, and spoke to her in the tongue of their ancestors, until the dying woman opened her eyes. Then from her pouch she took the medicinal herbs needed to save her, boiled them in a clay olla over the brazier that warmed the room, and gave them to her to drink. The entire house was saturated with the odor of sage.

In the meantime, Ana, with her habitual good nature, had taken Regina's child, whimpering with hunger, to her breast; thus Diego and Bernardo, Ana's son, began their lives with the same milk and in the same arms. That made them milk brothers for as long as they lived.

Once White Owl found that her daughter could stand, and that she could eat without being nauseated, she put her plants and belongings back into her pouch, took one look at Diego and Bernardo, who were sleeping side by side in the same cradle—without showing the least sign that she was curious about which of the two was her grandson—and left without a good-bye. Alejandro de la Vega watched her go with great relief. He was grateful that she had saved Regina from certain death, but he was happier to be grateful from a distance; he felt uncomfortable under that woman's influence, and worse, the Indians on the ranch were becoming insolent. They appeared for work in the morning with faces streaked with paint, at night they danced like sleepwalkers to the sound of mournful ocarinas, and in general they ignored his orders as if they had lost their Spanish.

Normality returned to the hacienda at the same rate that Regina recovered her health. By the following spring, everyone except Alejandro de la Vega had forgotten that Regina had had one foot in the grave. It did not require medical training to deduce that she could not have any more children. Without his realizing, this knowledge began to come between Alejandro and his wife as he turned his devotion to Diego. He had dreamed of a large family, like those of other dons in the region. One of his friends had fathered thirty-six legitimate children in addition to the bastards that he didn't bother to count. He had twenty children from his first marriage in Mexico, and sixteen from the second, the last five born in Alta California, one per year. The fear that something bad would happen to that one irreplaceable son, as it did to so many small children who died before they learned to walk, kept de la Vega awake at night. He formed the habit of praying aloud, kneeling beside his son's bed, crying out to heaven to watch over him. Emotionless, arms folded across her breast, Regina observed her humbled husband from the doorway. In those moments she thought she despised him, but later, in bed, surrounded by the warmth and scents of their intimacy, they found a short-lived reconciliation. At dawn Alejandro dressed and went down to his office, where an Indian girl served him his hot chocolate, thick and bitter the way he liked it. He began the day by meeting with his foreman to give him instructions about the ranch, then turned to his multiple duties as alcalde. Husband and wife spent the day apart, in their own occupations, until sunset marked the hour to meet again. In summer they dined on the terrace of the bougainvillea, always accompanied by musicians playing their favorite songs. In winter they ate in the Sewing Room, where no one had ever sewed on so much as a button; the name came from a painting of a Dutch woman embroidering by the light of a candle. Often Alejandro stayed overnight in Pueblo de los Angeles because it grew late at a fiesta, or because he was playing cards with other dons. The round of dances, cards, musical evenings, and get-togethers went on every day of the year. There was nothing else to do, other than the outdoor sports that both men and women engaged in. Regina was not involved in any of it; she was a solitary soul, and except for her husband and Padre Mendoza, she distrusted anyone Spanish on principle. Neither did she have any interest in accompanying Alejandro on his trips or in the American ships that brought in contraband; she had never gone on board to negotiate with the sailors. At least once a year Alejandro went to Mexico City on business, absences that tended to last a couple of months. He returned from them laden with gifts and new ideas, but these too failed to move his wife. Regina went back to her long horseback rides, with her son in a kind of papoose basket on her back, and she lost the slight interest she'd had in the domestic chores now delegated to Ana. She fell into her old habit of visiting the Indians, even those not on their ranch, with the aim of identifying their problems and, if possible, easing them. As the colonists continued to divide up the land and subdue the tribes of the region, a system of obligatory service developed that was different from slavery only in that the Indians too were subjects of the king of Spain, and in theory had certain rights. In practice they were dirt-poor; they worked in exchange for food, liquor, tobacco, and permission to raise a few animals. In general the ranchers were benevolent patriarchs, more interested in their pleasures and passions than in the land and their peons, but occasionally a rancher came along who had a bad temper, and then the *indiada*, as the Indian population was called, went hungry or was pitilessly beaten. The neophytes at the mission were just as poor; they lived with their families in round huts built of sticks and straw, they worked from sunup to sunset, and they were totally dependent on the mission brothers for their livelihood. Alejandro de la Vega tried to be a good *patron*, as he wrote in a letter to Eulalia de Callís, but it annoyed him that Regina kept asking for more for the Indians, even after he had explained to her that they could not treat them any differently from those on other ranches because that would cause problems in the colony. Padre Mendoza and Regina, unified by the same desire to protect the Indians, had become friends. He had forgiven her for attacking the mission, and she was grateful because he had brought Diego into the world. The *patrones* stayed out of their way; the missionary had moral authority and she was the wife of the alcalde. On the occasions that Regina wanted to launch one of her campaigns for justice, she dressed in Spanish style, combed her hair into a severe bun, wore an amethyst cross upon her breast, and attended functions in an elegant carriage, a gift from her husband, abandoning the spirited mare she usually rode. Even so, she was coolly received, because she was not one of them. No rancher would admit to having an Indian ancestor. To a man, they claimed Spanish heritage: white skin and pure blood. That Regina did not even try to hide her origins was not something they could forgive, although that was what Padre Mendoza most admired about her. When they learned that Regina's mother was an Indian, the Spanish colony turned its back on her, though no one dared snub her to her face, out of respect for her husband's position and fortune. They continued to invite her to parties and balls with the tranquil assurance that they would not see her there. Her husband would come alone.

De la Vega did not have a lot of time for his family, busy as he was with running the town, his hacienda, and business affairs, and with settling disputes, of which there seemed to be no shortage among the townspeople. Every Tuesday and Thursday, without fail, he went to Pueblo de los Angeles to fulfill his political obligations, a prestigious burden with more duties than satisfactions but one he refused to give up out of a sense of service. He was not greedy, he did not abuse power, and authority came naturally to him, but he was not a man with grand vision. He never questioned the ideas he had inherited from his ancestors, even though sometimes they were not appropriate to the reality of America. To Alejandro, everything came down to a question of honor, pride in being who he was—an exemplary Catholic hidalgo—and in holding his head high. He worried that Diego, too tied to his mother's apron strings, to Bernardo, and to the Indian servants, would not assume the position that was his by birth, but he reasoned that the boy was still very young, there would be time to guide him. He told himself he would start directing his son's manly formation as soon as possible, but that moment always got put off; there were other more urgent matters to attend to. Sometimes the desire to protect his son and make him happy moved him to tears. His love for the child perplexed him; it was like being stabbed in the heart. He outlined lofty plans for him: he would be brave, a good Christian, loyal to the king like every male de la Vega before him, and wealthier than any of his relatives had ever been: the master of vast, fertile lands with a temperate climate and abundant water, where nature was generous and life was sweet, not as it was on the barren estates of his ancestors in Spain. He would have more herds of cattle, sheep, and swine than King Solomon; he would breed the best bulls and the most elegant Arabian horses; he would become the most influential man in Alta California; he would be governor. But that would be later. First he had to grow up, go to the university or to military school in Spain. De la Vega anticipated that by the time Diego was old enough to travel, Europe would be in better shape. Peace was too much to expect, since there never was peace on the old continent, but he could hope that level heads had prevailed. The news they were receiving was disastrous. He explained all this to Regina, but she did not share his ambitions for her son, and cared even less about problems on the other side of the ocean. She could not conceive of a world beyond limits she could travel to by horseback, say nothing of worry about events in France. Her husband had told her that in 1793, precisely the year they were married, King Louis XVI had been beheaded before a mob screaming for revenge and blood. José Díaz, a friend of Alejandro's and a ship's captain, had given him a miniature guillotine, an awesome toy he used to cut off the tips of his cigars and, in passing, illustrate how the heads of nobles had rolled in France, a terrible example that to Alejandro's way of thinking could sink Europe into absolute chaos. That little machine seemed a tempting idea to Regina, for she speculated that if the Indians had it, whites would respect them, but she had the good sense not to share those musings with her husband. There was cause enough for bitterness between them; it wasn't smart to add another. She was shocked by how much she had changed. She looked at herself in the mirror and could find no trace of Toypurnia; she saw only a woman with hard eyes and clenched lips. The need to live in a world foreign to her, and to stay out of trouble, had made her cautious and underhanded; she rarely confronted her husband, she preferred to act behind his back. Alejandro de la Vega never suspected that she was talking to Diego in her own tongue, so he was unpleasantly surprised when the first words out of his son's mouth were in the Indian language. If he had known that his wife used each of his absences to take the child to visit his mother's tribe, he would have exerted his authority.

Whenever Regina appeared in the Indian village with Diego and Bernardo, grandmother White Owl abandoned her chores and devoted herself completely to them. The tribe had been reduced through mortal illness and by the number of braves who had been recruited by the Spanish; barely twenty families remained, more miserable every day. The grandmother filled the young boys' heads with myths and legends of her people; she cleansed their hearts with the smoke of the sweet grass she used in her ceremonies and took them with her to pick magical plants. As soon as they were able to stand firmly on their two feet and hold a stick, she had the braves teach them to fight. They learned to fish with sharpened wands, and to hunt. She gave each of them a whole deerskin, complete with head and horns, to wear during the hunt; that was how they would stalk a deer. They waited, motionless, until their prey wandered near, and then shot their arrows. The growing presence of the Spanish had made the Indians submissive, but when Toypurnia-Regina was around, their blood was fired with the memory of the war of honor she had led. Their awed respect for her was translated into affection for Diego and Bernardo. They treated both as their sons.

It was White Owl who took the boys to explore the caves near the de la Vega hacienda. She taught them to read the symbols carved on the walls a thousand years before, and showed them how to use them as a map. She explained that the caves were divided into seven sacred directions, a basic map for spiritual journeys, which is why in ancient times initiates had gone there to seek their own centers, which ideally should coincide with the center of the world, where life originates. When that correspondence was reached, the grand-mother informed them, a luminous flame from the bowels of the earth blazed up and danced in the air for a long while, bathing the initiate with light and warmth. She explained that the caves were natural temples, and that they were protected by a higher energy, and that was why they should enter them only with good in mind. "Whoever goes in with bad intentions will be swallowed up, and after a while the cave will spit out his bones," she told them. She added that if you help others, as the Great Spirit commands, a space in your body opens to receive blessings; that is the only way to pre-pare yourself for *okahué*.

"Before the whites came, we went to those caves to seek harmony and find *okahué*, but no one goes now," White Owl told them.

"What is *okahué*?" Diego asked.

"The five basic virtues: honor, justice, respect, dignity, and courage."

"I want all those, Grandmother."

"You must pass many tests, without crying," White Owl replied curtly.

From that day on, Diego and Bernardo began to explore the caves on their own. Before they were able to memorize the petroglyphs to guide them, as their grandmother had told them to do, they marked their route with pebbles. They invented their own ceremonies, inspired by what they had heard and seen in the tribe, and by the stories of White Owl. They asked the Great Spirit of the Indians, and Padre Mendoza's God, to allow them to be granted *okahué*, but they never saw the flames blaze up and dance in the air, as they hoped. Their curiosity, however, did lead them to a natural passage. They had moved some rocks to lay out a medicine wheel on the ground, like the ones the grandmother traced: thirty-six stones in a circle and one in the center, out of which led four straight roads. When they moved a round stone that they had intended to set in the center of the circle, several others rolled away, uncovering a small entrance. Diego, who was slimmer and more agile, crawled inside and discovered a tunnel that quickly opened up enough for him to stand. The boys returned with candles and picks and shovels, and in the following weeks worked at widening the passageway. One day the tip of Bernardo's pick opened a little hole that let in a ray of light; enchanted, the boys discovered that they had come out smack in the rear of the huge fireplace in the living room of the de la Vega hacienda. A few mournful chimes from the grandfather clock welcomed them. Many years later they would learn that the site of the house had been chosen by Regina precisely because it was close to the sacred caves.

After their discovery, Diego and Bernardo set about strengthening the tunnel with boards and rocks, since the clay walls tended to crumble, and they also opened a hidden door in the bricks of the fireplace to connect the caves with the house. The hearth was so tall, wide, and deep that a cow could stand inside, a fitting dimension for the dignity of that room, which was never used to entertain guests but sometimes accommodated Alejandro de la Vega's political meetings. The furniture, rough and uncomfortable, like that in the rest of the house, was lined up around the walls, as if they were for sale in a carpenter's shop, accumulating dust and that rancid smell old furniture gets. The most prominent object in the room was an enormous oil of Saint Anthony—ancient, bone-thin, covered with sores, and wearing rags—in the act of rejecting Satan's temptations, one of those horrors commissioned by the square unit in Spain and greatly appreciated in California. In a corner of honor, where they could be admired, were the staff and trappings of the alcalde's office, which the owner of the house used in performing official duties. Those ranged from major matters, such as laying out streets, to trivial ones like granting permission for serenades; after all, if that were left to the wishes of smitten suitors, no one in the town would have slept. Hanging from the ceiling above a great table of cedar wood was an iron lamp the size of a cart wheel; it was set with one hundred and fifty candles that had never been lit because no one had the spirit to lower the huge contraption to light them. On the few occasions the room was opened they used oil lamps. The fireplace was never lighted either, although a fire was always laid with large logs. Diego and Bernardo got into the habit of coming back from the beach by using a shortcut through the caves, emerging like ghosts into the dark hollow of the fireplace. They had sworn, with the solemnity of children absorbed in their games, never to share that secret with anyone. They had also promised White Owl that they would enter the caves for good purposes only, and not for trivial games, but for them everything they did there was part of their training for *okahué*.

†

More or less during the same period that White Owl was nourishing the children's indigenous roots, Alejandro de la Vega was beginning Diego's education as an hidalgo. That was the year two trunks arrived from Europe, sent by Eulalia de Callís as gifts. Her husband, the former governor Pedro Fages, had dropped dead in Mexico City, felled by one of his rages. He collapsed like a sack at his wife's feet during one of their fights, ruining her digestion forever because she blamed herself for having killed him. After spending a lifetime arguing with him, Eulalia sank into a deep depression when she found herself widowed; finally she realized how much she would miss her rotund husband. She knew that no one could replace such a stupendous man, a bear hunter and a great soldier, the only man she had ever known who could stand up to her. The tenderness she had never felt for him when he was alive smote her like a plague when she saw him in his coffin, and for her remaining years would continue to haunt her with memories that grew more vivid over time. Finally, weary of weeping, she followed the advice of her friends and her confessor and returned to Barcelona, where she had been born, and where she could enjoy the support of her fortune and her powerful family. From time to time she remembered Regina, whom she thought of as her protégée, and she wrote her on fine Egyptian paper imprinted with her coat of arms in gold. In one of those letters they learned that the Fages's son had died of the plague, leaving Eulalia even more disconsolate.

The two trunks were quite battered by the time they arrived; they had left Barcelona nearly a year before and had sailed on different ships across many seas before they reached Pueblo de los Angeles. One was filled with gorgeous dresses, high-heeled shoes, plumed hats, and fripperies that Regina rarely had occasion to wear. The other, intended for Alejandro de la Vega, contained a black silk-lined cape with silver buttons from Toledo, a few bottles of the best Spanish brandy, a set of dueling pistols with mother-of-pearl handles, an Italian fencing sword, and Maestro Manuel Escalante's *Treatise on Fencing and Dueling*. Just as the first page explained, this was a compendium of the "most useful instructions to ensure that one never hesitates when it is necessary to defend one's honor with Spanish sword or épée." Eulalia de Callís could not have sent a more appropriate present. It had been years since Alejandro de la Vega had held a sword, but thanks to the manual he was able to refresh his knowledge and teach fencing to a son who still could not blow his own nose. He ordered a child-sized épée, a quilted vest, and a mask for Diego, and from that moment formed the habit of practicing with him a couple of hours every day. Diego demonstrated the same natural talent for fencing that he had for all athletic activities, but he did not take it seriously, as his father wanted him to; for him it was just another of the many games he shared with Bernardo. That unwavering complicity between the boys worried Alejandro de la Vega. To him it seemed a weakness in his son's character, who was by now old enough to assume the role his destiny decreed. De la Vega was fond of Bernardo, and favored him among the Indian servants—after all, he had seen him born—but he could not forget the differences that existed between social levels. He maintained that without those differences, set out by God for a clear purpose, chaos would reign in this world. His favorite example was France, where everything had been turned topsy-turvy by that accursed revolution. In that country no one knew any longer who was who; power was passed from hand to hand like a coin. Alejandro prayed that something like that would never happen in Spain. Even though a succession of inept monarchs was leading the empire to inevitable ruin, Alejandro had never questioned the divine legitimacy of the monarchy, just as he never questioned the hierarchical order in which he had grown up or the absolute superiority of his race, his nation, and his faith. Diego and Bernardo were different by birth; they would never be equals, and it was his opinion that the sooner they understood that, the fewer problems they would have in the future. Bernardo knew without having to have it drummed into his head, but it was a subject that drew tears from Diego when his father brought it up. And far from seconding her husband in his didactic aims, Regina continued to treat Bernardo as if he were her son, too. In her tribe no person was superior to another because of birth, only for their courage or wisdom, and in her mind it was still very early to know which of the two boys was the more courageous or wise.

Diego and Bernardo parted only at bedtime, when each went to his mother's room. The same dog bit them both, they were stung by bees from the same honeycomb, and they got the measles at the same time. When one did something mischievous, no one bothered to identify the culprit; they made them both bend over to receive identical switchings, and they took their punishment without protest, as seemed perfectly fair. Everyone except Alejandro de la Vega thought of them as brothers, not only because they were insep+arable, but because at first sight they looked very much alike. The sun had burned their skin to the same wood tone, Ana made them identical linen trousers, and Regina cut their hair in the Indian style. The observer had to look carefully to see that Bernardo had noble Indian features, while Diego was tall and fine-boned, with his mother's caramel-colored eyes. In the years that followed, they learned to flourish the épée according to Maestro Escalante's impec+cable instructions, to gallop bareback on their horses, to use the whip and lasso, and to hang by their feet like bats from the eaves of the house. The Indians taught them to dive and rip shellfish from the rocks, to follow a prey for days to get a kill, to craft bows and arrows, and to endure pain and fatigue without complaining.

Alejandro de la Vega took them on the roundup when it was time to brand the cattle, each with his own riata so they could help in the task. It was the only manual labor considered proper for a gentleman, more sport than work. All the dons of the region brought their sons and vaqueros and Indians. They rounded up the cattle, separated them, and put their brands on them, which after+ward were listed in a book to prevent confusion and cattle rustling. That was also the time for slaughtering, and after skinning the steers they rolled up the hides, salted down the meat, and rendered the fat. The *nuqueadores,* fabulous horsemen able to kill a steer by planting a dagger in its nape while riding at full tilt, were the kings of the roundup and tended to be signed up a year in advance. They came from Mexico and from the American prairies, with their trained horses and their long two-edged daggers. As soon as a steer was down, the *peladores* ran to them to skin them, stripping off the whole hide in a matter of minutes; then came the *tasajeros,* responsible for butchering the meat, and last the Indian women whose humble task it was to cut off the tallow, render it in enormous kettles, and then store it in *botas* made from bladders, intestines, or stitched skins. It was also the women's responsibility to tan the hides, scraping the raw side with sharp knives, spending endless hours on their knees. The smell of blood maddened the herd, and there were always gutted horses and one or two vaqueros trampled or gored to death. The monster formed of thousands of head of cattle racing by, bawling and heaving, raising a hell of dust, was a sight to be seen; the vaqueros in their white sombreros, glued to their mounts, whistling lassos dancing over their heads and gleaming knives in their waistbands, were something to be admired; the thunder of the herd shaking the ground, the yells of the fired-up men, the whinnying horses and barking dogs, were sounds never to be forgotten; and the smells—the steam rising from the hide of foam-flecked mounts, the acrid smell of the vaqueros, and the disturbing, warm, secret scent of the Indian women—would linger forever in the men's minds.

At the end of the roundup, everyone went into town to celebrate a task well done. Rich and poor, white and Indian, young and the few elderly in the colony, all joined in a spree that lasted several days. There was a wealth of food and drink; couples danced to music from Mexico till the last pair dropped; they bet on fistfights, rat fights, cockfights, dogfights, and bear-and-bull fights, and in one night they might lose everything they had earned during the roundup. On the third day, the fiesta ended with a mass officiated by Padre Mendoza, who used a coachman's whip to herd the drunks off to the church, and then, musket in hand, forced the seducers of his young neophytes to marry them; he had counted, and nine months after every roundup a scandalous number of fatherless babies were born.

One year during a bad drought the ranchers had to kill off the wild horses to guarantee pasture for their cattle. Diego rode with the vaqueros, but for once Bernardo refused to go with him; he knew what they were going to do and he couldn't bear to watch it. The riders encircled herds of horses, spooked them with gunpowder and dogs, chased them at full gallop toward the cliffs, and then drove them over in a blinding stampede. Horses jumped off by the hundreds, falling on top of one another, necks and legs broken by the fall into the bottom of the ravine. The fortunate died on the spot; others agonized for days amid a cloud of flies and a stench of carrion that attracted bears and buzzards.

Twice a week Diego had to make the trip to the San Gabriel mission to receive the rudiments of a proper education from Padre Mendoza. Bernardo always went with him, and the missionary eventually allowed him into the class despite his belief that it was unnecessary, and even dangerous, to give Indians too much learning; it put bold ideas into their heads. The boy did not have Diego's mental quickness and tended to get behind, but he was stubborn and did not back down, though it meant spending his nights burning the candle down to the end. He had a reserved and quiet nature that contrasted with Diego's explosive happiness. He backed his friend with unquestionable loyalty in all the pranks Diego thought up and, when he had to, resigned without fuss to being punished for something that had been Diego's idea, not his. Ever since he could walk, Bernardo had assumed the role of protecting Diego, who he believed was destined for great things, like the heroic warriors in White Owl's storehouse of myths.

Diego, for whom being quiet and indoors was torture, often schemed to slip away from Padre Mendoza's lessons and get out in the open. He put as much energy into games as Bernardo did into studying. The lessons came in one ear and he recited them quickly, before they went out the other. He was so good at bluffing that he succeeded in fooling Padre Mendoza, but afterward he would have to teach Bernardo the lesson word for word, and it was by this repetition that he learned. After much discussion they reached an agreement: he would instruct Bernardo, and he in turn would practice the lasso, whip, and sword with Diego.

"I don't see why we work so hard to learn things we won't ever use," Diego complained one day after he had been repeating the same Latin phrases for hours.

"Sooner or later you use everything," Bernardo replied. "It's like the sword. I will probably never be a dragoon, but it is still good to learn fencing."

Very few citizens of Alta California knew how to read and write, except the missionaries; they were rough men, nearly all from the country, but they at least had a varnish of culture. There were no available books, and on the rare occasions that a letter arrived, it was assumed that it contained bad news, so the addressee was in no rush to take it to a friar and ask him to decipher it. Alejandro de la Vega, however, had a fancy for education, and for years he had tried to attract a teacher from Mexico City. By then, Pueblo de los Angeles had grown to more than the town with four streets that he had seen born; it had become a required stop for travelers, a place for sailors from the merchant ships to rest ashore, and the center of the region's commerce. Monterey, the capital, was a long way away, so most matters of government were aired in Pueblo de los Angeles. Except for authorities and military officers, the population was mixed, referred to as *gente de razón*, respectable people, to distinguish them from Indians and servants. Pure-blooded Spaniards were a class apart. The town now had a bull ring, a brand-new brothel staffed by three half-Mexican girls of negotiable virtue, and an opulent mulatto from Panama, whose price was fixed and not cheap. There was now a building for the meetings of the alcalde and the councilman, which also acted as a courthouse and theater where light operas, moralistic plays, and patriotic ceremonies were presented. A bandstand had been built in the Plaza de Armas, and musicians enlivened the evening hour of the paseo when, under the watchful eyes of their parents, young promenaders, looking their very best, strolled around the plaza, the girls in one direction and the boys in the other. But hotel? There still was none; it would be ten years before the first was built. Travelers took lodging in the homes of wealthy citizens, where there was always food and a bed to welcome anyone in need of hospitality. In view of such progress, Alejandro de la Vega considered it indispensable for the town to have a school. No one shared his concern. With his own money then, completely on his own, he founded the first school in the province, and for many years it would be the only one. It opened its doors just as Diego turned nine and Padre Mendoza announced that he had taught the boy everything he knew, except for saying mass and exorcising demons. The building was as dark and dusty as the jail, located on a corner of the main plaza and furnished with a dozen iron benches; a menacing-looking whip hung beside the blackboard. The teacher turned out to be one of those insignificant little men whom the slightest hint of authority converts into a brutal tyrant. Diego had the bad fortune to be one of his first students, along with a handful of other male children, the budding sprouts of the well-to-do families of the town. Bernardo was not allowed to attend, even though Diego begged his father to let him come. Alejandro de la Vega found Bernardo's ambition praiseworthy, but he decided not to make an exception; if one Indian were accepted, others would have to be let in, and the teacher had already announced, with unmistakable clarity, his intention to leave if any Indian so much as stuck his nose into his "honorable establishment of learning." The need to teach Bernardo, more than the intimidating whip, motivated Diego to pay attention in his classes. Among the students was a certain García, son of a Spanish soldier turned tavern owner, a fat boy, not overly bright, with flat feet and a foolish smile, the teacher's favorite victim—and that of the students, who tormented him ruthlessly. Through some desire for justice that he himself could not explain, Diego became García's defender, winning the pudgy boy's fanatic admiration.

✝

For Padre Mendoza the years were taken up by many chores—farm-ing, herding cattle, and Christianizing Indians—and he still had not repaired the church roof that had been damaged during Toypurnia's attack, when the explosion had shaken the building to its founda-tions. Every time the good father held up the host to consecrate it during mass, his eyes inevitably fell on the weakened beams; he would promise himself with alarm to fix them before they crashed down upon his small congregation, but just as inevitably he had to tend to other matters and would forget his intentions till the next mass. Worse, termites were devouring the wood in the building, so it should have been no surprise when finally the accident Padre Men-doza had feared happened. Fortunately, it was not when the entire congregation was present, something that would have been cata-strophic. It came during one of the many temblors that frequently shook the area—it wasn't for nothing that their river was named Jesús de los Temblores. The roof collapsed on a single victim, Padre Alvear, a sainted brother who had traveled from Peru to visit the San Gabriel mission. The noise of the roof's giving way and the cloud of dust brought the neophytes running, and they immediately started clawing at the rubble to unearth the unfortunate visitor. They found him squashed like a cockroach beneath the main beam. In all logic he should have died, because it took them most of the night to res-cue him, and all the while the poor man's lifeblood was oozing away. But God performed a miracle, as Padre Mendoza explained, and when finally they pulled the victim from the ruins, he was still breathing. Padre Mendoza needed only one glance to recognize that his meager knowledge of medicine would not save the wounded man, however much help he received from the divine power. With-out a moment's hesitation, he sent a neophyte with two horses to look for White Owl. Over the years he had become convinced that the Indians' veneration of the woman was fully justified.

By chance, Diego and Bernardo arrived at the mission the day after the earthquake, bringing two fine horses that Alejandro de la

Vega had sent as a gift to the missionaries. Since no one came out to greet them or thank them—everyone was occupied in sifting through the damage from the quake and tending to the dying Padre Alvear—the boys left the horses in the corral and stayed on to watch the spectacle. Consequently, they were there when White Owl came galloping up, following the neophyte who had gone to fetch her. Even with her face furrowed with new wrinkles, and with her hair even whiter, she had changed very little; she was the same strong, eternally young woman who ten years before had come to the de la Vega hacienda to save Regina's life. Now she had come on a similar mission, and again she had brought her pouch of medicinal plants. Since she refused to learn Spanish, and Padre Mendoza's vocabulary in her tongue was very limited, Diego offered to interpret. They had laid the patient on the unfinished dining room table, and everyone who lived at the mission gathered around. White Owl carefully examined Padre Alvear's wounds, which Padre Mendoza had bandaged but had not dared stitch up because he could see shattered bones sticking through. The *curandera* palpated his entire body with her expert fingers and took an inventory of what treatments she would have to make.

"Tell the white man that it can all be mended, except this leg; it is rotten. First I cut it, then I take care of the rest," she announced to her grandson.

Diego translated without taking the precaution of lowering his voice, because Padre Alvear was nearly dead anyway, but the minute he repeated his grandmother's diagnosis, the dying man's fiery eyes flew open.

"Blast it! I prefer to die and get it over," he said forcefully.

White Owl ignored him, while Padre Mendoza forced the poor man's mouth open, as he did the children's who refused to drink their milk, and stuck in his famous funnel. Then they poured in two spoonfuls of a thick reddish syrup White Owl had brought in her pouch. In the time it took to wash a wood saw with lye and tear some rags for bandages, Padre Alvear had sunk into a deep sleep from which he would awake ten hours later, lucid and tranquil, some time after the stump of his leg had stopped bleeding. White Owl had treated the dozen or so injuries on his body and had packed them with spiderwebs and mysterious salves and bandaged them. For his part, Padre Mendoza had arranged for the neophytes to take turns praying, so prayer would be continuous, day and night, until the patient was healed. The method had good results. Against all expectations, Padre Alvear got well quickly, and seven weeks later, carried on a hand litter, he was able to take a ship back to Peru.

Bernardo would never forget the shock of seeing Padre Alvear's amputated leg, and Diego would never forget the incredible power of his grandmother's potion. In the following months he went many times to her village to beg her for the secret, but she refused time and time again, arguing that a medicine so magical should not be in the hands of a mischievous boy who undoubtedly would use it for some prank. On an impulse, like so many that he later paid for with whippings, Diego stole a gourd containing the sleeping elixir, promising himself that he would not use it to amputate human limbs but only for a good purpose. As soon as he had the treasure in his hands, nevertheless, he began to plan ways to have fun with it. The opportunity presented itself one hot June day when he and Bernardo were coming home from swimming—the one sport that Bernardo could best him in because of his staying power, his calm, and his strength. While Diego wore himself out thrashing through the waves, Bernardo maintained an unhurried rhythm for hours, breathing slowly and letting himself be carried by the mysterious currents of the sea. If the dolphins showed up, they soon clustered around Bernardo, just as horses did, including the ones no one could break. When no vaquero dared go near an enraged colt, Bernardo would walk up to it cautiously, lay his face against its ear, and whisper secret words until it calmed down. No one could break a colt as quickly, or as well, as that Indian boy.

That sunny afternoon on their way home, the boys were stopped by the sound of García's terrified screams, once again being tormented by the bullies from school. There were five of them, led by Carlos Alcázar, the oldest and most feared of all the students. He had the intellectual capacity of a louse, but he shone in cooking up new ways to be cruel. This time they had stripped off García's clothes and tied him to a tree, and then had slathered him from head to toe with honey. García was screeching at the top of his lungs, and now his five tormentors watched with fascination as a cloud of mosquitoes and columns of ants began to attack. Diego and Bernardo made a quick evaluation of the situation and realized that they were at a distinct disadvantage. They could not take on Carlos and his four buddies, but neither could they leave to go for help; that would be cowardly. Diego walked toward them with a smile, while just behind him, Bernardo clenched his teeth and his fists.

"What are you doing?" Diego asked, as if it weren't obvious.

"Nothing that concerns you, moron—that is, unless you want to end up like García," Carlos replied, backed by the guffaws of his gang.

"You're right. It doesn't concern me, except that I was planning to use this tub of lard to catch a bear. It's a shame to waste good bait on ants," Diego said indifferently.

"Bear?" Carlos grunted.

"I'll trade you García for a bear," Diego proposed off-handedly, as he cleaned his fingernails with a sharpened stick.

"Where are you going to get a bear?" the bully asked.

"That's my business. I plan to bring it in alive, and wearing a hat besides. I can give it to you, if you'd like, Carlos, but to do it I will need García," Diego repeated.

The five boys consulted in whispers, as García felt the trickle of icy sweat and Bernardo scratched his head, figuring that this time Diego had gone too far. The usual method for trapping the live bears they used for fighting bulls required strength, skill, and good horses. Several expert horsemen would lasso the animal and control it by keeping the ropes taut, while another vaquero, acting as a lure, would go ahead, teasing it. That way they would jockey it into the corral, but the diversion often cost dear, because occasionally the bear, which could run faster than any horse, managed to get free and turn on whoever was closest.

"And who's going to help you?" Carlos asked.

"Bernardo."

"That dumb Indian?"

"Bernardo and I can do it ourselves, as long as we have García as bait," said Diego.

In two minutes' time they had closed the deal and the tormentors had gone off. Diego and Bernardo untied García and helped him wash off the honey and clean his snot-smeared face in the river.

"How are we going to get a live bear?" Bernardo asked.

"I don't know yet, I have to think about it," Diego answered, and his friend never doubted that he would find the solution.

The rest of the week went by in gathering the necessary tools for the hoax they were hoping to bring off. Finding a bear was the least of their worries; as many as a dozen at a time hung around the place where the steers were slaughtered, drawn by the scent of red meat, but the boys had to be careful not to engage more than one, and especially not a female with cubs. They had to find a solitary bear, but that would not be difficult, they were everywhere in the summer. García declared that he was not well, and refused to leave his house for several days, but Diego and Bernardo forced him to come with them, using the convincing argument that if he didn't, he would end up in the hands of Carlos Alcázar and the other bullies again. Joking, Diego told him that they needed him for bait, but when he saw how García's knees were knocking, he took pity and told him the details of the plan he had worked out with Bernardo. The three boys told their mothers that they were going to spend the night at the mission, where, as he did every year, Padre Mendoza was celebrating the feast of Saint John. They left very early, armed with several lassos and riding in a cart pulled by a pair of ancient mules. García was dying of fright, Bernardo was deep in thought, and Diego was whistling. As soon as they had left the house behind and turned off the main road, they headed onto the Sendero de las Astillas, the "splinter path" the Indians believed was bewitched. The age of the mule team and the rough terrain forced them to a crawl, but that gave them time to read the tracks on the ground and the slash marks on the bark of the trees. They were getting near Alejandro de la Vega's sawmill, which provided the lumber for dwellings and for repairing ships, when the braying of the terrified mules warned them that a bear was nearby. All the workers at the sawmill had gone to the fiesta, and there was no one in sight, only abandoned saws and axes and tree trunks piled near a rustic board building. They unhitched the mules and tugged them into the shed to protect them. Then Diego and Bernardo set about rigging their trap, while García watched from his refuge a short distance away. He had brought an abundant supply of food, because he got hungry when he was nervous, and had been chewing on something ever since they left that morning. From his hiding place he watched his friends, who were throwing ropes over the largest branches of two trees; they laid out the lariats as they had watched the vaqueros do, and in the center arranged some branches they covered with the deerskins they wore when they went hunting with the Indians. They laid a freshly killed rabbit under the skins, along with a ball of lard soaked in the grandmother's sleeping potion. Then they went into the shed to share García's lunch.

The three conspirators were prepared to spend a couple of days, but they didn't have to wait that long; in no time at all the same bear the mules had scented earlier came ambling up. It was a ponderous male, a quivering mass of fat and dark fur waddling from side to side with unexpected agility and grace. The boys were not deceived by the animal's attitude of mild curiosity; they knew what it was capable of, and they prayed that the breeze would not carry their scent or that of the mules to it. If the bear charged the shed, the door would not hold. The behemoth made a couple of circuits of the area and suddenly sighted what looked like a downed deer. It rose up on its hind legs and stretched out its front paws. The boys could see it then: the whole bear, a giant several heads taller than a grown man. It roared, freezing their blood, slashed menacingly at the air, and hurled all its enormous weight upon the hide, smashing the light frame that held it. The bear was puzzled at finding itself flat on the ground, but sprang up immediately. Again it clawed at the false deer, and discovered the hidden rabbit and the lard, which it devoured in two gulps. It shredded the hide, looking for more substantial fare, and when it didn't find anything again rose to its full height, furious. It took one step forward and tripped the ropes, activating the trap. The ropes tightened, and in the blink of an eye the bear was hanging upside down between the two trees. The boys' celebration was short-lived, because the weight of the bear, swinging in the air, broke the branches. Frightened for their lives, Diego, Bernardo, and García barricaded themselves inside the shed with the mules, looking for something to defend themselves with, while the bear, spread-eagled on the ground, was trying to kick its right hind foot free of the lasso that still bound it to one of the broken tree branches. It struggled for quite some time, getting more and more entangled and more and more infuriated; then, finding that it couldn't get loose, it started forward, dragging the branch.

"And now?" asked Bernardo, feigning calm.

"Now we wait," Diego replied.

When García felt something warm between his legs and saw the stain spreading down his pants leg, he lost his head and started sobbing at the top of his lungs. Bernardo jumped on him and clamped his hand over his mouth, but it was too late. The bear had heard. It started toward the shed, and once there it slashed at the door, shaking the fragile construction so badly that boards fell off the roof. Inside, Diego was waiting beside the door with his whip in one hand, while Bernardo was waving a crowbar he had found in the shed. To their good fortune, the beast was dazed by its fall from the tree and hampered by the heavy branch it was dragging. After one last halfhearted feint at the door, it stumbled off toward the woods, but it didn't get far because the branch caught in some of the logs stacked near the sawmill, stopping it short. The boys couldn't see the bear, but for a long time they heard its frustrated roars, until they subsided into resigned sighs, and finally ceased altogether.

"And now?" Bernardo asked again.

"Now we have to get it into the cart," Diego announced.

"Are you crazy? We can't leave the shed!" yelled García, whose pants by now were darkly stained and stinking.

"I don't know how long it will be asleep. It's really big, and we have to suppose that my grandmother's sleeping potion is meant for a human. We have to work fast, because if it wakes up, our hide is cooked," Diego ordered.

Bernardo followed him without asking for further explanation, as he always did, but García stayed behind, miserable in the muck of his own filth and moaning with what little breath he had left. Diego and Bernardo found the bear on its back a short distance from the shed, just where it had dropped after being walloped by the drug. In Diego's plan, the animal was to have been strung up in the trees during the time it was unconscious; that way the boys could pull the cart beneath it and drop it down. Now they would have to hoist the gargantuan animal into the cart. They prodded the bear with a pole and, as it didn't move, felt brave enough to go right up to it. It was older than they'd thought: two claws were missing on one paw, several teeth were broken, and it was stippled with old scars. The dragon breath issuing from its open jaws struck them full in the face, but this was no time to retreat; they tied up its snout and roped its four paws together. At first they worked slowly, blocking out defense moves that would have been completely useless had the beast wakened, but once they were convinced that it was as good as dead, they moved quickly. Soon they had the bear immobilized, and went to look for the terrorized mules. Bernardo used his method of whispering into their ears, as he did with wild horses, and convinced them to obey. García approached with caution, after being assured that the bear's snores were legitimate, but he was shaking, and smelled so bad that they sent him to wash himself and his trousers in a nearby stream. Bernardo and Diego followed the vaquero's method for lifting huge weights: they secured two ropes to one end of the tipped-over cart, passed them beneath the bear, pulled them back over it in the opposite direction, then tied the ends to the mules' harness and ordered them to pull. At the second try, they succeeded in rolling the beast over, and in that way worked it into the cart. They were panting when they finished their backbreaking task, but they had achieved their goal. They hugged each other and leaped around like lunatics, prouder than they had ever been before. The proud boys hitched up the mules, and were ready to start back to town, but not before Diego had pulled out the bucket of tar he'd collected in the pits near his house and used it to paste a sombrero onto the bear's head. The boys were exhausted, bathed in sweat, and saturated in the stench of the beast. García, for his part, was a bundle of nerves; he could barely stand, he still smelled like a pigsty, and his clothes were soaking wet. Their adventure had taken most of the afternoon, but when finally they headed the mules back down the Sendero de las Astillas, they had a couple of hours of daylight left. They urged the team on, and reached the Camino Real just as it grew dark. From there on, the long-suffering mules found their way by instinct, while the bear wheezed in its prison of rope. It had woken from the lethargy brought on by White Owl's potion, but was still muddled. When they drove into Pueblo de los Angeles, it was pitch-black night. By the light of a pair of oil lanterns they untied the animals' rear feet, but left its front paws and snout bound. They prodded it until they got it out of the cart and onto two feet, dizzied but with every ounce of fury intact. The boys started yelling, and soon people were pouring out of their houses carrying lamps and torches. The whole town came out to see what was going on, and the street filled with people admiring the bizarre spectacle: Diego de la Vega leading a huge bear wearing a sombrero, of all things, and staggering along on its hind feet with Bernardo and García poking it from the rear. Applause and cheers echoed for weeks in the ears of the three boys, and by then they'd had plenty of time to consider how foolish they had been and to recover from their well-deserved punishment. Nothing could dim the radiance of that victory. Carlos and the other bullies never bothered them again.

✝

The exploit of the bear, exaggerated and embellished to the point of impossibility, spread by word of mouth; with time, it crossed the Bering Strait, carried by traders in otter skins, and circulated as far away as Russia. Diego, Bernardo, and García were not excused from the whipping administered by their parents, but no one could contest their fame as champions. They were very careful, oh yes, very careful not to mention White Owl's sleeping potion. Their trophy was exhibited in a corral for several days, exposed to the jeers and rocks of the curious, while promoters looked for a bull worthy of fighting it, but Diego and Bernardo took pity on the captive and the night before the fight set it free.

In October, when the town was still talking about nothing else, they were attacked by pirates. They had sailed along the coast by night and at dawn they came ashore without warning, with the experience of many years of marauding. Their ship was a brigantine armed with fourteen light cannons; it had made the voyage from South America by swinging around Hawaii to take advantage of the prevailing winds that blew toward Alta California. They were on the prowl for ships laden with treasures from America destined for the royal coffers in Spain. These buccaneers rarely attacked on dry land—the important cities could defend themselves, and the others were too poor—but they had been at sea for an eternity without any luck, and the crew needed to take on fresh water and release a little energy. The captain decided to put in at Pueblo de los Angeles, although he didn't expect to find anything interesting there, only basic supplies, liquor, and a little diversion for the lads. They were counting on not meeting any resistance, preceded as they were by the reputation they themselves made sure was well known, spine-chilling tales of blood and ashes, of how they chopped men into little pieces, gutted pregnant women, and strung children on grappling hooks and hung them from the masts like trophies. They liked being thought of as barbaric. When they struck, all they had to do was announce their presence by firing off a few cannons, or come howling onto the scene, and the whole town would desert, leaving the pirates to sack the place without the inconvenience of a fight. They dropped anchor near Pueblo de los Angeles and readied their assault. In this case, the brigantine's cannons were useless; the shot would not reach that target. They disembarked in launches, knives between their teeth and swords in hand, like a horde of demons. Halfway to town they came across the de la Vega hacienda. The large adobe house, with its red roof tiles and purple bougainvillea creeping up the walls, its orange grove, its unmistakable air of prosperity and peace, was irresistible to those rough sailors, who for months had seen nothing but mossy water, wormy biscuits, and smelly dried beef. In vain their captain bawled that their objective was the town; his men rushed toward the hacienda, kicking aside dogs and shooting point-blank a pair of Indian gardeners who had the bad luck to get in their way.

Alejandro de la Vega was in Mexico City at the time, buying furniture more graceful than the crude pieces in his home, gold velvet for drapes, heavy silver for the table, place settings of English china, and crystal glasses from Austria. He hoped to impress Regina with these queenly gifts, to see whether she would give up her Indian ways and return to the European refinement he wanted for his family. His business affairs were thriving, and for the first time he could treat himself to living in the way a man of his breeding deserved. He had no way to suspect that as he was bargaining over the price of Turkish rugs, thirty-six soulless pirates were invading his home.

Regina was awakened by the furor of the dogs' barking. Her room was in a small tower, the only bold feature in the low profile of the house. Through her window, which had neither drapes nor shutters, she could see the timid light of early morning streaking the sky with orange. She threw a shawl around her shoulders and went out on the balcony in her bare feet to see what was disturbing the dogs, just as the first marauders forced open the wooden gate of the garden. It never occurred to her that they were pirates—she had never seen one in the flesh—but she didn't stop to identify them. Diego, who at ten still shared his mother's bed when his father wasn't there, saw her race by in her nightgown. As she flew past,

Regina seized a well-kept sword and a dagger that had been hanging on the wall since her husband left his military career behind, and ran down the stairway yelling for the servants. Diego leaped out of bed and followed her. The doors of the house were oak, and in the absence of Alejandro de la Vega they had been bolted from the inside with an iron bar. The pirates' rush was stopped by that invulnerable obstacle, and that gave Regina time to hand out the firearms stored in big chests and prepare a defense. Diego, still not completely awake, found himself watching a woman who looked only vaguely familiar to him. In seconds, his mother had been transformed into Daughter-of-Wolf. Her hair was standing on end and the ferocious gleam in her eyes gave her the look of a woman possessed; her jaw was set and her lips drawn back, and she was foaming at the mouth like a rabid dog. Toypurnia barked orders to the servants in the Indian tongue, and was brandishing a sword in one hand and a dagger in the other when the shutters that protected the windows on the main floor gave way and the first pirates spilled into the house. Even over the clamor of the assault, Diego heard a cry, more jubilation than terror, issue from the earth, course through his mother's body, and shake the walls of the house. The sight of that woman barely covered by the thin cloth of a nightgown rushing to meet them and wielding two weapons with a strength impossible in someone her size shocked the pirates for a second or two. In that time, the servants fired their weapons. Two pillagers fell face forward, and a third staggered, but there was no time to reload; another dozen were already swarming through the windows. Diego picked up a heavy iron candlestick and ran to his mother's defense as she retreated toward the big hall. She had lost the sword and was holding the dagger in both hands, swinging blindly against the vandals closing in on her. Diego thrust the candlestick between the legs of one man, throwing him to the floor, but before he could club him, a brutal kick to his chest slammed him against the wall. He never knew how long he lay there, befuddled, because later versions of the attack were contradictory. Some said it lasted for hours, but others said that within a few minutes the pirates had killed or wounded everyone in their path, destroyed what they couldn't carry, and before they continued on to Los Angeles set fire to the furniture.

When Diego regained consciousness, the ruffians were still running through the house looking for loot, and smoke from the fire was drifting into the room. Despite the tremendous pain in his chest, which left him gasping for breath, Diego got to his feet and stumbled forward, coughing and calling his mother. He found her beneath the large table in the great hall, with her batiste gown soaked in blood, but lucid and with open eyes. "Hide, son!" she ordered in a strong voice, and promptly fainted. Diego took her arms and with a superhuman effort, considering the broken ribs, tugged her to the fireplace. He managed to open the secret door that only he and Bernardo knew existed, and dragged her into the tunnel. He closed the false door from the other side and sat there in the dark with his mother's head in his lap, whispering, "Mama, Mama," and weeping and praying to God and the spirits of her tribe not to let her die.

Bernardo, too, was in bed when the pirates attacked. He slept in his mother's room in the servants' quarters at the opposite end of the hacienda. Their space was larger than the windowless cells of the other domestic workers because it was also used as the ironing room, a task that Ana never delegated. Alejandro de la Vega demanded that his tucked shirtfronts be perfect, and she took pride in ironing them personally. Aside from the narrow bed with its straw mattress, and a battered chest in which they kept their few belongings, the room was furnished with a long worktable and a metal container for the coals that heated the irons, along with a pair of enormous baskets of clean wash that Ana planned to iron the next day. The floor was dirt; a wool serape served as a door; light and air entered through two small windows. Bernardo had not been awakened by the yells of the pirates or by the shots on the far side of the house, only when Ana shook him. He thought the earth was quaking, as it had before, but his mother gave him no time to speculate; she grabbed his arm, swept him up with the strength of a tornado, and in one stride was across the room. With a brutal shove she stuffed him inside one of the large baskets. "Whatever happens, don't move. You hear me?" Ana's tone was so forbidding that it seemed to Bernardo that she was speaking to him with a hidden loathing. He had never seen her agitated. His mother's sweet nature was legend; she was always quiet and content, even though she had few reasons to be happy. She devoted herself exclusively to the task of adoring her son and serving her *patrones*, in line with her humble existence and with no resentment in her heart. In that moment, however, the last she would ever share with Bernardo, she was hard as ice. She took a handful of clothing and covered the boy, pushing him down in the basket. From there, wrapped in the white shadows of the clothing, choked with terror and the smell of starch, Bernardo heard the cries, cursing, and loud laughter of the men who surged into the room where Ana was waiting with death already inscribed upon her forehead, ready to distract the men for as long it took to keep them from finding her son.

The pirates were in a rush, and one look around told them that there was nothing of value in that servant's room. Maybe they would just have glanced in and turned away, but there stood that brown-skinned woman, arms akimbo, defying them with suicidal determination: round Indian face, midnight black mantle of hair, generous hips, and firm breasts. For a year and four months they had been roving the seas without the consolation of even looking at a woman. For an instant they thought they were seeing a mirage, like so many that had tormented them on the high seas, but then Ana's sweet scent enveloped them and they forgot their hurry. They tore off the rough penitent's gown that covered her body and threw themselves on her. Ana did not struggle. She bore in dead silence everything they wanted to do to her. When she fell, her head was so close to Bernardo's basket that he could count, one by one, his mother's faint sighs eclipsed by the brutish panting of her assaulters.

At no moment did the boy move beneath the pile of clothes that covered him; there, paralyzed with horror, he lived the torture of his mother. He was curled up in the basket, his mind a blank, sweating bile, shaken with nausea. After an eternity, he became aware of a deathly silence and the smell of smoke. He waited until he couldn't wait any longer because he was choking, then quietly called Ana. No answer. He called a couple of times more; still nothing. Finally he dared peek out. Clouds of smoke were billowing through the doorway, but as yet there was no fire. Numb from tension and immobility, Bernardo had to struggle to climb out of the basket. He saw his mother where the men had forced her to the floor, naked, her long black hair spread out like a fan on the ground and her neck slit from ear to ear. The boy sat down beside her and took her hand, calm, and silent. He would not speak again for many years.

That was how they found him, mute and stained with his mother's blood, hours later when the pirates were already back at sea. The town of Pueblo de los Angeles was putting out fires and counting its dead. No one thought of going to see what had happened at the de la Vega hacienda until Padre Mendoza, struck by a premonition so vivid that he could not ignore it, went with half a dozen neophytes to take charge. Flames had burned the furniture and licked some of the beams, but the house was sound, and by the time he arrived the fire was burning itself out. The assault left a balance of several wounded and five dead, including Ana, whom they found just as her murderers had left her.

"God help us!" Padre Mendoza exclaimed when he came upon that tragedy.

He covered Ana's body with a blanket and picked Bernardo up in his strong arms. The child was petrified, his eyes staring and his face frozen in a spasm that locked his jaws. "Where are Regina and Diego?" the missionary asked, but Bernardo gave no sign of hearing. The priest left the boy in the hands of an Indian servant, who cuddled him in her lap, rocking him like a baby as she sang a mournful song in her native tongue, while Padre Mendoza went through the house, searching for the missing.

†

Time passed without change in the tunnel; because there was no daylight, it was impossible to judge time in that eternal darkness. Diego could not tell what was going on in the house because he couldn't hear sounds or smell the smoke of the fire. He waited without knowing what he was waiting for, while Regina slipped in and out of consciousness, drained. Inconsolable, fearing he would disturb his mother, the boy sat motionless despite the nearly unbearable prickling in his legs and the daggerlike stab in his chest every time he drew a breath. From time to time he would be overcome by fatigue, but he would immediately awaken, sunk in darkness and dizzy with pain. He felt as if he were freezing, and several times he tried to flex his arms, but he would sink back into a hopeless languor and start to nod again, floating in a cottony fog. This semiconscious state lasted most of the day, until finally Regina moaned and moved. That startled him awake. Knowing that his mother was alive gave him new life; a wave of happiness swept over him, and he bent to cover her face with delirious kisses. With infinite care, Diego lifted her head, which had turned to marble, and lowered it gently to the ground. After several minutes of trying to move his legs, he was able to crawl off and look for the candles that he and Bernardo had stored in their ongoing quest for *okahué*. He heard his grandmother's voice asking in her Indian tongue what the five essential virtues were, but the only one he could remember was courage.

Regina opened her eyes to the light of a candle, and found herself in a cave with her son. She didn't have the strength to ask what had happened, or to console him with lies; she merely indicated that he should rip her gown and use it to bandage the wound in her chest. With trembling fingers, Diego did as she directed, and found that his mother had a deep knife wound below the collarbone. Not knowing what else to do, he simply waited.

"My life is draining away, Diego, you must go for help," Regina murmured after a while.

The boy estimated that if he went through the caves to the beach, from there he could run for help without being seen, but it would take time. On an impulse, he decided that it was worth the risk to peek through the door in the fireplace and see what the situation was in the house. The opening was well disguised behind the high stack of logs in the fireplace and he could look out without being seen, even if someone was in the great room.

The first thing that greeted him when he cracked open the false door was a blast of smoke and the acrid odor of scorched wood. At first it drove him back, but then he realized that the smoke would hide him. Silent as a cat, he slipped through the secret door and crouched behind the logs. The rug and several chairs were smoking, the oil of Saint Anthony was completely destroyed, and the walls and ceiling beams were blackened, but the flames had died down. There was an abnormal quiet in the house, and he assumed that no one was there, which gave him the courage to come out. Cautiously he felt his way along the walls, eyes tearing from the smoke, and, one by one, went through the rooms on the main floor. He had no idea what had happened, whether everyone was dead or whether they had escaped. The entry hall looked like the aftermath of a shipwreck, and he saw blood, but the bodies of the men he himself had seen fall early that morning were no longer there. Confused by doubts, he thought he must be caught in a terrifying nightmare, one he would be awakened from by the sound of Ana's affectionate voice calling him for breakfast. He continued exploring in the direction of the servants' rooms, choked by the gray fog of the fire, which jumped out at him when he opened a door or turned a corner. He remembered his mother, who would surely die without help, and decided that he had nothing to lose. Forgetting all caution, he started running back down endless corridors, almost blindly, until he crashed into a solid body and two powerful arms that locked around him. He screamed with fright and the pain of the broken ribs, felt a surge of nausea, and nearly fainted. "Diego! God be praised!" He heard the huge voice of Padre Mendoza and smelled his musty old cassock; he felt the priest's scratchy beard against his forehead, and then, like the child he still was, he let go and began crying and vomiting.

Padre Mendoza had sent the survivors to the San Gabriel mission.

The only explanation he could come up with for the absence of Regina and her son was that they had been kidnapped by the pirates, although nothing like that had ever been heard of in their part of the world. He knew that in other places they took captives for ransom or to sell as slaves, but that had never happened on this remote American shore. He did not know how he would give the terrible news to Alejandro de la Vega. Aided by the two other Franciscans who lived at the mission, he had done everything he could to bind up wounds and console the other victims of the raid. The next day he would have to go to Pueblo de los Angeles, where the heavy burden of burying the dead awaited him, and make an inventory of the destruction. He was wrung out, but he felt so uneasy that he could not go with the others to the mission; he needed to stay and go through the house one more time. That is what he was doing when Diego collided with him.

Regina survived, thanks to the fact that Padre Mendoza wrapped her in blankets, put her in his carriage, and drove to the mission. There wasn't time to summon White Owl; the deep wound was bleeding profusely and Regina was growing weaker before their eyes. By candlelight, the missionaries gave her a pint of rum, washed the wound, and with pliers used for twisting wire removed the tip of the pirate's dagger, which had broken off in Regina's clavicle. They cauterized the wound with white-hot iron, as Regina clenched a stick between her teeth, as she had when giving birth to Diego. Her son covered his ears to blot out her choked moans, crushed with guilt and shame at having wasted in a childish prank the sleeping potion that could have saved his mother such torment. Her pain was his punishment for having stolen the magic medicine.

When they took off Diego's shirt, his skin was purple from his neck to his groin. Padre Mendoza was sure that the vicious kick had broken several ribs, and he himself fashioned a leather corset reinforced with lengths of cane to stabilize them. The boy couldn't stoop down or lift his arms, but thanks to the corset, within a few weeks he could breathe normally. Bernardo, on the other hand, did not recover from his injuries; they were much more serious than Diego's. He spent several days in the same frozen state that Padre Mendoza had found him in, staring straight ahead with his teeth clenched so tight that the priest had to use the funnel to feed Bernardo a little mush. The boy attended the collective funeral of the pirates' victims, and without a single tear watched as the coffin containing his mother's body was lowered into a hole in the ground. By the time people began to notice that Bernardo hadn't spoken for weeks, Diego, who had been with his friend day and night, not leaving him for an instant, had already accepted that he might never speak again. The Indians said that he had swallowed his tongue. Padre Mendoza began by forcing him to gargle with honey and wine from the mass; then he painted his throat with borax, put warm poultices around his throat, and gave him ground beetles to eat. When none of these improvised remedies for muteness worked, he decided to take drastic measures and try exorcism. He had never been called on to expel demons, and did not feel qualified for so difficult an undertaking, even though he knew the procedure. There was no one else for leagues around, however, who could do it. To find an exorcist authorized by the Inquisition, they would have to travel to Mexico City, and in all truth, the missionary did not think it was worth the effort. To prepare, he diligently studied the pertinent texts and fasted for two days; then he locked himself inside the church with Bernardo to go head to head with Satan. To no avail. Defeated, Padre Mendoza concluded that the trauma had shocked the poor boy senseless, and gave up. He delegated the nuisance of the funnel to a neophyte and went about his responsibilities. His time was absorbed by his duties at the mission, by the spiritual task of helping Pueblo de los Angeles recover from its misfortunes, and by the bureaucratic details his superiors in Mexico City demanded of him—always the most burdensome part of his ministry. By the time White Owl showed up at the mission to take Bernardo to her village, everyone else had given up on him, branding him as a hopeless idiot. The missionary turned him over to her because he didn't know what else to do, though he was confident that the medicine woman's magic could not achieve a cure where exorcism had failed. Diego was dying to go with his milk brother, but he didn't have the heart to leave his mother, who was still in convalescence, and besides, Padre Mendoza had forbidden him to ride while he was still wearing the corset. For the first time since they'd been born, the boys were separated.

Once White Owl was satisfied that Bernardo had not swallowed his tongue—there it was, intact, in his mouth—she diagnosed that his muteness was a form of mourning: he wasn't speaking because he didn't want to. She believed that beneath the unvoiced rage devouring the boy lay a fathomless ocean of sadness. She did not try to console him or cure him—in her opinion Bernardo had every right in the world not to speak—but she taught him to communicate with the spirit of his mother by observing the stars, and with other people through the sign language used for trading among tribes. She also taught him to play a delicate reed flute. With time and practice, the boy would learn to draw almost as wide a range of sounds from it as that of the human voice. Once everyone had left him alone, Bernardo began to come around. The first symptom was a voracious appetite—there was no need to force-feed him now—and the second was the timid friendship he struck up with Light-in-the-Night. The girl was two years older than Bernardo, and she was given that name because she had been born on a stormy night. She was small for her age, and she wore the pleasant expression of a squirrel. She treated Bernardo normally, without any notice of his speech problem, and she became his constant companion, unknowingly replacing Diego. They were apart only at night, when he had to go to White Owl's hut, and she to her family's. Light-in-the-Night took Bernardo to the river, where she stripped off her clothes and dived in headfirst, while he tried to find something else to look at; even though he was only ten, Padre Mendoza's teachings on the temptations of the flesh had made an impact. Bernardo would dive in after her, still wearing his pants, and wonder at the fact that, like him, she could swim like a fish in the icy water. She knew the mythic history of her people by heart, and never tired of telling it to Bernardo, just as he never tired of listening. The girl's voice was a balm to the sorrowing boy, who listened in a trance, not realizing that his love for her was beginning to melt the glacier of his heart. He began to act again like any boy his age—except that he didn't speak and he didn't cry. Together they tagged after White Owl, helping her in her duties as a healer and shaman, gathering curative plants and preparing potions. When Bernardo started smiling again, the grandmother decided that she had done all she could for him and that the time had come to send him back to the de la Vega hacienda. She was occupied in the rites and ceremonies that would acknowledge Light-in-the-Night's first menstrual period; nearly overnight she was an adolescent. That sudden transition did not distance her from Bernardo; on the contrary, it seemed to bring them closer together. As a farewell, she took him once again to the river and on a rock, using her menstrual blood, drew two birds in flight. "This is us, we will always fly together," she told him. Bernardo spontaneously kissed her and then ran off like the wind, with his body aflame.

Diego, who had been awaiting Bernardo's return with the sadness of an abandoned pup, saw him in the distance and ran to welcome him, whooping with joy. When he stood in front of him, however, he understood that this friend who was like a brother to him was a different person. He was riding a borrowed horse; he was larger, and rugged-looking. He could have passed for a man. His hair had grown long, his face was that of an adult Indian, and the unmistakable light of a secret love blazed in his eyes. Diego stopped short, but Bernardo dismounted and embraced him, easily lifting him off his feet, and they were once again the inseparable twins of before. Diego felt as if he had gained back half his soul. He didn't care a whit that Bernardo didn't speak, because neither of them had ever needed words to know what the other was thinking.

Bernardo was amazed that the burned-out property had been completely restored in the months he was gone. Alejandro de la Vega had determined to erase every sign of the pirates' passing, and he seized the excuse of the damage to improve his house. When he had returned to Alta California six weeks after the assault, with his load of luxury goods to surprise his wife, there hadn't been so much as a barking dog to welcome him. The home was completely abandoned, its contents turned to ash, and his family gone. The one person who came to greet him was Padre Mendoza, who brought him up to date on what had happened and took him to the mission, where Regina was taking her first steps as a convalescent, still heavily bandaged and with her arm in a sling. The experience of having peered into the far side of death had erased her freshness with a single stroke. Alejandro had left a young wife, but upon his return he found a woman with streaks of gray in her hair, a woman who was only thirty-three, but past her youth, and who showed no interest in Turkish carpets or engraved table silver. The news was bad, but as Padre Mendoza told him, it could have been much worse. Alejandro de la Vega vowed to put it all behind him since there was no possibility of punishing renegades, who by now must be halfway to the China seas, and turned his energies toward restoring the hacienda. In Mexico, he had seen how people of means lived, and he had determined to imitate them—not to be ostentatious, he would say as an excuse for his extravagance, but because in the future Diego would inherit the mansion and fill it with grandchildren. He ordered building materials and sent to Baja California for craftsmen—smiths, ceramists, woodcarvers, painters—who in no time at all added a second floor, long arched corridors, tile floors, a balcony in the dining room, a bandstand in the patio, the better to enjoy the musicians, small Moorish fountains, wrought-iron railings, carved wood doors, and windows with painted panes. In the main garden he installed statues, stone benches, birdcages, pots of flowers, and a marble fountain topped with a Neptune and three sirens that the Indian craftsmen copied directly from an Italian painting. When Bernardo came back, the mansion's red tile roofs had been restored, the second coat of peach-colored paint had been applied to the walls, and bales and bundles from Mexico City were being opened to decorate the house. "As soon as Regina gets well, we will have a housewarming this town will remember for a hundred years," Alejandro de la Vega announced. But that day would be long in coming, because his wife found excuse after excuse for putting off the fiesta.

Bernardo taught Diego the Indians' sign language, which they then enriched with their own additions and used for communicating when telepathy and the flute failed. Sometimes, when dealing with more complicated matters, they took recourse to slate and chalk, but they did it secretly because they did not want to be thought conceited. With the help of his whip, the schoolmaster had drilled the alphabet into the heads of a few privileged boys, but between there and reading freely lay an abyss, and in any case, no Indian went to school. Diego, despite himself, ended up becoming a good student, at which point he understood for the first time his father's mania for education. He began to read everything he could get his hands on. Maestro Manuel Escalante's *Treatise on Fencing and Dueling* was revealed to him as a collection of ideas very similar to the Indians' *okahué*; it, too, spoke of honor, justice, respect, dignity, and courage. Before, he had limited himself to absorbing his father's fencing lessons and imitating the movements illustrated in the pages of the manual, but after he started reading it, he learned that fencing was not only skill in handling the épée and the sword, but also a spiritual art. About that same time, Captain José Díaz sent Alejandro de la Vega a crate of books a passenger had left on his ship somewhere near Ecuador. The crate was sealed tight as a drum when it arrived, but when opened, it revealed a fabulous cargo of epic poems and novels, yellowed, dog-eared volumes that smelled of honey and wax. Diego devoured them, even though his father scorned novels as a minor genre plagued with inconsistencies, basic errors, and personal dramas that were none of his business. The books became an addiction for Diego and Bernardo; they read them so often that they could recite them by heart. The world they lived in grew very small, and they began to dream of countries and adventures beyond the horizon.

When Diego was thirteen, he still looked like a child, while

Bernardo, like most boys of his race, had reached his full growth. The passivity of his coppery face softened during times that he and Diego were spinning a plot, or when he was gentling the horses, or in the many times he rode off to visit Light-in-the-Night. The girl grew very little during that period; she was short and slim, with an unforgettable face. Her happiness and beauty had attracted wide attention, and on her fifteenth birthday the fiercest warriors of several tribes were competing for her. Bernardo lived with the terrible fear that one day he would go to visit her and find her gone. His appearance was deceptive; he was not overly tall or muscular, but he had surprising strength and the physical endurance of an ox. His muteness also gave a false impression, not just because people thought he was stupid, but also because it made him seem sad. In fact he wasn't, but the people close to him, who knew the real Bernardo, could be counted on the fingers of one hand. He always wore the linen pants and shirt of the neophytes, with a sash about the waist and, in winter, a striped serape. The band across his forehead and long braid that fell halfway down his back proclaimed his pride in being Indian.

Diego, in contrast, had the rather deceptive air of a young gentleman, despite his athleticism and sun-warmed skin. From his mother he had inherited his eyes and rebelliousness; from his father, long bones, chiseled features, natural elegance, and the love of learning. Both had bequeathed him an impetuous bravery that on occasion verged on dementia, and no one knew where his playful charm came from, something none of his ancestors, a rather tight-lipped people, had ever shown. Just the opposite of Bernardo, who was amazingly serene, Diego could not be still for more than a minute; so many ideas poured from his brain that a lifetime would not be enough to put them into practice. He now bested his father in swordplay and no one surpassed him with the bullwhip. Bernardo had made him one of braided cowhide, which Diego wore coiled at his waist. He never missed an opportunity to practice. With its tip he could flick out a candle or cut off a flower without damaging a petal. He could also have plucked the cigar from his father's mouth, but such insolence never entered his mind. His relationship with Alejandro de la Vega was one of timid respect. He addressed him as "señor" and never questioned his authority to his face, although behind his back he nearly always got away with doing whatever he wanted. He was, however, more mischievous than rebellious and had assimilated his father's severe lectures about honor. Diego was proud of being a descendent of the legendary Cid, an hidalgo whose lineage was without a blot, but he never denied his Indian blood because he was also proud of his mother's warrior past. While Alejandro de la Vega, always conscious of his social class and his faultless ancestors, tried to hide his son's mixed blood, Diego acknowledged it with his head held high. Diego's bond with his mother was intimate and affectionate, but he was never able to deceive her, as occasionally he did his father. Regina had a third eye in the back of her head that saw what no one else could see, and was as unyielding as a rock when it came to being obeyed.

Alejandro de la Vega's role as alcalde obliged him to visit the seat of government in Monterey regularly. Regina took advantage of one of those absences to take Diego and Bernardo to White Owl's village. She believed that the boys were at an age to become men. However, to avoid problems, she did not tell her husband. As the years went by, their differences had grown; the nighttime embraces were no longer enough to reconcile them. Only their nostalgia for a lost love helped them stay together, though now they lived in worlds very far apart and had nothing to say to one another. Early in their marriage, Alejandro's passion had been so strong that more than once he turned around halfway into one of his trips and galloped several leagues just to be a couple of hours longer with his wife. He never grew tired of admiring her regal beauty, which always lifted his spirits and inflamed his desire, though it was also true that he was ashamed that she was a mestiza. Because he was proud, he pretended not to notice that a narrow-minded colonial society ostracized her, but with time he began to blame her: she did nothing to apologize for her mixed blood, she was thorny and defiant. Regina had at first tried very hard to adjust to her husband's customs, to his language of harsh consonants, to his chiseled-in-stone ideas, to his dark religion, to the thick walls of his house, to too-tight clothing and kid boots, but the effort cost her too much and eventually she admitted defeat. For love's sake, she had tried to renounce her origins and become a Spanish lady, but she could not; she never stopped dreaming in her own language.

Regina did not tell the boys the reasons for their trip to the Indian village because she did not want to alarm them in advance, but they sensed that it was something special and secret. White Owl was waiting for them halfway there. The tribe had had to move farther away, pushed toward the mountains by the whites who kept taking over their land. The colonists were more and more numerous, and they were insatiable. The immense virgin territory of Alta California began to seem too small for so much cattle and so much greed. Once the hills had been covered with grass, always green and tall as a man; there had been waterfalls and streams everywhere, and in spring the fields were covered with flowers, but the colonists' herds trampled the ground and the hills dried up. White Owl saw the future in her shamanic journeys; she knew that there was no way to hold back the invaders; soon her people would disappear. She counseled the tribe to seek new pasturelands farther away from the whites, and she herself supervised moving the village. The grandmother had prepared a broader program for Diego and Bernardo than the tests of bravery for warriors. She did not think it necessary to suspend them from a tree with hooks through their chest muscles; they were too young for that, and besides, they did not have to prove their courage. Instead, she proposed to put them in contact with the Great Spirit so their destinies would be revealed to them. Regina told the boys good-bye with no show of emotion, telling them that she would come for them in sixteen days, when they had completed the four stages of their initiation.

White Owl threw the pouch containing the tools of her office— musical instruments, pipes, medicinal plants, magical relics—over her shoulder and started off toward the virgin hills with the long strides of the practiced walker. Diego and Bernardo, who followed without a single question, carried nothing but woolen blankets. In the first stage of the journey they walked four days through thick woods, sustained only by sips of water, until hunger and fatigue produced an abnormal state of lucidity. Nature revealed herself in all her mysterious glory. For the first time they really noticed the boundless variety of the forest, the concert of the breeze, the close proximity of the wild animals that sometimes followed them for long stretches. At the beginning they suffered from scrapes and scratches, from the unnatural weariness of their bones, from the bottomless void in their stomachs, but by the fourth day they were walking as if floating in a mist. The grandmother decided that the boys were ready for the second phase of the rite, and she ordered them to dig a waist-deep hole that was half again as big around. She built a fire to warm some stones and had the boys cut and peel supple tree branches to construct a dome over the hole, which they then covered with their blankets. In that round shelter, symbolic of Mother Earth, they were to purify themselves and undertake a voyage in search of a vision, guided by the spirits. White Owl lit a sacred fire ringed with rocks, which represented the creative force of life. All three drank water and ate a handful of nuts and dried fruit, and then the grandmother ordered them to take off their clothing. Accompanied by the sound of her drum and rattle, they danced frenetically for hours and hours, until they dropped with exhaustion. She led them to the refuge that now held the burning-hot stones, and gave them *toloache* to drink. The boys submersed themselves in the vapor of the steaming rocks, the smoke of their pipes, the aroma of the magical herbs, and the images invoked by the drug. In the following four days they came out from time to time to breathe fresh air, to renew the sacred fire, to heat up the stones, and eat a few seeds. At times, sweating, they slept. Diego dreamed that he was swimming in ice-cold water with dolphins, and Bernardo dreamed of the contagious laughter of Light-in-the-Night. White Owl guided them with prayers and chants, while outside spirits from all times circled the blanket-covered dome. During the day, deer, rabbits, mountain lions, and bears nosed around the camp; and at night they heard the howls of wolves and coyotes. An eagle glided overhead, watching them, until they were ready for the third part of the ritual, then disappeared.

The grandmother handed each boy a knife, allowed them to take their blankets, and sent them off in opposite directions, one to the east and the other to the west, with instructions to feed themselves on what they could find or hunt—except for mushrooms of any kind—and to come back in four days. If the Great Spirit so pleased, she said, they would encounter their vision during that period, otherwise, it would not happen during this trial and they would have to wait four years before they tried again. When they returned, they would have the last four days to rest and to ready themselves for normal life before going back to the village. Diego and Bernardo had lost so much weight during the first stages of their initiation rites that when they saw each other in the splendid light of the dawn, they did not recognize one another. They were dehydrated, their eyes were sunk deep in their sockets, and they had the burning gaze of the mad; their ashen skin was stretched tight over their bones, and they had such an air of desolation that despite the gravity of their parting they burst out laughing. They hugged, deeply moved, and each went his way.

Separately, they wandered aimlessly, not knowing what they were looking for, hungry and frightened, living on tender roots and seeds, until hunger prodded them to hunt mice and birds with bows and arrows they fashioned from branches. When it grew too dark to continue, each built a fire and lay down to sleep, shivering with cold, surrounded by spirits and wild animals. And each awoke stiff from the frost and aching in every bone, with the startling clairvoyance that tends to come with extreme fatigue.

A few hours into his march, Bernardo realized that he was being followed, but when he turned and glanced over his shoulder, he saw nothing but trees watching over him like quiet giants. In this forest he was embraced by ferns with shining leaves, surrounded by twisted oaks and fragrant firs and quiet, green space lighted with splashes of light that filtered through the leaves. It was a sacred place. It would be most of the day before the shy creature accompanying him would show itself. It was an orphaned foal, still so young that its legs, black as night, were wobbly. Despite its newborn delicacy and its orphan's sense of solitude, Bernardo could see what a magnificent horse it would grow into. Horses travel in herds, and always in open country; what was it doing alone in the woods? He called it with the finest sounds of his flute, but it would stop some distance away, eyes suspicious, nostrils flaring, legs trembling, too skittish to come closer. The boy plucked a handful of moist grass, sat down on a rock, put it in his mouth and chewed it, spit it into the palm of his hand, then offered it to the beautiful little creature. Time passed before the foal decided to take a few hesitant steps forward, observing Bernardo through clear chestnut eyes, weighing his intentions and reckoning its retreat in case of danger. It must have liked what it saw, because soon its velvety muzzle touched the extended hand to taste the strange food. "It isn't the same as your mother's milk, but it will do," Bernardo murmured. Those were the first words he had spoken in three years. He felt each one take shape in the pit of his stomach, rise like a cottony ball up his throat, roll around a bit in his mouth, and then, well chewed, be spit out like the mash for the foal. Something broke inside his chest, something thick and heavy, and all his rage and guilt and his oaths of terrible revenge poured out in an uncontainable torrent. He fell to his knees on the ground, crying and vomiting a bitter green mud, shaken by the memory of that fateful morning when he had lost his mother, and with her, his childhood. His retching turned his stomach inside out and left him empty and clean. The foal retreated, frightened, but did not go away, and when finally Bernardo grew calm, able to get to his feet and look for water to wash in, the foal followed close behind. They were together for the next three days. Bernardo taught it to use its hooves to paw down to the tenderest grass, he held it until its legs were steady and it could trot, he slept with his arms around it at night to keep it warm, and he entertained it with his flute. "You will be called

Tornado—that is, if you like that name—so you will run like the wind," he proposed with his flute, because after that one sentence he had again retreated into silence. He intended to tame the foal and give it to Diego; he could not think of a more appropriate fate for such a noble creature, but when he woke on the fourth day, the foal was gone. The mist had burned off and the sun was painting the hills with the white light of dawn. Bernardo looked for Tornado in vain, calling it in a voice hoarse from lack of use, until he understood that the animal had not come to him in search of an owner, but to show him the path he should follow in life. He knew then that his spirit guide was the horse, and that he should develop the horse's virtues: loyalty, strength, and endurance. He decided that his planet would be the sun, and his element the hills, where at that moment Tornado was surely trotting back to the herd.

Diego's sense of direction was not as good as Bernardo's, and he was quickly lost. He also had less skill in hunting, and all he could catch was a tiny mouse, which after it was skinned was reduced to a handful of pathetic bones. He ended up devouring ants, worms, and lizards. He was so weak from hunger and the demands of the previous eight days that he did not have the strength to foresee what dangers lay in store, but he was determined not to give in to the temptation to go back. White Owl had impressed upon him that the purpose of that long test was to leave childhood behind and become a man, and he did not mean to fail his grandmother halfway through; nonetheless, the urge to break into tears was growing stronger than his determination. He had never known solitude. He had grown up beside Bernardo, surrounded with friends and people who cherished him, and his mother was never far away. For the first time, he was alone, and it had to happen just when he was deep in the wilderness. He was afraid that he would never find the way back to White Owl's small campsite, and it occurred to him that he could spend the next four days sitting under the same tree, but his natural impatience pushed him forward. Soon he was completely lost in the vastness of the hills. He came upon a stream, and seized the opportunity to drink and bathe; then he ate some unfamiliar fruit he picked from trees. Three crows, birds venerated by his mother's tribe, circled a few times low over his head. He took that as a sign, and it gave him spirit to go on. At nightfall he found a hollow protected by two rocks; he lit a fire, wrapped himself in his blanket, and was instantly asleep, praying that his lucky star would not fail him—Bernardo said it would always light his way—because it would not be at all funny to have come so far only to die in the claws of a mountain lion. He was wakened in the middle of the night by the regurgitated acid of the fruit he had eaten and the howls of nearby coyotes. Only timid coals remained of the fire, but he fed it with a few sticks, speculating that such a ridiculous little fire would not do much to keep away wild beasts. He remembered that earlier they had seen several kinds of animals that had roamed nearby but hadn't attacked, and he sent up a prayer that they wouldn't know that he was alone. But at that exact moment, in the light of the flames, he saw a pair of red eyes watching him with ghostly intensity. He clutched his knife, thinking that it must be a particularly bold wolf, but when he sat up and could see it better, he recognized it as a fox. So what are you doing here, *zorro*? he wondered. It seemed strange that it didn't move but just sat there like a cat warming itself by the embers of the fire. He called, but it did not come, and when he tried to approach it, the fox retreated with caution, always maintaining the same distance between them. Diego tended the fire for a while, until weariness overcame him and he dropped back to sleep despite the faraway howling of coyotes. Each time Diego snapped awake, not knowing where he was, he would see the strange fox in the same place, like a watchful spirit. The night seemed eternal, but finally the first rays of the sun backlighted the profile of the mountains. The fox was gone.

In the next three days nothing happened that Diego could interpret as a vision, except the presence of the fox, which arrived at nightfall and remained with him until dawn, always quiet and watchful. On the third day, bored and faint with hunger, Diego tried to find his way back but could not locate the site. He decided that it would be impossible to find White Owl, but that if he headed downhill, sooner or later he would come to the sea, and there find the Camino Real. So he started walking, thinking how frustrated his grandmother and his mother would be when they learned that all their preparations for those rites had not provided a vision, only dejection, and he wondered whether Bernardo had been luckier than he had been. He did not get very far because as he stepped over a fallen tree trunk he stepped on a snake. He felt a stab on his ankle, and in a couple of seconds heard the unmistakable sound of a rattlesnake and was fully aware of what had happened. No room for doubt: the serpent had a slim neck and triangular head. Fear struck him in the stomach like the unforgettable kick from the pirate. He jumped back a few steps, away from the viper, at the same time reviewing a few vague facts about rattlesnakes. He knew that the venom is not always lethal, that it depends on the amount of poison released from the fangs, but he was in a weakened state and far from any kind of help. Death seemed probable, if not from the poison, from starvation and weakness. He had seen a vaquero dispatched to the other world by one of those reptiles; the man lay down in a haystack to sleep, and never woke up. According to Padre Mendoza, God had called him to his blessed bosom—where, incidentally, he would never again beat his wife—through the perfect combination of poison and alcohol. Diego also remembered the drastic treatments for such cases: cutting the puncture wounds with a knife or burning them with a live coal. He could see that his leg was turning purple, he felt his mouth filling with saliva, his face and hands prickled, and he was shaking with cold. He realized that he was panicked, and that he had to do something soon, before his thoughts clouded over completely. If he moved, the venom would circulate more rapidly through his body, and if he didn't, he would die right there. He chose to keep going, even though his knees were rubbery and his eyelids were so swollen he couldn't see. He began stumbling downhill, calling his grandmother in a sleepwalker's voice as his last strength drained away.

Diego fell facedown. Slowly, painfully, he rolled over and lay beneath the bright morning sun with his face to the sky. He was panting and tormented by a sudden thirst; he was sweating quicklime and at the same time shivering with the chill of the tomb. He damned the Christian God for abandoning him, and the Great Spirit who instead of offering him a vision, as promised, was mocking him. Diego lost touch with reality, but also with fear. He was floating on a hot wind, as if miraculous air currents were lifting him, spiraling him toward the light. Suddenly elated at the possibility of dying, he relaxed into a perfect peace. The blistering whirlwind kept rising toward the heavens, then suddenly the wind veered, hurling him like a rock to the depths of an abyss. In a flash of consciousness, before he sank into total delirium, he saw the red eyes of the *zorro*, looking at him from the other side of death.

For the next few hours, Diego floundered around in the tar pit of his nightmares, and when finally he struggled free and rose to the surface, he remembered only his consuming thirst and the unblinking eyes of the fox. He woke wrapped in a blanket, lighted by the flames of a campfire, and accompanied by Bernardo and White Owl. He was slow to come back to his body, to take inventory of his pains and reach a conclusion.

"The rattlesnake killed me," he said as soon as he had his voice back.

"You are not dead, son, but you nearly were." White Owl smiled.

"I did not pass the test, grandmother," the boy said.

"But you did, Diego," she informed him. "You passed."

Bernardo had found Diego and carried him back to the camp. He was on his way to meet White Owl when a fox appeared before him. He had no doubt that it was a signal; it was most unusual for such a nocturnal animal to run between his legs, especially in broad daylight. Instead of obeying his first instinct to hunt it, he stopped and observed it. The fox did not flee but sat down a short distance away and looked back at Bernardo, ears pricked and snout trembling. Under different circumstances, Bernardo would simply have noted the animal's strange behavior, but he was in a visionary state, with his senses fever-hot and his heart open to signs. Unhesitatingly, he followed where the fox wanted to lead, and only a short distance farther he came upon Diego's inert body. He saw his brother's monstrously swollen leg and knew immediately what had happened. He did not have an instant to waste; he threw Diego over his shoulder like a sack of flour and hurried straight to White Owl, who applied herbs to her grandson's leg that made him sweat out the poison. Finally he opened his eyes.

"The fox saved you. That *zorro* is your totemic animal, your spiritual guide," she explained. "You must cultivate its skill, its cleverness, its intelligence. Your mother is the moon, and your home, the cave. Like the fox, you will discover what cannot be seen in the dark, you will disguise yourself, and you will hide by day and act by night."

"To do what?" asked Diego, confused.

"One day you will know—you cannot rush the Great Spirit. In the meantime, prepare, so you will be ready when that day comes," his Indian grandmother instructed him.

Out of prudence, the boys kept the rites White Owl had conducted secret. The colony considered the traditions of the Indians to be absurd, if not savage, acts of ignorance. Diego did not want any whispers to reach his father. He confessed his strange experience with the fox to Regina, without going into detail. No one asked Bernardo anything, since his muteness made him invisible, an unexpectedly advantageous situation. People talked and behaved in front of him as if he did not exist, giving him the opportunity to observe and learn about the duplicity of human beings. He began to practice his skill at reading people's actions, and in that way discovered that words do not always correspond to intentions. He realized that bullies generally are easy to cow, that the loudest are the least sincere, that arrogance is a quality of the ignorant, and that flatterers tend to be vicious. Through systematic and quiet observation, he learned to read character, and he applied that knowledge to protecting Diego, who was trusting by nature: he could not imagine in others defects he himself did not have. The boys did not see the black foal or the fox again. Bernardo thought that he sometimes caught a glimpse of Tornado galloping in the middle of a herd of wild horses, and once in the woods Diego came upon a cave with a clutch of newborn fox kits. They could not, however, relate either of these encounters to the visions attributed to the Great Spirit.

In any case, White Owl's ritual marked a milestone. Both of the boys had the impression that they had crossed a threshold and left childhood behind. They did not as yet feel they were men, but they knew that they were taking the first steps along the hard road of manhood. Together they awakened to the urgent demands of carnal desire, much less tolerable than the vague, sweet affection Bernardo had felt for Light-in-the-Night since he was ten years old. It never occurred to them to satisfy their yearnings among the willing Indian girls in White Owl's tribe, where the rules the missionaries imposed on the neophytes were unknown. Diego held back because of his great respect for his grandmother, and Bernardo was reined in by his puppy love for Light-in-the-Night. Bernardo had no hope that his love would be returned; he realized that the one he loved had grown into a woman, and was courted by half a dozen braves who traveled from distant tribes to bring her gifts, while he was a clumsy adolescent with nothing to offer, besides being mute as a hare. Neither did the boys call on the beautiful mulatta or the more ordinary girls in the house of pleasure in Pueblo de los Angeles. They feared them more than a runaway bull; with their crimson-painted mouths and their dead jasmine scent, they were creatures from an unknown land. Like all the other boys of their age—except Carlos Alcázar, who boasted about having passed the test—they looked at those women from afar, with veneration and fear. Diego went with the other boys from "good" families to the Plaza de Armas at the hour of the paseo. With every circuit of the plaza he passed girls of his social class and his age strolling in the opposite direction; they cast sidelong glances, their faces half hidden by a fan or a mantilla, while the boys sweated out their impossible love in their Sunday suits. They didn't talk back and forth, but some, the most daring, asked the alcalde for permission to serenade beneath the girls' balconies, an idea that made Diego cringe with embarrassment—partly because the alcalde was his own father. He could imagine, however, that he might want to try that method in the future, so every day he practiced romantic ballads on his mandolin.

Alejandro de la Vega took enormous satisfaction from the fact that his son, whom he had thought to be hopelessly irresponsible, was finally turning into the heir he had dreamed of from the day the boy was born. He renewed his plans to educate him to be a gentleman, plans that had been postponed during the whirlwind of restoring the hacienda. He had considered sending his son to a Catholic school in Mexico City, since the situation in Europe was still unstable—now thanks to Napoleon Bonaparte—but Regina stirred up such a fuss at the idea of being separated from Diego that Alejandro did not bring the subject up again for two years. In the meantime he involved his son in running the hacienda, and found that he was much cleverer than his performance in school would suggest. Not only did he untangle the jumble of notes and numbers in the account books, he increased the family income by perfecting his father's formula for soap and the recipe for smoking meat that he had produced only after countless attempts. Diego cut back on the lye in the soap and added milk, and suggested that they give samples to the ladies of the colony, who acquired such luxuries from the American sailors, violating the ban on commerce that Spain had imposed on her colonies. It didn't matter that the soap was smuggled, everyone looked the other way; the inconvenience came from having to wait so long for the boats. The milk soaps were a great success, and the same was true of the smoked meat once Diego was able to dilute the odor of mule sweat. Alejandro de la Vega began to treat his son with respect, and to consult him on certain matters.

During that period, Bernardo told Diego in their private sign language, and with notes on the slate, that one of the ranchers, Juan Alcázar, Carlos's father, had expanded his boundaries beyond what was shown on paper. The Spaniard had herded his cattle into the mountains where one of the many tribes displaced by the colonists had taken refuge. Diego rode out there with his brother, and they got there in time to see the trail bosses, backed by a detachment of soldiers, burn the Indians' huts. Nothing was left of the village but ashes. Despite their terror at having witnessed such a scene, Diego and Bernardo ran to intervene. Without consulting one another, as if of one will, they placed themselves between the horses of the aggressors and their Indian victims. They would have been trampled unmercifully had one of the riders not recognized the son of Alejandro de la Vega. Even so, they drove them out of their way with their whips. From a short distance, the two boys watched, horrified, as the few Indians who stood firm were beaten down. The chief, an old man, was hanged from a tree as a warning to the others. The attackers rounded up the men capable of working in the fields or serving in the army and led them away, roped together like animals. The elders, the women, and the children were driven off to wander through the forests, hungry and desperate. Nothing of this was new; it happened more and more frequently, and no one dared intervene—except Padre Mendoza, but his charges fell on the deaf ears of the creaking and remote bureaucracy in Spain. Documents that took years by sea were lost on the dusty desks of judges who had never set foot in America and were entangled in the flimflam of petty lawyers, and in the end, even if the magistrates ruled in favor of the Indians, there was no one on the other side of the ocean to carry out justice. In Monterey, the governor ignored complaints because Indians were not his priority. The officials in charge of the garrison were part of the problem, as they lent the services of their soldiers to the white settlers. They did not doubt the moral superiority of the whites who, like them, had come from far away with the sole intention of civilizing and Christianizing that savage land. Diego went to talk with his father. He found him, as always in the late afternoon, studying long-ago battles in his huge books, the one remnant of the military ambitions of his youth. He liked to set up his armies of lead soldiers on a long table according to the descriptions in the books, a passion he had never been able to interest Diego in. The boy blurted out what he had seen with Bernardo, but Alejandro de la Vega's indifference quickly deflated him.

"What do you propose that I do, son?"

"But, señor, you are the alcalde."

"The division of land is not in my jurisdiction, Diego, and I do not have any authority to control the soldiers."

"But el s-señor Alcázar killed and kidnapped Indians!" Diego stuttered, choked with emotion. "Forgive my insistence, señor, but how can you permit such abuses?"

"I will speak with Don Juan Alcázar, but I doubt that he will listen," Alejandro replied, moving a line of his soldiers.

Alejandro de la Vega kept his promise. He did more than speak with the rancher; he took his complaint to the garrison, where he wrote a report to the governor and sent the accusation to Spain. At every step he kept his son informed, since he was doing it only because of him. Alejandro knew the class system too well to harbor any hope of righting the wrong. Pressed by Diego, he tried to help the victims, who had been turned into miserable vagabonds, by offering them protection on his own hacienda. Just as he expected, it was all in vain. Juan Alcázar annexed the Indians' lands, the tribe disappeared without a trace, and the matter was never mentioned again. Diego de la Vega never forgot that lesson; the bad taste of justice denied would remain forever in the deepest part of his memory, and would emerge again and again, determining the course of his life.

The celebration of Diego's fifteenth birthday was cause for the first party held in the big house of the hacienda. Regina, who had always been opposed to opening her doors, decided that this was the perfect occasion to make all the mean-spirited people who had scorned her for so many years bite their tongues. She not only agreed that her husband should invite anyone he pleased but herself took the responsibility of organizing the festivities. For the first time in her life she visited the smuggler's boats to stock up on necessities, and she set a dozen women to sewing and embroidering. It did not escape Diego that it was also Bernardo's birthday. Alejandro de la Vega pointed out that although the mute boy was like a member of the family, he could not offend their guests by seating them with an Indian. For once, he said, Bernardo would have to take his place among the servants. They never had to discuss the matter further because Bernardo eliminated the problem by writing on his slate that he planned to visit White Owl's village. Diego did not try to change his mind; he knew that his brother wanted to see Light-in-the-Night, and he also knew that he should not push his father, who had already agreed to let Bernardo travel to Spain with him.

Plans to send Diego to school in Mexico City had changed with the arrival of a letter from Tomás de Romeu, Alejandro de la Vega's oldest friend in the world. When they were young, they had fought together in the war in Italy, and for more than twenty years they had kept in touch through sporadic letters. While Alejandro was fulfilling his destiny in America, Tomás had married a Catalan heiress and had devoted himself to the good life, until she died in childbirth, at which point he had no alternative but to come to his senses and take charge of his two daughters and what little remained of his wife's fortune. In his letter, Tomás de Romeu commented that Barcelona was still the most interesting city in Spain, and that it offered the best possible education for a young man, because they were living in fascinating times. In 1808 Napoleon had invaded Spain with a hundred and fifty thousand men; he forced the king to abdicate in favor of his own brother, Joseph Bonaparte, all of which had seemed outrageous to Alejandro de la Vega until he received his friend's letter. Tomás explained that only the primitive patriotism of ignorant masses stirred up by minor clergy and a few fanatics could oppose the liberal ideas of the French, who wanted to bring an end to feudalism and religious oppression. Their influence, he said, was a fresh, renewing wind that was sweeping away medieval institutions like the Inquisition and the privileges of nobles and military. In his letter, Tomás de Romeu offered Diego the hospitality of his home, where he would be looked after and loved like a son. He could complete his education in the School of Humanities, which although religious in orientation—and he was no friend of the cassock—had an excellent reputation. He added, as the final enticement, that the boy could study with the famed fencing master Manuel Escalante, who had settled in Barcelona after traveling through Europe, teaching his art. That last carrot was all Diego needed to keep begging his father so insistently to let him go to Spain that in the end Alejandro relented, but his surrender was more the result of exhaustion than conviction, since his friend Tomás could not offer any argument that lessened his dismay at knowing that his country was invaded by foreigners. Father and son were very careful not to tell Regina that, worse yet, Spain was overrun by guerrilla fighters—a bloody form of warfare devised by the people to combat Napoleon's troops. Though not effective in recapturing territory, the guerillas could dart out and sting the enemy like wasps, exhausting their resources—and their patience.

The birthday *sarao* began with a mass conducted by Padre Mendoza, horse races, and a bullfight, in which Diego himself made several passes with the cape before the professional torero entered the ring. Those events were followed by a performance of itinerant acrobats, and the festivities ended with artificial fireworks and a ball. Meals were served to five hundred guests for three days in accordance to social class: pure-blooded Spanish, comfortably shaded beneath a grape-laden arbor, at the main tables set with tablecloths embroidered in Tenerife; "decent people" dressed in their Sunday best at tables to the side but still in the shade; Indians in full sun on the patios where the meat was roasted, the tortillas toasted, and pots of chili and *mole* simmered all day. The guests came from the four cardinal points, and for the first time in history there was congested carriage traffic along the Camino Real. Not one girl from a respectable family missed the party; every mother had an eye on the only heir of Alejandro de la Vega—even though he had one-quarter Indian blood. Among the candidates was Lolita Pulido, the niece of Don Juan Alcázar, a gentle, coquettish fourteen, very different from her cousin Carlos. Even though Alejandro de la Vega detested

Juan Alcázar because of the incident with the Indians, he had to invite him and all his family because he was one of the important men of the town. Diego did not speak to the rancher or his son Carlos, but he was attentive to Lolita. He did not see any reason that the girl should be punished for the sins of her uncle. Besides, she had been sending him love notes for a year through her chaperone, which he had not answered, partly out of shyness but also because he had wanted to stay as far away as possible from any member of the Alcázar family, even a niece. The mothers of marriageable girls were greatly disappointed when they realized that Diego was not even remotely ready to think about a sweetheart; he was much younger than one might expect of a fifteen-year-old. At a time when other sons of dons were growing mustaches and serenading, Diego still had not started shaving, and he swallowed his tongue when he had to talk to a girl.

The governor came from Monterey, bringing with him a Count Orloff, a relative of the czarina of Russia and the man she had put in charge of the Alaska territory. He was nearly seven feet tall, with impossibly blue eyes, and he was decked out in the colorful uniform of the Hussars: all in scarlet, a short, white-fur-trimmed jacket over his shoulder, his chest adorned with ornamental gold cord, and a plumed bicorne in his hand. He was quite the handsomest man ever seen in that part of the world. In Moscow Orloff had heard the story of a pair of white bears that Diego de la Vega had trapped alive and dressed in women's clothing when he was only eight years old. Diego saw no reason to relieve him of his error, but Alejandro, with his overzealous love of precision, hastened to explain that it wasn't two bears, but one, and one with dark fur at that—there was no other kind in California; that Diego had not captured it alone, but with the help of two friends; that he had pasted the hat on with tar; and that he had been ten, not eight, as the story went. Carlos Alcázar and his gang, by then infamous bullies, passed almost unnoticed in the mass of guests, but not García, who had had a few too many drinks and was publicly wailing over Diego's leaving. At that time, the tavern owner's son was the size of a buffalo, but he was still the same frightened little boy, and he still admired Diego with the same bedazzled allegiance. The presence of the splendid Russian nobleman and the enormous expense of the party had temporarily silenced the evil tongues in the colony. Regina took pleasure in seeing the same snobs who had always disdained her bow and kiss her hand. Alejandro de la Vega, completely alien to such pettiness, walked among his guests with pride in his social position, his hacienda, his son, and for once, his wife, who appeared at the ball dressed like a duchess in a blue velvet dress and a lace mantilla from Brussels.

Bernardo had galloped two days up into the mountains to his tribe's village to say good-bye to Light-in-the-Night. She was waiting for him; the Indians' "mail" had spread the news of his coming trip throughout the province. She took his hand and led him to the river to ask what lay beyond the sea and when he thought to return. He sketched a rough map on the ground with a stick but he could not help her understand the enormous distances that separated her village from that mythic land of Spain, because he himself could not imagine them. Padre Mendoza had showed him a globe of the world, but that painted sphere had no connection with reality. As for when he would return, he signed to her that he wasn't sure, but that it would be many years. "In that case, I want you to take something of me to remember," said Light-in-the-Night. With eyes gleaming with ageless wisdom, the girl took off her necklaces of seeds and feathers, the red sash around her waist, her rabbit-skin boots, and her kidskin tunic, and stood naked in the golden light filtering through the leaves of the trees. Bernardo felt that his blood was turning to molasses, that amazement and gratitude were strangling him, that his soul was escaping in sighs. He did not know what to do, standing before that extraordinary creature, so different from him, so absolutely beautiful, and offering herself like the most extraordinary gift. Light-in-the-Night took one of his hands and placed it on her breast. She took the other hand and slipped it behind her waist, then she lifted her arms and began to undo her hair, which fell like a cascade of crow feathers across her shoulders. Bernardo sobbed and murmured her name—"Light-in-the-

Night"—the first words she had ever heard from him. She welcomed the sound of her name with a kiss, and she went on kissing Bernardo and bathing his face with before-the-fact tears because she was missing him even before he left. Hours later, when Bernardo emerged from his undreamed-of bliss and was able to think again, he dared suggest the unthinkable to Light-in-the-Night: that they spend their lives together. She answered with a happy laugh and told him that he was still a runny-nosed boy; maybe the voyage would help him become a man.

Bernardo spent several weeks with his tribe, and during that time things very basic to his life happened, but he has not wished to tell me about them. What little I know, I was told by Light-in-the-Night. Although I can easily imagine the rest, I shall not, out of respect for Bernardo's reserved character. I do not want to offend him. He returned to the hacienda in time to help Diego pack their things for the journey in the same trunks Eulalia de Callís had sent many years before. As soon as Bernardo appeared, Diego knew that something fundamental had changed in the life of his milk-brother, but when he tried to find out what it was, he was met with a stone face that forestalled any further inquiry. Then he guessed that the secret had to do with Light-in-the-Night, and he stopped asking questions. For the first time in their lives there was something they could not share.

Alejandro de la Vega had ordered a prince's wardrobe for his son from Mexico City, which he completed with a new sword, dueling pistols inlaid with mother-of-pearl, and the silk-lined black cape with silver buttons from Toledo that had been Eulalia's gift. Diego added his mandolin, a very useful instrument should he ever conquer his shyness with women, his fencing épée, his cowhide whip, and Maestro Manuel Escalante's book. By contrast, Bernardo's luggage consisted of the clothes he was wearing, an identical set to change into, a black mantle of Castillian wool, and boots large enough for his wide feet, which Padre Mendoza gave him because he thought he should not go barefoot in Spain.

The day before the boys' departure, White Owl came to tell

them good-bye. She would not come into the house because she knew that it embarrassed Alejandro de la Vega that she was his mother-in-law, and she did not want to cause trouble for Regina. She met the two boys on the patio, far from listening ears, and gave them the presents she had brought them. For Diego she had a flask filled with the sleeping potion, with the warning that he use it only to save human life. By the look on her face, Diego realized that she knew he had stolen the magic potion five years before. Hot with shame, he assured her that she could rest easy; he had learned his lesson. He would guard the mixture like a treasure, and he would never steal again. She brought Bernardo a leather pouch containing a braid of black hair. Light-in-the-Night had sent it with a message: that he go in peace and take his time becoming a man, because even if many moons went by, on his return she would be waiting with her love intact. Deeply touched, Bernardo asked the grandmother with gestures how it could be that the most beautiful girl in the universe would love him, that he was a flea, and she answered that she didn't know, that women were strange that way. Then she added, with a mischievous wink, that any woman would fall in love with a man who spoke only for her. Bernardo put the pouch around his neck and beneath his shirt, where it lay next to his heart.

The de la Vegas, mother and father, with their servants, and Padre Mendoza with his neophytes, came down to the beach to give the boys a good send-off. A yawl carried them out to the three-masted schooner *Santa Lucía*, under the command of Captain José Díaz, who had promised to deliver them safe and sound to Panama, the first stage of the long voyage to Europe. The last Diego and Bernardo saw before climbing aboard was the proud figure of White Owl in her rabbit-skin mantle and with her untamable hair blowing in the wind, waving good-bye from a rock cliff near the sacred caves of the Indians.

PART TWO

Barcelona, 1810–1812

*I* am encouraged to continue. I do so with a light heart, since you have read this far. The part to come is more important than what happened before. A person's childhood is not easy to recount, but it is necessary if I am to give you the full picture. Childhood is a miserable period filled with unfounded fears, such as being afraid of imaginary monsters, and of ridicule; from the literary point of view it has no suspense, since children tend to be a little dull. Furthermore, they have no power; adults decide for them, and they do it badly; they drive home into their little ones their own mistaken ideas about reality, and then their offspring spend the rest of their lives trying to break free of those beliefs. That was not necessarily the case with Diego de la Vega, our Zorro, because from an early age he did more or less what he pleased. He was fortunate in that the people around him, preoccupied with their own passions and concerns, paid little attention to him. He reached the age of fifteen with no great vices or virtues, except for a disproportionate love of justice, though whether that is a vice or a virtue, I am not sure. Let us just say that it is an integral part of his character. I could add that another of his qualities is vanity, but that would be to get ahead of the story; that developed later, when he realized that the number of his enemies was swelling—always a good sign—and that of his admirers as well, especially those of the female gender. Now he is a fine-looking man, but at fifteen, when he arrived in Barcelona, he was still a stripling with protruding ears, and his voice had not yet changed. The problem of the ears was the inspiration for wearing a mask; it filled the dual purpose of hiding both his identity and those fawn-like appendages. Had Moncada seen those ears on Zorro, he would have recognized immediately that his detested rival was Diego de la Vega.

And now, if you will allow me, I shall continue my narration, which about here becomes interesting, at least for me, since it was during this time that I met our hero.

The merchant ship *Santa Lucía*—which sailors called *Adelita* both out of affection and because they were sick of vessels with saints' names—made the journey between Pueblo de los Angeles and Panama City in a week's time. Captain José Díaz had been sailing up and down the Pacific coast of America for eight years, and during that time had accumulated a small fortune with which he planned to find a wife thirty years younger than he and then retire to his village in Murcia. Alejandro de la Vega felt a twinge of unease as he entrusted his son Diego to Díaz; he thought of the captain as a man of pliable morals. It was said that he had made his money from smuggling and dealing in women of carefree reputation. The phenomenal Panamanian woman whose unfettered love of life lighted the nights of gentlemen in Pueblo de los Angeles had come there via the *Santa Lucía.* However, Diego decided, that was no reason to be uneasy; better that Diego be in the hands of someone he knew, however questionable, than sail alone across the world. Diego and Bernardo would be the only passengers on board, and he was confident that the captain would watch them closely. The crew consisted of twelve experienced men divided into two groups called "port" and "starboard" to differentiate them, though those classifications had no meaning in this case. While one shift worked their four-hour watch, the other rested and played cards. Once Diego and Bernardo got over their seasickness and grew accustomed to the motion of the ship, they were able to join in normal shipboard life. They made friends with the sailors, who were kind to and protective of them, and spent their time in the same activities as the men. Most of the day the captain was locked in his stateroom with a mestiza woman, completely unaware that the boys in his charge were leaping around like monkeys in the rigging, risking skull fractures.

Diego turned out to be as skillful in acrobatics on the ropes—hanging by a hand or a leg—as he was in cards. He had luck in being dealt good hands, and he was terrifyingly slick in his play. With a face of purest innocence he fleeced the expert players; had they been betting money, they would have been bled dry, but they bet only beans or shells. Money was prohibited on board ship, precisely to avoid having the crew massacre one another over gambling debts. A heretofore unknown side of his milk brother was being revealed to Bernardo.

"We will never go hungry in Europe, Bernardo, because there will always be someone to beat at cards, and then it will be gold doubloons and not beans. How about that? Don't look at me like that, for God's sake—you would think I'm a criminal. The bad thing about you is that you're so holier-than-thou. Don't you see that at last we're free? There's no Padre Mendoza around to threaten us with hell."

Diego laughed; he was used to talking to Bernardo and answering himself.

As they approached Acapulco, the sailors began to suspect that Diego was doing a little double-dealing, and they threatened to throw him overboard when the captain wasn't looking; fortunately along came the whales and distracted them. They came by the dozens, colossal creatures whispering in a chorus of love and stirring up the sea with their impassioned leapings. The whales would swim so near the *Santa Lucía* that the men could count the yellowish crustaceans on their backs. Their skin, dark and slightly textured, told the complete story of each of those giants and that of their ancestors from centuries back. Once in a while one of them breached, falling gracefully back into the water. Their spouts sprinkled the ship with a fine, cool spray. In the effort of dodging the whales and the excitement of reaching port in Acapulco, the sailors forgave Diego, but they warned him to be careful: it is easier to die from being a card shark, they said, than being a soldier in war. Furthermore, Bernardo, with his telepathic scruples, would not leave him alone, and Diego had to promise that he would not use his new proficiency to make himself rich at the cost of others, as he had been planning.

The best thing about life on shipboard, aside from being taken to their destination, was the freedom the boys had to attempt athletic feats that only tried-and-true sailors and freaks in the fair could perform. As children they had hung upside down from the eaves by their feet, a sport that Regina and Ana vainly tried to discourage with swipes of their brooms. On the *Santa Lucía* there was no one to forbid the boys to take risks, and they seized the opportunity to develop the latent abilities they had had since childhood, talents that would serve them well in the world. They learned to swing like trapeze artists, swarm up the rigging like spiders, keep their balance eighty feet in the air, descend from the top of the mast holding onto the ropes, and slide along a tightrope to furl sails. No one paid the least attention to them, and in truth no one cared if they did fall and split their heads open. The sailors gave them some basic lessons. They taught them to tie seamen's knots, to sing in chorus when more strength was needed, to knock their biscuits to loosen the weevils, never to whistle under sail, because it would cause the wind to shift, to sleep in short snatches, like newborn babies, and to drink rum laced with gunpowder to prove their manliness. Neither of them passed this last test; Diego nearly died from nausea, and Bernardo wept all night after he saw his mother. The first mate, a Scotsman named McFerrin, who was much more expert in matters of navigation than the captain, gave them their most important counsel: "One hand for sailing, the other for you." He told them that at every moment, even in calm water, they should hold on to something. Once when Bernardo had gone out on the poop deck to see whether sharks were following, he forgot. He could not see them anywhere, but he had the feeling that as soon as the cook threw the scraps overboard, they would appear. He was thinking about that, distractedly scanning the surface, when the ship unexpectedly lurched and threw him overboard. He was a good swimmer, and by luck someone had seen him fall and raised the alarm; if they hadn't, that would have been the end of it, because not even in those circumstances could he get out a sound. His dunking gave rise to a disagreement. Captain José Díaz thought that in view of the nuisance and the loss of time, it was not worth the trouble to stop and lower a dinghy to look for him. If it had been the son of Alejandro de la Vega, perhaps he would not have been so hesitant, but this was only a dumb Indian—in both senses of the word. He would have to be stupid to have fallen overboard, he argued. While the captain hesitated, pressed by McFerrin and the rest of the crew, for whom rescuing anyone who falls overboard was an inalienable principle of sailing, Diego dived in after his brother. He closed his eyes and jumped without thinking, because from the ship the distance down to the water looked enormous. He also remembered the sharks, which, if not there at that moment, were never too far away. The shock of the cold waves left him dazed for a few seconds, but Bernardo reached him in a few strokes and held him with his nose above water. Given that his prize passenger ran the risk of being gobbled up if he didn't act soon, José Díaz authorized the rescue. The Scotsman and three other men had already lowered the boat by the time the first sharks appeared and began their eager dance around the two bobbing figures. Diego yelled until he choked and swallowed water, while Bernardo calmly held him with one arm and stroked with the other. McFerrin fired his pistol at the nearest shark, and immediately the sea was tinged with a brushstroke the color of rust. That caught the attention of the other predators, which fell upon the wounded killer with the clear intention of having it for lunch, giving time to the sailors to help the boys. The applause and whistles of the crew celebrated the maneuver.

Between lowering the boat, locating the boys, beating off the boldest sharks with their oars, and returning to the ship, a lot of time was lost. The captain considered it a personal insult that Diego had jumped in after Bernardo, forcing his hand, and as reprisal he forbade him to climb the masts—but it was too late, because by then they were off Panama, where he was to leave his passengers. The youths sadly bid the crew of the *Santa Lucía* farewell and went ashore with their luggage, armed with the dueling pistols, the sword, and Diego's whip—as deadly as a cannon—as well as Bernardo's slaughtering knife, a weapon useful for everything from cleaning fingernails and slicing bread to hunting large game. Alejandro de la Vega had warned them to trust no one. The natives had a reputation for thievery, and so they would take turns sleeping and not let their trunks out of sight for a minute.

Panama City seemed magnificent to Diego and Bernardo—compared to the small Pueblo de los Angeles, anything would have. For three centuries the riches of the Americas had passed through there, destined for the royal coffers of Spain. From the port goods were transported in mule trains through the mountains, and then in boats down the Chagres River to the Caribbean Sea. The importance of that port, like that of Portobelo on the Atlantic coast of the isthmus, had declined at the same rate that shipments of gold and silver from the colonies dwindled. It was possible to go from the Pacific Ocean to the Atlantic by sailing around the extreme southern tip of the continent at Cape Horn, but a mere glance at the map illustrates what an endless journey that was. As Padre Mendoza explained to the boys, Cape Horn lies where the world of God ends and the world of ghosts begins. Trekking across the narrow waist of the isthmus of Panama, a trip that takes only a couple of days, saves months of sailing, which was why Emperor Charles V, as early as 1534, had dreamed of digging a canal to join the two oceans, a preposterous idea, like so many that occur to certain monarchs. The major drawback in Panama was the miasma—the gaseous emanations rising from rotten jungle vegetation—and the quagmires of the rivers, sources of horrifying plagues. A sobering number of travelers in that country died from yellow fever, cholera, and dysentery. Some also went mad, it was said, but I suppose that applied to fanciful people little fitted for wandering around in the tropics. So many died in epidemics that the gravediggers did not shovel dirt over the common graves piled with corpses because they knew that more would be added in the next hours. To protect Diego and Bernardo from such dangers, Padre Mendoza gave each of them a medal of Saint Christopher, the patron saint of travelers and sailors. Those talismans gave miraculous results, and both survived. A good thing, too, because otherwise I would not be telling this story. The stifling tropical heat took the boys' breath, and the mosquitoes were so big they had to swat them with their boots, but everything else went well. Diego was enchanted with the city, where no one was watching them and where there were so many temptations to choose from. Only Bernardo's sanctimoniousness saved his brother from ending up in some gambling den or in the arms of a woman of goodwill and bad reputation, where he might have perished from a knifing or some exotic illness. Bernardo did not close his eyes that night, not so much to defend them from bandits as to look after Diego.

The two milk brothers and friends ate at the port, then passed the night in a cheap inn where travelers made themselves as comfortable as possible on pallets on the floor. By paying double, they were entitled to hammocks covered with filthy mosquito nets, where they were more or less safe from rats and cockroaches. The next day they started across the mountains toward Cruces on a good cobbled road the width of two mules, which with their characteristic lack of invention regarding names, the Spanish called the Camino Real. In the high country the air was not as heavy and humid as at sea level, and the view of the countryside below was a true paradise. Against the unbroken green of the jungle, richly colored butterflies and jewel-bright birds flashed like magical brushstrokes. The natives were extremely decent; instead of taking advantage of the two young travelers, which they had a reputation for doing, they offered them fish with fried plantain and put them up in a hut that was crawling with vermin but at least offered protection from the torrential rains. The boys were advised to stay away from tarantulas and the green toads that spit in the eyes of the unwary, blinding them. They were also warned of a variety of nut that burns the enamel off teeth and produces lethal stomach cramps.

In some stretches the Chagres River was a dense swamp, but in others the water was crystal clear. River passengers were transported in canoes or flat boats with a capacity of eight or ten passengers along with their baggage. Diego and Bernardo had to wait a whole day, until there were enough people to fill a boat. They wanted to take a dip in the river to cool off—the blazing heat had stunned the snakes and silenced the monkeys—but as soon as they put a toe in the water, the caimans that had been dozing beneath the surface, blending into the slime, came to life. The boys beat a quick retreat, accompanied by the hoots of the natives. Neither of them dared drink the water their amiable hosts offered—it was green with tadpoles—they simply bore their thirst until other passengers, rough merchants and adventurers, shared their bottles of wine and beer. The boys accepted so eagerly and drank with such gusto that afterward neither of them could remember that part of the trip, except for the strange way the natives had of navigating the river. Six men equipped with long poles were stationed on two long narrow catwalks on either side of the boat. Facing the bow, they buried the tips of the poles in the riverbed and then pushed with all their might to move the boat forward. Because of the infernal heat, they were entirely naked. The trip took about eighteen hours, which Diego and Bernardo passed in a state of anesthetized hallucination, spread-eagled on their backs beneath a canvas protecting them from a merciless sun. When they reached their destination, the other travelers, elbowing each other and laughing, had to push them off the boat. That was how, in the twelve leagues between the mouth of the river and the city of Portobelo, they lost the trunk containing most of the princely wardrobe Alejandro de la Vega had acquired for his son. It was actually a lucky stroke, because the latest European fashions had not as yet reached California. Diego's clothing was frankly laughable.

Portobelo, founded in 1500 on the Gulf of Darien, was an essential city; treasures going to Spain were shipped from there, and merchandise from Europe was received. In the opinion of the captains of the time, it was the most efficient and secure port in the Indies, defended by several forts in addition to barriers of coral reefs. The Spanish constructed the forts with coral mined from the depths of the sea, workable when it was still wet, but so resistant when it dried that cannonballs scarcely made a dent in it. Once a year, when the Royal Treasure Fleet arrived, there was a fair that lasted forty days; at that time the population grew by thousands and thousands of visitors. Diego and Bernardo had heard that in the Casa Real del Tesoro, gold bars were stacked up like firewood, but they were in for a disappointment: the city had declined in recent years, partly because of attacks by pirates, but most of all because the American colonies were not as profitable for Spain as they had been. The city's wood and stone dwellings were discolored by rain, the public buildings and storehouses were overgrown with weeds, and the forts languished in an eternal siesta. Despite all that, there were several ships in the port and swarms of slaves loading precious metals, cotton, tobacco, and chocolate, as well as unloading crates for the colonies. Among the vessels was the *Madre de Dios,* "Mother of God," on which Diego and Bernardo would cross the Atlantic. That ship, constructed fifty years before but still in excellent condition, was a three-masted square-rigger, larger, slower, and heavier than the schooner *Santa Lucía,* and better suited for ocean travel. Her crowning glory was a spectacular figurehead in the form of a siren. Sailors believed that bare breasts calmed the sea, and those of this marvel were voluptuous. The captain, Santiago de León, appeared to be a man of unique personality. He was short and wiry, with carved features in a face weathered by many seas. He limped, owing to a clumsy operation to remove a musket ball from his left leg; the surgeon had not been able to extract it, and the attempt had left the captain crippled and in pain for the rest of his days. The man was not given to complaining; he gritted his teeth, dosed himself with laudanum, and found distraction in his collection of fabulous maps. These charts pinpointed the places that voyagers tried to locate for centuries, with little success, like El Dorado, the city of pure gold; Atlantis, the sunken continent whose inhabitants are human but have gills like fish; the mysterious islands of Luquebaralideaux in the Mer Sauvage, populated by enormous boneless sausages with sharp teeth that move in herds and feed on the mustard that flows in the streams and is said to cure even the worst wounds. The captain entertained himself by copying the maps and adding sites of his own invention, with detailed descriptions, then selling them for a king's ransom to antique dealers in London. He was not deceiving anyone; he always signed them in his own hand and added a mysterious phrase that anyone in the know would recognize: "A numbered work from the *Encyclopedia of Desires,* complete version."

By Friday the cargo was on board, but the *Madre de Dios* did not set sail because Christ had died on a Friday. That was a bad day to begin a voyage. On Saturday the forty-man crew refused to leave port because a redheaded man had walked by them on the dock and a dead pelican had dropped onto the ship's bridge—two ominous signs. Finally on Sunday, Santiago de León got his men to unfurl the sails. The only passengers were Diego, Bernardo, an auditor returning from Mexico to his own country, and his whiney, ugly thirty-year-old daughter. This señorita fell in love with each and every one of the rough sailors, but they fled from her as if from the devil; everyone knows that virtuous women on board ship attract bad weather and other calamities. The men reached the conclusion that her virtue was the result of lack of opportunity, not her nature. The auditor and his daughter shared a tiny stateroom, but Diego and Bernardo, like the crew, slept in hammocks strung in the foul-smelling mess deck of the ship. The captain's cabin on the quarter-deck served as office, command center, dining room, and game room for officers and passengers. The door and the furniture folded for convenience, like most things on board, where space was the greatest luxury. During their several weeks at sea, the boys did not have an instant of privacy; the most basic functions were performed on a bucket in full view of everyone, if the seas were running high, or if calm, perched on a board projecting out over the water and fitted with a hole. No one knew how the modest daughter of the auditor managed, because no one ever saw her empty a chamber pot. The sailors laid bets about it, at first laughing boisterously but later sobered by fear: constipation that lasted that long had to be the work of witchcraft. Aside from the constant movement and the crowding, the most notable thing about the ship was the noise. Wood creaked, metal clinked, barrels rolled, ropes moaned, and water lashed the hull. For Diego and Bernardo, accustomed to the solitude, space, and silence of California, adjusting to life on shipboard was not easy.

Diego liked to sit on the shoulders of the figurehead, a perfect place to gaze at the infinite line of the horizon, be splashed with salt water, and watch the dolphins. He would put an arm around the wooden damsel's head and grip her nipples with his toes. Considering the boy's athleticism, the captain limited himself to ordering him to tie a rope around his waist; if he fell from there, the ship would pass right over him. Later, however, when he caught Diego at the tip of the mainmast, more than a hundred feet in the air, he said nothing. He had decided that if the boy was fated to die young, he could not prevent it. There was always activity on the ship, and it went on through the night, though most of the work was done during the day. Bells signaled the first watch at noon, when the sun was at its zenith and the captain took a sighting to fix their location. At that hour the cook handed out a pint of lemonade per man, to prevent scurvy, and then the mate distributed rum and tobacco, the only vices allowed on board, where betting money, fighting, falling in love, or even blaspheming was forbidden. At nautical twilight, that mysterious hour of dawn and evening when stars twinkle in the heavens but the line of the horizon is visible, the captain took new sightings with his sextant and consulted his chronometers and the large book of celestial ephemerides that indicate the position of the stars at every moment. For Diego, that geometric operation was fascinating; all the stars looked alike to him, and in every direction he saw nothing but the same lead-colored sea and the same white sky, but before long he learned to observe with the eyes of a navigator. The captain also constantly consulted the barometer that signaled the changes in air pressure that heralded storms and the days when his leg would be more painful.

At first, milk, meat, and vegetables were served at meals, but before a week had gone by, everyone aboard was limited to beans, rice, dried fruit, and the eternal hard-as-marble biscuits seething with weevils. There was also salted meat, which the cook soaked a couple of days in water and vinegar before tossing it into the pot, hoping it would be less like saddle leather. What a great business deal his father could make with his smoked meat, Diego thought, but Bernardo pointed out that it was a pipe dream to think they could get sufficient supplies to Portobelo. At the captain's table, to which Diego, the auditor and his daughter—though not Bernardo—were always invited there was also pickled cow's tongue, olives, cheese from La Mancha, and wine. The captain put his chessboard and his cards at the passengers' disposal, along with a handful of books that only Diego was interested in. Among them he found a couple of essays about possible independence for the colonies. Diego admired the example of the United States, which had freed itself from the English yoke, but it had not occurred to him that similar aspirations on the part of Spanish colonists in America might be praiseworthy until he read the captain's publications.

Santiago de León turned out to be such an entertaining conversationalist that Diego sacrificed hours of happy acrobatics in the rigging in order to talk with him and study his fantastic maps. The captain, a solitary man, discovered the pleasure of sharing his knowledge with a young and inquisitive mind. The man was a tireless reader and always carried boxes of books that he exchanged in every port. He had been around the world several times, and he knew lands as strange as those described on his fabulous maps; he had been near death so many times that he had lost any fear of living. The most revealing thing to Diego, who was accustomed to absolute truths, was that this man with a Renaissance mentality doubted nearly everything that formed the intellectual and moral world of Alejandro de la Vega, Padre Mendoza, and Diego's schoolmaster. At times Diego had questioned the rigid precepts hammered into his brain since his birth, but he had never dared challenge them aloud. When some rule made him too uncomfortable, he quietly ignored it; he never rebelled openly. With Santiago de León he dared for the first time to talk about subjects he had never discussed with his father. He was amazed to discover that there were many ways to think. De León opened his eyes to the fact that the Spanish were not the only ones who claimed superiority over the rest of humanity; every nationality suffered from the same delusion. In wars, the Spanish committed exactly the same atrocities as the French, or any other army: they raped, robbed, tortured, and murdered; Christians, Moors, and Jews all maintained that their God was the only true God, and held other religions in contempt. The captain was in favor of abolishing the monarchy and making the colonies independent, two concepts that were revolutionary to Diego, who had been raised with the belief that the king was holy and the obligation of every Spaniard was to conquer and Christianize other lands. Santiago de León exalted the equality, liberty, and fraternity of the French revolution, though he had never accepted the French invasion of Spain. On this subject he showed signs of fierce patriotism: he would rather see his country sunk in the obscurantism of the Middle Ages, he said, than awake to the triumph of modern ideas if they were imposed by foreigners. He could not forgive Napoleon, who had forced the king of Spain to abdicate and then replaced him with his brother, Joseph Bonaparte, whom the people had nicknamed Pepe Botellas after his love of the bottle.

"All tyranny is abominable, my boy," the captain concluded. "Napoleon is a tyrant. What good was the revolution if an emperor replaced the king? Nations should be governed by a council of learned men who must answer to the people for their actions."

"The kings' authority is divine in origin, Captain," Diego argued weakly, repeating his father's words without really understanding what he was saying.

"Who has proved that? As far as I know, young de la Vega, God has not spoken to that subject."

"According to the Holy Scriptures—"

"You have read them?" Santiago de León interrupted decisively. "Nowhere in the Scriptures does it say that the Bourbons are to rule in Spain, or Napoleon in France. Besides, there is nothing holy about Holy Scriptures. They were written by men, not God."

It was night, and the two were walking back and forth on the bridge. The sea was calm, and above the eternal creaking of the ship Bernardo's flute could be heard with hypnotic clarity, seeking his mother and Light-in-the-Night in the stars.

"Do you believe that God exists?" the captain asked Diego.

"Of course, Captain!"

With a sweep of his arm, Santiago de León indicated the dark firmament sprinkled with constellations. "If God exists, I am sure He is not interested in designating kings for every star in the heavens," he said.

Diego de la Vega protested in horror. Doubting God was the last thing on his mind, a thousand times more serious than doubting the divine mandate of the monarchy. The feared Inquisition had burned people at the stake for much less, something that seemed not to worry the captain in the least.

Tired of winning beans and shells from the sailors, Diego turned to frightening them with spine-chilling tales drawn from the captain's books and fantastic maps, which he embellished by drawing from his inexhaustible imagination, in which there were gigantic octopuses with tentacles capable of destroying a ship as large as the *Madre de Dios,* carnivorous salamanders the size of whales, and sirens that from a distance looked like seductive maidens but were in fact monsters with snakelike tongues. Never go near them, Diego warned the sailors, because they hold out their smooth arms to embrace an unwary seaman, kiss him, and then slip their lethal tongues down the poor fool's throat and devour him from the inside out, leaving nothing but a skeleton covered with hide.

"Have you seen those glittering lights on the waves? You know, of course, that they signal the presence of the living dead, Christian sailors who have drowned in attacks by Turkish pirates. Since they were not able to receive absolution for their sins, their souls could not find the way to purgatory. They lie trapped in the wrecks of their ships on the bottom of the ocean and don't even know that they are dead. On nights like this, those wandering souls rise to the surface. If by any chance a ship sails past, the living dead climb on board and steal anything they can find: anchor, wheel, the captain's instruments, ropes, even the masts. But that isn't the worst, my friends— they also need sailors. Any they can catch, they drag down to the depths to help them salvage their boats and sail to Christian shores. I hope that doesn't happen on this voyage, but we must be on guard. If you see any stealthy black figures, you can be sure they are the living dead. You will know them by their capes, which they wear to cloak the rattling of their poor bones."

Diego found, to his delight, that his eloquence produced collective terror. He told his tales at night, after dinner, at the hour when the men were savoring their pint of rum and chewing their tobacco, because it was much easier to make their hair stand on end when it was dark. After laying the groundwork with several days of hair-raising stories, he was ready for the coup de grâce. Dressed entirely in black, wearing gloves and the cape with the buttons from Toledo, he made sudden brief appearances in the darkest corners of the ship. In that getup he was nearly invisible at night, except for his face, but Bernardo had the idea of covering it with a black kerchief in which he cut two holes for the eyes. Several sailors swore they saw at least one of the living dead. Instantly, word traveled that the ship was bewitched, and they laid that at the door of the auditor's daughter, who had to be possessed by a devil, since she never used the chamber pot. She was the only one who could have attracted the ghosts. The rumor reached the ears of the nervous spinster and triggered such a brutal headache that the captain had to sedate her for two days with massive doses of laudanum. When Santiago de León learned what had happened, he summoned the sailors to the bridge and threatened to cut off all liquor and tobacco if they continued to spread such poppycock. Those dancing lights, he told them, were a natural phenomenon caused by weather, and the apparitions they thought they were seeing were the products of suggestion. No one believed the captain, but he had imposed order. Once a semblance of calm had been restored, he led Diego by one wing to his stateroom and when they were alone warned him that if any living dead turned up again on the *Madre de Dios,* he, the captain, would have no reluctance to have Diego flogged.

"I have the right of life or death on my ship; and I'm even more entitled to scar your back for your lifetime. Do we understand one another, young de la Vega?" he growled between clenched teeth, accentuating each word.

It was as clear as day to Diego, but he didn't answer because he was distracted by the glimpse of a medallion hanging around the captain's neck; gold and silver, it was engraved with strange symbols. When Santiago de León noticed that Diego had seen it, he hurriedly tucked it inside and buttoned his jacket. His action was so abrupt that the boy was afraid to ask the significance of the jewel. Once his anger was spent, the captain was gentler.

"If we have favoring winds, and do not run into pirates, this voyage will last six weeks. You will have more than enough opportunity to be bored, my boy. I suggest that instead of terrorizing my men with childish pranks, you spend your time studying. Life is short; there is never enough time to learn."

Diego rapidly figured that he had read nearly everything on board that interested him and by now had conquered the sextant, nautical knots, and sails, but he nodded in agreement; he had another science in mind. He went down to the suffocating hold of the ship, where the cook was preparing Sunday dessert, a pudding of molasses and nuts that the crew eagerly awaited all week. The cook was a man from Genoa who had signed onto the Spanish merchant marine to avoid going to prison, where in all justice he should be for having hacked his wife to death. He had an unsuitable name for a sailor: Galileo Tempesta. Before he took over the galley on the *Madre de Dios,* Tempesta had been a magician, earning his living wandering from market to fair with his sleight-of-hand tricks. He had an expressive face, prominent eyes, and the hands of a virtuoso, with fingers like tentacles. He could make a coin disappear so smoothly that standing only a handspan away, it was impossible to discover how the devil he did it. He used breaks in his labors in the kitchen to practice; when he wasn't palming coins or cards and making daggers disappear, he was sewing secret pockets into hats, boots, linings, and jacket cuffs that he used for hiding multicolored handkerchiefs and live rabbits.

"Señor Tempesta, the captain sent me to ask you to teach me everything you know," Diego blurted out in one breath.

"I don't know much about cooking, boy."

"But I was referring to your magic."

"You don't learn that talking, that you learn doing," Galileo Tempesta replied.

The rest of the voyage he devoted himself to teaching Diego his tricks for the same reason that the captain told the boy about his voyages and showed him his maps: because those men had never enjoyed as much attention as they received from Diego. At the end of the crossing, forty-one days later, Diego, among other amazing feats, could swallow a gold doubloon and pull it whole from one of his notable ears.

The *Madre de Dios* left the city of Portobelo behind and, taking advantage of the Gulf currents, swung north, sailing along the coast of the United States. At about the latitude of Bermuda, she headed into the Atlantic and three weeks later called at the Azores to stock up on water and fresh food. That archipelago of nine volcanic islands belonging to Portugal was an obligatory stop for whalers of every nationality. They arrived at Flores Island—well named, since it was covered with hydrangeas and roses—on the day of a national fiesta. First the crew filled up on wine and the island's typical hearty soup, then played around a while getting into fistfights with American and Norwegian whalers, and finally set off in a group to take part in the running of the bulls. The whole male population of the island, plus visiting sailors, raced in front of the bulls through the steep streets of the town, yelling the obscenities that Captain Santiago de León prohibited on board. The beautiful local women, with flowers in their hair and at their necklines, cheered from a prudent distance, while the priest and two nuns prepared bandages and the sacraments to tend the wounded and dying. Diego knew that any bull is always quicker than the swiftest human, but if it charges blind with anger it is possible to outwit it. The boy had seen so many bulls in his short life that he was not overly afraid. Thanks to his experience, he saved Galileo Tempesta by a hair when a pair of horns aimed at his backside were ready to spear him. Diego ran and whipped the beast with a stick to head it off as the magician dived headfirst into a clump of hydrangeas amid the applause and laughter of the crowd. Then it was Diego's turn to bolt like a buck, with the bull at his heels. Although there was a lot of battering and bruising, no one died of being gored that year. It was the first time in history that had happened, and the people of the Azores did not know whether to take it as a good omen or a warning of disaster. That remained to be seen. In any case, the bulls made a hero of Diego. And Galileo Tempesta, deeply grateful, gave the boy a Moroccan dagger fitted with a hidden spring that allowed the blade to retract into the handle.

The *Madre de Dios* sailed with the trade winds for a few weeks more. Coasting Spain, she passed Cadiz without stopping and headed toward the Strait of Gibraltar, the entrance to the Mediterranean controlled by the English, who were allies of Spain and enemies of Napoleon. With no major alarms, they followed the coast without putting into port, and finally arrived at Barcelona, the end of Diego and Bernardo's journey. To their eyes, the ancient Catalan port resembled a forest of masts and sails. There were ships of every origin, shape, and size. If the youths had been impressed by the little town of Panama, imagine the effect Barcelona had on them. The city lay proud and massive against a leaden sky accented with turrets, towers, and walls. From the harbor it looked like a splendid city, but in the dark of night the face of Barcelona changed. They were not able to debark until the next morning, when Santiago de León lowered dinghies to ferry his impatient crew and passengers ashore. In the greasy harbor hundreds of little launches were circulating among the larger vessels, and thousands of gulls filled the air with their squawking.

Diego and Bernardo bid farewell to the captain, Galileo Tempesta, and the sailors who were pushing and shoving to get into the yawl, in a frenzy to spend their pay on liquor and women. The auditor, meanwhile, had to carry his daughter, who had swooned from the foul odors in the air. And with good reason. When they reached shore, a beautiful and lively but unhealthful port awaited; deep in garbage, it was crawling with rats as big as dogs that boldly darted between the legs of a hurried throng. Wastewater ran in open gutters where barefooted children splashed in play and women emptied chamber pots from upper-story windows, yelling "Heads up!" to passersby, who had to jump aside to keep from being drenched with urine. Barcelona, with its hundred and fifty thousand inhabitants, was one of the most densely populated cities in the world. Encircled by thick walls, guarded by the sinister La Ciudadela fort, and trapped between the ocean and the mountains, it had nowhere to grow but up. Garrets were added to houses, and rooms were subdivided into tiny cubicles where tenants crowded together without fresh air or clean water. Foreigners in assorted attire walked around the docks, insulting one another in incomprehensible tongues: sailors wearing striped stocking caps and sporting parrots on their shoulders, stevedores rheumatic from carrying too-heavy loads, rude vendors selling jerked beef and biscuits, beggars bubbling with lice and pustules, derelicts with ready knives and desperate eyes. Prostitutes of the lowest degree mingled with the crowd, while the more pretentious among them rode in carriages, competing in splendor with distinguished ladies. French soldiers trooped around prodding pedestrians with the butts of their muskets for the pure pleasure of annoying them. Behind their backs, women cursed them and spit on the ground. Nothing, however, could dim the incomparable elegance of that city bathed in the silvery light of the sea. When they stepped onto shore, Diego and Bernardo were so unaccustomed to walking on land that they staggered and nearly fell, just as they had on Flores

Island. They had to hold one another up until they could control the trembling of their knees and focus their eyes.

"And what do we do now, Bernardo? I agree with you that the first thing would be to rent a coach and try to locate the home of Don Tomás de Romeu. You say that first we ought to claim what is left of our luggage? Yes, you're right."

So they pushed their way through the crowd, Diego talking to himself and Bernardo a step behind, alert, fearing that someone would grab his distracted friend's purse. They passed the market, where bovine old women were selling the produce of the sea, standing in puddles of fish heads and guts that were soaking into the ground beneath a cloud of flies. It was here they were intercepted by a tall man with the profile of a buzzard. In Diego's eyes, judging from the blue velvet uniform, the gold epaulets of his jacket, and three-cornered hat perched on his white wig, he had to be an admiral. He greeted the man with a deep bow, sweeping the cobbles with his California sombrero.

"Señor Diego de la Vega?" the stranger inquired, visibly taken aback.

"At your service, caballero," Diego replied.

"I am no caballero, sir. I am Jordi, Don Tomás de Romeu's coachman. I was sent to look for you. I will return later for your luggage," the man clarified with a frown, thinking that the youngster from the Indies was making fun of him.

Diego's ears were beet red, and as he clapped his hat back on his head and prepared to follow, Bernardo was choking with laughter. Jordi led them to a slightly shabby carriage where the family majordomo was waiting. They rolled through tortuous cobbled streets leading away from the port, and soon came to a neighborhood of elegant homes and somber mansions. They turned into the patio of the residence of Tomás de Romeu, a large, dark, three-story house sitting between two churches. The majordomo commented that they were no longer disturbed by bells pealing at all hours because the French had removed the clappers as reprisal against the priests responsible for stirring up the guerrilla fighters. Diego and Bernardo, intimidated by the size of the house, did not even notice how run-down it was. Jordi led Bernardo to the servants' quarters, and the majordomo escorted Diego up the exterior stairs to the *piso noble*, or main floor. They walked through salons in eternal shadow and icy corridors hung with threadbare tapestries and arms from the time of the Crusades. Finally they came to a dusty library badly lighted by a few candles and a dying fire in the fireplace. Tomás de Romeu was waiting there. He welcomed Diego with a fatherly embrace, as if he had known him always.

"I am honored that my good friend Alejandro has entrusted his son to me," he proclaimed. "As of this instant you are a member of our family, Diego. My daughters and I will see to your comfort and contentment."

De Romeu was a ruddy-faced, paunchy man of about fifty, with a roaring voice and thick sideburns and eyebrows. His lips curved upward in an involuntary smile that softened his rather haughty aspect. He was smoking a cigar and holding a glass of sherry in his hand, he asked a few courteous questions about the voyage and about the family Diego had left behind in California, then pulled a silk cord to summon the majordomo, whom he ordered in Catalan to take his guest to his rooms.

"We will dine at ten. You need not dress, we will be just family," he said.

That night in the dining room, an immense hall with ancient furniture that had served several generations, Diego met the daughters of Tomás de Romeu. He needed only one glance to decide that Juliana, the elder, was the most beautiful woman in the world. Possibly he exaggerated, but it was true that the girl had the reputation of being one of the belles of Barcelona, as alluring, everyone said, as the celebrated Madame de Récamier of Paris had been in her day. Her elegant bearing, her classic features, and her raven black hair, milky skin, and jade green eyes were unforgettable. She had so many suitors that the family, and the merely inquisitive, had lost count. Gossip had it that they had all been rejected because her ambitious father wanted to climb a couple of rungs of the social ladder by marrying her to a prince. They were mistaken; Tomás de Romeu was not capable of schemes of that nature. In addition to her remarkable physical attributes, Juliana was cultivated, virtuous, and sentimental; she also played the harp with tremulous fairy fingers and performed charitable works among the poor. When she wafted into the dining room in a delicate white Empire-style batiste gown caught beneath her breasts with a watermelon-colored sash, a fashion that exposed her long neck and round alabaster arms, with her feet shod in satin and a diadem of pearls in her black curls, Diego felt his knees turn to rubber and all reason flee. He bent to kiss her hand, and in his stupefaction at touching her sprayed her with saliva. Horrified, he sputtered an apology, but Juliana smiled like an angel and quietly wiped the back of her hand on her nymph's dress.

Isabel, in contrast, was so ordinary that she did not seem to be of the same blood as her dazzling sister. She was eleven, and not even a good eleven. Her teeth had not quite settled into place, and her bones poked out in various angles. From time to time one eye wandered slightly, which gave her a distracted and deceptively sweet expression—because she was of rather peppery nature. Her chestnut hair was a rebellious tangle barely controlled by a half dozen ribbons; she had nearly outgrown the yellow dress she was wearing, and to complete her orphanlike looks, she was wearing high-buttoned shoes. As Diego would tell Bernardo later, poor Isabel looked like a skeleton with four elbows, and she had enough hair for two heads. Diego, blinded by Juliana, barely glanced in her direction all night, but Isabel observed him openly, taking a rigorous inventory of his antiquated suit, his strange accent, his manners—as out of date as his clothing—and of course his protruding ears. She concluded that this young man from the Indies was mad if he thought he would impress her sister, a conviction underscored by his comical behavior. Isabel sighed, thinking that Diego was going to be a long-term project; he would have to be remade almost entirely, but fortunately she had good raw material to work with: pleasant personality, well-proportioned body, and those amber eyes.

Dinner consisted of mushroom soup, a succulent plate of gems of land and sea—in which the fish rivaled the meat—salads, cheeses, and to end, *crème Catalan,* all washed down with a red wine from the family vineyards. Diego calculated that with that diet, Tomás de Romeu would never grow to be an old man, and his daughters would end up as fat as their father. While the ordinary Spaniard was going hungry, the tables of the well-to-do were always well supplied. After the meal they went into one of the many inhospitable salons, where Juliana delighted them until after midnight with her harp, accompanied, unmusically, by the groans Isabel tore from a badly tuned harpsichord. At that hour, early for Barcelona and late for Diego, Nuria, the chaperone, arrived to suggest to the girls that they should retire. She was a straight-backed woman of near forty, her fine features marred by a hard expression and the harsh severity of her attire: a black dress with starched collar and a black cap with a satin bow tied beneath the chin. The rustling of her petticoats, her tinkling keys, and her squeaking boots announced her presence before she came into sight. She greeted Diego with a barely perceptible bow, after examining him from head to toe with aloof disapproval.

"What am I to do with that boy named Bernardo, that Indian from the Americas?" she asked Tomás de Romeu.

"If it were possible, sir, I would like for Bernardo to share my room. In fact, we are like brothers," Diego intervened.

"Of course, señor. Do whatever needs be done, Nuria," de Romeu ordered, somewhat surprised.

As soon as Juliana retired, Diego felt the onslaught of accumulated fatigue and the weight of dinner in his stomach, but he had to stay another hour, listening to his host's ideas on politics.

"Joseph Bonaparte is an educated and sincere man; I am happy to tell you that he even speaks Spanish and attends the bullfights," said de Romeu.

"But he has usurped the throne of the legitimate king of Spain," Diego rejoined.

"King Charles IV turned out to be an unworthy descendent of

men as outstanding as his father and grandfather. The queen is friv-
olous, and the heir, Ferdinand, is inept; even his parents have no
faith in him. They do not deserve to reign. The French, on the other
hand, have brought modern ideas with them. If this country would
allow Joseph I to govern, instead of waging war against him, it
would leave its backwardness behind. The French army is invincible;
ours, in contrast, is in ruins: no horses, weapons, boots—and our
soldiers are surviving on bread and water."

"Nonetheless," Diego interrupted, "the Spanish people have
resisted the occupation for two years."

"It is true that gangs of armed civilians are waging an insane
guerrilla war, urged on by fanatics and by ignorant clergy. These
masses are striking out blindly; they have no ideas, only resentment."

"I have heard stories about the cruelty of the French."

"Atrocities are committed by both sides, young de la Vega. The
guerrillas are murdering Spanish civilians who refuse to help them,
as well as the French. The Catalans are the worst; you cannot imagine the cruelty they are capable of. Maestro Francisco Goya has
painted those horrors. Is his work known in America?"

"I believe not, señor."

"You must see his paintings, Don Diego, in order to understand
that in this war there are no good men, only bad," sighed de Romeu,
and held forth on other subjects until Diego's eyes closed.

In the next months Diego de la Vega got a glimpse of how volatile and
complex the situation in Spain had become, and how far behind the
news lagged at home. His father reduced politics to black and white,
because that was how it was in California, but in the confusion of
Europe tones of gray predominated. In his first letter, Diego told his
father about the voyage and his impressions of Barcelona and the Catalans, whom he described as zealous regarding their freedom, explosive
in temperament, sensitive in questions of honor, and as hardworking as
draft mules. They themselves cultivated their reputation for being tight-
fisted, he said, but in private they were generous. He added that there

was nothing they resented so much as taxes, especially when they had to pay them to the French. He also described the de Romeu family, omitting his ridiculous love for Juliana, which might be interpreted as an abuse of hospitality. In his second letter he tried to explain the political situation, though he suspected that when his father received it in a few months' time, it would all have changed.

*Esteemed Sir: You find me well and I am learning a lot, especially philosophy and Latin in the School of Humanities. It will please you to know that Maestro Manuel Escalante has accepted me in his Academy and honors me with his friendship, an undeserved honor, of course. Allow me to tell you something about the situation here. Your close friend, Don Tomás de Romeu, is a great aficionado of all things French—shall we say a Francophile. There are other liberals like himself who share his political ideas but still detest the French. They fear that Napoleon will convert Spain into a satellite of France, which apparently Don Tomás de Romeu would look upon with favor.*

*Just as you told me to do, I have visited Her Excellency Doña Eulalia de Callís. Through her I have learned that the nobility, like the Catholic Church and the common people, await the return of King Fernando VII, whom they call "The Desired." The people, who distrust in equal measure the French, the liberals, the nobles, and change in any form, are determined to expel the invaders and fight with whatever they have at hand: axes, clubs, knives, picks, and hoes.*

Diego found these topics quite interesting—they talked of nothing else in the School of Humanities and in the house of Tomás de Romeu—but he did not lose any sleep over them. He had a thousand different things on his mind, the main one being contemplation of Juliana. In that enormous house, impossible to light or heat, the family used only a few rooms on the main level and a wing of the second floor. More than once Bernardo caught Diego hanging like a fly from the balcony to spy on Juliana when she was sewing with Nuria or studying her lessons. The girls had been spared the convent school where daughters of fashionable families were educated, thanks to their father's antipathy to religious instruction. Tomás de Romeu said that behind the convent shutters poor young girls were fodder for evil nuns who filled their heads with demons, and for clergy who pawed them under the pretext of confessing them. He assigned his girls a tutor, an emaciated little fellow with a pockmarked face, who swooned in Juliana's presence and whom Nuria watched like a hawk. Isabel was also his student, although the teacher ignored her so totally that he never learned her name.

Juliana treated Diego like an unbalanced younger brother. She called him by his given name and spoke warmly to him, following the example of Isabel, who was affectionate from the beginning. Much later, when their lives became more complicated and they went through difficult times together, Nuria, too, warmed up to him. She came to love him like a nephew, but in that period she still addressed him as Don Diego: a simple first name was used only among family members or when speaking to an inferior. It was several weeks before Juliana suspected that she had broken Diego's heart, just as she never realized she had done the same to her unhappy tutor. When Isabel pointed it out to her, she laughed with surprise; fortunately Diego never knew that until several years later.

It was only a brief time before Diego realized that Tomás de Romeu was neither as noble nor as rich as he had at first seemed. The mansion and lands had belonged to his deceased wife, the heiress to a bourgeois family that had made a fortune in the silk industry. Upon his father-in-law's death, Tomás was left to handle the business affairs, but he was not especially gifted in commerce, and he immediately began to lose what he had inherited. Contrary to the reputation of most Catalans, Don Tomás knew how to spend money with grace, but he did not know how to earn it. Year after year his income had decreased, and at the rate he was going, he soon would be obliged to sell his house and descend in social level. Among Juliana's numerous suitors was one Rafael Moncada, a noble with a considerable fortune. An alliance with him would resolve Tomás de Romeu's problems, but in his defense I have to say that he would never press his daughter to accept Moncada. Diego estimated that his father's hacienda in California was worth several times more than the properties of de Romeu, and he wondered whether Juliana might consider going to the New World with him. He laid that plan before Bernardo, and in his private language, his brother made Diego see that if he didn't hurry, another more mature, handsome, and interesting candidate would make off with his damsel. Accustomed to Bernardo's sarcasm, Diego was not disheartened, but he decided to speed up his education as much as possible. He could see the day when he could claim to be a true Spanish gentleman. He dedicated himself to learning Catalan, a tongue that he thought very melodious, he attended the School of Humanities, and he went every day to classes at Maestro Manuel Escalante's Fencing Academy for the Instruction of Nobles and Caballeros.

The picture that Diego had in mind of the celebrated maestro did not coincide in any way with reality. After having studied Escalante's manual down to the last comma, he imagined him to be an Apollo, a compendium of virtues and manly beauty. He turned out to be a disagreeable, meticulous, spruce little man with the face of an ascetic, disdainful lips, and pomaded mustache, a man to whom fencing seemed to be the one true religion. His students were of the finest lineage—all except Diego de la Vega, whom Escalante accepted less on Tomás de Romeu's recommendation than because Diego passed the admission examination with honors.

The maestro handed Diego a foil. "En garde, monsieur!"

Diego adopted the preparatory position: right foot forward, the left at a right angle to the body, knees slightly bent, torso half turned, face forward, right arm extended over the right foot, the left held behind the body at approximately the same angle as the foil arm.

"Lunge! Recovery! Thrust! Engage! Coupé! Press! Bind!"

Soon the maestro stopped issuing instructions. From feints they passed quickly through the entire array of attacks and parries in a violent and macabre dance. Diego warmed to the test and began to fight as if his life were at stake, with a fervor near anger. For the first time in many years Escalante felt sweat running down his face and soaking his shirt. He was pleased, and the trace of a smile began to lift the corners of his thin lips. He never praised anyone easily, but he was impressed with the speed, precision, and strength of this young man.

"Where did you say you had learned to fence, caballero?" he asked after crossing foils with him for a few minutes.

"With my father, in California, maestro."

"California?"

"To the north of Mexico—"

"You need not explain, I have seen a map," Manuel Escalante interrupted curtly.

"B-beg pardon, maestro," Diego stammered. "I have studied your book and practiced for years—"

"I see that. You are a diligent student, it seems. But you must curb your impatience and acquire elegance. You have the style of a pirate, but that can be remedied. First lesson: calm. You must never fight in anger. The firmness and stability of the blade depend on equanimity of mind. Do not forget that. I shall receive you Monday through Saturday mornings on the stroke of eight. If you miss even one time, you need not return. Good afternoon, sir."

With that, he dismissed him. Diego had to struggle not to whoop with joy, but once outside he jumped up and down around Bernardo, who was waiting at the door with the horses.

"We will become the best swordsmen in the world, Bernardo. Yes, my brother, you heard me right, you will learn what I learn. Oh, you are right, the maestro will not accept you as a student, he is very particular. If he knew that I have one-fourth Indian blood, he would kick me out of his academy. But don't worry, I intend to teach you everything I learn. The maestro says I lack style. What is that?"

Manuel Escalante fulfilled his promise to polish Diego's art, and Diego kept his to pass on those skills to Bernardo. They practiced fencing every day in one of the large, empty salons in the home of

Tomás de Romeu, almost always with Isabel present. According to Nuria, that girl had a devilish curiosity about men's ways, but she covered up Isabel's antics because she had taken care of her ever since her mother had died at her birth. The brash girl talked Diego and Bernardo into teaching her to handle a fencing épée and to ride astride, as women did in California. With Maestro Escalante's manual, she spent hours practicing alone before a mirror, under the patient gaze of her sister and Nuria, who were working their cross-stitch embroidery. Diego had a selfish reason for resigning himself to the younger girl's company: she had convinced him that she could intercede on his behalf with Juliana—something she never did do. Bernardo, on the other hand, seemed always pleased to have her around.

Diego's milk brother had an equivocal position in the hierarchy of the house, where about eighty people lived, counting servants, employees, secretaries, and "distant cousins," as the poor relatives that Tomás de Romeu housed under his roof were called. He slept in one of the three rooms placed at Diego's disposal but did not go into the family salons unless summoned, and he ate in the kitchen. He had no particular responsibilities, and had time left over to wander around the city. He came to know the different faces of boisterous Barcelona, from the castles and mansions of Catalan nobles to the crowded rat- and lice-infested rooms of the lower classes, a hotbed of fights and epidemics; he roamed the ancient section constructed upon Roman ruins, a labyrinth of twisting alleyways scarcely wide enough for a burro to pass through, the popular markets, artisans' shops, the stalls where Turkish merchants sold baubles and bibelots, and the always bustling docks. Sundays after mass, he lingered to admire the groups dancing delicate *sardanas*, which to him seemed a perfect reflection of the solidarity, order, and lack of ostentation of the people of Barcelona. Like Diego, he learned Catalan; otherwise he could not have understood what was happening around him. Spanish and French were the languages of high society and the government; Latin was used for academic and religious matters, and Catalan for everything else. Bernardo's silence, and the dignity he conveyed, won the respect of everyone in the de Romeu mansion. The servants, who affectionately called him *el Indiano*, were not sure whether he was deaf, but they assumed he was, and so spoke freely in front of him, which allowed him to learn many things. Tomás de Romeu was entirely unaware of his existence; for him servants were invisible. Nuria was intrigued by the fact that he was an Indian, the first she had met face to face. Thinking he would not understand her, for the first few days she made monkey faces and gestured theatrically, but when she learned that he wasn't deaf, she began speaking normally to him. And as soon as she was told that he had been baptized, she began to like him. She had never had a more attentive listener. Convinced that Bernardo could not betray her confidence, she fell into the habit of telling him her dreams, true epic fantasies, and of inviting him to listen to Juliana read aloud at the hour for chocolate. As for Juliana, she addressed him with the same gentleness she exhibited with everyone. She understood that he was not Diego's servant but his brother, having shared Bernardo's mother's milk, but she made no effort to communicate with him because she supposed that they had little to say to one another. Not so with Isabel; Bernardo became her best friend and ally. She learned the Indians' sign language and how to interpret the inflexions of his flute, though she was never able to participate in the telepathic dialogues Bernardo shared with Diego. It didn't matter anyway. They didn't need words; they understood each other perfectly. They came to love each other so much that over the years Isabel became Diego's rival for second place in Bernardo's heart. Light-in-the-Night always came first.

In the spring, when the air in the city smelled of ocean and flowers, strolling groups of students came out to fill the night with music; besmitten suitors offered their serenades, watched from a distance by French soldiers, because even that innocent diversion might mask sinister designs on the part of the guerrillas. Diego practiced songs on his mandolin, but it would have been ridiculous to plant himself beneath Juliana's window and serenade her when he lived in the same house. He tried to accompany her after-dinner harp concerts, but she was a true virtuoso, and he was so clumsy on his instrument—like Isabel on the harpsichord—that they left their audience with migraines. The best he could do was entertain Juliana with the magic tricks he'd learned from Galileo Tempesta, added to and perfected during months of practice. The day he stood before her prepared to swallow Tempesta's Moroccan dagger, Juliana felt faint and nearly fell, while Isabel examined the weapon, looking for the spring that hid the blade in the haft. Nuria, outraged, warned Diego that if he tried a cheap sorcerer's trick like that again in the presence of her girls, she herself would stick that Turk's knife down his gullet. In the first weeks Diego was in the house, the woman had declared an unvoiced war of nerves with him; somehow she had found out that he was a mestizo. It seemed the last straw that her master would take a youth into the bosom of the family who did not have pure Spanish blood, and as if that weren't enough, one who had the brass to fall in love with Juliana. However, as soon as Diego set his mind to it, he won the chaperone's dried-up heart with little attentions: flowers, marzipan, a print of some saint. Although she continued to answer him with grumbles and sarcasm, she could not help but laugh—trying to hide it—when he did something clownish like climb up on the roof and threaten to jump headfirst if she didn't make him some pastries.

One night Diego had to suffer through a serenade Rafael Moncada, accompanied by several musicians, gave beneath Juliana's window. To his chagrin, Diego learned that not only did his rival have a seductive tenor voice, but more impressive yet, he sang in Italian. He tried to make Moncada look ridiculous to Juliana, but his strategy failed; for the first time she seemed charmed by Moncada's attention. She felt conflicting emotions when she was around her suitor, a mixture of instinctive distrust and cautious curiosity. When he was present, she felt bothered and naked, but she was also attracted by the self-confidence he exuded. She did not like the scornful and cruel expressions she sometimes glimpsed on his face, a look that did not correspond with how generous he was when he distributed coins among the beggars after mass. Whatever her feelings, her admirer was twenty-three years old and had been courting her for some months; soon she would have to give him an answer. Moncada was wealthy, he came from an impeccable family, and he made a good impression on everyone except her sister Isabel, who detested him without hiding or explaining it. There were solid arguments in favor of his suit; Juliana held back only because of an inexplicable presentiment of disaster. In the meantime, Moncada continued his siege with delicacy, fearful that the least pressure would frighten her. They saw one another at church, at concerts and plays, during the paseos in the parks and streets. He often sent her gifts and tender notes, but nothing compromising. He had not succeeded in being invited to Tomás de Romeu's home or in getting his aunt Eulalia de Callís to include the de Romeus among her guests. His aunt had stated with her habitual firmness that Juliana was a very bad choice: "Her father is a traitor, a lover of the French and all their ways, and that family has no rank, no fortune—nothing to offer," was her jewel-hard judgment. But Moncada had had his eye on Juliana for a long time; he had watched her blossom and had determined that she was the only woman worthy of him. He thought that with time Eulalia would yield before Juliana's undeniable virtues; it was all a question of manipulating the matter diplomatically. He was not disposed to give Juliana up, and certainly not his inheritance, but he never doubted he could have both.

Rafael Moncada was too old to be serenading and too proud for that kind of exhibitionism, but he found a way to do it with humor. When Juliana came out on her balcony that night, she saw him costumed as a Florentine prince with a lute in his hands, all brocade and silk from head to toe, his doublet trimmed with otter and his hat with ostrich plumes. Several servants were holding elegant crystal lanterns to illuminate him, and at his side the musicians, attired as operetta pages, strummed melodic chords on their instruments. The crowning effect, however, was undoubtedly Moncada's extraordinary voice. Hidden behind a curtain, Diego burned with humiliation, knowing that Juliana was on her balcony comparing Moncada's magnificent warbling with the hesitant mandolin he had tried to impress her with. He was muttering curses when Bernardo came and signaled him to follow and bring his sword. His brother led him to the servants' floor—where Diego had never been, even though he had lived in that house nearly a year—and from there through a service gate to the street. Hugging the wall, they arrived unseen at the place where his rival had stationed himself to thrill Juliana with his ballads in Italian. Bernardo pointed to a portal behind Moncada, and Diego's fury melted into diabolic glee: it was not Moncada singing, but another man hidden in the shadows.

Diego and Bernardo waited to the end of the serenade. The group broke up and drove off in a pair of coaches as the last servant handed some coins to the real tenor. After making sure that the singer was alone, the youths took him by surprise. He hissed like a serpent and put his hand to the curved knife waiting in his sash, but Diego was faster, and touched the tip of his sword to the substitute's neck. The man retreated with awesome agility, but Bernardo tripped him and threw him to the ground. He cursed when again he felt the tip of Diego's rapier pricking his throat. At that hour the only light in the street came from a timid moon and the lamps of the house—enough to see that the man was a strong, dark-skinned Gypsy, nothing but pure muscle, sinew, and bone.

"What the devil do you want of me?" he spit out insolently.

"Nothing but your name. You may keep that dishonestly earned money," Diego replied.

"Why do you want my name?"

"Your name, I say!" Diego demanded, increasing the pressure of the sword tip enough to draw a few drops of blood.

"Pelayo," the Gypsy replied.

Diego dropped his weapon, and the man stepped back and disappeared into the shadows of the street with the stealth and speed of a cat.

"Let us remember that name, Bernardo. I think that we will run into that ruffian again. I can say nothing of this to Juliana—she will think I am acting out of pettiness or jealousy. I must find another way to let her know that the voice is not Moncada's. Can you think how? Well, when something occurs to you, let me know," Diego concluded.

†

One of the most faithful visitors to the home of Tomás de Romeu was Napoleon's chargé d'affaires in Barcelona, Monsieur Roland Duchamp, known as Le Chevalier. He was the éminence grise behind the visible officialdom, with more influence, it was said, than King Joseph I himself. Since he no longer needed his brother to perpetuate the Bonaparte dynasty, Napoleon had begun withdrawing power from him. Now he had a son, a frail child nicknamed "The Eaglet" and crushed since infancy beneath the title King of Rome. Le Chevalier directed a vast network of spies, who kept him informed about the plans of his enemies even before they had formulated them. He held the rank of ambassador, but in truth everyone up to the highest army officers reported to him. His life in Barcelona, where the French were detested, was far from pleasant. The best society ostracized him even though he courted the leading families with balls, receptions, and theater performances, just as he tried to win over the masses by handing out loaves of bread and authorizing bullfights, which had previously been banned. No one wanted to seem loyal to the French. Nobles like Eulalia de Callís were afraid not to greet him, but neither did they accept his invitations. Tomás de Romeu, on the other hand, was honored by his friendship, since he admired everything that came from France, from its philosophical ideas and refinement to Napoleon himself, whom he compared to Alexander the Great. He knew that Le Chevalier was in league with the secret police, but he discredited rumors that he was responsible for the torture and executions in La Ciudadela. He could not believe that a person that refined and cultivated would be involved in the barbarities attributed to the military. The two of them discussed art, books, new scientific discoveries, and advances in astronomy, and they commented on the situation of the colonies in America, such as Venezuela, Chile, and others that had declared their independence.

While the two caballeros shared pleasant hours over their glasses of French cognac and their Cuban cigars, Agnès Duchamp,

Le Chevalier's daughter, amused herself reading French novels with Juliana behind the back of Tomás de Romeu, who never would have tolerated such behavior. The girls suffered the torment of the ill-starred love affairs of the characters and sighed with relief at the happy endings. Romanticism was not as yet in vogue in Spain, and before Agnès appeared in her life, Juliana had had access only to a few classic authors in the family library that had been selected by her father for educational purposes. Isabel and Nuria sat in on the readings. Juliana's younger sister made fun of her books, but did not miss a word, and Nuria sobbed uncontrollably. The girls explained to her that none of those things had really happened, that they were only the lies of the author, but she didn't believe them. The unhappiness of the characters caused her such distress that the girls changed the plots of the novels so as not to sour her on life. The chaperone did not know how to read, but she had a sacred respect for the printed word. From her wages she bought illustrated booklets of the lives of martyrs, true compilations of savagery that the girls had to read to her again and again. She was sure that each saint was a wretched compatriot tortured by the Moors in Granada. It was pointless to explain to her that the Roman Colosseum was right where its name indicated: in Rome. She was also convinced, like any good Spanish woman, that Christ did not die on the cross for the good of all humanity, but specifically for Spain. To her, the most unforgivable fact about Napoleon and the French was that they were atheists, and after each visit she sprinkled the chair Le Chevalier had sat in with holy water. She attributed her employer's failure to believe in God to the premature death of his wife, the mother of the girls. She was sure that Don Tomás was suffering through a temporary condition: on his deathbed he would come to his senses and call for a confessor to absolve him of his sins, as everyone did in the end, however much they claimed to be atheists when in good health.

Agnès was a small girl, smiling and vivacious, with transparent skin, a mischievous glint in her eye, and dimples in her cheeks, knuckles, and elbows. She had matured early because of the novels she'd read, and at an age when other girls still were not allowed out of the house, she lived the life of an adult woman. She accompanied her father to social events wearing the most daring Paris styles. When she attended a ball, she dampened her frock so that the cloth would cling to her body and no one could miss appreciating her rounded buttocks and virginal but bold nipples. Diego caught her eye at their first meeting; during that year he had left the blandness of adolescence behind and had spurted up like a colt: he was as tall as Don Tomás and thanks to the hearty Catalan diet and Nuria's coddling, he had gained weight—something he greatly needed. His features were taking on their definitive form, and at Isabel's suggestion he was wearing his hair cut to cover his ears. To Agnès he seemed not at all bad. He was exotic, and she could imagine him in the wild lands of the Americas surrounded by submissive, naked Indians. She never tired of questioning him about California, which she confused with a mysterious, steamy island like the one where the ineffable Josephine Bonaparte had been born. Josephine was her ideal, and she tried to imitate her with her diaphanous dresses and violet scent. Agnès had met the empress in Paris, in Napoleon's court, when she was a child of ten. While the emperor was off conducting some war, Josephine had honored Le Chevalier Duchamp with a friendship approaching amour. Agnès would always carry the image of that woman in her memory. Though she was neither young nor beautiful, her sinuous walk, her dreamy voice, and her fleeting fragrance made her seem so. That had been more than four years ago. Josephine was no longer the empress of France because Napoleon had replaced her with an insipid Austrian princess whose one good point, according to Agnès, was that she had given him a son—as if fertility were not too, too vulgar. When Agnès learned that Diego was the sole heir of Alejandro de la Vega, the lord of a ranch the size of a small country, it took little effort for her to imagine herself as the mistress of that fabulous territory. She waited for the opportune moment and whispered to Diego, behind her fan, that he should come visit her so they could talk alone, since in Tomás de Romeu's home Nuria was always hovering over them. In Paris no one had a chaperone—that was the epitome of antiquated customs, she added. To seal her invitation, she handed him a lace and linen handkerchief bearing her full name embroidered by the nuns and perfumed with violet. Diego did not know what to answer. For a whole week he tried to make Juliana jealous by talking about Agnès and waving her handkerchief in the air, but that ploy backfired when his enchantress offered amiably to help him along in his love life. In addition, Isabel and Nuria teased him unmercifully, so he ended up throwing the handkerchief away. Bernardo retrieved it and kept it, faithful to his theory that you never know when something may be useful.

Diego frequently was in the company of Agnès Duchamp, who had become a faithful visitor to the house. Though she was younger than Juliana, she nevertheless left her behind in exuberance and experience. Had the circumstances been different, Agnès would not have lowered herself to cultivate a friendship with a girl as naive as Juliana, but her father's situation had closed many doors to her, and she had few friends. Besides, in her favor Juliana had her reputation as a beauty, and although in principle Agnès preferred to avoid competition, she soon realized that the mere name Juliana de Romeu drew men's interest and that she benefited indirectly. To rid himself of Agnès's sentimental insinuations, which were increasing in intensity and frequency, Diego tried to change the image the girl had formed of him. No more daydreams of a rich, courageous rancher galloping across the valleys of California with his sword at his side; instead he began reporting scraps of supposed letters from his father that announced, among other calamities, the family's imminent financial ruin. At that moment he had no idea how close to the truth those lies would be within a few years. Then, as a finishing touch, he started imitating the precious mannerisms and tight trousers of Juliana and Isabel's dance instructor. He responded to Agnès's novel-inspired gazes with little affectations and sudden headaches, until he planted the suspicion in Agnès's mind that she was pursuing an effeminate *artiste*. That game of deceit suited his histrionic personality perfectly. "Why are you acting like such an idiot?" Isabel, who from the first had treated him with a frankness bordering on rudeness, asked more than once. Juliana, distracted as she always was in the world of Agnès's novels, never noticed how Diego changed when Agnès was present. Compared with Isabel, who could see right through Diego's theatrics, Juliana revealed a distressing innocence.

Tomás de Romeu fell into the habit of inviting Diego for an after-dinner drink with Agnès's father, once he realized that the older man was interested in his young guest. Le Chevalier would inquire about the activities of the students in the School of Humanities, the political tendencies of young Catalans, and the rumors Diego heard in the street and from the servants, but Diego, aware of the man's reputation, was cautious in his replies. If he told the truth, he might put more than one person in jeopardy, especially his companions and professors, blood enemies of the French, although most agreed with the reforms they had imposed. As a precaution, in Le Chevalier's company Diego feigned the same affected, dimwitted mannerisms he adopted around Agnès, with such success that the father ended up dismissing him as a spineless dandy. The Frenchman was hard put to understand his daughter's interest in de la Vega. In his eyes the young man's hypothetical fortune could not compensate for his staggering frivolity. Le Chevalier was an iron man—otherwise he would not have been able to maintain his stranglehold on Catalonia—and he was quickly bored with Diego's trivialities. He stopped asking him questions and sometimes made comments he would have kept to himself had he thought better of him.

"On my way back from Gerona yesterday I saw pieces of bodies the guerrillas had hung from trees and speared on pikes. The buzzards were having a feast. I still have the stench on me," Le Chevalier commented.

"How do you know that was the work of guerrillas, not French soldiers?" Tomás de Romeu asked.

"I have good information, my friend. In Catalonia the guerrillas are ferocious. Thousands of contraband weapons pass through this city; there are arsenals even in the church confessionals. The guerrillas cut the supply routes, and the population goes hungry when vegetables and bread don't get through."

"Let them eat cake, then." Diego smiled, echoing Queen Marie

Antoinette's famous remark as he tossed an almond bonbon into his mouth.

"This is not a time to make jokes, sir," Le Chevalier replied, annoyed. "Starting tomorrow it will be forbidden to light torches at night because they are used to send signals, or wear a cape because muskets and knives can be hidden beneath them. What would you say, caballeros, if I told you that there are plans to infect the prostitutes who service the French troops with smallpox!"

"Please, Chevalier Duchamp!" Diego exclaimed with a scandalized air.

"Women and priests hide weapons in their clothing and use children to carry messages and light explosives. We will have to search the hospital because they hide weapons beneath the bedcovers of women who are supposedly in labor."

Only one hour later, Diego de la Vega had managed to warn the director of the hospital that the French would be arriving from one moment to the next. Thanks to the information provided by Le Chevalier, he was able to save more than one of his companions from the School of Humanities and a number of endangered neighbors. On the other hand, he sent an anonymous note to Le Chevalier when he learned that bread destined for a barracks had been poisoned. His intervention foiled the attempt, saving thirty enemy soldiers. Diego was not sure of his reasons, but he detested treachery of any kind, and he simply liked the game and the risk. He felt the same revulsion for the guerrillas' methods that he did for those of the occupation troops.

"There's no point in looking for justice, Bernardo, because there is none, anywhere. The only positive thing to do is to try to prevent more violence. I am sick of so much horror, so many atrocities. There is nothing noble or glorious about war."

The guerrillas relentlessly harassed the French and stirred up the people. Farmers, bakers, masons, craftsmen, merchants—ordinary people during the day, they fought by night. The civilian population protected them, furnished them with food, information, mail, hospitals, and clandestine cemeteries. The tenacious popular resistance wore down the occupation troops, but it also kept the country in ruins. To the Spanish cry, "Blood and guts!" the French responded with identical cruelty.

For Diego, the fencing lessons were his most important activity, and he never arrived late for a class, knowing that the master would dismiss him and never take him back. At fifteen minutes before eight he was at the academy; five minutes later a servant opened the door, and at eight on the dot he was standing before his fencing master, foil in hand. At the end of the lesson the maestro often asked him to stay a few minutes and discuss the nobility of the art of fencing, pride in strapping on the sword, the military glories of Spain, and the obligation of every caballero with a sense of honor: to defend his good name, even though duels were banned by law. Those themes led to others more profound, and during those discussions that sober little man, who had the starched and prissy demeanor of a fop and was sensitive to the point of absurdity when it came to his own honor and dignity, revealed the other side of his character. Manuel Escalante was the son of a merchant from Asturias, but he had escaped the undistinguished fate of his brothers because of his genius with a sword. Fencing elevated him in rank, allowed him to invent a new persona and to travel throughout Europe rubbing elbows with gentlemen and nobles. His obsessions were not historical duels or titles of nobility, as it seemed at first view, but justice. He sensed that Diego shared his concerns, although being so young, he did not as yet know how to articulate them. The master felt that finally his life had a high purpose: to guide this young man to follow in his footsteps, to convert him into a paladin of just causes. Escalante had taught fencing to hundreds of young caballeros, but none had proved worthy of that distinction. They lacked the burning flame that he immediately recognized in Diego because he himself had it. He did not want to be carried away by his initial enthusiasm; he decided he would get to know this youth better and put him to the test before he shared his secrets with him. He sounded him out during their brief conversations over coffee. Diego, inclined always to be frank and open, told him, among other things, about his childhood in California, the escapade of the bear with the hat, the pirates' attack and Bernardo's muteness, and the day the soldiers burned the Indians' village. His voice trembled as he remembered how they had hanged the tribe's ancient chieftain, beat the men, and taken them off to work for the whites.

On one of his courtesy visits to Eulalia de Callís's palace, Diego ran into Rafael Moncada. He called on Her Excellency from time to time, more the result of his parents' requests than his own initiative. Her mansion was on Calle Eulalia, and at first Diego believed that the street had been named for his family's old friend. It was a year before he found out that the mythic Eulalia was the favorite saint of Catalonia, a virgin martyr whose torturers, according to legend, cut off her breasts and made her roll in a tunnel of slivers of glass before they crucified her. The mansion of the former governor of California's wife, one of the city's architectural jewels, was decorated inside with an excess that shocked the sober Catalans, for whom ostentation was an inarguable sign of bad taste. Eulalia had lived in Mexico for a long time and had been infected with that country's taste for the baroque. In her personal retinue were several hundred people whose livelihood came primarily from chocolate. Before he died of apoplexy in Mexico, Doña Eulalia's husband had set up an operation in the Antilles to supply the chocolate shops of Spain, and the family fortune ballooned. Eulalia's titles were neither very old nor very impressive, but her money more than compensated for what she lacked in bloodlines. While the nobility were losing their income, privileges, lands, and sinecures, Eulalia was growing increasingly wealthy thanks to the aromatic river of chocolate flowing from America directly into her coffers. In other times the most aristocratic nobles, those who could prove that their blue blood dated from before 1400, had sneered at Eulalia, who belonged to the self-made peerage, but these were not times to quibble. What counted now, more than ancestors, was money, and she had plenty of that. Other landowners complained that their campesinos refused to pay taxes and rents, but she did not have that problem—she entrusted a carefully selected group of thugs with collections. Another factor in her favor was that most of her income came from outside the country. Eulalia had become one of the most recognizable citizens of the city. She made a grand entrance wherever she went, including church, with several carriage loads of servants and dogs, her retainers outfitted in sky-blue livery and plumed hats that she herself, finding her inspiration at the opera, had designed. Over the years she had gained weight and lost originality, and she was now a gluttonous matriarch robed in eternal black mourning and surrounded by priests, pious old women, and Chihuahua dogs, horrid little beasts that looked like skinned rats and relieved themselves on the draperies. She was completely divorced from the fine passions that had tormented her during her resplendent youth, when she colored her hair red and luxuriated in milk baths. Now her interests had dwindled to defending her lineage, selling chocolate, ensuring a place in paradise after she died, and working every way she could to obtain the return of Fernando VII to the throne of Spain. She loathed the liberal reforms.

Because of his father's orders, and in gratitude for how well Her Excellency had treated his mother Regina, Diego de la Vega tried to visit Eulalia on a regular basis, even though that obligation seemed like a major sacrifice. He had nothing to say to the widow, except for three or four formulas of courtesy, and he never knew in what order to use the forks and spoons at his place at table. He knew that Eulalia de Callís strongly disliked Tomás de Romeu, for two reasons: first, because he admired all things French, and second, because he was the father of Juliana, with whom, to her chagrin, Rafael Moncada, her favorite nephew and principal heir, was in love. Eulalia had seen Juliana at mass and had to admit that she was far from ugly, but she had much more ambitious plans for her nephew. She was discreetly negotiating an alliance with one of the daughters of the duke of Medinacelli. The desire to prevent Rafael from marrying Juliana was the one thing she and Diego had in common.

On Diego's fourth visit to Doña Eulalia's palace, several months after the incident of the serenade beneath Juliana's window, he had occasion to get to know Rafael Moncada better. He had come across him several times at social and sporting events, but except for nodding to him in greeting had had no further relations. Moncada thought that Diego was a humdrum young fellow. Except that he lived beneath the same roof as Juliana de Romeu, nothing else made him stand out from the design of the carpet. That night Diego was surprised to find that Doña Eulalia's palace was extravagantly lighted, and dozens of carriages were lined up in the courtyards. Until then, she had invited him only to gatherings of artists and to one intimate dinner, during which she questioned him about Regina. Diego thought she was ashamed of him, not so much because he came from the colonies as because he was a mestizo. Eulalia had treated his mother very well in California, even though Regina was more Indian than white, but after living a while in Spain, she had been infected with the scorn the Spanish felt for the people of the New World. The widely held opinion was that because of the climate and contact with Indians, criollos—the Spanish born there—had a natural predisposition toward barbarism and perversion. Before introducing Diego to her select friends, Eulalia wanted to have a very good sense of who he was, so she ran a few trials to be sure that he looked white, dressed well, and had passable manners.

That night Diego was shown to a splendid salon where the cream of Catalan nobility was gathered, presided over by the matriarch—dressed, as always, in black velvet as a sign of her unrelieved mourning for Pedro Fages, but dripping with diamonds, and seated in a huge chair with a bishop's canopy. Other widows buried themselves in life beneath a dark veil that covered them from the combs in their hair to their elbows, but not Doña Eulalia. Her jewels were displayed on the opulent bosom of a well-fed hen, her décolletage revealing the beginnings of enormous breasts as smooth and round as summertime melons. Diego could not tear his eyes away, dizzied by the glitter of the diamonds and the abundance of flesh. Her Excellency offered a plump hand, which he kissed as required; she asked about his parents and without waiting for the answer waved him away.

In the adjoining salons, most of the gentlemen discussed politics and business, while young couples, overseen by the mothers of the young ladies, danced to the strains of an orchestra. There were gaming tables in one of the rooms, gambling being the most popular entertainment in European courts, where there was no other way to combat tedium, aside from intrigue, hunting, and brief affairs. Fortunes were bet, and professional players traveled from one grand home to another to fleece the idle nobles, who, if they could find no players of their own class to lose money to, enriched unsavory characters in gambling dens and dives. And there were hundreds of those in Barcelona. At one of the tables Diego saw Rafael Moncada playing blackjack with a group of caballeros, one of whom was Count Orloff. Diego recognized him immediately by his magnificent bearing and those blue eyes that had inflamed the imagination of so many women during his visit to Los Angeles, but he did not expect the Russian nobleman to recognize him. He had seen him only once, when he was a boy. "De la Vega!" Orloff called out, getting to his feet and embracing him enthusiastically. Surprised, Rafael Moncada looked up from his cards and for the first time truly registered the fact that Diego existed. He looked him over from head to foot as the handsome count recounted to one and all how this young man had captured several bears when he was barely a pup. This time Alejandro de la Vega was not present to correct the count's epic version of events. The men applauded amiably and turned back to their cards. Diego stationed himself near the table to observe the particulars of the game, not daring, though the men were only mediocre players, to ask whether he could join in because he did not have the funds to match their bets. His father sent him money regularly, but he was not generous: he believed that privation shaped character. After only five minutes, Diego realized that Rafael Moncada was cheating, as he knew perfectly well how to do that himself. In another five he decided that although he could not show Moncada up without causing a scandal that Doña Eulalia would never forgive, he could at least put a spoke in his wheels. The temptation to humiliate his rival was irresistible. He planted himself beside Moncada and watched him so insistently that the man became uncomfortable.

"Why don't you go dance with the pretty young things in the other room?" asked Moncada, making no attempt to veil his insolence.

"Because, caballero, I am intensely interested in your very peculiar style of playing. I have no doubt that I can learn a great deal from you," Diego replied, smiling with equal insolence.

Count Orloff immediately caught the intent of those words, and nailing Moncada with his gaze, he let him know, in a tone as icy as the steppes of his country, that his luck with cards was truly miraculous. Rafael Moncada did not answer, but from that moment he was unable to pull any tricks, since the other players were watching him with conspicuous attention. For an hour Diego did not move from Moncada's side but stood looking over his shoulder until the game was over. Count Orloff saluted, clicking his heels together, and retired with a small fortune in his purse, prepared to spend the rest of the night dancing, well aware that not a single woman at the party had failed to take notice of his elegant bearing, his sapphire eyes, and his spectacular imperial uniform.

It was one of those leaden Barcelona nights, cold and damp. Bernardo was waiting for Diego in the courtyard, sharing his wineskin and hard cheese with Juanillo, one of the many lackeys attending the carriages. The two had been keeping warm by dancing on the brick paving. Juanillo, an irrepressible talker, had finally found a person who would listen without interrupting him. He identified himself as the servant of Rafael Moncada—something Bernardo already knew, the reason in fact that he had approached him—and launched into an endless story filled with gossip, the details of which Bernardo classified and stored in his memory. He had proved before that any information, even the most trivial, could at some point become useful. He was still talking when Rafael Moncada, in a foul humor, came out and called for his carriage.

"I have forbidden you to speak with the other servants!" he spit at Juanillo.

"He's just an Indian from the Americas, Excellency, the servant of Don Diego de la Vega."

Following an impulse to avenge himself upon Diego, who had put him on the spot at the table, Rafael Moncada whirled around, lifted his cane, and brought it down hard across Bernardo's shoulders, dropping him to his knees, more surprised than hurt. Bernardo heard him order Juanillo to get Pelayo, but Moncada did not make it into his carriage because Diego had come out into the courtyard in time to see what happened. He pushed Moncada's footman aside, grabbed the door of the coach, and confronted Moncada.

"What do you want?" the latter asked, taken aback.

"You struck Bernardo!" Diego exclaimed, livid with rage.

"Who? Are you referring to that Indian? He was disrespectful, he raised his voice to me."

"Bernardo could not raise his voice to the devil himself—he's mute. You owe him an apology, sir," Diego demanded.

"Have you lost your mind?" Moncada cried, incredulous.

"When you struck Bernardo, sir, you injured me. You must apologize, or my seconds will call on you," Diego replied.

Rafael Moncada burst out laughing. He could not believe that this criollo who had neither education nor class would challenge him to a duel. He slammed the door and ordered the coachman to leave. Bernardo took Diego by the arm and held him back, pleading with his eyes for him to calm down, that it wasn't worth making such a fuss, but Diego was beside himself, trembling with indignation. He shook off his brother's grip, mounted his horse, and galloped off toward the home of Manuel Escalante.

† 

Ignoring the inappropriateness of the hour, Diego beat on Manuel Escalante's door with his cane until it was answered by the same aged retainer who served coffee after his lessons. The servant led Diego to the second floor, where he had to wait half an hour before the maestro appeared. Escalante had been in bed for some time, but when he presented himself he was, as always, trim: spotless dressing gown, his mustache neatly slicked with pomade. Diego poured out what had happened and asked Escalante to serve as his second. He had twenty-four hours in which to formalize the duel, and it had to be done discreetly, behind the back of the authorities, because the penalty was the same as for any homicide. Only members of the aristocracy could duel without consequence; their crimes were treated with an impunity Diego did not enjoy.

"A duel is a serious matter that concerns a gentleman's honor. It has a very strict etiquette and norms. A caballero does not fight a duel over a servant," said Manuel Escalante.

"Bernardo is my brother, maestro, not my servant. But even if he were, it isn't fair to mistreat someone who is unarmed."

"Not fair, you say? Do you truly believe that life is fair, Señor de la Vega?"

"No, maestro, but I plan to do everything in my power to make it so," Diego replied.

The procedure turned out to be more complex than Diego had imagined. First Manual Escalante had him write a letter asking for an explanation, which he personally carried to the home of the offender. From that moment on, the maestro dealt with Moncada's seconds, who did everything they could to prevent the duel, as was their duty, but neither of the adversaries wanted to back down. In addition to seconds for both parties, a discreet physician and two impartial witnesses were required who had cool heads and familiarity with the rules. Manuel Escalante was responsible for finding those parties.

"Just how old are you, Don Diego?" the maestro asked.

"Almost seventeen."

"Then you are not old enough to fight a duel."

"Maestro, I beg you, let us not make a mountain out of *that* grain of sand. What difference do a few months make? My honor is at stake, and that is not limited by age."

"Very well, but Don Tomás de Romeu must be informed. It would be insulting not to tell him, considering that he has honored you with his confidence and hospitality."

So de Romeu was also designated to serve as a second for Diego. He tried his best to dissuade him, for if the youth should be killed, he could not imagine how he would explain it to his father—but he pleaded in vain. He had attended two or three of Diego's fencing classes in Escalante's academy, and he did not doubt the young man's skill, but his relative tranquility was shattered when Moncada's seconds notified them that he had sprained an ankle and could not duel with a sword. They would use pistols.

The time and place were set for the Montjuic forest at five in the morning; at that hour there was a little light, and because the curfew was lifted, they could travel freely through the city. A light mist was rising from the ground, and a delicate dawn light was filtering through the trees. The countryside was so peaceful that the encounter seemed even more grotesque, but none of those present, except Bernardo, noticed it. In his role as servant, the Indian stood a certain distance away, not participating in the strict ritual. In accord with the protocol, the adversaries greeted each other; then witnesses checked their bodies to be sure that they were not wearing protection against bullets. They drew lots to see who would face the sun, and Diego lost, though he believed that his good vision would compensate for that disadvantage. As the person offended, Diego had the choice of pistols, and he chose the ones that Eulalia de Callís had sent his father in California many years before, now cleaned and oiled for the occasion. He smiled at the irony of Eulalia's nephew being the first to use them. The witnesses and the seconds checked the weapons and loaded them. They had agreed that it would not be a duel to draw first blood; both combatants would have the right to shoot in turn even if they were wounded, as long as the physician authorized them to continue. Moncada chose his pistol, since the weapons were not his. Then they drew lots again to determine who would shoot first—Moncada won that, too—and measured the fifteen paces that would separate them.

At last Rafael Moncada and Diego de la Vega faced one another. Neither of the two was a coward, but they were pale, and their shirts were soaked with icy sweat. Diego had reached this point out of rage, and Moncada out of pride; it was too late now, they could not consider the possibility of withdrawing. At that moment they realized that they were gambling their lives without being sure of the cause. Just as Bernardo had earlier pointed out to Diego, the duel was not because of the blow Moncada had struck, but because of Juliana, and although Diego had emphatically denied it, in his heart he knew Bernardo was right. A closed coach was waiting some distance away to bear off the corpse of the loser with as little fuss as possible. Diego did not think of his parents or of Juliana. In the instant that he took his position, with his body in profile so as to present the minimum target to his opponent, the image of White Owl came to his mind with such clarity that he actually saw her standing beside Bernardo. His strange grandmother looked just as she had when she waved good-bye to them as they left California: the same pose, the same rabbit-skin cloak. White Owl raised her shaman's staff with a haughty gesture that he had seen her make many times and shook it vigorously. Diego felt invulnerable; his fear magically disappeared, and he could look Moncada in the face.

One of the witnesses, the one who had been named director for the duel, clapped his hands once to set them on their marks. Diego took a deep breath and without blinking an eye faced Moncada's pistol, which he had raised to fire. The director clapped twice for him to aim. Diego smiled at Bernardo and his grandmother, readying himself for the shot. The hands clapped three times, and Diego saw a spark and simultaneously heard gunpowder exploding and felt a burning pain in his left arm.

He swayed, and for a long moment it seemed that he would fall, as the sleeve of his jacket pooled with blood. In that misty dawn, a pale watercolor in which the outlines of trees and men were a wash of faint color, the red stain gleamed like lacquer. The director indicated to Diego that he had but one minute to respond to his opponent's shot. He nodded, and assumed the position to fire with his right hand as blood dripped from his left, which hung useless at his side. Opposite him, Moncada, diminished, trembling, standing sideways, squeezed his eyes shut. The director clapped once, and Diego raised his weapon: two, and he pointed; three . . . Fifteen paces away, Rafael Moncada heard the shot and felt the impact of a cannonball. He fell to his knees, and several seconds passed before he realized that he was not injured: Diego had fired into the ground. Then he vomited, shivering as if from a high fever. His seconds, embarrassed, went to him to help him to his feet, and to tell him quietly that he must control himself.

In the meantime, Bernardo and Manuel Escalante were helping the physician rip open Diego's jacket sleeve; he was on his feet and seemingly calm. The bullet had grazed the meaty part of his upper arm without touching the bone or doing great harm to the muscle. The doctor applied a cloth and bound the arm to staunch the bleeding until he could clean and stitch it later. As the etiquette of the duel demanded, the combatants shook hands. They had cleansed their honor; there were no unresolved offenses.

"I give thanks to God that your wound was slight, sir," said Rafael Moncada, by now in total control of his nerves. "And I ask you to forgive me for having struck your servant."

"I accept your apology, caballero, and remind you that Bernardo is my brother," Diego replied.

Bernardo took him by his sound arm and practically carried him to the coach. Later Tomás de Romeu asked Diego why he had challenged Moncada if he was not prepared to shoot him. Diego replied that he had never intended to carry a death on his conscience; all he had wanted was to humiliate him.

†

The two men made a pact that they would say nothing to Juliana and Isabel about the duel. That was a man's matter, and they must not offend feminine sensibilities. Neither of the girls believed the story that Diego had fallen off his horse. Isabel pestered Bernardo so unrelentingly that he ended up telling her with a few gestures what had happened. "I have never understood all the fuss about male honor. You have to be slow in the head to risk your life over a trifle," Isabel commented, but she was impressed; Bernardo could tell because her eye wandered when she was emotional. From that instant, Juliana, Isabel, even Nuria, fought over the privilege of carrying Diego's food to him. The physician had prescribed rest for a few days, to prevent complications. These were the happiest four days in the young man's life; he would gladly have fought a duel every week if it earned him Juliana's attention. His room filled with a supernatural light when she entered. He awaited her in an elegant smoking jacket, sitting in a chair with a book of sonnets on his knees pretending to read, although all he had been doing was counting the minutes she had been gone. On those occasions, his arm was so painful that Juliana had to spoon the soup into his mouth, cool his brow with orange-blossom water, and entertain him for hours playing her harp, reading Lope de Vega to him, and playing girls' games.

Distracted by Diego's wound, which though not serious was nonetheless of concern, Bernardo had forgotten that he'd heard Rafael Moncada ask his servant to summon Pelayo, remembering only when he learned through the servants, several days later, that Count Orloff had been assaulted on the night of Eulalia de Callís's party. The noble Russian had stayed at the palace until very late, then called for his carriage and started back to the residence he had rented for his brief stay in the city. On the way, a group of armed ruffians had stopped his coach in an alleyway and easily subdued the four footmen. After stunning the count with a vicious blow to the head, they took his purse, his jewels, and the chinchilla cape he always wore. The attack had been attributed to guerrillas, although that had never been their mode of operation. The general reaction was that all traces of order in the city had evaporated. What good was it to have a safe-conduct for the curfew if decent people were no longer safe in the streets? It was the last straw that the French could not maintain a scintilla of security! Bernardo reported to Diego that the stolen purse contained the gold Count Orloff had won from Rafael Moncada at the gaming table.

"Are you sure you heard Moncada name Pelayo? I know what you are thinking, Bernardo. You think that Moncada had some role in the assault on the count. That is a bit strong, don't you think? We don't have proof, but I agree with you that it is a suspicious coincidence. Even if Moncada had nothing to do with this, he is still a rogue. I do not want to see him anywhere near Juliana, but I don't know how to stop him," Diego admitted.

In March of 1812, in Cadiz, the Spanish approved a liberal constitution based on the principles of the French Revolution, though with the difference that it designated Catholicism as the official state religion and outlawed the practice of any other faith. As Tomás de Romeu often said, there was no reason to keep fighting Napoleon when, after all, they agreed on the essential points. "It won't get any farther than paper and ink, because Spain is not ready for modern ideas," was the opinion of Le Chevalier, and he added with a gesture of impatience that it would be fifty years before Spain crept into the nineteenth century.

While Diego spent long hours studying in the ancient halls of the School of Humanities, practicing his fencing, and inventing new magic tricks to seduce the immovable Juliana, who as soon as his wound healed had gone back to treating him like a brother, Bernardo explored Barcelona, dragging Padre Mendoza's heavy boots, which he never could get used to. Around his neck was the magic pouch containing Light-in-the-Night's black braid, which by now held the warmth and odor of his skin; it was part of his own body, an appendage of his heart. His self-imposed muteness had refined his other senses. He could follow a course by scent and hearing. He was solitary by nature, and in his situation as a foreigner he was even more alone, but he liked that. He was not oppressed by a crowd because in the midst of all the hullabaloo he always found a quiet place for his soul. He missed the open spaces of his early years, but he also liked this city with the patina of centuries: the narrow streets, the stone buildings, the dark churches that reminded him of Padre Mendoza's faith. He liked best the port, where he could gaze out at the ocean and communicate with dolphins from distant seas. He walked silently, invisibly, among the throng, taking the pulse of Barcelona and the nation. It was during one of his wanderings that he saw Pelayo again.

A filthy, beautiful Gypsy woman was standing at the entrance of a tavern, tempting passersby, in her broken Spanish, to let her reveal their destinies, which she could read in the cards or in the map of their hands. Moments before, she had told a drunken sailor, to console him, that a treasure awaited him on a distant beach when in fact she had seen the cross of death in his palm. A few minutes later the man realized that his money pouch was missing and concluded that the Gypsy had stolen it. He rushed back in a mood to get what was his. His eyes were smoldering, and he was foaming like a rabid dog as he grabbed the supposed thief by the hair of her head and began shaking her. Her yelps emptied the tavern of its customers, who began jeering and cursing—if one thing united a crowd, it was their blind hatred of the Romany, and to make things worse, thanks to the war it took very little to fire up a mob. They accused the woman of every vice known to humanity, including stealing Spanish children to be sold in Egypt. Grandfathers could recall lively fiestas when the Inquisition had burned heretics, witches, and Gypsies alike. Just at the instant the sailor opened his knife to carve the woman's face, Bernardo intervened, butting him like a mountain goat and shoving him to the ground, where he lay weakly kicking amid a cloud of alcohol fumes. Before the crowd could react, Bernardo seized the Gypsy by the hand, and they ran for their lives. They didn't stop until they reached the barrio of La Barceloneta, where they were more or less safe from the enraged crowd. There Bernardo dropped her hand and turned to leave, but she insisted that he follow her several blocks to where a wagon brightly painted with arabesques and hitched to a sad, big-hoofed Percheron was sitting in a side street. The inside of that vehicle, battered by the abuse of several generations of nomads, was a Turkish cave crammed with strange objects: a waterfall of colored kerchiefs, a jumble of little bells, and a museum of almanacs and religious images in little boxes nailed everywhere, even on the ceiling. Bernardo breathed in a mixture of patchouli perfume and dirty clothes. A mattress strewn with ostentatious brocade cushions was the only attempt at furniture. With a gesture the woman invited Bernardo to make himself comfortable and immediately sat down before him with her legs tucked beneath her, studying him with her piercing gaze. She pulled out a liquor flask, took a swallow, and passed it to him, still breathing heavily from their escape. She had dark skin, a muscular body, fierce eyes, and hennaed hair. She was barefoot and was wearing two or three long ruffled skirts, a faded blouse, and a short jacket with crisscrossing laces; a shawl was tossed over her shoulders, and she had tied a kerchief around her head—in her tribe the sign of a married woman, although she was a widow. A dozen bracelets tinkled at her wrists in chorus with little silver bells on her ankles and gold coins sewn onto the kerchief across her forehead.

She told Bernardo that she used the name Amalia among the *gadje,* that is, people who weren't Gypsies. Her mother had given her another name at birth, which only she knew; its purpose was to mislead evil spirits by keeping the girl's true identity a secret. She also had a third name, one she went by among the other Gypsies. Ramón, the man of her life, had been cudgeled to death by farmers in the market in Lérida, accused of stealing hens. She had loved him since she was a girl, and their families had arranged the marriage when she was only eleven years old. Her in-laws had paid a high price for her because she had good health and a strong character, and she was well trained for domestic chores. In addition to those selling points, she was a true *drabardi;* she had been born with a natural gift for telling fortunes and for healing with spells and herbs. When she was young, she had looked like a wet cat, but beauty had nothing to do with selecting a wife. Her husband had a pleasant surprise, then, when the pile of bones turned into an attractive woman, but that pleasure was countered when they discovered that Amalia could not have children. Her people considered children a blessing; a sterile womb was grounds for a divorce, but Ramón loved her too much. At the death of her husband, Amalia sank into a long period of mourning, from which she would never recover. She was not supposed to utter the dead man's name, in order not to summon him from the other world, but secretly she wept for him every night.

For centuries her people had roamed throughout the world, persecuted and despised. The ancestors of her tribe had left India several hundred years before and made their way through all of Asia and Europe before ending up in Spain, where they were treated as badly as in other places. The climate lent itself to their nomadic life, however, so they had settled in the south of that country. There were few nomadic families like Amalia's left. Hers had met adversity again and again, and so Bernardo's unexpected intervention had touched Amalia's heart. Her people never had relations with the *gadje* unless for commercial reasons, otherwise the purity of their breed and their traditions would be endangered. Out of basic caution, the Romany stayed out of the mainstream; they never trusted strangers, and they reserved their loyalty for their clan. But it seemed to Amalia that this young man was not exactly a *gadje*; he was from another planet, a foreigner everywhere. Maybe he was a Gypsy from a lost tribe.

Amalia, it turned out, was Pelayo's sister, which Bernardo would discover that same day when Pelayo himself came to the wagon. He did not recognize Bernardo; the night they had caught him singing to Juliana in Italian, on Moncada's behalf, he had seen nothing but Diego and felt the sword tip pressing against his throat. Amalia explained what had happened to Pelayo in the brittle sounds of Romany, her Sanskrit-derived language. She asked her brother's pardon for having violated the taboo of not mixing with *gadje*. That grievous sin could condemn her to *marimé*, a state of impurity that warranted rejection by the entire community, but she was counting on the fact that rules had been relaxed since the beginning of the war. The clan had suffered greatly during that time, and families had been scattered. Pelayo reached the same conclusion, and instead of scolding his sister, as he would have before, he calmly thanked Bernardo. He was as surprised as Amalia at the Indian's generosity, since they had never been treated well by a foreigner. They had realized that Bernardo was mute, but they did not make the common mistake of thinking he was also deaf and slow-witted. As a group, they scrambled to survive by taking on any job that fell into their hands; usually that meant selling and breaking horses, as well as treating them if they were sick or injured. They also made money with their small forges, working metals—iron, gold, silver—to fashion everything from horseshoes to swords and jewelry. The war frequently made them move on, but at the same time it worked in their favor, because in the furor of killing each other both French and Spanish ignored them. On Sundays and feast days the Gypsies would set up a ragged tent in some plaza and put on a small circus. Bernardo would soon meet the rest of the group, among whom a certain Rodolfo stood out, a giant covered with tattoos, who coiled a fat snake around his neck and lifted a horse with his bare hands. Over sixty years old, he was the eldest of the large family, and therefore the one with the most authority. Petrina, a tiny nine-year-old girl who folded herself like a handkerchief to fit inside a vessel for storing olives, was the main attraction of the pathetic Sunday circus. Pelayo did an acrobatic act on one or more galloping horses, and other members of the family delighted their public by throwing daggers at one another with their eyes blindfolded. Amalia sold raffle tickets, read horoscopes, and told fortunes with a classic glass ball, all with such unerring intuition that she frightened herself with her lucid successes. She knew that the ability to foretell the future can be a curse, since if it is not possible to change what is to happen, it is better not to know at all.

As soon as Diego de la Vega learned that Bernardo had struck up a friendship with the Gypsies, he insisted on meeting them so that he could learn more about Pelayo's dealings with Rafael Moncada. He never imagined that he was going to take a liking to them and feel so comfortable in their company. By that time in Spain most of the tribes of the Roma people, as they called themselves, were living a sedentary life. They set up their camps on the outskirts of towns and cities. Little by little they became part of the landscape, until the local population got used to seeing them and stopped bothering them, although they were never accepted. In Catalonia, on the other hand, there were no fixed camps; the Romany of that part of the world were nomadic. Pelayo and Amalia's tribe was the first to come along that wanted to stay in one place; they had been there for three years. Diego realized from the first moment that it was not a good idea to ask questions about Moncada, or anything else, because the Gypsies had very good reason to be suspicious and to keep their secrets to themselves. Once the wound on his arm had completely healed, and Pelayo had forgiven him for the nick his sword had made on his neck, Diego was able to get his permission to join the improvised circus, along with Bernardo. They made one brief appearance, which was not as stunning as they had hoped because Diego's arm was still weak, but it was good enough to allow them to join as acrobats. With the help of the rest of the company, they put together an ingenious tangle of posts, ropes, and trapezes modeled on the rigging of the *Madre de Dios*. They entered the ring wearing black capes that they removed with a grand flourish, revealing tights of the same color. In that garb they flew through the air quite reck-lessly, as they had on a pitching ship at twice the height. Diego also made a dead hen disappear and then pulled it from the neck of Amalia's blouse, and with his whip he put out a candle placed on the head of the gigantic Rodolfo, without disturbing a hair. They never mentioned these activities outside the world of the Gypsies; Tomás de Romeu's tolerance had its limits, and he surely would not have approved. There were many things that de Romeu did not know about his young guest.

One Sunday Bernardo peeked from behind the artists' curtain and saw that Juliana and Isabel, accompanied by their chaperone, were in the audience. On the way back from mass, where Nuria insisted on taking them even though the idea greatly displeased

Tomás de Romeu, the girls had seen the circus and insisted on going in. The tent, patched together from yellowed pieces of sail discarded in the port, had a center straw-covered ring, some wood benches for the moneyed spectators, and space in the rear for the hoi polloi, who had to stand. In that ring the giant lifted his horse, Amalia squeezed Petrina into the olive vessel, and Diego and Bernardo did their trapeze act. In the same spot, at night, Pelayo organized cockfights. It was not a place where Tomás de Romeu would have wanted to see his daughters, but Nuria could not stand firm when Juliana and Isabel joined together to bend her will.

"If Don Tomás finds out that we're involved in this, he will send us back to California on the first available ship," Diego whispered to Bernardo, aghast to see the girls in the tent.

Then Bernardo remembered the mask they had used to frighten the sailors on the *Madre de Dios*. He cut holes for eyes in two of Amalia's kerchiefs, and they tied those on to cover their faces, praying that the de Romeu sisters would not recognize them. Diego decided to cancel his magic act, since he had often performed it in the girls' presence. Even so, they had the impression that the girls recognized them, until later that evening when he heard Juliana reporting the details of the spectacle to Agnès Duchamp. Whispering, behind Nuria's back, she told her friend about the intrepid black-clad acrobats who risked their lives on the trapezes, and she added that she would give each one a kiss if only they would show their faces.

Diego was not as lucky with Isabel. He was celebrating their escapade with Bernardo when the girl came into the room without announcing herself, as she often did despite her father's strict prohibition not to get too friendly with Diego. She planted herself before them, arms akimbo, and announced that she knew who the trapeze artists were and that she was ready to expose them unless they took her the next Sunday to meet the Gypsies. She wanted to see whether the giant's tattoos, which looked as if they were painted on, were real, and whether the lethargic snake might not be embalmed.

In the following months, Diego, whose blood was boiling with the pent-up desires of his seventeen years, found relief in Amalia's bosom. They met at tremendous risk. By making love with a *gadje* she was violating a basic taboo, for which she could pay dearly. She had been a virgin when she married, the custom among the women of her people, and she had been faithful to her husband till the day he died. Widowhood had left her in a kind of never-never land: still young, she would be treated like a grandmother until Pelayo, charged with finding her another husband once she dried the last tear of her mourning, fulfilled his obligation. Lives were lived in full view of the clan. Amalia did not have time or a place to be alone, but occasionally she was able to meet Diego in some quiet alleyway: there she would take him in her arms, always with the insufferable fear of being caught. Amalia did not entangle Diego with romantic demands; after the ugly murder of her husband, she had resigned herself to being alone forever. She was twice Diego's age and had been married for more than twenty years, but she was not expert in matters of love. With Ramón she had shared a deep and faithful affection absent raptures of passion. They had been married in a simple rite in which they shared a piece of bread anointed with drops of their blood. That was all that was required. The mere fact that they had made the decision to live together sanctified the union, but they gave a bountiful wedding banquet anyway, with music and dance that lasted three whole days. Afterward, they took a place in a corner of the communal tent. From that moment on they were never apart; they traveled the roads and byways of Europe together, they went hungry in hard times, they fled aggression in many places, and they celebrated at the slightest excuse. As Amalia told Diego, she had had a good life. She knew that Ramón, whole again, was waiting for her somewhere, miraculously recuperated from his martyrdom. When she had seen his body, mutilated by the hoes and spades of his murderers, the flame that lighted her within had gone out, and she had never again given a thought to sensual pleasure or the consolation of an embrace. She had decided to invite Diego to her wagon out of simple friendship, and when she saw how on edge he was for want of a woman, it had occurred to her to help him; that was the extent of it. She ran the risk that the spirit of her husband would return, transformed into a *muló*, to punish her for her posthumous infidelity, but she hoped that Ramón would understand her motives: she was not motivated by lust, only generosity. A bashful partner, she made love in the dark, without taking off her clothes. Sometimes she quietly wept. Then Diego would dry her tears with soft kisses, deeply moved. With her he learned to decipher some of the hidden mysteries of a woman's feminine heart. Despite the severe sexual norms of her tradition, Amalia, moved by unselfish sympathy, might have done Bernardo the same favor if he had given her so much as a hint, but he never did; the memory of Light-in-the-Night was always foremost in his mind.

Manuel Escalante watched Diego de la Vega for a long time before deciding to talk to him about the most important thing in his life. At first he had distrusted the youth's arresting magnetism. To Escalante, a man of funereal seriousness, Diego's lightheartedness was a character flaw, but he had been forced to revise that judgment the morning he witnessed the duel with Moncada. Escalante knew that the purpose of a duel is not to win, but to confront death with nobility and thereby gauge the quality of the soul. For the master, fencing—and with even greater reason a duel—was an infallible formula for revealing the true measure of a man. In the fever of combat, the essential personality emerges: there is little advantage in being expert with the blade if the swordsman is not imbued with sufficient courage and serenity to confront danger. Escalante realized that in the twenty-five years he had been teaching his art, he had never had a student like Diego. He had seen others with similar talent and dedication, but none had a heart as strong as the hand that held the sword. The admiration he felt for the young man turned into affection, and fencing became the excuse to see him every day. He was ready long before eight, but he was too disciplined and too proud to come into the room one minute before the stroke of the hour. The lesson was always conducted with the greatest formality, and almost in silence; however, during the conversations that followed he shared his ideas and personal aspirations with Diego. Once class was over they washed off with wet towels, changed their clothes, and went up to the second floor, where the maestro lived. There they took their usual seats in uncomfortable carved wood chairs in a dark modest room ringed with books on sagging shelves and polished weapons aligned on the walls. The same ancient servant, who never stopped mumbling to himself, as if endlessly praying, served them black coffee in small rococo porcelain cups. Soon they passed from subjects connected with fencing to others. The maestro's family, Spanish and Catholic for four generations, nevertheless, could not claim purity of blood because their ancestors had been Jewish. Escalante's great-grandparents had converted to Catholicism and changed their name to escape persecution. They had succeeded in eluding the merciless harassment of the Inquisition, but in the process they had lost the fortune accumulated over more than a hundred years of good business dealings and modest habits. By the time Manuel was born, there was only a vague memory of a past of comfort and refinement; nothing was left of their properties, artworks, or jewels. His father had made his living in a small shop in Asturias, two of his brothers were craftsmen, and the third had disappeared in north Africa. The fact that his closest relatives were devoted to commerce and the manual trades embarrassed the maestro. He believed that the only occupations worthy of a gentleman were those without tangible products. He was not alone. In Spain in those years only poor campesinos worked, each of them providing food for thirty idlers. But Diego learned of his maestro's past only much later. When Escalante first told him about La Justicia, and showed him his medallion, he had said nothing about his Jewish heritage. That morning in the *sala*, as they were drinking their coffee, Manuel Escalante took a key from a fine chain around his neck, went to a small bronze coffer on his desk, solemnly opened it, and showed what it contained to his student: a gold and silver medallion.

"I have seen one like this before, maestro," Diego murmured, recognizing it.

"Where?"

"Don Santiago de León, the captain of the ship that brought me to Spain, wore one."

"I know Captain de León. Like me, he is a member of La Justicia."

Escalante's secret society was one of many in Europe during that time. It had been founded two hundred years earlier in reaction to the power of the Inquisition, the fearsome arm of the church that since the sixteenth century had labored to defend the spiritual unity of Catholics by persecuting Jews, Lutherans, heretics, sodomites, blasphemers, sorcerers, seers, devil worshipers, warlocks and witches, astrologers, and alchemists, as well as anyone who read banned books. The wealth of the condemned passed into the hands of their accusers, so that many victims burned at the stake because they were wealthy, not for any other reason. For more than three hundred years of religious fervor, the people celebrated autos-da-fé, cruel orgies of public executions, but in the eighteenth century the strength of the Inquisition had begun to wane. The trials continued for a while, but behind closed doors, until the entire institution was abolished. The work of La Justicia had been to save the accused, smuggling them out of the country when possible and helping them begin a new life elsewhere. They provided clothing and food, obtained false documents, and when possible paid ransoms. During the period when Manuel Escalante recruited Diego, the orientation of La Justicia had changed; it combated not only religious fanaticism but other forms of oppression as well, such as that of the French in Spain and of slavery in foreign lands. La Justicia was a hierarchical organization with a military discipline, in which women had no place. Each step of the initiation had its colors and symbols, the ceremonies were held in secret places, and the only way to be admitted was through another member who acted as sponsor. The participants swore to pledge their lives to the service of the noble causes embraced by La Justicia, never to accept payment for their services, to keep their secret at any price, and to obey the orders of their superiors. The oath was elegantly simple: "To seek justice, nourish the hungry, clothe the naked, protect widows and orphans, give shelter to the stranger, and never spill innocent blood."

Manuel Escalante had no difficulty convincing Diego de la Vega to stand as a candidate for membership in La Justicia. Mystery and adventure were irresistible temptations for Diego: his only uncertainty had to do with the clause about blind obedience, but after he was convinced that no one would order him to do anything against his principles, he overcame that stumbling block. He studied the coded texts the maestro gave him and subjected himself to training for a unique form of combat that demanded both mental agility and extraordinary physical skill. A precise series of movements with swords and daggers were performed on a design laid out on the floor; this was called the Circle of the Maestro and was the same design reproduced on the gold-and-silver medallions that identified the members of the organization. First Diego learned the sequence and technique of the combat; then he devoted himself for months to practicing with Bernardo, until he could perform the movements without thinking. As Manuel Escalante had indicated, he would be ready only when he could catch a fly on the wing with a single casual swoop. Otherwise he would never best a longtime member of La Justicia, as he would have to do to be accepted.

Finally the day came when Diego was ready for the ceremony of initiation. The fencing master led him through places unknown even to the architects and builders who prided themselves on knowing the city like the palms of their hands. Barcelona had grown upon successive layers of ruins: the Phoenicians and Greeks had passed through without leaving much trace; then came the Romans, who *had* left their mark on the city but were replaced by the Goths and finally the conquering Saracens, who remained for several centuries. Each culture contributed to the city's complexity; from the archaeological point of view the city was like a layered phyllo pastry. The Jews had dug out refuges and tunnels in which to hide from the agents of the Inquisition. When they abandoned them, those mysterious passageways became caves for bandits, until gradually La Justicia and other secret sects took over the buried entrails of the city.

Diego and his maestro wove through a labyrinth of sinuous alley-ways deep into the barrio of the ancient Goths; they passed beneath hidden gateways, descended stairs worn by time, dove into under-ground recesses, clambered through cavernous ruins, and crossed canals where no water ran, only a dark viscous liquid that smelled of rotten fruit. Finally they stopped before a door marked with cabalis-tic signs; it opened to them after the maestro gave the password, and they walked into a room with the look of an Egyptian temple. Diego found himself in the company of twenty men wearing brightly col-ored tunics adorned with a variety of symbols. All were wearing medallions similar to those of Maestro Escalante and Santiago de León. He was in the sect's tabernacle, the heart of La Justicia.

The initiation ritual lasted through the night, and during those long hours Diego met all the challenges to which he was subjected, one after another. In an adjoining space, perhaps the ruin of a Roman temple, the Circle of the Master was drawn on the floor. A man stepped forward to challenge Diego, and all the rest gathered around as judges. The man introduced himself as Julius Caesar, his code name. Diego and his oppo-nent shed shirts and shoes, stripping to their trousers. Their bout demanded precision, speed, and a cool head. They would engage one another with sharp daggers, with the apparent intention to kill, attack-ing as if to sink their daggers to the hilt but at the last fraction of a sec-ond holding back. The tiniest scratch on the nearly naked body of the opponent meant that the attacker was immediately eliminated. Neither could step outside the area of the design on the floor. The winner would be the one who could pin his opponent's shoulders to the ground in the very center of the circle. Diego had trained for months, and he had great confidence in his agility and endurance, but the moment the fight began, he realized that he had no real advantage over his antagonist. Julius Caesar was forty, slimmer and shorter than Diego, but very strong. He stood with his feet planted and elbows out, neck rigid, all the mus-cles of his torso and arms tensed, veins swollen, dagger gleaming in his right hand, but his face was absolutely calm. He was a formidable adver-sary. At the order to commence, the two began to dance around the circle, seeking the best angle to attack. Diego made the first move, throwing himself forward, but Caesar gave a great leap and, as if he were flying, flipped in the air and came down behind Diego, giving him barely enough time to whirl and crouch down to avoid the weapon slashing toward him. Three or four passes later, Julius Caesar shifted the dagger to his left hand. Diego was ambidextrous himself, but he had never had to fight anyone who was, and for an instant he lost his focus. His opponent seized that moment to aim a kick at Diego's chest that tumbled him to the ground, but Diego immediately sprang back up and using that momentum thrust his knife toward Caesar's neck; had it been actual combat he would have sliced the older man's throat, but Diego's hand stopped short, as demanded, and he believed he had scored. As judges did not intervene, he assumed there had been no contact, but he had no opportunity to make sure because the man had locked him in a wrestling hold. Each defended himself from the other's dagger while with legs and free arm he struggled to force his opponent to the ground. Diego managed to break free and again circled, readying himself for a new charge. He felt on fire; he was red in the face and streaming sweat, but his adversary was not even breathing hard and his face was as tranquil as it had been at the beginning of the match. Manuel Escalante's words came to mind: never fight in anger. Diego drew two deep breaths, giving himself a moment to calm down, though watching Julius Caesar's every move. As his mind cleared he realized that just as he had not expected an ambidextrous opponent, neither had his antagonist. He shifted the dagger to his other hand with the quickness he had learned for Galileo Tempesta's magic tricks and attacked before the other man realized what had happened. Caught by surprise, Caesar stepped back, but Diego thrust a foot between his legs and pushed him off balance. As soon as he fell, Diego was on him, pressing with all his strength, his right arm across the man's chest and his left fending off the struggling man's dagger. For a long moment they rocked back and forth, muscles taut as steel, eyes burning into the opponent's, teeth clenched. Diego not only had to hold his man down, he also had to drag him toward the center of the circle, a difficult task given that his opponent was scrapping with all his strength to prevent it. Out of the tail of his eye, Diego calculated the distance, which seemed enormous; never had an arm's length seemed so long. There was only one way to do it. He rolled over. Now Caesar was on top of him, and he could not contain his grunt of triumph at having gained the advantage. But with superhuman strength Diego rolled once again, and that placed his adversary precisely on the symbol that marked the center of the circle. Julius Caesar's calm changed to something difficult to read, but it was enough to tell Diego that he had won. With one last effort he pinned his adversary's shoulders to the ground.

"Well done," said Julius Caesar with a smile, dropping his dagger.

After that, Diego had to take on two more members with his sword. The judges tied one hand behind his back to give the advantage to his opponents, as neither of those men knew as much about fencing as he. Manuel Escalante's training paid off royally, and he was able to vanquish his challengers in fewer than ten minutes. Intellectual challenges followed the physical ones. After demonstrating that he knew the history of La Justicia, he was given difficult problems for which he had to offer original solutions demanding wit, courage, and knowledge. Finally, when he had successfully overcome every obstacle, he was led to an altar. There he saw the symbols he must venerate: a loaf of bread, a scale, a sword, a chalice, and a rose. The bread symbolized the obligation to help the poor; the scale represented the determination to fight for justice; the sword represented courage; the chalice held the elixir of compassion; and the rose reminded the members of the secret society that life is not only sacrifice and labor, it is also beautiful, and for that reason alone must be defended. At the conclusion of the ceremony, Maestro Manuel Escalante, as Diego's sponsor, placed the medallion around his neck.

"What will your code name be?" asked the Supreme Defender of the Temple.

"Zorro," Diego replied without hesitation.

He had not been thinking about it, but in that instant he had a clear vision of the red eyes of the fox he had seen during another rite of initiation many years before in the forests of California.

"Welcome to La Justicia, Zorro," said the Supreme Defender of the Temple, and all the members chorused his name.

Diego de la Vega was so euphoric that he had passed the tests, so awed by the solemnity of the sect's members, and so overwhelmed by the complex steps of the ceremony and the high-flown names of the hierarchy—Caballero of the Sun, Templar of the Nile, Maestro of the Cross, Guardian of the Serpent—that he could not think clearly. He agreed with the dogma of the sect and felt honored that he had been admitted. Only later, as he remembered the details and recounted them to Bernardo, would he judge the rite a little childish. He tried to make fun of himself for having taken it so seriously but his brother didn't laugh. He simply pointed out how similar the principles of La Justicia were to those of the *okahué* of his tribe.

One month after being accepted by the assembly of La Justicia, Diego surprised his maestro with an outlandish idea: he planned to free a group of hostages. Every attack launched by the guerrillas immediately unleashed a barbaric reprisal from the French. Soldiers would take four times as many hostages as they had lost and hang or shoot them in a public place. This swift response did not dissuade the Spanish—it merely fueled their hatred, but it broke the hearts of the unfortunate families trapped in the middle.

"This time they've taken five women, two men, and an eight-year-old boy, maestro, who will pay for the death of two French soldiers. They already killed the parish priest in the doorway of his church. They are holding these prisoners in the fort and are going to shoot them Sunday, at twelve o'clock noon," Diego explained.

"I know that, Don Diego, I have seen the notices all around the city," Escalante replied.

"We have to save them, maestro."

"To attempt that would be madness. La Ciudadela is impregnable. And in the hypothetical case that you succeeded in your mission, the French would execute two or three times that many hostages, I assure you."

"What does La Justicia do in such a situation, maestro?"

"There are times that one must resign oneself to the inevitable. Many innocents die in a war."

"I will remember that."

Diego was not inclined to resign himself; among other reasons, Amalia was one of those who had been taken, and he could not desert her. Through one of those blunders of fate that her cards had forgotten to warn her about, the Gypsy happened to be in the street at the time of the roundup by the French and was captured along with other persons as innocent as she. When Bernardo brought him the bad news, Diego gave no thought to the obstacles he would face, only the necessity of intervening and the irresistible thrill of adventure.

"In view of the fact that it is impossible to get inside La Ciudadela, Bernardo, I will have to settle for the palace of Le Chevalier Duchamp. I want to have a private conversation with him. How does that seem? Ah, I see that you don't like that idea, but I can't think of another. I know what you are thinking: that this is some kind of schoolboy prank, like that time with the bear when we were boys. No, this is serious—there are human lives to consider. We can't allow them to shoot Amalia. She is our friend. Well, in my case, she's something more than a friend, but that isn't the point. Unfortunately, brother mine, I cannot count on La Justicia, so I am going to need your help. It will be dangerous, but not as much as it would appear. Here is my plan. . . ."

Bernardo threw his hands up in a gesture of surrender and prepared to back his brother, as he had since they were born. Occasionally, when he was especially tired and lonely, he was convinced that it was time to return to California and face the undeniable truth that their childhood was behind them; Diego did show regrettable signs of being an eternal adolescent. Bernardo wondered how they could be so different and yet love each other so much. While for him destiny was a heavy weight on his shoulders, his brother was as carefree as a lark. Amalia, who knew how to read the enigmas of the stars, had explained why they had such different personalities. She said that they were born under two different signs of the Zodiac, although in the same place and during the same week. Diego was a

Gemini, and he was a Taurus, and that was what determined their temperaments. Bernardo listened to Diego's plan with his usual patience, without showing the doubts that troubled him, because deep down he had faith in his brother's inconceivable good luck. He knew that Diego arrived at his own conclusions, and then did something about them.

Bernardo carried out his assignment, which was to strike up a friendship with a French soldier and get him to drink until he passed out. He then removed the man's uniform and donned it himself: a dark blue jacket with a crimson military collar, white breeches and shirt, black leggings and tall headgear. In that uniform he was able to lead a team of horses into the palace gardens without attracting the attention of the night guards. Security around the sumptuous residence of Le Chevalier was somewhat lax because it had never occurred to anyone to attack it. At night, guards were posted with lanterns, but with the tedious passing of the hours their vigilance relaxed. Diego, dressed in his black acrobat costume, with cape and mask, the attire that he called his Zorro disguise, used the dark shadows to approach the building. With a spark of inspiration, he had pasted on a mustache he found in the costume trunk of the circus, a black tracing on his upper lip. The mask covered only the upper part of his face, and he was afraid that Le Chevalier could recognize him; the fine mustache was to distract and confuse him. Diego used his whip to pull himself up onto a balcony on the second floor; once he was inside, it was not difficult to locate the wing of the family's private quarters, since he had been there several times with Juliana and Isabel. It was about three in the morning, an hour when no servants were around and the guards were nodding at their posts. The palace was decorated not with typical Spanish sobriety but in the French manner, with so much furniture, draperies, plants, and statues that Diego had no difficulty moving through the palace unseen. He went down countless corridors and opened twenty doors before he came to the bedchamber of Le Chevalier, which turned out to be unexpectedly simple for someone of his power and rank. Napoleon's personal representative was sleeping on a hard soldier's cot in a nearly bare room lighted by a candelabrum in one corner. Diego knew, from indiscreet comments Agnès Duchamp had made, that her father suffered from insomnia and took opium in order to get some rest. One hour before, his valet had helped him disrobe, brought him a glass of sherry and his opium pipe, and then installed himself in a chair in the corridor, as he always did, in case his master needed him during the night. The valet slept very lightly, but that night he never noticed when someone brushed by him. Once inside Le Chevalier's room, Diego tried to exercise the mental control shown by the members of La Justicia; his heart was galloping, and his brow was wet. If he were caught in this room, he was as good as dead. Political prisoners were swallowed up in the dungeons of La Ciudadela forever, and better not even think of the stories of torture. Suddenly the thought of his father struck him like a blow. If Diego died, Alejandro de la Vega would never know why, only that his son was caught like a common thief in someone else's home. He took a minute to calm himself, and when he was sure that his will, his voice, and his hand would not tremble, he went over to the cot where Duchamp was floating in the lethargy of opium. Despite the drug, the Frenchman was immediately awake, but before he could yell, Diego covered his mouth with a gloved hand.

"Silence, or you will die like a rat, Excellency," he whispered.

He touched the tip of his sword to the chest of Le Chevalier, who sat up as far as the sword would allow and nodded that he had understood. In a whisper, Diego laid out what he wanted.

"You give me too much credit. If I order those hostages to be released, the *comandante* of the plaza will take others tomorrow," Le Chevalier answered in the same low tone.

"It would be a pity if that should occur. Your daughter Agnès is very precious, and we do not want to hurt her, but as Your Excellency knows, many innocents die in a war," said Diego.

He put his hand to his silk jacket, pulled out the lace handkerchief Bernardo had retrieved, and waved it in the face of Le Chevalier; though he could not see his daughter's embroidered name in the pale light, her father had no difficulty recognizing it from the unmistakable scent of violets.

"I suggest that you not summon your guards, Excellency, because at this moment my men are already in your daughter's room. If anything happens to me, you will not see her alive again. They will leave only when I give the signal," Diego said in the most amiable tone in the world, sniffing the handkerchief and stuffing it back into his jacket.

"You may escape with your life tonight," Le Chevalier growled, "but we will track you down, and then you will regret you were ever born. We know where to find you."

"I think not, Excellency. I am not a guerrilla, and neither do I have the honor of being one of your personal enemies." Diego smiled.

"Who are you, then?"

"Shhhh! Do not raise your voice. Remember that Agnès finds herself in good company. . . . My name is Zorro, caballero. At your service."

Forced by his captor, the Frenchman went to his desk and scribbled a brief note on his personal stationery, ordering the release of the hostages.

"I would be grateful if you would add your official seal, Excellency," Diego indicated.

Grumbling, Le Chevalier did as Diego directed, then called his valet, who came to the doorway. Behind the door, Diego held his sword pointed at the servant, ready to eliminate him at the first suspicious move.

"Send a guard to La Ciudadela with this letter," Le Chevalier ordered. "And tell him he must bring it back to me immediately, signed by the officer in charge, so I can be sure I am being obeyed. Is that clear?"

"Yes, Excellency," the man replied, and hurried off.

Diego suggested that Le Chevalier should return to bed and keep warm. It was a cold night, and they might have a long wait. He regretted, he added, that it was necessary to impose in this manner, but he would have to stay with him until the signed letter was returned. Did he have a chessboard or some cards with which they could pass the time? The Frenchman did not deign to reply. Furious, he slipped beneath the covers, watched by the masked man, who

made himself comfortable at the foot of the bed, as if they were intimate friends. They tolerated one another in silence for more than
two hours, and just when Diego had begun to fear that something
had gone wrong, the valet knocked at the door and handed his master the paper signed by a Captain Fuguet.

"*Hasta la vista,* Excellency." And Zorro's parting words were,
"Please be kind enough to give my greetings to the beautiful Agnès."

He felt sure that Le Chevalier believed his threat and would not
raise the alarm before he was safely away, but as a precaution he
bound and gagged him. With the tip of his sword he traced a large
letter *Z* on the wall, then with a mocking bow bid his host farewell
and dropped from the palace wall to the ground. There he found his
horse where Bernardo had hidden it, its hooves wrapped in rags to
silence sound. He rode away without raising an outcry because no
one was in the streets at that hour. The next day soldiers pasted
notices on the walls of public buildings that as a sign of goodwill on
the part of the authorities, the hostages had been pardoned. At the
same time, a secret hunt was begun to find the dastardly sneak who
called himself Zorro. The last thing the leaders of the guerrilla
forces could understand was this sudden mercy for hostages, and
they were so confused that for a week no new attempts against the
French were carried out in Catalonia.

Le Chevalier could not prevent the news from spreading that an
insolent brigand had gained entry to his very bedchamber, first
among the servants and the palace guards, then everywhere. The
Catalans howled with laughter at what had happened, and the name
of the mysterious Zorro passed from mouth to mouth for several
days, until other matters engaged the public's attention, and he was
forgotten. Diego heard about it in the School of Humanities, in the
taverns, and in the de Romeu home. He bit his tongue not to boast
of his exploit in public, and he never confessed to Amalia. The
Gypsy believed she had been saved by the miraculous power of the
talismans and amulets she always wore and the timely intervention
of her husband's ghost.

# PART THREE

# Barcelona, 1812–1814

cannot give you any further details about Diego's relationship with Amalia. Carnal love is one aspect of Zorro's legend that he has not authorized me to divulge, not so much out of fear of being the butt of jokes or accused of lying as from a sense of gallantry. It is common knowledge that no man that women flock to boasts of his conquests. Those who do, lie. And besides, I take no pleasure in prying into others' intimate moments. If you are expecting spicy pages from me, you will be disappointed. All I can say is that in the period when Diego was disporting himself with Amalia, his heart was given wholly to Juliana. So what were those embraces with the Gypsy widow like? One can only imagine. Perhaps she closed her eyes and thought of her murdered husband, while Diego abandoned himself to a fleeting pleasure with his mind a blank. Those clandestine meetings did not muddy the limpid adoration the chaste Juliana inspired in Diego; his emotions were compartmentalized, parallel lines that never crossed. I suspect that that has often been the case throughout Zorro's long life. I have observed him for three decades, and I know him almost as well as Bernardo does, which is why I dare make that statement. Thanks to his natural charm—which is more than a little—and his awesome good luck, he has been loved by dozens of women, usually without inviting it. A vague hint, a look out of the corner of his eye, one of his radiant smiles, is ordinarily enough to make even women with virtuous reputations invite him to climb to their balcony at questionable hours of the night. However, Zorro does not fall for them—he prefers impossible romances. I would swear that as soon as he jumps from the balcony to terra firma, he forgets the lady he was embracing only moments before. He himself does not know how many times he has fought a duel with a vindictive husband or offended father, but I have kept count—not for reasons of envy or jealousy, but because of my thoroughness as a chronicler. Diego remembers only women who tortured him with their indifference—like the incomparable Juliana. Many of his feats during those years were frantic attempts to attract that young lady's attention. When he was with her, he did not play the role of the faint-hearted fop that he adopted to deceive Agnès Duchamp, Le Chevalier, and others. To the contrary, in her presence he fanned out all his feathers like a peacock. He would have done battle with a dragon for her, but there were none in Barcelona, and he had to settle for Rafael Moncada. And now that I have mentioned him, it seems only fair to do justice to the man. Every story must have a villain. In fact, his wickedness is essential, for there are no heroes without enemies of their own stature. Zorro was fortunate to have a rival like Rafael Moncada; otherwise I would not have much to tell in these pages.

Juliana and Diego slept beneath the same roof, but they led separate lives, and there were few reasons for them to meet in that mansion with so many empty rooms. Only rarely were they alone, because Nuria watched Juliana and Isabel spied on Diego. Sometimes he waited hours to catch her alone in a corridor and walk a few steps with her without witnesses. They happened upon one another in the dining room at dinner hour, in the salon during harp concerts, Sundays at mass, and in the theater when there was a play by Lope de Vega or Molière, writers who delighted Tomás de Romeu. In church as well as in the theater, men and women were seated separately, so that Diego had to be satisfied with observing the back of his beloved's neck. He lived in the same house with her for more than four years, pursuing her with a hunter's dogged determination, without a single episode worthy of mention, until tragedy struck the family and the scales tipped in Diego's favor. Up until then, Juliana had responded to his siege with so little emotion that it was as if she didn't see him—but he needed very little to feed his illusions. He believed that her indifference was a stratagem intended to mask her true feelings. Someone had told him that women do such things. He was pitiful to see, poor man; it would have been better had Juliana loathed him. The heart is a capricious organ that can make a sudden turn, but warm, sisterly affection is nearly impossible to reverse.

The de Romeu family made occasional trips to Santa Fe, where they owned a semi-abandoned property. The patriarchal home was a square building on the point of a cliff, where the grandparents of Tomás de Romeu's deceased wife had ruled over their children and their peasants. The view was magnificent. Once those hills had been covered with vineyards that produced a wine comparable to the best of France, but during the war no one had tended them, and now nothing was left but dried-up, insect-infested runners. The house itself was taken over by the famous Santa Fe rats, well-fed, bad-tempered vermin that the campesinos had been known to eat during times of hardship. With garlic and leeks, they are not half bad. Two weeks before going there, Tomás would send a crew of servants to smoke out the rooms, the only way to make the rodents retreat temporarily. Those excursions were less frequent now; the roads had become too dangerous. One could feel the hatred of the country folk in the air like hot breath, exhalations of bad omen that raised the hair on the back of one's neck. Tomás de Romeu, like many landowners, scarcely dared leave the city, say nothing of trying to collect rents from his tenants, for fear of having his throat slit. In the country Juliana read, played her music, and tried to charm the campesinos like a fairy godmother to gain their affection, with little success. Nuria criticized the climate and complained about everything. Isabel entertained herself painting watercolor landscapes and portraits. Have I told you that she was a good artist? I think I forgot to mention that—an unpardonable omission, seeing that it was her only talent. On the whole, her art won more sympathy among the humble than all Juliana's charitable works. She could capture a remarkable likeness, but she made her subjects better-looking than they were, giving them more teeth, fewer wrinkles, and a dignified expression they seldom possessed.

But let us go back to Barcelona, where Diego kept busy with his classes, La Justicia, the taverns where he met with other students, and his swashbuckling adventures, which was his romantic way of referring to his escapades. In the meantime Juliana was living the idle life of young women of the period. She could go nowhere, not even to confession, without a chaperone. Nuria was her shadow. Neither could she be seen talking alone with any man under sixty. She went to balls with her father, sometimes accompanied by Diego, whom they introduced as a cousin from the Indies. Juliana showed no sign of being in any hurry to marry, despite the long line of eager suitors. It was her father's responsibility to arrange a good marriage for her, but he seemed incapable of choosing a son-in-law worthy of his marvelous daughter. In two years Juliana would be twenty, the allowable limit for finding a fiancé; if she was not engaged by then, the odds of her marrying would plummet month by month. With his unquenchable optimism, Diego was making the same calculations, and he concluded that time was working in his favor: once Juliana saw that she was withering on the vine, she would marry him to keep from becoming an old maid. He tried to use this curious argument to convince Bernardo, the one person patient enough to listen to his constant ranting about his desperate love.

As 1812 came to a close, Napoleon Bonaparte met defeat in Russia. The emperor had invaded that enormous country with his Grande Armée of nearly two hundred thousand men. The invincible French armies operated under an iron discipline, and they moved at a forced march, much more quickly than their enemies because they carried very little weight and lived off the land they conquered. As they advanced toward the interior of Russia, towns emptied, their inhabitants evaporated, and farmers burned their harvests. With every advance, Napoleon left behind scorched earth. The invaders triumphantly marched into Moscow, where they were welcomed by apocalyptic flames and the isolated fire of sharpshooters hidden in the smoking ruins, ready to die killing. The Muscovites, imitating the example of the brave farmers, had burned their possessions before evacuating the city. No one was left to give the keys of the city to Napoleon, not a single Russian soldier to humiliate, only a few tired prostitutes resigned to entertaining the conquerors now that their usual clients had decamped. Napoleon found himself isolated in the midst of a mountain of ashes. He waited, not knowing what he was waiting for, through the summer. By the time he decided to return to France, the rains had begun, and soon the soil of Russia would be covered with snow as hard as granite. The emperor could never have imagined the terrible trials that his men would have to bear. Added to harassment from the Cossacks and ambushes by farmers, they suffered hunger and a lunar cold that none of his soldiers had ever experienced. Thousands of the French army were turned into statues of eternal ice and left stationed along the ignominious route of the retreat. Soldiers were forced to eat their horses, their boots, at times even the corpses of their comrades. Only ten thousand men, defeated and disillusioned, made it back to their homeland. When he saw his destroyed army, Napoleon knew that the star that had shone so brightly in his prodigious ascent to power was beginning to fade. He had to pull back the troops occupying a large part of Europe. Two-thirds of those sent to Spain were recalled. At last the Spanish could glimpse a victorious end after years of bloody resistance, but that triumph would not come until sixteen months later.

That year, during the same period that Napoleon was licking his wounds after the disastrous retreat to France, Eulalia de Callís sent her nephew Rafael Moncada to the Antilles on a mission to expand her chocolate enterprise. She planned to sell cocoa, almond paste, preserved nutmeats, and refined aromatic sugar to chocolatiers in Europe and the United States. She had heard that all Americans had a sweet tooth. Her nephew's mission was to weave a network of business contacts in important cities from Washington to Paris.

Moscow was put on hold, since it was in ruins, but Eulalia was confident that as soon as the smoke of war cleared, the Russian capital would be rebuilt in all its previous splendor. Rafael set out on an eleven-month tour, plowing oceans and pounding his kidneys on horseback, all to establish the aromatic brotherhood of chocolate imagined by Eulalia.

Before he left for the Antilles, and without saying a word of his intentions to his aunt, Rafael requested an audience with Tomás de Romeu. He was not received in the de Romeu home but on the neutral terrain of the Geographic and Philosophic Society, of which the older man was a member. The club ran an excellent restaurant on the second floor, and Tomás de Romeu's admiration for France did not extend to its exquisite cuisine. No canary tongues for him—he preferred robust Catalan dishes: *escudella,* a soup to raise the dead, *estofat de toro,* a stew with the firepower of a bomb, and the divine *butifarra del obispo,* a blood sausage blacker and fatter than most. Rafael Moncada, facing his host across a mountain of meat and fat, was a little pale. He barely tasted the meal because he had a delicate stomach and was nervous as well. He laid out his personal circumstances to Juliana's father, from his titles to his financial solvency.

"I deeply regret, Señor de Romeu, that we had to meet on the unfortunate occasion of the duel with Diego de la Vega. He is an impetuous young man, and I myself, I must admit, am often inclined to impulse. We had words, and ended up on the field of honor. Happily, there were no serious consequences. I hope that the incident does not weigh negatively in the judgement you hold of me, sir," said the candidate for the role of son-in-law.

"Not at all, caballero. The purpose of a duel is to cleanse a stain. Once two gentlemen have fought, no rancor remains between them," de Romeu replied amiably, although he had not forgotten the details of that particular match.

With the dessert, *postre de music,* filled with so many dried fruits and nuts that they stuck in one's teeth, Moncada expressed his desire to ask for Juliana's hand as soon as he returned from his journey. For a long time, without intervening, Tomás had observed the strange relationship between his daughter and her tenacious suitor. He found it difficult to talk about emotions, and he had never made the effort to approach his daughters. Woman's talk flustered him, and he preferred to delegate that to Nuria. He had watched Juliana toddle down the stone corridors of his icy home when she was small, had noticed when her permanent teeth came in, and had watched her shoot up in a spurt and navigate through the graceless years of puberty. Then one day she stood before him with little-girl curls and a woman's body, her dress bursting at the seams. At that point he ordered Nuria to have a proper wardrobe made for her, hire a dancing master, and not let his daughter out of her sight. Now here he was being accosted by Rafael Moncada, among other well-placed caballeros, asking for Juliana's hand in marriage, and he did not know what to say. Such an alliance would be ideal; any father in his situation would be pleased; but de Romeu did not like Moncada, less because of differences in their ideological positions than for the disturbing gossip he had heard about the man's character. The generally held opinion was that marriage is a social and financial arrangement in which sentiment plays little part—that part of marriage irons out over the years—but de Romeu did not agree. He had married for love, and he had been very happy, so much so that he never found a woman to take his wife's place. Juliana was like him, and to make matters worse, she had filled her head with romantic novels. He was held in check by the enormous respect he had for his daughter. He would have to twist her arm to get her to marry someone she didn't love, and he did not feel capable of doing that; he wanted her to be happy, and he doubted that Moncada was the man who could achieve that. He would have to report their conversation to Juliana, but he didn't know how; her beauty and virtue intimidated him. He felt more comfortable with Isabel, whose obvious imperfections made her much more accessible. He realized that he could not put things off, so that very night he communicated Moncada's proposal to her. She shrugged and without missing a stitch in her embroidery commented that many people had died of malaria in the Antilles, so there was no need to hurry a decision.

Diego was happy. The journey of his dangerous rival presented him with a unique opportunity to gain ground in the race for Juliana's hand. The girl showed no reaction to Moncada's absence, but neither did she seem to note Diego's advances. She continued to treat him with the same tolerant and distracted affection she had always shown, without demonstrating the least curiosity about his mysterious activities. She was similarly unimpressed with his poems. She could not imagine that the teeth like pearls, emerald eyes, and ruby lips of those verses were to be taken seriously. Looking for more excuses to spend time with Juliana, Diego joined dancing classes and turned out to be an elegant and spirited dancer. He was even able to convince Nuria to rattle a bone or two to the tune of a fandango, although he could never get her to intercede with Juliana; on that point, the good woman was always as insensitive as Isabel. Hoping to capture the admiration of the women of the house, Diego cut candles in half with his fencing foil, with such precision that the flame never wavered and the parts of the candle remained in place. He could also extinguish them with the tip of his whip. He perfected the sleight of hand he had been taught by Galileo Tempesta, and performed true miracles with cards. He also juggled lighted torches and escaped unaided from a trunk closed with a padlock and chain. When he ran out of tricks, he tried to impress his beloved with his adventures, including some he had promised Bernardo and Maestro Manuel Escalante never to mention. In one moment of weakness, he hinted about the existence of a secret society to which only a select number of men belonged. Juliana congratulated him, thinking he was referring to a student club that wandered through the streets playing love ballads. Juliana's attitude was not one of disdain—she was fond of Diego—nor of maliciousness, of which she was incapable: it was merely the effect of the novels. She was waiting for the hero from her books, courageous and tragic, who would rescue her from everyday boredom, and it never occurred to her that that person might be Diego de la Vega. Or Rafael Moncada.

Every day it became more evident that the end of the war was near. Eulalia de Callís was impatiently preparing for that moment while her nephew secured their business affiliations outside the country. Malaria did not resolve Juliana de Romeu's problem with Moncada, and in November 1813 he returned, wealthier than ever because his aunt had allocated a high percentage of the bonbon business to him. He had been successful in the best circles in Europe, and in the United States he met no lesser a personage than Thomas Jefferson, to whom he suggested the idea of planting *cacao* trees in Virginia. As soon as he brushed off the dust of the road, Moncada communicated with Tomás de Romeu, repeating his intention to pay suit to Juliana. He had been waiting for years, and he was not inclined to accept another evasion. Two hours later, Tomás summoned his daughter to the library, the place where he settled most of his affairs and clarified his existential doubts with the help of a glass of cognac, and transmitted her suitor's message to her.

"You are at an age to marry, my dear daughter. Time passes for everyone," he argued. "Rafael Moncada is a true gentleman, and upon the death of his aunt he will become one of the wealthiest men in Catalonia. I do not judge people by their financial position, as you know, but I have to think of your security."

"An unhappy marriage is worse than death for a woman, Father. There is no way out of it. The idea of obeying and serving a man is terrible if there is no trust and affection."

"That grows after you marry, Juliana."

"Not always, sir. Besides, there are your needs and my duty to consider. Who will care for you when you grow old? Isabel does not have the temperament for that."

"For God's sake, Juliana! I have never suggested that my daughters should look after me in my old age. What I want are grandchildren, and to see you both well placed. I cannot die in peace without leaving you protected."

"I do not know whether Rafael Moncada is the man for me. I cannot imagine any kind of intimacy with him," she murmured, blushing.

"You are no different from other girls in that respect, daughter. What virtuous young woman *can* imagine that?" Tomás de Romeu replied, as embarrassed as she was.

That was a subject he had never expected to discuss with his daughters. He supposed that at the right moment Nuria would explain what they needed to know, although the chaperone probably was as ignorant about such matters as the girls. Juliana did not choose to tell her father that she talked about those things all the time with Agnès Duchamp, and that she had learned everything she needed to know in her romantic novels.

"I need a little more time to decide, Father," Juliana pleaded.

Tomás de Romeu had never missed his departed wife so badly; she would have handled the problem wisely and with a firm hand, as mothers do. He was weary of so much hot and cold. He spoke with Rafael Moncada to ask for another postponement, and Moncada had no choice but to agree. Then Tomás ordered Juliana to talk things over with her pillow, and told her that if she did not have an answer in two weeks' time, he would accept Moncada's proposal, and that would be the end of that. It was his last word, he concluded, though his voice quavered as he said it. By then Moncada's long offensive had reached the level of a personal challenge; people were talking about it in the stateliest salons and in the servants' patios as well, how this young girl who had no fortune and no titles was humiliating the best catch in Barcelona. If his daughter kept asking him to put it off, Tomás de Romeu would be facing a serious confrontation with Moncada, but undoubtedly he would have continued to find excuses had a strange event not precipitated the outcome.

That day de Romeu's two daughters had gone with Nuria to dispense charity, as they always did the first Friday of the month. There were fifteen hundred acknowledged beggars in the city, and several thousand indigents that no one took the trouble to count. For five years, always on the same day and at the same time, Juliana, flanked by the stiff figure of her chaperone, could be seen visiting houses of charity. Out of a sense of decorum and a wish not to offend with a display of ostentation, they covered themselves from head to foot in mantillas and dark coats and visited the barrio on foot. Jordi waited for them with the trap in a nearby plaza, combating his boredom with his flask of liquor. These excursions took all afternoon; in addition to succoring the poor, the women visited the nuns who ran the hospices. That year Isabel had started to accompany them. At fifteen, she was old enough to learn compassion instead of wasting time spying on Diego and fighting a duel with herself before a mirror, as Nuria put it. They had to walk through narrow alleyways in barrios of raw poverty, where even the cats were on guard to keep from being caught and sold as hares. Juliana submitted with exemplary rigor to that heroic penance, but it made Isabel ill, not simply because the sores and boils, the rags and crutches, the toothless mouths and noses eaten by syphilis frightened her, but because that form of charity seemed a cruel joke. She believed that all the *duros* in Juliana's purse would do nothing to help the enormity of the misery.

"To do nothing is worse," her sister would reply.

They had begun their round a half hour before and had visited only one orphanage when as they came to a corner, they saw three dangerous-looking men coming toward them. The men's eyes were barely visible because they were wearing kerchiefs around their faces and hats pulled down to their eyebrows. Despite the official ban on wearing a cape, the tallest of them was wrapped in a cloak. It was the dead hour of the siesta, when very few people were about. The alley was bounded on either side by the massive stone walls of a church and a convent; there was not even a door recess to take refuge in. Nuria began to scream, but one of the rapscallions silenced her with a slap on the face that knocked her to the ground. Juliana opened her coat and tried to hide the purse with the money as Isabel glanced around, searching for a source of help. One of the footpads grabbed the purse, and another was just about to tear off Juliana's pearl earrings when he was stopped by the sound of a horse's hooves. Isabel yelled at the top of her lungs, and an instant

later no other than Rafael Moncada made a providential appearance. In a city as densely populated as Barcelona, his riding to the
rescue was little less than a miracle. Moncada needed only a glance
to appraise the situation, to unsheathe his sword and confront the
lowlifes. Two of them had already pulled out their curved knives, but
two slashes of Moncada's sword and his determined manner made
them hesitate. Their rescuer looked enormous and noble on his
steed: black boots gleaming in silver stirrups, tightly fitting, snow-
white trousers, dark green velvet astrakhan-trimmed jacket, long
sword with its rounded gold-engraved guard. From that vantage,
Moncada could have dispatched more than one adversary without
trying, but he seemed to enjoy intimidating them. With a fierce
smile on his lips and his sword glinting in the air, he could have been
the central figure in a battle painting. The aggressors huffed and
panted as he goaded them mercilessly from on high. The horse,
whirling in the midst of the fracas, reared, and for a moment it
seemed that it would throw its rider, but Moncada merely gripped
tighter with his legs. It was a strange and violent dance. In the center of the circle of daggers the steed circled, whinnying with terror,
as Moncada reined it in with one hand and flourished his weapon in
the other, surrounded by ruffians looking for the moment to sink
their knives into him but not daring to step within his reach. Nuria
added her yells to Isabel's, and soon people came out to look, but
when they saw iron gleaming in the pale light of day, they kept their
distance. One boy went running to get the constables, but there was
no hope that they would get there in time to help. Isabel took
advantage of the confusion to yank the money purse from the hands
of the cloaked man, then grabbed her sister by one arm and Nuria by
the other and urged them to run. She could not move them; they
were glued to the paving stones. The whole episode was very brief,
but the minutes dragged by in the unreal time of nightmares. Finally
Rafael Moncada swatted one of the men's dagger from his hand, and
with that the three attackers realized that they would do better to
retreat. The rescuing caballero made a sign of pursuing them but

stopped when he saw how upset the women were and leapt from his mount to calm them. A red stain was spreading down the white cloth of his trousers. Juliana ran to take comfort in his arms, trembling like a rabbit.

"You are wounded!" she cried when she saw the blood on his leg.

"Only a scratch," he replied.

All the commotion was too much for the girl. Her vision clouded, and her knees buckled, but before she hit the ground, Moncada's waiting arms swept her up. Isabel grumbled impatiently that this was all they needed to complete the picture: her sister swooning. Moncada ignored her sarcasm and, limping slightly but never stumbling, carried Juliana to the plaza. Nuria and Isabel followed, leading the horse and surrounded by a crowd of curiosity seekers, each of whom had an opinion about what had happened and all of whom wanted to have the last word on the subject. When Jordi saw that procession, he jumped from the driver's seat and helped Moncada get Juliana inside the carriage. Loud applause burst out among the onlookers. Seldom did anything as quixotic and romantic happen in the streets of Barcelona; there would be something to talk about for days. Twenty minutes later, Jordi drove into the patio of the de Romeu home, followed by Moncada on horseback. Juliana was sniffling from nerves, Nuria was counting with her tongue the teeth loosened by the blow to her face, and Isabel was shooting sparks and holding on to the purse.

Tomás de Romeu was not a man to be impressed with aristocratic surnames—in truth, he hoped to see them abolished from the face of the earth—or with Moncada's fortune—because he was open-handed by nature—but he was moved to tears when he learned that this caballero, who had suffered so many rebuffs from Juliana, had risked his life to protect his daughters from irreparable harm. Although he professed to be an atheist, he fully agreed with Nuria that divine providence had sent Moncada in time to save them. He insisted that the hero of the day come in and rest while Jordi went for a doctor to tend his wound, but Moncada preferred to retire discreetly. Except for an occasional sharp intake of breath, nothing suggested that he was injured. Everyone commented that his sangfroid in the face of pain was as admirable as his courage facing danger. Isabel was the only one who showed no signs of gratitude. Instead of joining in the flood of emotion flowing from the rest of the family, she merely clicked her tongue several times with disgust, something that was ill received. Her father sent her to her room and told her not to stick her nose out until she apologized for her vulgarity.

Diego had to listen with disciplined patience to Juliana's detailed account of the assault, in addition to speculations about what would have happened had her savior not intervened in time. Nothing so dangerous had ever happened to the girl before. The figure of Rafael Moncada grew in her eyes, adorned with virtues that she had not perceived until then: he was strong and handsome, he had elegant hands and wavy hair. A man with good hair has a head start in this life. She suddenly noticed that he resembled the most famous torero in Spain, a long-legged, fiery-eyed man from Cordoba. This suitor, she decided, was really not so bad. With all the excitement, however, she was running a fever, and she went to bed early. That night the doctor had to sedate her, after applying a tincture of arnica to Nuria's face, which had swollen like a squash.

In view of the fact that he would not see his beauty at dinner, Diego, too, retired to his rooms, where Bernardo was waiting. For the sake of decency, the girls were not allowed in the wing of the house where the men had their rooms, the one exception being the time when Diego was convalescing from the wound he suffered in the duel, but Isabel had never paid much attention to rules, just as she did not fully obey punishments her father set. That night she ignored his order to stay in her room and appeared in Diego's and Bernardo's without warning, as she often did.

"Didn't I tell you to knock? One day you are going to find me naked," Diego scolded.

"I don't think that would be such a memorable sight," she replied.

She plopped down on Diego's bed with the smug expression of someone who has something to tell but won't say it, waiting to be begged; Diego successfully refused to play her game, and Bernardo was busy tying knots in a rope. A long minute went by, and finally her eagerness to tell them was too great. In the unladylike language she used out of Nuria's hearing, she said that her sister must be a dumbass not to suspect Moncada. She added that the whole thing smelled of rotten fish; one of the three attackers had been Rodolfo, the giant from the circus. Diego jumped up like a monkey, and Bernardo dropped the rope he was knotting.

"Are you sure? Didn't all of you say that those ruffians had their faces covered?" Diego protested.

"Yes, and besides that, he was wrapped in this cloak, but he was huge, and when I grabbed the purse I saw his arms. They were tattooed."

"It might have been a sailor, Isabel. Lots of them have tattoos," Diego contended.

"They were the same ones the giant has, I am absolutely sure, so you'd better believe me," she answered.

From there to deducing that the Gypsies were involved was but a step, which Diego and Bernardo immediately took. They had known for a long time that Pelayo and his friends did Moncada's dirty work, but they couldn't prove it. They never dared bring the subject up with the giant, who was very close-mouthed and would never have confessed to them. Neither did Amalia respond to Diego's subtle questions; even in moments of greatest intimacy she guarded the family's secrets. Diego could not take a suspicion of that nature to Tomás de Romeu without proof, and if he did, he would have to confess his own connections with the tribe. He decided, nevertheless, to take action. As Isabel said, they could not allow Juliana to end up married to Moncada out of mistaken gratitude.

The next day they managed to convince Juliana to get up out of bed, control her nerves, and go with them to the barrio where Amalia usually posted herself to tell the fortunes of the passersby. Nuria went with them, as was her duty, though her face looked worse even than it had the day before. One cheek was purple, and her eyelids were so swollen that she looked like a toad. It took less than half an hour to find Amalia. While the girls and their chaperone waited in the carriage, Diego, calling upon an eloquence he did not know he possessed, urged the Gypsy to save Juliana from a terrible fate.

"One word from you will prevent the tragedy of a loveless marriage between an innocent young girl and a heartless man. You must tell her the truth," he pled dramatically.

"I don't know what you are talking about," Amalia replied.

"Oh, yes, you know. The men who attacked the girls were from your clan. I know one of them was Rodolfo. I think that Moncada set the stage to look like a hero in front of the de Romeu sisters. It was all arranged, wasn't it?" he insisted.

"Are you in love with her?" Amalia asked, with no malice.

Caught off guard, Diego had to admit that he was. Amalia took his hands, studied them with an enigmatic smile, and then wet the tip of a finger with saliva and traced the sign of the cross on his palms.

"What are you doing? Is this some kind of curse?" Diego asked, frightened.

"It's a prediction. You will never marry her."

"You mean that Juliana is going to marry Moncada?"

"That I do not know. I will do what you ask, but have no illusions—that woman must live out her destiny, just as you must, and nothing I say will change what is written in the heavens."

Amalia climbed into the carriage, nodded to Isabel, whom she had seen several times with Diego and Bernardo, and took her seat across from Juliana. Nuria held her breath, frightened, because she believed that Gypsies were descendents of Cain, as well as professional thieves. Juliana dismissed her chaperone and Isabel, who complained but got out of the coach. When they were alone, the two women looked one another over for a long minute. Amalia made a detailed inventory: the classic face framed by black curls, the green cat's eyes, the slender neck, the short fur cape and hat, the delicate kid boots. For her part, Juliana studied the Gypsy with curiosity; she had never seen one so close before. If she had been in love with Diego, her instinct would have warned her that this was her rival, but that thought never crossed her mind. She liked Amalia's smoky scent, her prominent cheekbones, her full skirts, the tinkling of her silver jewelry. She thought she was beautiful. Impulsively, she removed her gloves and took Amalia's hands in hers. "Thank you for talking with me," she said. Disarmed by Juliana's spontaneity, Amalia decided to violate the basic rule of her people: never to trust a *gadje,* especially if it endangered the tribe. In a few words she described the dark side of Moncada; she told Juliana that, yes, the assault had been planned, that she and her sister had never been in danger, and that the stain on Moncada's pant leg was not from a wound but from a piece of sheep gut filled with chicken blood. She said that once in a while one or two men of her tribe did jobs for Moncada, usually unimportant things; only in a handful of instances had they done something bad like the attack on Count Orloff. "We are not criminals," Amalia explained, and added that she was sorry that the Russian and Nuria had been struck; violence was prohibited in their law. And as the real coup de grâce, she informed Juliana that it was Pelayo who had sung the serenade because Moncada was as tone-deaf as a duck. Juliana listened to the entire confession without a single question. The two women nodded and said good-bye. Amalia left the carriage; then Juliana burst into tears.

That same afternoon Tomás de Romeu formally received Rafael Moncada, who had informed him in a brief note that he found himself recovered from loss of blood and hoping to pay his respects to Juliana. That morning his footman had delivered a bouquet of flowers for her and a box of almond nougats for Isabel, delicate, modest attentions for which Tomás gave the suitor good marks. Moncada arrived dressed with impeccable elegance, leaning on a cane. Tomás welcomed him in the main salon, dusted in honor of his future son-in-law. He offered him a glass of sherry, and once they had taken a seat thanked him again for his timely intervention. Then he sent for his daughters. Juliana looked strained, and was wearing a dark dress more appropriate for a nun than for an important occasion like this. Her sister Isabel's eyes were blazing, and the corners of her lips lifted in a mocking smile; she held Juliana's arm in such a strong grasp that she seemed to be dragging her along. Rafael Moncada attributed Juliana's ravaged countenance to nerves. "It is no wonder, after the terrible experience you have been through—" he began before she interrupted to announce in a trembling voice, but with iron conviction, that not even dead would she marry him.

After hearing Juliana's emphatic no, Rafael Moncada left the house fuming, although still in control of his good manners. In his twenty-six years he had encountered a few obstacles but he had never failed in anything. He was not going to give up. He still had a few tricks up his sleeve: that was what social position, money, and connections were for. He had refrained from asking Juliana for her reasons; intuition warned him that it would be very bad strategy. She knew enough to have doubts, and he could not run the risk of being exposed. If Juliana suspected that the assault in the street had been a farce, there could be only one reason: Pelayo. He did not think the man would have dared betray him—there was no profit in it for him—but he might have been careless. There were no secrets in Barcelona; the servants had a much more efficient information network than the French spies in La Ciudadela. Just one wrong word from any of the conspirators and it would have reached Juliana's ears. He had used the Gypsies on various occasions precisely because they were nomads; they came and went with no interchange with anyone outside their tribe; they had no friends or acquaintances in Barcelona; they were discreet out of necessity. During the time that he was away on his journey, he had lost contact with Pelayo, and in a certain way he was relieved. Dealings with such people made him uncomfortable. When he got back, he thought that he could start with a clean slate, forget the peccadilloes of the past and start anew, detached from the underhanded world of hired skullduggery, but his vow to be a new man lasted barely a few days. When Juliana had asked for another two weeks to respond to his proposal of marriage, Moncada suffered a panic very rare in him; he prided himself on dominating even the monsters of his nightmares. During his absence he had written Juliana several letters, which she had not answered. He attributed her silence to shyness; at an age when her contemporaries were already mothers, Juliana behaved like a schoolgirl. In his eyes that innocence was the girl's best quality; it guaranteed that when she did give herself to him, she would do so without reserve. But with the new postponement his certainty faltered, and that was when he had decided to put on some pressure. A romantic exploit like one of those in the books she treasured would be his most effective move, he calculated, but he could not hope that the opportunity would happen on its own—he had to speed things up. He would get what he wanted without harming anyone; it would not actually be deceiving her, because should footpads attack Juliana—or any other decent woman—he would rush to their defense. It did not seem necessary to explain those arguments to Pelayo, of course; he simply gave the orders and they were carried out without a hitch. True, the scene the Gypsies staged was briefer than he had planned because the knaves broke and ran after a few minutes, when they feared that Moncada's sword was overly enthusiastic. That had not given him time to act with the dramatic splendor he had envisioned, which is why when Pelayo came to collect, he felt it was fair to haggle over the price. They argued, and Pelayo ended by accepting the lower amount, but Rafael Moncada was left with a bitter taste in his mouth; the man knew too much, and he might be tempted to blackmail him. Definitely, he concluded, it was bad for a man of that stripe, who respected no law or moral code, to have power over him. He must get rid of him as quickly as possible, him and his whole tribe.

As for Bernardo, he was very familiar with the tight network of gossip that people of Moncada's class were so in fear of. With his tomblike silence, his dignified Indian ways, and his willingness to do favors, he had endeared himself to many people: the women in the market, the stevedores in the port, the artisans in the barrios, and the coachmen, lackeys, and servants in the homes of the rich. He stored information in his prodigious memory, divided into compartments as if in an enormous archive that contained orderly facts and lists to use at the proper time. He had not stored the night he had met Juanillo in Eulalia de Callís's courtyard under "blow received" but, rather, under "attack on Count Orloff." He had kept in contact with Juanillo, and in that way followed Moncada's movements from afar. The footman was not very bright, and he detested anyone who was not a Catalan, but he tolerated Bernardo because he never interrupted him, and he knew that the Indian had been baptized. Once Amalia acknowledged Moncada's dealings with the Gypsies, Bernardo had decided to find out more about him. He made a visit to Juanillo, taking as a gift a bottle of Tomás de Romeu's best cognac that Isabel had slipped to him when she learned that it would be used for a good purpose. The footman did not need liquor to loosen his tongue, but he was grateful nonetheless, and soon he was telling Bernardo the latest news: he himself had carried a missive from his master to the military chief of La Ciudadela, a letter in which Moncada accused the tribe of Gypsies of smuggling contraband weapons into the city and of conspiring against the government.

"Those Gypsies are eternally cursed because they forged the nails for Christ's cross. They deserve to be burned at the stake. Give them no mercy, that's what I say," was Juanillo's conclusion.

Bernardo knew where to find Diego at that hour. He headed straight for the open country outside the walls of Barcelona, where the Gypsies had their filthy tents and beat-up wagons. In the three years they had been there, the camp had taken on the look of a village of rags. Diego de la Vega had not renewed his trysts with Amalia because she was afraid that she would endanger her own fate forever. She had been saved from being executed by the French; that was more than enough proof that the spirit of her husband Ramón was protecting her from the Other Side. It was not a good idea to provoke his anger by continuing to bed a young *gadje*. It was also in her heart that Diego had confessed his love for Juliana to her; in that case they were both being unfaithful: she to the memory of her deceased husband, he to the chaste maiden.

Just as Bernardo had supposed, Diego had gone to the camp to help his friends set up the tent for the Sunday circus, which that day would not be in a plaza, as usual, but right in the camp. They had several hours yet, since the spectacle would not begin until four. When Bernardo arrived, Diego and the other men were singing a tune that Diego had learned from the sailors on the *Madre de Dios* while heaving on the ropes to tighten the canvas. He had sensed his brother across the distance and was expecting him. He did not need to see Bernardo's troubled expression to know that something was amiss. The smile that was always dancing on his lips vanished when he heard what Bernardo had learned from Juanillo. Immediately, he called the tribe together.

"If this information is accurate, you are in grave danger. I wonder why they haven't arrested you before this," he said.

"That must mean that they plan to come during the performance, when we are all together and they have an audience," Rodolfo theorized. "The French like to set examples; this will keep people frightened, and what better way than to use us."

They began gathering up the small children and animals. In silence, with the stealth of centuries of persecution and nomadic living, the Gypsies tied up bundles of things they could not do without, climbed onto their horses, and in less than half an hour had ridden off in the direction of the mountains. As they left, Diego told them to send someone the next day to the old cathedral. "I will have something for you," he told them, and added that he would try to entertain the soldiers and give them time to get away. The Gypsies lost everything. Behind them they left a desolate camp with its sad circus tent, wagons without horses, still-smoking bonfires, abandoned tents, and a sprawl of pots and pans, mattresses, and rags. In the meantime, Diego and Bernardo were parading through nearby streets, beating on drums and wearing clown hats to attract potential showgoers and lead them back to the circus. Soon there was a goodly number of spectators waiting beneath the canvas. When Diego appeared in the ring dressed as Zorro, with mask and mustache, he was greeted with impatient whistles. As he juggled three lighted torches, passing them between his legs and behind his back before tossing them up again, his public did not seem too impressed and began to shout crude remarks. Bernardo took away the torches, and Diego asked for a volunteer for a trick of great suspense. A husky, pugnacious sailor came forward and, following instructions, stood a few paces away with a cigarette in his lips. Diego snapped his whip on the ground a couple of times before flicking the tip. When the volunteer felt the air whistle by his face he reddened with anger, but as tobacco flew through the air and he realized that the whip had not touched his skin, he and the crowd bellowed with laughter. At that same moment someone remembered the story that had circulated around the city about a certain Zorro who dressed in black and wore a mask and who had dared get Le Chevalier out of bed to save some hostages. "Zorro? A fox? A *fox*?" flashed through the audience, and someone pointed to Diego, who made a deep bow and then scurried up the ropes toward the trapeze. At the precise instant that Bernardo gave the signal, Diego heard the horses' hooves. They had been waiting for that. Diego did a somersault on the bar of the trapeze, dropped, and hung by his feet, swinging through the air above the heads of the audience.

Instants later a group of French soldiers burst into the tent with drawn bayonets, led by an officer bawling threats. Panic broke out as people tried to escape, a moment Diego seized to slide down a rope to the ground. Several shots were fired, and a monumental panic ensued as spectators, shoving to get out, stumbled into and over the soldiers. Diego slipped away like a weasel before they could lay a hand on him, and with Bernardo's help cut the ropes that held up the tent. The canvas dropped onto the people trapped inside, soldiers and public alike. In the confusion the two milk brothers jumped onto their horses and set off at a gallop for Tomás de Romeu's home. On the way, Diego shed the cape, sombrero, mask, and mustache. They calculated that it would take the soldiers a good long while to fight their way out of the tent, realize that the Gypsies had fled, and organize a party to give chase. Diego knew that the next day the name of Zorro would again be on everyone's lips. Bernardo threw Diego an eloquent look of reproach; his arrogance could cost him dear, since the French would be moving heaven and earth to find this mysterious Zorro. The brothers reached their destination without incident, went inside through the service entrance, and shortly afterward were having chocolate and biscuits with Juliana and Isabel. They did not know that at that moment the Gypsy camp was going up in smoke. The soldiers had set fire to the straw in the ring, which burned like dry tinder, reaching the ancient canvas in only minutes.

The following day at noon Diego took up a position in a nave of the cathedral. Gossip about the second appearance of Zorro had made the complete rounds of Barcelona and come back to his ears. In one day the enigmatic hero had captured the people's imagination. The letter Z had been scratched with a knife on several walls, the work of small boys inflamed with the desire to imitate Zorro.

"That is just what we need, Bernardo, *many* foxes to distract the hunters."

At that hour the church was empty except for a pair of sacristans changing the flowers on the main altar. It was dark and cold, and quiet as a tomb; the brutal sunlight and noise of the street did not penetrate that far. Diego sat waiting on a bench, surrounded by statues of saints and breathing the unmistakable metallic scent of incense that had impregnated the walls. Timid, reflected colors filtered through the venerable stained-glass windows, bathing the interior with unreal light. The calm of that moment brought memories of his mother. He knew nothing of how she was; it was as if she had vanished. It surprised him that neither his father nor Padre Mendoza mentioned her in their letters, and that she herself had never written him two lines, but he wasn't worried. If something bad happened to his mother he would feel it in his bones. One hour later, when he was about to leave, convinced that no one would be coming to the rendezvous now, the slim figure of Amalia materialized like a ghost. They greeted one another with their eyes, without touching.

"What is to become of you now?" Diego whispered.

"We're moving on until things calm down. Soon everyone will forget all about us," she replied.

"They burned the camp; you have nothing left."

"That is nothing new, Diego. We Roma are accustomed to losing everything; it has happened to us before, and it will again."

"Will I see you someday, Amalia?"

She smiled and shrugged her shoulders. "That I do not know, I do not have my crystal ball."

Diego gave her everything he had been able to gather in the few hours since he had seen her: most of the money he had left from an allowance his father had sent and also what the de Romeu girls had been able to contribute once they knew what had happened. From Juliana he had also brought a package wrapped in a handkerchief.

"Juliana asked me to give you this as a remembrance," said Diego.

Amalia untied the handkerchief to find a delicate pearl diadem, the one Diego had seen Juliana wear several times; it was the most valuable jewel she owned.

"Why?" Amalia asked, surprised.

"I suppose it must be because you saved her from marrying Moncada."

"That may not be certain. Her destiny may be to marry him anyway—"

"Never!" Diego interrupted. "Juliana knows now what a swine he is."

"The heart is fickle," Amalia replied. She hid the jewel in a pouch tucked among the folds of her full overskirts, wagged her fingers at Diego in a gesture of farewell, and faded into the icy shadows of the cathedral. Instants later she was running through the alleyways of the barrio toward the *ramblas*.

Shortly after the exodus of the Gypsies, but before Christmas, a letter arrived from Padre Mendoza. The missionary wrote every six months to send news of the family and of his mission. He would report, for example, that the dolphins had returned to the coast, that the year's wine was acid, that soldiers had arrested White Owl because she assaulted them with her staff while defending an Indian but through Alejandro de la Vega's intervention had been released. Since then, he added, they had seen no sign of her. Padre Mendoza's precise and energetic style moved Diego much more than that of Alejandro de la Vega, whose letters were sermons salted with moral advice, little different from the tone Alejandro always used with his son. This time, however, Padre Mendoza's brief missive was addressed not to Diego but to Bernardo, and the flap was closed with sealing wax. Bernardo broke the seal with his knife and sat down near a window to read it. Diego, who was watching from across the room, saw him pale as his eyes followed the missionary's angular writing. Bernardo read it two times and then handed it to his brother.

> *Yesterday, the second day of August of the year eighteen-thirteen, a young woman of White Owl's tribe came to visit me at the mission. She brought her son, who was a little more than two, a boy she called simply "Niño." I offered to baptize him, as was proper, and I explained that otherwise the soul of that innocent child would be in danger, for if God decides to take him he will not go to heaven but spend eternity in limbo. The girl declined to have him baptized. She said she would wait for the father to return so that he can choose the name. She also refused to listen to my teachings about Christ or come to the mission where she and*

*her son would live a civilized life. She gave me the same reason:*
*when the father of the boy returns, she will make up her mind on*
*that question. I did not insist, because I have learned to wait*
*patiently for the Indians to come here of their own accord, other-*
*wise their conversion to the True Faith is a mere coat of varnish.*
*The name of the woman is Light-in-the-Night. May God bless*
*you and guide your footsteps always, my son.*

> *Embracing you in the name of Christ Our Lord is*
> *Padre Mendoza*

Diego handed the letter back to Bernardo, and both sat in silence as the daylight faded from the window. Bernardo's face, usually so expressive in mute communications, seemed sculpted in granite. He began to play a sad melody on his flute, taking refuge in it to avoid explaining further. Diego did not ask for clarifications, he felt his brother's pounding heart in his own chest. The time had come for them to go separate ways. Bernardo could not continue to live like a boy; his roots were calling him, he wanted to return to California and assume his new responsibilities. He had never felt comfortable away from his home country. He had lived several years counting the days and hours in that city of stone and icy winters because of the loyalty that bound him to Diego, but he could not do it any longer; the hollow in his chest was expanding into a limitless cavern. The absolute love he felt for Light-in-the-Night now had taken on a terrible urgency; he hadn't a shadow of a doubt that the child was his. Diego accepted his brother's unvoiced arguments though a claw was ripping through his gut, and answered with a burst of words that issued from his soul. You will have to go alone, my brother; it will be several months before I graduate from the School of Humanities, and during that time I intend to convince Juliana to marry me. First, however, before I declare myself and ask Don Tomás for her hand, I must wait for her to recover from the disillusion inflicted by Rafael Moncada. Forgive me, brother, I am very selfish; this is no time to bore you once again with my fantasies of love. We need to talk about you.

All these years I have played around like a spoiled child while you have been sick with longing for Light-in-the-Night, even without knowing that she has given you a son. How have you put up with so much? I do not want you to go, but your place is in California, there can be no question about that. I understand now why my father, even you, Bernardo, have always said that we have separate destinies. I was born with wealth and privileges you do not have. It isn't fair, because we are brothers. One day I will be owner of the de la Vega hacienda, and then I will be able to give you the half that belongs to you. In the meantime, I will write my father and ask him to provide you with enough money to make a home with Light-in-the-Night and your son, wherever you want—you do not have to live at the mission. I promise you that as long as I am able, your family will never lack for anything material. I don't know why I am crying like a baby, it must be that I am already missing you. What will I do without you? You have no idea how much I need your strength and your wisdom, Bernardo.

The two young men embraced, first emotionally and then with forced laughter; they prided themselves on not being sentimental. A phase of their youth had ended.

Bernardo could not leave immediately, as he would have liked. He had to wait until January to catch a merchant ship that would take him to America. He had very little money, but the captain allowed him to pay his passage by working on board as a sailor. He left Diego a letter asking him to beware of Zorro, not merely for the risk of being discovered, but also because the character would end by taking him over. "Never forget that you are Diego de la Vega, a flesh-and-blood person, while that Zorro is a creature of your imagination," he wrote in the letter. It was difficult for him to say goodbye to Isabel, whom he had come to love like a younger sister; he was afraid he would never see her again, even though she promised a hundred times that she would come to California the minute her father gave her permission.

"We will see each other again, Bernardo, even if Diego never marries Juliana. The world is round, and if I travel around it one day I will come to your house," Isabel assured him, blowing her nose and wiping away a torrent of tears.

The year 1814 dawned filled with hope for the Spaniards. Napoleon was weakened by his defeats in Europe and the internal situation in France. In January, Le Chevalier ordered his majordomo to pack up the contents of his mansion—not an easy task, since he had furnished it with princely splendor. He suspected that Napoleon had very little time left in power, and in that case his own destiny was in danger; in his position as the emperor's trusted confidant he would have no place in any future government. Not wanting to upset his daughter, he presented the journey as a promotion in his career: at last they were returning to Paris. Agnès threw her arms around his neck, delighted. She was bored with the somber Spanish, the muted bells, the dead streets during curfew, and especially, she was tired of having garbage hurled at her carriage, and being snubbed. She loathed the war, the privation, the frugality of the Catalans, and Spain in general. She threw herself into frantic preparations for the journey. In her visits to Juliana's home, she chattered excitedly over the prospect of the social life and diversions of France. "You must come visit me in summer, that is the most beautiful time in Paris. By then Papa and I will be in a suitable residence. We shall live very close to the Louvre palace." In passing, she also extended their hospitality to Diego; in her opinion, he could not possibly go back to California without having known Paris. Everything important took place in that city: fashion, art, and ideas, she said. Even the American revolutionaries had been formed by France. Wasn't California a colony of Spain? Ah! Then they must win their independence. Perhaps in Paris Diego would get over his finicky ways and his headaches and become a famous military man like that one in South America they called the Liberator: Simón Bolívar, wasn't that his name?

Meanwhile in the library, Le Chevalier Duchamp was sharing his last cognac with Tomás de Romeu, the closest thing to a friend he had had during his stay in that hostile city. Without revealing any strategic information, he gave Tomás an overview of the political situation and suggested that he might want to take advantage of the moment to take his daughters abroad. The girls were at a perfect age to discover Florence and Venice, he said; no one who appreciated culture could afford not to know those cities. Tomás replied that he would think about it. It was not a bad idea . . . perhaps in the summer.

"The emperor has authorized the return of Ferdinand VII to Spain. That can happen at any moment. I believe it would be just as well if you were not here at that time," Le Chevalier hinted.

"Why is that, Excellency?" Tomás de Romeu replied. "You know how much I have celebrated France's influence here, but I also believe that El Deseado, the desired one, as the people call him, will mean an end to the guerrilla warfare that has lasted six years now; that will allow this country to reorganize. Ferdinand VII will be obliged to govern under the liberal Constitution of 1812."

"So I hope, my friend. For the good of Spain and of yourself."

Shortly afterward, Le Chevalier Duchamp went back to France with his daughter Agnès. Their convoy of carriages was intercepted at the foothills of the Pyrenees by a band of fervent guerrillas, among the last remaining. They were well informed; they knew the identity of the elegant traveler, and they knew that he was the éminence grise of La Ciudadela, the person responsible for countless tortures and executions. They were not able to take revenge, as they intended, because Le Chevalier was traveling with a contingent of armed guards, who met the guerrillas with ready muskets. The first salvo left several Spaniards in a pool of blood; more perished by sword. The encounter lasted fewer than ten minutes. The surviving guerrillas scattered, leaving behind several wounded, who were impaled on French blades without mercy. Le Chevalier, who had not moved from his carriage, and who had seemed more bored than frightened, would have had no reason to remember the skirmish had a stray bullet not wounded Agnès. It struck her in the face, destroying one cheek and part of her nose. The horrible scar would change the girl's life. She closed herself in her family summer home in Saint-Maurice for many years. At first she sank into the absolute depression of having lost her beauty, but with time she stopped weeping and began to read something more than the sentimental novels she had shared with Juliana de Romeu. One by one she read all the books in her father's library, and then asked for more. During the solitary afternoons of her youth, cut short by that wild musket ball, she studied philosophy, history, and politics. Later she began to write under a male pseudonym, and today, many years later, her work is known in many parts of the world . . . but that is not our story. We need to return to Spain and to the period that concerns us.

Despite Bernardo's advice, that year Diego de la Vega found himself involved in events that would change him into Zorro forever. The French troops abandoned Spain, some by ship, others by land, moving like a shambling beast harassed by the insults and stones of the people. In March, Ferdinand VII, El Deseado, returned from his golden exile in France. Led by the long-awaited monarch, the royal cortege crossed the border in April, entering the country through Catalonia. Finally the people's long struggle to drive out the invaders had ended. At first the nation's jubilation was uncontainable and unconditional. From the nobility down to the last peasant, and including most of the intellectuals like Tomás de Romeu, the nation celebrated the king's return, happy to overlook the major character flaws that had been in evidence since he was a youth. It was supposed that exile would have matured that less-than-brilliant prince and that he would have returned cured of his jealousy, pettiness, and passion for court intrigue. That was not the case. Ferdinand VII was still a weak man who saw enemies everywhere and surrounded himself with fawning courtiers.

One month later, Napoleon Bonaparte was forced to abdicate. The most powerful monarch in Europe succumbed, defeated by an imposing coalition of political and military forces. Added to rebellion in conquered countries like Spain was the alliance composed of

Prussia, Austria, Great Britain, and Russia. He was deported to the island of Elba, though he was allowed to keep the now ironic title of emperor. The day following his abdication, Napoleon tried, unsuccessfully, to kill himself.

In Spain, within weeks, the general elation over the return of El Deseado turned to violence. Isolated by the Catholic clergy and the most conservative wings of the nobility, army, and public administration, the restored king revoked the Constitution of 1812, along with liberal reforms, within the period of a few months, sending the country back to the feudal era. The Inquisition was reinstituted, as were the privileges of the nobility, clergy, and military, and a heartless persecution was unleashed against dissidents, opponents, liberals, Francophiles, and former collaborators in the government of Joseph Bonaparte. Magistrates, ministers, and deputies were arrested, twelve thousand families had to seek refuge across the border in foreign countries, and the repression expanded to such a degree that no one was safe; the least suspicion or unfounded accusation was reason enough for being arrested and executed without further formalities.

Eulalia de Callís was in her glory. She had long awaited the king's return to regain her former privileged status. She did not like the insolence of the masses, or the disorder; she preferred the absolutism of a monarch, however mediocre. Her watchword was, Everyone in his place, and a place for everyone. Hers was at the top, naturally. Unlike other nobles who had lost their fortunes in those revolutionary years because they had clung to tradition, she had no scruples in adopting bourgeois methods for accumulating wealth. She had a nose for business. She was richer than ever, powerful, with friends in the court of Ferdinand VII, and she was eager to see the systematic elimination of the liberal ideas that had placed a good part of what sustained her in jeopardy. Even so, some of her former generosity was hibernating in the crannies of her corpulent humanity; when she saw the great suffering around her she opened her coffers to help the hungry, without asking their politics. She ended up hiding more than one family in her summer homes, or finding some way to smuggle them into France.

Though he did not need to, since his situation was already exemplary, Rafael Moncada immediately joined the army corps of officers, where his titles and his aunt's connections guaranteed a rapid ascent. It lent him prestige to announce to the four winds that at last he was able to serve Spain in a monarchical, Catholic, and traditional army. His aunt agreed; she was of the opinion that even the most stupid man looked good in a uniform.

Tomás de Romeu came to understand what fine counsel his good friend Le Chevalier Duchamp had given him when he suggested he take his daughters abroad. He summoned his accountants for the purpose of reviewing the state of his holdings and discovered that his income was not sufficient for them to live decently in another country. He also feared that if he were too far away, the government of Fernando VII would confiscate what few properties he had left. After having broadcast his scorn for material rewards for a lifetime, now he must cling to his possessions. The idea of poverty horrified him. He had never worried much about the systematic reduction of the fortune he had inherited from his wife; he had assumed that there would always be enough to support him in the style to which he was accustomed. He had never seriously considered the possibility of losing his social position, and he could not imagine his daughters deprived of the comfort they had always enjoyed. He decided that the best solution would be to go somewhere and wait for the wave of violence and persecution to pass. At his age, he had seen a lot. He knew that sooner or later the political pendulum would swing in the opposite direction; it was all a question of making himself invisible until the situation stabilized. He could not consider going to his family home in Santa Fe, where he was too well known, and hated, but then he remembered some land his wife had owned on the road to Lérida, a place he had never visited. This property, which had produced no income, only problems, might now be his salvation. It lay on hills planted with ancient olive trees and sustained a few very poor and backward families. It had been so long since they had seen a *patron* that they believed they didn't have one. On the estate was a frightful house in near ruin, constructed sometime around the year 1500, a massive cube sealed up like a tomb to protect its inhabitants from the dangers of the Saracens, soldiers, and bandits who had laid waste to the region for centuries. Tomás, however, quickly decided that it was preferable to prison. He could stay there a few months with his daughters. He dismissed most of his servants, closed half the mansion in Barcelona, left the other half in the care of his majordomo, and set out in a large number of coaches, many carrying basic items of furniture.

Diego witnessed the exodus of the family with a sense of doom, but Tomás de Romeu soothed him with the argument that he had never held a position in the Napoleonic administration, and also that very few people knew of his friendship with Le Chevalier. There was nothing to fear. "For once I am happy not to be an important person," he said, smiling as he said good-bye. Juliana and Isabel had no idea that they might be in danger, and left as if they were heading for some strange vacation. They barely understood their father's reasons for taking them so far from civilization, but they were used to obeying and asked no questions. Diego kissed Juliana on both cheeks and whispered into her ear not to despair, their separation would be short-lived. She answered with a puzzled glance. Like so many things Diego hinted at, this one was incomprehensible.

Nothing would have pleased Diego more than to accompany the family to the country, as Tomás de Romeu had asked. The idea of spending some time far from the world and in Juliana's company was very tempting, but he could not leave Barcelona. The members of La Justicia were very active; they had to use every resource in aid of the mass of refugees trying to leave Spain: hide them, find transport, get them into France by way of the Pyrenees, or send them to other countries in Europe. England, which had fought Napoleon so fiercely until he was defeated, now supported King Ferdinand VII and, with few exceptions, offered no protection to the enemies of his government. As Maestro Escalante had reported to Diego, La Justicia had never before been so near to being discovered. The Inquisition had come back stronger than ever, given full powers to defend the faith at any price, and since the dividing line between heretics and opponents of the government was blurred, anyone might fall into their grasp. During the years the Inquisition had been abolished, the members of La Justicia had become careless in matters of security, convinced that in the modern world there was no place for religious fanaticism. They believed that the days of burning people at the stake were gone forever. Now they were paying the consequences of their excessive optimism. Diego was so absorbed in the missions of La Justicia that he stopped attending the School of Humanities, where education, like everything else in the country, was censored. Many of his professors and companions had been arrested for expressing their opinions. In those days, the pompous rector of the Universidad de Cervera proclaimed before the king a phrase that defined academic life in Spain: "The last thing we espouse is the unfortunate mania for thinking."

In early September, a member of La Justicia who had hidden for several weeks in the home of Maestro Manuel Escalante was arrested. The Inquisition, being an arm of the church, preferred not to spill blood. Their most frequent methods of interrogation were to disjoint their victims on the rack or brand them with red-hot iron. As predicted, the miserable prisoner gave up the names of those who had helped him, and shortly afterward, the fencing master was arrested. Before he was dragged into the constables' sinister coach, he had barely enough time to advise his servant, who carried the bad news to Diego. At dawn the following morning, the former pupil was able to confirm that Escalante had not been taken to La Ciudadela, as was normal in the case of political prisoners, but to a barracks in the port, from which they intended to take him to Toledo, the forbidding center of the bureaucracy of the Inquisition. Diego immediately contacted Julius Caesar, the man with whom he had dueled in the tabernacle of the secret society as a part of his initiation.

"This is very grave. They may arrest all of us," said Caesar.

"They will never make Maestro Escalante confess," Diego declared.

"They have infallible methods they have developed over the centuries. Several of our members have been arrested, so they have a great deal of information. The circle is closing around us. We will have to dissolve the society temporarily."

"And Don Manuel Escalante?"

"I hope for the good of all that he can find a way to end his days before he is subjected to torture," sighed Julius Caesar.

"They are holding the maestro in a local barracks. It isn't La Ciudadela, we must try to rescue him," Diego contended.

"Rescue him? Impossible!"

"Difficult, but not impossible. I will need the help of La Justicia. We will do it this very night," Diego replied, and explained his plan.

"It seems madness to me, but it is worth the attempt. We will help you," his companion decided.

"It will be necessary to get the maestro out of the city immediately."

"Of course. We can have a boat with a trustworthy oarsman waiting in the port. I think we can slip through the guards. The boatman will row the maestro to the ship that is sailing at dawn for Naples. There he will be safe."

Diego sighed, thinking once again how badly he needed Bernardo. This was more serious than slipping into Le Chevalier's mansion. It was no joke to attack a barracks, overcome the guards— he had no idea how many there were—free the prisoner, and get him to a boat unharmed before the law sank its claws into them.

Diego rode to Eulalia de Callís's mansion, whose layout he had carefully studied every time he visited. He left his horse in the street and crept unseen through the gardens to the service patio, where chickens and small animals were wandering among blocks for slaughtering hogs, laundry troughs, large vats for boiling sheets, and clotheslines hung with wash. In the rear were the carriage house and stables. Cooks, footmen, and servant girls were everywhere, all busy at their chores. No one even glanced at him. He went into the shed, concealed by the coaches, chose one that suited him, and waited, crossing his fingers that no stable hand would discover him. He knew that at five the bells rang to call the servants to the kitchen; Eulalia de Callís herself had told him that. It was the hour when the matriarch offered a treat to her army of retainers: cups of foaming chocolate and bread to dunk in them. Half an hour later, Diego heard the bells ring, and in a trice the patio was emptied of people. The breeze carried the delicate aroma of chocolate, and he felt his mouth fill with saliva. Ever since the family had left for the country, he had eaten very poorly in the de Romeu house. Diego, aware that he had only ten or fifteen minutes, quickly pried the coat of arms off the door of a carriage and took a pair of jackets from their hangers: footmen's elegant livery of sky-blue velvet with crimson collar and lining, gilded buttons and epaulets. He left behind the lace-collared shirts, white trousers, patent leather shoes with silver buckles, and red brocade sashes that completed the uniforms. As Tomás de Romeu had said, not even Napoleon Bonaparte was outfitted as elegantly as Eulalia's servants. Once Diego was sure that the patio was empty, he left with his bundle, darting among the bushes, and found his horse. Soon he was trotting toward home.

Among the things in storage there he found a battered old carriage too old and fragile to take to the country. Compared with any of those in Doña Eulalia's shed, it was ruinous, but Diego was praying that with the darkness no one would notice what bad shape it was in. He would have to wait until sunset and calculate his time with care; the success of his mission depended on it. After nailing the shield onto the carriage, he went down to the wine cellar, which the majordomo kept tightly locked—a minor hindrance for Diego, who had learned to pick any kind of lock. He opened the door, chose a cask of wine, and rolled it away in plain view of the servants, who asked no questions, believing that Don Tomás had given Diego the key before he left.

For more than four years Diego had safeguarded the treasure of the sleeping potion his grandmother, White Owl, had given him as a farewell gift after making him promise that he would use it only to save lives. And that was exactly what he intended to do with it. Many years before, Padre Mendoza had amputated a leg using that potion, and he himself had stunned a bear. He did not know how powerful the drug might be when diluted in that amount of wine; it might not have the effect he hoped, but he had to try. He poured the contents of the flask into the cask and sloshed it around to mix it. Shortly afterward, two accomplices from La Justicia arrived; they put on the white wigs of footmen and the livery from the house of Callís. Diego himself was dressed like a prince in his best coffee-colored velvet jacket with fur collar and gold and silver passementerie lace; his formal starched tie was held with a pearl stickpin, and butter yellow trousers, foppish shoes with gilded buckles, and top hat completed the ensemble. In this attire he was driven by his comrades to the barracks. It was the dark of night when he knocked at a door badly lighted by lanterns. In the ringing voice of someone accustomed to giving orders, Diego ordered the two guards to call their superior officer. He turned out to be a young second lieutenant with a strong Andalusian accent, who was flabbergasted by Diego's stunning elegance and the coat of arms on the carriage.

"Her Excellency, Doña Eulalia de Callís, is sending a barrel of the best wine from her cellar, so that you and your men may toast her tonight," Diego announced with a superior air. "It is her birthday."

"It seems a little strange," the amazed man managed to stammer out.

"Strange? You must be new to Barcelona!" Diego interrupted. "Her Excellency has always sent wine to the troops on her birthday, and she has even greater reason now that our country has been liberated from the atheist despot!"

Still bewildered, the lieutenant ordered his subalterns to retrieve the cask from the carriage, and even invited Diego to toast with them, but he excused himself, alleging that he had to deliver similar gifts to La Ciudadela.

"Soon Her Excellency will be sending you her favorite stew: pigs' feet and turnips. How many mouths to feed here?" Diego asked.

"Nineteen."

"Fine. Good evening."

"Your name, señor, please—"

"I am Don Rafael Moncada, nephew of Her Excellency Doña Eulalia de Callís," Diego replied, and rapping on the carriage door with his cane, he ordered the false coachman to drive on.

At three in the morning, when the city was asleep and the streets were empty, Diego prepared to carry out the second phase of his plan. He was banking on the fact that at that hour the men in the barracks would have drunk their wine, and if not asleep they would at least be stunned. That was his one advantage. He had changed his clothes and dressed as Zorro. He carried his whip, a pistol, and his sharp sword. To avoid attracting attention with the sound of horse's hooves, he went on foot. Hugging the walls, he made his way through the alleyways to the barracks, where he verified that the same guards, yawning with fatigue, were still standing beneath the lanterns. Apparently they had not had their share of the wine. Julius Caesar and two other members of La Justicia were waiting in the shadows of an entryway, disguised as sailors, as they had agreed. Diego gave them their instructions, which included the categorical order not to intervene and come to his aid, whatever happened. Each man should look out for himself. They wished one another luck in the name of God, and separated.

The "sailors" staged a drunken brawl near the barracks while Diego, hidden in the darkness, awaited his chance. The ruckus attracted the attention of the guards, who briefly abandoned their posts to check out the source. They found the spurious drunks and warned them to move on or they would be arrested, but the offenders continued swinging blindly at each other, as if they hadn't heard. Their staggering and the nonsense they were shouting was so comic that the guards burst out laughing, but when they tried to disperse the supposedly drunk men, they miraculously regained their equilibrium and redirected their blows. Caught by surprise, the soldiers did not have a chance to defend themselves. The "sailors" overcame them in an instant, then took them by the ankles and dragged them unceremoniously down a nearby alley to a dwarf-sized door set back from the street, beneath an arch. Diego's comrades from La Justicia knocked three times; a peephole opened, they gave the password, and a sixtyish woman dressed in black opened the door. They stooped down to go in, to avoid banging their heads against the low door frame, and pulled their inert prisoners into a coal bin. There they left them with their hands bound and hoods pulled over their heads—after taking their clothes. The former sailors were quickly transformed into guards and hurried back to the barracks to take up posts beneath the lanterns. In the few minutes it had taken to replace the guards, Diego had gained entrance to the barracks, sword and pistol in hand.

Inside, the building seemed deserted; the quiet of the graveyard reigned, and there was very little light because the oil in half the lanterns had burned out. Invisible as a ghost—only the gleam of his blade betrayed his presence—Zorro crossed through the entry hall. Cautiously, he pushed open a door and peered into the hall used as an armory; it was here the contents of the barrel had been dealt out, because he found a half dozen men snoring on the floor, including the lieutenant. Diego satisfied himself that none of them was awake, and then checked the cask. They had emptied it to the last drop.

"To your health, señores!" he exclaimed with satisfaction, and on a playful impulse traced the letter Z on the wall with three strokes of his sword. Bernardo's warning that Zorro would ultimately take over came to his mind, but it was too late.

Quickly, he gathered up firearms and swords, piled them into the chests in the entry hall, then continued his exploration of the building, extinguishing lights and candles as he went. Shadows had always been his best allies. He found three more men felled by White Owl's potion and calculated that unless the lieutenant had lied, there were eight left. He hoped to find the prisoners' cells without running into guards, but he heard voices nearby and realized he had to hide. He found himself in a large, nearly empty room. There was nothing to crouch behind, and there was no time to douse the two lanterns on the opposite wall, fifteen paces away. The only things that might be of use were the heavy ceiling beams, but they were too high to jump up to. He sheathed his sword, put his pistol in his waistband, unrolled his whip, and with a flick wrapped the tip around one of the beams, tugged to tighten it, and pulled himself up, as he had done so often in the ship's rigging and in the Gypsies' circus. Once there, he coiled his whip and flattened himself along the beam, at ease, knowing that the light of the torches did not reach him. At that moment two men sauntered in, jabbering; judging by their behavior, they had not drunk their ration of wine.

Zorro decided to stop them before they reached the armory where their companions lay sprawled in a deep sleep. He waited until they were beneath the beam, then swooped down on them like an enormous black bird, cape flapping and whip in hand. Paralyzed, the men were slow to draw their swords, giving him time to buckle their knees with two swift blows of the whip.

"Good evening to you, señores!" he said, making a mocking bow to his victims, now on their knees. "I beg you, please place your swords on the ground . . . oh so carefully."

He snapped his whip as a warning and drew his pistol from his sash. The men did exactly as he said, and he kicked their swords into a corner.

"Perhaps you will assist me, Your Mercies. I assume that you do not wish to die, and for me it would be an annoyance to have to kill you. Tell me, where is the best place to incarcerate you so that you will not cause problems?" he asked sarcastically.

The soldiers gaped at him in a daze; they had no idea what he meant. They were ignorant conscripts, a pair of peasants who in their brief lives had witnessed horrors, survived the killing of war, and nearly starved. They were not up to riddles. Zorro simplified his question, accentuating his words with snaps of his whip. One of them, too frightened to speak, pointed to the door they had come through. He suggested that they say their prayers, because if they were deceiving him they would die. The door opened onto a long bare corridor that they marched down in single file, the captives ahead and Zorro behind. At the end, the passageway split. To the right was a battered door; the one to the left was in better condition and bore a lock that opened from the other side. He motioned to his prisoners to open the one to the right. That revealed a nauseating latrine composed of four holes in an excrement-covered floor, a few pails of water, and a lantern swarming with flies. There was no way out other than a small opening with iron bars.

"Perfect! I regret that the fragrance is not that of gardenias. Perhaps in the future you will swab this down more carefully, caballeros," he commented, and with his pistol indicated that the terrified men should go in.

He bolted the toilet and walked to the other door. The lock on the door to the left was very simple; he was able to open it in seconds with the steel pin he always hid in the seam of a boot to perform his magic tricks. He opened the door with caution and stole down a stairway, reasoning that it led underground, the most likely place for the cells. At the end of the stairway he pressed himself against the wall and glanced around the corner. A single torch lighted a small airless room guarded by one man; he, too, seemed not to have tasted the wine laced with the potion, as he was sitting cross-legged on the ground, laying out a game of solitaire. His gun was within reach of his hand, but he did not have time to pick it up before Zorro leaped toward him and with one kick to the chin tumbled him backward, then with a second kick sent his weapon flying. The stench in the place was so foul that Diego was nearly driven back, but this was no moment for queasiness. He took the torch from the wall and started looking into the cramped, damp, vermin-ridden, pestilent cells where the prisoners were jammed together in darkness; skeletons with the eyes of madmen. There were three or four to a cell so small that they had to take turns standing and sitting. The fetid air pulsed with the panting breath of those miserable wretches. Zorro called for Manuel Escalante, and a voice answered from one of the cells. He raised the torch and saw a man clinging to the bars, so badly beaten that his face was a shapeless purple mass in which no features were distinguishable.

"If you are the executioner, you are welcome," said the prisoner, and Zorro recognized his maestro from his dignified bearing and firm voice.

"I have come to free you, maestro. I am the fox. Zorro."

"Good idea. The keys are near the door. And on your way, it would be wise to tend to the guard; he is beginning to come to," Manuel Escalante calmly replied.

His disciple found the key ring and opened the maestro's barred door. The three prisoners who shared his cell rushed out, pushing and scrambling like animals, maddened by a mixture of terror and gut-wrenching hope. Their rescuer stopped them with his pistol.

"Not so fast, caballeros; first you must help your comrades," he ordered.

The menacing aspect of the large pistol had the virtue of restoring some of the men's lost humanity. While they struggled with keys and locks, Zorro shoved the guard into the empty cell, and Escalante took his gun. Once all the cells were open, the two of them led away those pathetic, ragged specters, uncombed and covered with dried blood, filth, and vomit. They went up the stairs, down the corridor, across the empty room where Diego had jumped from the beam, and got as far as the armory before coming upon a group of guards alerted by the noise from the dungeon. They had come prepared, swords in hand. Zorro fired the single shot of his weapon, hitting one of the guards, who dropped like lead, but Escalante found that his own musket was not loaded, and he had no time to do it. He gripped it by the barrel and erupted like a tornado, swinging blows in every direction. Zorro had drawn his sword, and he too attacked. He managed to hold back the onslaught long enough for Escalante to pick up one of the swords that had been taken from the men Zorro had locked in the latrine. Between the two of them, they created more noise and harm than a battalion. Zorro had plied his foil every day since he was a boy, but he had never had to use it in a serious fight. His one duel to the death had been with pistols, and had been much cleaner. He found that there is nothing honorable in a real combat, where rules count for nothing. The only standard is to win, whatever the cost. The blades did not ring in an elegant choreography, as they did in fencing classes, but were aimed directly at the enemy to run him through. Gentlemanly conduct was forgotten; blows were ferocious and gave no quarter. The sensation he experienced as steel pierced flesh was indescribable. He was suffused with a blend of unholy exaltation, repugnance, and triumph; he lost all notion of reality and was transformed into an animal. The cries of pain and bloodstained clothing of his adversaries made him grateful for the techniques gleaned from his associates in La Justicia, as infallible on the Circle of the Master as in all-out, hand-to-hand combat. Afterward, when he had time to think, he appreciated the months of practice with Bernardo, when he was so worn out after finishing that his legs barely held him. In the process, he had developed very quick reflexes and peripheral vision: he sensed instinctively what was happening behind his back. In a fraction of a second he was able to parry the simultaneous moves of several opponents, judge distances, calculate the velocity and direction of every thrust, defend himself, attack.

Maestro Escalante showed himself to be as effective as his former student despite his age and the terrible beating he had suffered at the hands of his torturers. He did not have the younger man's agility and strength, but his experience and calm more than compensated for those deficiencies. In the heat of the fray, Zorro was sweating and panting, while his maestro was brandishing his sword with the same decisiveness but with much more elegance. Within a few minutes the two of them had disabled, disarmed, or wounded every guard. Only when the field had been won did the rescued prisoners dare come near. None had had the courage to help their rescuers, but now they were more than willing to drag the vanquished guards to the cells that they themselves had occupied only minutes before, insulting and punching them as they pushed them inside. Only after their victims were gone did Zorro recover his senses and look around him. There were pools of blood on the floor, blood spattered on the walls, blood on his sword . . . blood everywhere.

"Holy Mother of God!" he exclaimed, frightened.

"Come along, we cannot stop to think about this now," said Maestro Escalante.

They left the barracks without encountering resistance. The freed prisoners disbanded and scurried through the dark streets of the city. Some were saved by fleeing the country, or hiding for years, but others were captured again and tortured before they were executed, in an attempt to extract details of how they had escaped. Those men were never able to tell who the daring masked man was who had set them free because they didn't know. They heard nothing but his name, Zorro, which explained the Z scored on the wall of the armory.

A total of forty minutes had passed between the moment the supposed drunks distracted the sentinels in front of the barracks and the time Zorro rescued his maestro. The comrades from La Justicia were waiting in the street, still wearing the guards' uniforms, and they conducted the fugitive to the port. When they said good-bye, Diego and Manuel Escalante embraced for the first and last time.

At dawn, once the soldiers had recuperated from the effects of the drug and could reorganize and tend to the wounded, the hapless second lieutenant had to report to his superiors. The one thing in his favor was that even with all that had happened, none of his men had died in the clash. He informed them that from what he had been told, Eulalia de Callís and Rafael Moncada were implicated because the fateful cask of wine that had intoxicated his troops had been a gift from them.

That same afternoon a captain, escorted by four armed guards, presented himself before the suspected culprits, though he was extremely obsequious and nothing but flattery rolled from his tongue. Eulalia and Rafael received him as they would a vassal, demanding that he apologize for disturbing them with his nonsense. The lady sent him to the carriage house to see for himself that their coat of arms had been ripped from one of the carriages, proof that the captain deemed insufficient, though he didn't dare say so. Rafael Moncada, arrayed in the uniform of the king's officers, was so intimidating that the lieutenant did not ask explanations of him. Moncada had no alibi, but with his social position he did not need one. In the blink of an eye the suspects were cleared of suspicion.

"The officer who allowed himself to be deceived in that manner is a dithering imbecile and should receive harsh punishment. I demand to know the meaning of that Z slashed on the wall of the barracks, and the identity of the bandit who dared use my name and that of my nephew for his villainy. Is that clear, officer?" Eulalia spit at the captain.

"Have no doubt, Excellency, that we will do everything possible to clear up this most unfortunate incident," he assured her, retreating toward the door with deep bows.

In October, Rafael Moncada decided that the moment had come to be more autocratic with Juliana, since diplomacy and patience had not given results. Perhaps she suspected that the incident in the street had been his work, but she had no proof, and the persons who could furnish it, the Gypsies, were long gone and would not dare return to Barcelona. In the meantime, he had investigated and found that Tomás de Romeu was insolvent. Times had changed; that family was no longer in any condition to make demands. His own status was exceptional, and the one thing he needed to hold the reins of his destiny in his hands was Juliana. True, he did not have Eulalia de

Callís's approval to court the girl, but he decided that he was past the age to be ordered about by his domineering aunt. However, when he tried to send a letter to Tomás de Romeu to request an appointment, it was returned; Romeu had already left the city with his daughters. No one knew where he had gone, but Moncada had ways to find out. By coincidence, Eulalia had that very day summoned him to set a day for her to introduce him to the daughter of the duke and duchess de Medinacelli.

"I am sorry, aunt. However suitable that union might be, I cannot be a party to it. As you know, I love Juliana de Romeu," Rafael announced with all the firmness he could muster.

"Get that girl out of your head, Rafael," Eulalia warned. "She never was a good match, but now marrying her would be social suicide. Do you think she would be received at court when it is known that her father is a French sympathizer?"

"I am prepared to run that risk. She is the only woman in my entire lifetime who has ever interested me."

"Your life has barely begun. You want her because she has snubbed you, not for any other reason. If you had won her, you would be bored with her by now. You need a wife of our station, Rafael. That girl is barely good enough to be a mistress."

"Do not speak that way of Juliana!" Rafael exclaimed.

"And why not? I say whatever I please, especially when I am right," the matriarch replied in a voice that brooked no disagreement. "With the titles of the Medinacelli and my fortune, you can go far. Ever since the death of my poor son, you have been my only family; that is why I look after you like a mother. But my patience has its limits, Rafael."

"As far as I am aware, your deceased husband, Pedro Fages, may God hold him in his sacred bosom, had no titles, *or* money, when you met him, aunt," her nephew accused.

"The difference is that Pedro was courageous; he had an impeccable military record, and he was willing to eat lizards in the New World if that is what it took to make a fortune. Juliana, on the other hand, is a spoiled little minx, and her father is a nobody. If you choose to ruin your life with her, you cannot count on me for help, is that clear?"

"Very clear, aunt. Good day."

Moncada clicked his heels, bowed, and left the salon. He looked splendid in his officer's uniform, with the tasseled sword at his side and his boots gleaming. Doña Eulalia did not change expression. She knew human nature, and she was confident that towering ambition always wins out over deranged passion. Her nephew's case would be no exception.

Only a few days later, Juliana, Isabel, and Nuria came rushing back to Barcelona in the family coach, with no escort but Jordi and two footmen. The sound of hooves and the noise in the courtyard alerted Diego, who was just getting ready to go out. The three women were covered with dust, and looked drained. They came with the news that Tomás de Romeu had been arrested. A detachment of soldiers had burst into the house, leveling everything in the place, and had taken him off without giving him time to pick up a coat. All the women knew was that he was accused of treason, and that he was being taken to the dreaded Ciudadela.

When Tomás de Romeu was arrested, Isabel had assumed the management of the family because Juliana, who was four years her senior, simply crumpled. With a maturity she had never shown until then, Isabel gave orders to pack up the necessities and close the country house. In less than three hours she and Nuria and her sister had hurried to Barcelona, pushing the horses to the limit. On the way they had time for the realization to sink in that they did not have a single ally. Their father, who, they believed, had never harmed anyone, now had nothing but adversaries. No one was going to compromise himself by lending a hand to a target of government prosecution. The one person whom they might go to was an enemy, not a friend, but Isabel did not hesitate one minute. Juliana would have to prostrate herself at the feet of Rafael Moncada, if it were necessary;

no humiliation could be too great when it was a matter of saving their father, she said. Melodramatic or not, she was right. Juliana herself admitted that, and afterward Diego would have to accept the decision; not even a dozen Zorros could rescue someone from La Ciudadela. No one could escape from that fort. It was one thing to worm his way into an unimportant barracks commanded by an inexperienced second lieutenant; it was something else to confront the king's troops in Barcelona. Nevertheless, the idea that Juliana was going to Moncada to beg horrified Diego. He insisted on going in her place.

"Don't be naive, Diego," Isabel replied firmly. "The one person who can get anything from that man is Juliana. You have nothing to offer him."

Isabel herself wrote a letter announcing that her sister would call, and sent a servant to take it to the house of the persevering suitor, then instructed her sister to bathe and dress in her best clothes. Juliana was insistent that only Nuria accompany her, because Isabel lost her head too easily, and Diego was not one of the family. Besides, he and Moncada hated each other. A few hours later, still with deep circles under her eyes from the fatigue of the trip, Juliana knocked at the door of the man she detested, defying norms of discretion established centuries before. Only a woman with the most questionable reputation would dare visit an unmarried man, even if accompanied by a strict chaperone. Though the winds of autumn were already blowing, beneath her black mantle Juliana wore a gauzy yellow summer dress and short jacket embroidered with bugle beads; her curls were covered with a bonnet the color of her dress, tied with a sash of green silk and trimmed with white ostrich plumes. From a distance she resembled an exotic bird, and when she came near, she was more beautiful than ever. Nuria waited in the vestibule while a servant led Juliana to the salon where the smitten suitor was waiting.

Rafael watched Juliana float in like a naiad in the quiet afternoon air, and he knew that he had been awaiting this moment for four years. The desire to make the girl pay for past humiliations nearly won out, but he sensed that he should not go too far: that fragile dove must be at the limits of her endurance. The last thing he had imagined was that the fragile dove would be as skillful in haggling as a Turk in the market. No one ever knew exactly the course of their negotiations; afterward Juliana explained only the basic points of the agreement they reached. Moncada would arrange for Tomás de Romeu to be freed and she, in exchange, would marry him. Not a gesture, not a word, betrayed Juliana's emotions. A half hour after she went in, she came out of the salon with perfect calm, walking beside Moncada, who was lightly holding her arm. She made a peremptory gesture to Nuria and went straight to the coach, where Jordi was dozing with exhaustion on the coach box. She left without a single glance at the man to whom she had promised her hand.

For more than three weeks, the de Romeu girls awaited the results of Moncada's efforts. The only times they had left the house were to go to church to pray to Santa Eulalia, the saint of the city, to help them. "We need Bernardo badly!" Isabel commented more than once during that time; she was convinced that he would have been able to find out what condition her father was in, even get a message to him. What could not be done from higher up, Bernardo frequently achieved through his connections.

"Yes, it would be good to have him here, but I am happy he's gone. Finally he is with Light-in-the-Night, where he has always wanted to be," Diego assured her.

"Have you had news of him? A letter?"

"No, not yet. It takes a long time."

"Then how do you know?"

Diego shrugged. He could not explain how what the whites in California called the "Indian mail" operated. It worked infallibly between Bernardo and him; since childhood they had been able to communicate without words, and there was no reason why they could not do it now. An ocean might separate them, but they stayed in contact as they always had.

Nuria bought a length of rough dark brown wool and stitched some pilgrim's robes. To reinforce Santa Eulalia's influence in the heavenly court, she also appealed to another saint, Santiago de Compostela. She promised him that if he freed her *patron*, she and the girls would make the pilgrimage to his sanctuary on foot. She had no idea how far that would be, but she assumed that if people went from France, it could not be far.

The situation of the family was at its lowest ebb. The major-domo had left without explanation as soon as his *patron* was arrested. The few servants left in the house went about with long faces, and they replied to any order with insolence because they had no hope of collecting back wages. The only reason they didn't leave was that they had nowhere to go. The money counters and pettifoggers who looked after Don Tomás's affairs refused to see his daughters when they came to ask for money for everyday expenses. Diego had no way to help; he had given almost everything he had to the Gypsies. He was expecting money from his father, but it had not arrived. In the meantime, he resorted to more earthly contacts than those Nuria was pursuing to find out what shape the prisoner was in. La Justicia was no help now. Its members had dispersed, the first time in two centuries that the secret society had suspended its activities; even at the worst moments in their history they had been able to function. Some of its members had fled the country; others were hiding, and the least fortunate among them had fallen into the grasp of the Inquisition, which no longer was burning its prisoners at the stake; now they simply disappeared without a trace.

At the end of October, Rafael Moncada came to speak with Juliana. He looked defeated. In those three weeks, he reported, he had discovered that his power was more limited than he had supposed. At the moment of truth he found that he could do nothing to move the heavy bureaucracy of the state. He had ridden at top speed to Madrid to intercede before the king in person, but His Excellency had shuffled him off on his secretary, one of the most powerful men at court, with the warning not to bother him with any more of his

nonsense. Moncada had made no headway with the secretary, however eloquent his plea, and he did not dare bribe the man; a mistake
would be very costly. He was notified that Tomás de Romeu, along
with a handful of traitors, was to die before a firing squad. The secretary added that if Moncada threw down the gauntlet to fate by
defending a vulture, he might regret it. The threat was clear. Upon
his return to Barcelona, he had barely taken time to bathe before
hurrying to tell the whole story to the girls, who wrung their hands
as they listened, but were strong. To console them, Moncada assured
them that he was not giving up; he would keep trying through every
means to have the sentence commuted.

"In any case, you ladies will not be alone in this world. You can
always count on my esteem and my protection," he added, looking
grieved.

"We shall see," Juliana replied, without a tear.

When Diego learned of the most recent developments, he
decided that if the heavenly Eulalia had not been able to do anything for them, he would have to go to the terrestrial Eulalia.

"That señora is very powerful. She knows the secrets of half the
world. Everyone is afraid of her. Besides, in this city money counts
above everything else. The three of us will go talk with her," said
Diego.

"Eulalia de Callís does not know my father and, from what they
say, she detests my sister," Isabel warned him. But he had to try.

The contrast between that excessively adorned mansion, reminiscent
of the most luxurious homes of the gilded age of Mexico, and
Barcelona sobriety in general and the de Romeu house in particular
was staggering. Diego, Juliana, and Isabel were led through enormous salons with frescoes and Flemish tapestries, oils of noble
ancestors, and paintings of epic battles. There were liveried servants
at every door, and maids dressed in Dutch laces taking care of horrid
Chihuahua dogs, who cast their eyes down when anyone of a higher
social status passed by. I am referring to the maids, of course, not the

dogs. Doña Eulalia received her visitors on the canopied throne in the main salon, decked out as if she were going to a ball, though as always she was in strict mourning. With her layer on layer of fat, her small head and beautiful eyes shining like olives through their long eyelashes, she looked like an enormous sea lion. If the elderly señora hoped to intimidate them, she succeeded. The young people were choking with shame in the cottony air of this mansion. They had never been in a situation like that; they had been born to give, not ask.

Eulalia had seen Juliana only from a distance, and she was curious to examine her more closely. She could not deny that the girl was attractive, but her looks did not justify her nephew's lunacy. She looked back in memory to her own early years and decided that she had been as beautiful as the de Romeu girl. Besides her flaming hair, she had had the body of an Amazon. Beneath the fat that now impaired her ability to walk, she held intact the memory of the woman she had once been: sensual, imaginative, filled with energy. It was not for nothing that Pedro Fages had loved her with inexhaustible passion and had been envied by scores of men. Juliana, in contrast, had the look of a wounded gazelle. Whatever did Rafael see in that pale, delicate girl who surely would have all the fire of a nun in bed? Men are a parcel of fools, she concluded. That other de Romeu girl, what was her name? She was the more interesting of the two. She seemed not at all timid, though her looks left a lot to be desired, especially in comparison with Juliana. The child had the bad luck to have a celebrated beauty for a sister, she thought. Under normal circumstances she would have at least offered sherry and tidbits to her visitors. No one could accuse Eulalia of being stingy with food—her house was famous for its cuisine—but she did not want them to feel comfortable, she needed to keep the upper hand for the bargaining that undoubtedly lay ahead.

Diego started by explaining the girls' father's situation, not omitting the fact that Rafael Moncada had ridden to Madrid for the purpose of interceding for him. Eulalia listened in silence, observing

each of them with her penetrating eyes and drawing her own conclusions. She could guess the deal that Juliana had made with her
nephew; otherwise he would never have risked his reputation to
defend a liberal accused of treason. That stupid move could cost him
the favor of the king. For a moment she was happy that Rafael had
not achieved his objective, but then she saw the tears in the girls'
eyes, and her old heart betrayed her once again. It often happened
that her common sense and her good judgment in business ran afoul
of her sentimentality. Emotion had its price, but she dispensed
money with grace; her spontaneous fits of compassion were the last
remaining vices from her lost youth. A long pause followed Diego
de la Vega's plea. At last the matriarch, moved despite herself, told
them that they had a very exaggerated notion of her influence. It
was not in her power to save Tomás de Romeu. She could do nothing that her nephew had not already done, she said, except bribe his
jailers to give the prisoner special considerations until the moment
of his execution. They must understand that there was no future for
Juliana and Isabel in Spain. They were daughters of a traitor, and
when their father died they would be daughters of a criminal with a
dishonored name. The crown would confiscate their wealth and they
would be put out in the street, unable to live in this or any other
country in Europe. What would become of them? They would have
to earn their living embroidering sheets for brides or as governesses
for other women's children. Of course, Juliana might persist in enticing some gullible man to marry her, including Rafael Moncada himself, but she was confident that at the hour of making such a grave
decision, her nephew, who was not totally devoid of brains, would
weigh in the balance his career and social position. Juliana was not
on the same level as Rafael. Furthermore, there was no greater nuisance than a too-beautiful woman, she said. No man should marry
one; they attracted all kinds of problems. She added that in Spain,
beauties without fortunes were fated for the stage or to being kept
by some benefactor. Everyone knew that. She wanted with all her
heart for Juliana to escape that fate. As the matriarch was building

her case, Juliana was losing the control she had striven to maintain throughout the hideous interview, and a river of tears washed down her cheeks and bosom. Diego decided they had heard enough, and wished that Doña Eulalia were a man, so he could have thrashed her right there. He took Juliana and Isabel by the arm and without so much as a good-bye propelled them toward the door. Before they got there, the voice of Eulalia stopped them.

"As I said, there is nothing I can do for Don Tomás de Romeu, but I can do something for you girls."

She offered to buy the family's properties, from the ruined mansion in Barcelona to the remote abandoned lands in the provinces, at a good price and with immediate payment. That way the girls would have the capital they needed to begin a new life somewhere far away, where no one knew them. She told them that she could send her notary the next day to examine the titles and prepare the necessary documents. She would arrange with the chief military officer in Barcelona to allow them to visit their father one last time, to say good-bye and to have him sign the papers of the sale, a transaction they should complete before the authorities intervened and confiscated everything.

"What you intend, Your Excellency, is to get rid of my sister so she will not marry Rafael Moncada!" Isabel accused, trembling with fury.

To Eulalia the insult was a slap in the face. She was not accustomed to having anyone raise her voice to her; no one had done that since her husband died. For a few seconds she couldn't breathe, but over the years she had learned to control her explosive temper and to appreciate the truth when it was right under her nose. Silently, she counted to thirty before she answered.

"You are in no position to refuse my offer. The deal is simple and straightforward: as soon as you get the money, you leave," she replied.

"Your nephew blackmailed my sister into saying she would marry him, and now you are blackmailing her not to!"

"That's enough, Isabel, please," Juliana murmured, drying her tears. "I have made a decision. I accept your offer, and I appreciate your generosity, Excellency. When may we see our father?"

"Soon, child. I will notify you when I arrange the interview," said Eulalia, well satisfied.

"Tomorrow at eleven, we shall receive your accountant. Good day, señora."

Eulalia kept her part of the bargain. The next morning at eleven o'clock on the dot three lawyers appeared at the residence of Tomás de Romeu; they went through all his papers, turned out the contents of his desk, checked through his slapdash accounting, and made an approximate evaluation of his holdings. They reached the conclusion that not only did he have much less than it appeared, but he was up to his neck in debt. As things were, the income for the girls would not be adequate to maintain them at their current level. The notary, nevertheless, had brought specific instructions from his *patrona*. When she made her offer, Eulalia was not thinking of the value of what she would acquire but, rather, of what the two girls would need to live. That is what she offered. To them it seemed neither too much nor too little. They had no idea even of what a loaf of bread cost, so they were not capable of comprehending the sum that the matriarch was prepared to give them. Diego similarly had no experience with finances and had nothing at that time to help Juliana and Isabel. The sisters accepted the stipulated amount without knowing that it was twice the value of their father's properties. As soon as the lawyers prepared the documents, Eulalia obtained permission for a visit at the prison.

La Ciudadela was a monstrous pentagon of stone, wood, and cement designed in 1715 by a Dutch engineer. It had been the heart of the military might of the Bourbon kings in Catalonia. Thick walls crowned by a bastion at each of its five angles encircled its vast grounds. From its height, it dominated the entire city. To construct the impregnable fortress, the armies of King Philip V had demolished entire barrios, hospitals, convents, twelve hundred houses, and several nearby forests. The massive edifice and its dismal legend hovered over Barcelona like a black cloud. It was the equivalent of the Bastille in France: a symbol of oppression. Inside its walls it had housed many armies of occupation, and thousands and thousands of prisoners had died in its cells. Bodies of the hanged were dangled from its bastions as an example to the citizenry. According to a popular saying, it was easier to escape from hell than from La Ciudadela.

Jordi drove Diego, Juliana, and Isabel to the main gate, where they presented the safe-conduct pass Eulalia de Callís had obtained for them. The coachman had to wait outside, so the three young people went in on foot, accompanied by four soldiers carrying rifles and fixed bayonets. The path ahead was ominous. Outside, it was a cold but splendid day with blue skies and clear air. The sea was a silver mirror, and sunlight painted festive reflections on the white walls of the city. Inside the fortress, however, time had stopped a century before, and the climate was an eternal winter dusk. It was a long walk from the heavy entry gate to the central building, but no one spoke a word. They went into the forbidding prison through a side door of thick oak studded with iron and were led down long passageways in which echoes returned the sound of their footsteps. Air whistled past them, and they smelled that peculiar odor of military installations. Humidity seeped from the ceiling, tracing mossy maps on the walls. They went through several open doors, but each one swung shut behind them. They had the sensation that every time one slammed, they were farther from the world of free men and known reality, venturing into the entrails of a gigantic beast. The two girls were trembling, and Diego could do nothing but wonder whether they would come out of that accursed place alive. They came to a vestibule where they had to stand and wait for a long time, watched by soldiers. Finally they were shown into a small room in which the only furnishings were a rough table and several chairs. The officer who received them glanced at the safe-conduct to confirm the seal and the signature, though it was doubtful that he knew how to read. He handed it back without comment. He was a smooth-shaven man of about forty, with iron gray hair and strangely blue, almost violet, eyes. He spoke to them in Catalan to advise them that they would have fifteen minutes to speak to the prisoner, and that they must not go near him but stand three paces away. Diego explained that Señor de Romeu had to sign some papers and would need time to read them.

"Please, sir." Juliana fell to her knees with a sob that caught in her throat. "This is the last time we will ever see our father. I beg you, let us hold him once more."

The officer stepped back with a blend of disgust and fascination; Diego and Isabel tried to get Juliana to stand up again, but she was nailed to the ground.

"In God's name! Get up, señorita!" the soldier exclaimed in a voice of command, but almost immediately he softened and, taking Juliana's hand, gently pulled her up. "I am not without heart, child. I am a father, too. I have several children and I understand how painful this situation is. Very well, I will give you half an hour, and you may be alone with him and show him your documents."

He ordered a guard to bring the prisoner. During that time Juliana was able to regain control of her emotions and prepare herself for the meeting. Shortly after, Tomás de Romeu was led in by two guards. He was bearded, dirty, and emaciated, but they had at least removed his shackles. He had not been able to shave or wash in weeks, he stank like a beggar, and he had the wild eyes of a crazed man. The meager prison diet had reduced his bon vivant paunch; his features had sharpened, his aquiline nose looked enormous in his greenish face, and his once ruddy cheeks were covered by a scrawny growth of gray beard. It took his daughters a few seconds to recognize him and throw themselves, weeping, into his arms. The officer and the guards left. The pain of that family was so raw, so intimate, that Diego wished he were invisible. He squeezed against the wall and stared at the floor, totally undone.

"Come, come, girls, calm down. Don't cry, please. We have very little time, and there is much to do," said Tomás de Romeu, wiping away his own tears with the back of his hand. "They told me that I have papers to sign."

Diego succinctly explained Eulalia's offer, and handed him the documents of sale, with the plea that he sign them and conserve his daughters' paltry patrimony.

"This confirms what I already know." The prisoner sighed. "I will not leave here alive."

Diego made it clear to him that even if a pardon from the king arrived in time, the family would have to leave the country in any case, and they could do that only with cash in their pockets. Tomás de Romeu took the pen and inkwell Diego had brought and signed the transferal of all his earthly possessions to the name of Eulalia de Callís. Then he calmly asked Diego to look after his daughters, to take them far away where no one would know that their father had been executed like a common criminal.

"In the years I have known you, Diego, I have come to trust in you as I would the son I never had. If my daughters are in your care, I can die in peace. Take them to your home in California. Ask my friend Alejandro de la Vega to care for them as if they were his own," he pleaded.

"We must not despair, father dear. Rafael Moncada assured us that he will use all his influence to win your freedom," Juliana moaned.

"The execution has been scheduled for two days from today, Juliana. Moncada will do nothing to help me, because it was he who denounced me."

"Father! Are you sure?" the girl cried.

"I have no proof, but that is what my captors told me," Tomás explained.

"But Rafael went to the king to ask for your pardon!"

"Do not believe it, daughter. He may have gone to Madrid, but it was for other reasons."

"Then it is my fault!"

"You do not bear the blame for the evil others do, child. You are not responsible for my death. Courage! I do not want to see any more tears."

De Romeu believed that Moncada had not denounced him for political motives or to avenge Juliana's rebuffs, but that it was a cold calculation. At their father's death his daughters would be alone in the world and would have to accept the protection of the first person to offer it. There Moncada would be, waiting for Juliana to fall like a turtledove into his hands; that was why Diego's role was so important at this moment, he added. Diego was about to fall to his knees, say that he adored Juliana and she would never fall into Moncada's power, and ask for her hand in marriage, but he swallowed the words. Juliana had never given him the slightest indication that she returned his love. This was not the moment to mention it. Besides, he felt like a charlatan; he could not offer the girls a modicum of security. His courage, his sword, his love, were of little value now. He realized that without the backing of his father's fortune, he could do nothing for them.

"You may be at peace, Don Tomás. I would give my life for your daughters. I shall watch over them always," he said simply.

Two days later at dawn, when the fog from the sea covered the city with a mantle of intimacy and mystery, eleven political prisoners accused of collaborating with the French were executed in one of the courtyards of La Ciudadela. A half hour earlier a priest had offered them extreme unction so that they might depart this world cleansed of sin, like newborn babes, as he phrased it. Tomás de Romeu, who for fifty years had railed against the clergy and the dogma of the church, received the sacrament with the other prisoners and even took communion. "Just in case, Father, it can't hurt," he commented jokingly. He had been sick with fear from the moment the soldiers had come to his country home, but now he was tranquil. His anguish had disappeared the moment he was able to say good-bye to his daughters. He slept the following two nights with no dreams, and passed the days in good spirits. He had surrendered himself to his approaching death with a placidity he had not possessed in life. He began to be pleased with the idea of ending his days with a shot, rather than gradually, ensnared in the inevitable advance of decrepitude. He thought of his daughters, delivered from their fate, hoping that Diego de la Vega would keep his word. He felt more distant from them than ever. In the weeks of his captivity he had been letting go of memories and emotions and in doing so had acquired new freedom: he had nothing left to lose. When he thought of his daughters, he could not visualize their faces or hear their voices; they were two motherless children playing with dolls in the dark rooms of his home. Two days earlier, when they visited the prison, he was astounded to see the women who had replaced the little girls in high-buttoned shoes, pinafores, and little topknots that he remembered. "Be damned," he said when he saw them, "how time flies." He had told them good-bye with a light heart, surprised by his detachment. Juliana and Isabel would make their lives without him; he could no longer protect them. From that moment on he was able to savor his last hours and observe with curiosity the ritual of his execution.

Before dawn on the day of his death, Tomás de Romeu received Eulalia de Callís's last present: a picnic basket containing a bottle of superlative wine and a plate of the most delicious bonbons in her chocolate collection. He was authorized to wash and shave, watched by a guard, and was given the change of clothing his daughters had sent. He was elegant and undaunted as he walked to the site of the execution; he took his place in front of a bloody post, to which he was tied, and refused a blindfold. The man in charge of the firing squad was the same blue-eyed officer who had greeted Juliana and Isabel in La Ciudadela. It was he who delivered a bullet to de Romeu's temple when he ascertained that though half his body had been shattered by the shots, he was still alive. The last thing the condemned man saw before the coup de grâce exploded in his brain was the golden light of dawn through the fog.

The officer, who was not easily moved, having suffered the war and the brutality of the barracks and prison, had not been able to forget the tear-stained face of the virginal Juliana, kneeling before him. Breaking his own rule of separating duty from his emotions, he went to give her the news in person. He did not want the daughters of the prisoner to learn through other means.

"He did not suffer, señoritas," he lied.

Rafael Moncada learned of Tomás de Romeu's death at the same time he found out about Eulalia's strategy to get Juliana out of Spain. The former was part of his plans, but the latter provoked a paroxysm of anger. He was careful, nonetheless, not to berate his aunt; he had not given up the idea of winning Juliana without losing his inheritance. He regretted that his aunt was in such good health; her family was noted for its longevity, and he had little hope that she would die early, leaving him wealthy and free to determine his destiny. He would somehow have to arrange for the matriarch to accept Juliana willingly; it was the only solution. The worst thing he could do would be to present the marriage as a fait accompli—she would never forgive him—but he had in mind a plan based on the legend that in California, when she was the wife of the governor, Eulalia had transformed a dangerous Indian warrior into a civilized Christian Spanish damsel. He could not suspect that that person was the mother of Diego de la Vega, but he had heard the tale several times from the mouth of Eulalia herself, who was infected with the vice of trying to control others' lives and when she did, boast of it. Moncada was hoping to talk her into taking the de Romeu girls into her court as protégées, seeing that they had lost their father and had no other family. To save them from dishonor and see them again accepted in society would be an interesting challenge for Eulalia, just as that Indian had been in California more than twenty years ago. When the mother-to-the-world opened her heart to Juliana and Isabel, as in the end she did with almost everyone, he would bring up the matter of the marriage again. However, if that intricate plan failed there was always the alternative suggested by Eulalia herself. His aunt's words had made an unforgettable impression: Juliana de

Romeu could be his mistress. Without a father to look out for her, the girl would end up being kept by some protector. No one better than himself for that role. Sterling plan. That would allow him to take a wife with social position, perhaps even La Medinacelli, without giving up Juliana. Anything is possible if done discreetly, he reasoned. With this in mind, he presented himself at the residence of Tomás de Romeu.

The house, which had always seemed run-down, now looked abandoned. In a few months' time, since the political situation had changed in Spain and Tomás de Romeu had sunk into his worries and debts, the residence had taken on the defeated and needy air of its owner. Weeds had invaded the garden, and ferns had dried in their pots; there were chickens and dogs, horse manure, and garbage in the main patio. Inside, dust and shadow ruled; the drapes had not been opened or a fire lighted in the fireplaces for months. The cold breath of autumn seemed trapped in the inhospitable rooms. There was no majordomo to answer the door. Nuria appeared instead, as dried-up and cross-looking as ever, and led him to the library.

The chaperone had tried to take the place of the majordomo and was doing everything possible to keep the near-foundering de Romeu vessel afloat, but she had no authority in dealing with the rest of the domestics. Nor did she have much money to work with; they had put away every last *maravedí* for the future, the only dowry Juliana and Isabel would have. Diego had taken Eulalia de Callís's notes of payment to a banker that she herself had recommended, a man of scrupulous honesty, who gave him the equivalent amount in precious stones and gold doubloons, with the advice to go home and have the girls sew the treasure into their underskirts. That was how Jews had preserved their money during centuries of persecution, he explained. Jewels and gold were the only things that could easily be carried and that had the same value in every country. Juliana and Isabel could not believe that that handful of small colored stones represented everything the family possessed.

While Rafael Moncada was waiting in the library, surrounded

by the leather-bound books that formed the private world of Tomás de Romeu, Nuria went to get Juliana. She was in her room, exhausted from weeping and praying for her father's soul.

"You have no obligation to speak to that heartless man, Juliana," said the chaperone. "If you want, I can tell him to go to hell."

"Hand me the cherry red dress and help me do my hair, Nuria. I do not want him to see me in mourning, or looking crushed," the girl decided.

Shortly afterward she appeared in the library, as dazzling as in her best times. In the flickering light of the candles, Rafael could not see the eyes reddened by tears or the pallor of sorrow. He sprang to his feet with his heart galloping, verifying yet one more time the unbelievable effect that maiden had on his senses. He expected to find her beaten down by sorrow; instead, there she was, as beautiful, haughty, and exciting as ever. When he could speak, he told her how deeply he regretted the horrible tragedy that had befallen her family, and reiterated that he had left no stone unturned in his quest to aid Don Tomás, but it had been for naught. He knew, he added, that his aunt Eulalia had counseled her and her sister to leave Spain, but he did not think that was necessary. He was convinced that soon the iron fist with which Ferdinand VII was strangling his opposition would loosen its hold. The country was in ruin; the people had suffered too many years of violence and now were clamoring for bread, employment, and peace. He suggested that Juliana and Isabel should henceforth use their mother's maiden name, since their father's was irrevocably stained, and that they should stay out of sight for a prudent amount of time, until the murmuring about Tomás de Romeu subsided. Perhaps then they could reappear in society. In the meantime, he would offer them his protection.

"What exactly are you suggesting, señor?" Juliana asked defensively.

Moncada repeated that nothing would make him happier than to have her for his wife, and that his previous offer still stood, but that given the circumstances it would be necessary to maintain appearances for a few months. He would also have to deal with Eulalia de Callís's opposition, but that was not an insurmountable problem. Once his aunt had the opportunity to know Juliana better, she would change her opinion. He supposed that now, after such devastating events, Juliana would have given serious thought to her future. Although he did not deserve her—no man on earth fully deserved her—he would place his life and his fortune at her feet. At his side, she would never want for anything. Even though the wedding would have to be postponed, he could offer her and her sister comfort and security. His was not an empty offer; he begged her to give it due consideration.

"I am not asking for an immediate answer. I fully realize that you are in mourning and that perhaps this is not the moment to speak of love—"

"We shall never speak of love, Señor Moncada, but perhaps we can talk business," Juliana interrupted. "I lost my father because you denounced him."

Rafael Moncada sucked in his breath and felt blood pounding in his temples.

"How can you accuse me of such villainy! Your father dug his own grave, with no help from anyone. I shall forgive that insult only because you are overcome with grief."

"How do you plan to compensate my sister and me for the death of our father?" Juliana insisted, with clearheaded fury.

Her tone was so disdainful that Moncada could not control his temper. It was ridiculous, he decided, to continue to feign an ineffectual chivalry. Apparently Juliana was one of those women who respond better to male domination. He took her by the arms and, violently shaking her, spit out that she was in no position to negotiate, she should be thanking him; perhaps she did not realize that she could end up in the street or in prison with her sister, just like her traitorous father. The military had been alerted, and only his timely intervention had prevented their arrest, but that could happen at any moment; only he could save them from poverty and jail. Juliana tried to pull away, and in the struggle the seam of her sleeve ripped, revealing her shoulder, and the pins flew out of her hair. Her black hair caressed Moncada's hands. Unable to contain himself, he grabbed a fragrant, silken fistful, pulled Juliana's head back, and kissed her hard on the mouth.

Diego had been spying on this scene from the partly opened door, quietly repeating, like a litany, the advice Maestro Escalante had given him in his first fencing lesson: never fight with anger. However, when Moncada threw himself on Juliana and forced a kiss, it was too much for Diego; he burst into the library with his sword in his hand, puffing with indignation.

Moncada released Juliana and pushed her toward the wall as he drew his sword. The two men faced one another, knees bent, swords in their right hands at a ninety-degree angle to their bodies, the other arm lifted high to maintain balance. The moment he adopted that position, Diego's fury evaporated, to be replaced by absolute calm. He took a deep breath, expelled it, and smiled with satisfaction. At last he was in control of his impulsive temperament, something his maestro had emphasized from the beginning. No losing his breath. Tranquility of mind, clear thinking, firm arm. That sensation of cold running down his spine like a wintry wind must precede the euphoria of combat. In that state, the mind ceased to think logically and the body responded reflexively. The finality of the rigorous training of La Justicia was that instinct and skill direct one's movements. The two men crossed swords twice, feeling one another out, then Moncada initiated the attack with a lunge, from which Diego retreated. From the first feints, Diego was able to evaluate the class of opponent he was facing. Moncada was a very good swordsman but Diego was more agile and more experienced; it was not for nothing that he had made fencing his first priority. Instead of quickly executing a riposte, he feigned clumsiness, retreating until his back was to the wall, on the defensive. He parried attacks with apparent effort, as if desperate, though Moncada had not been able to touch him anywhere.

Later, when he had time to evaluate what had happened, Diego realized that, without planning it, he was playing the part of two different persons, determined by the circumstances and the clothing he was wearing. That lowered his enemy's defenses. He knew that Rafael Moncada scorned him; he himself had encouraged that by affecting the mannerisms of a dandy when he was around. His motives were the same they had been with Le Chevalier and his daughter Agnès: a mode of defense. In their pistol duel Moncada had seen Diego's courage, but conveniently had tried to forget it. Later they met on several occasions, and each time Diego reinforced the negative impression his rival had of him, in that way lulling the unscrupulous Moncada into a false security. And now he had decided to employ cleverness rather than heroics. On his father's hacienda, Diego had seen foxes dance to attract lambs, and when the innocents' curiosity brought them closer, they were devoured. Adopting the tactic of playing the buffoon, he threw Moncada off, confusing him. Until that moment Diego had not been conscious of his dual personality: one part Diego de la Vega, elegant, affected, hypochondriac, and the other part El Zorro, audacious, daring, playful. He supposed that his true character lay somewhere in between, but he didn't know who he was: neither of the two nor the sum of both. He wondered, for example, how Juliana and Isabel saw him, and concluded that he did not have the least idea. Perhaps he had overplayed the theatrics, and had given them the impression he was a poseur. But there was no time to ponder those questions now. Events had become very convoluted and required immediate action. He would assume that he was two persons and turn that to his advantage.

Diego raced around among the tables and chairs of the library, pretending to escape from Moncada's attacks and at the same time provoking him with sarcastic comments, as blows rained and steel sparked. He succeeded in enraging him. Moncada lost the cool head he made so much of. He was breathing heavily, and the perspiration running down his forehead was blinding him. Diego judged that now he had his rival on the run. Like a bull in the ring, he first had to tire him.

"Take care, Excellency, you might hurt someone with that sword!" Diego cried.

By then Juliana had somewhat recovered, and she shouted for them to put down their weapons, for the love of God and respect for the memory of her father. Diego made another half-hearted thrust or two, then put down his weapon and raised his hands above his head, signaling for a truce. It was a risk, but he was sure Moncada would not kill an unarmed man in front of Juliana. He was wrong; his adversary was upon him with a shout of triumph and the momentum of his full weight. Diego dodged the blade, which grazed one hip, and in two leaps was at the window, taking cover behind the heavy floor-length velvet drapes. Moncada's sword pierced the cloth, loosing a cloud of dust, but it caught in the fabric, forcing the entangled swordsman to struggle to withdraw it. Those few instants gave Diego the advantage, and he threw the curtain over Moncada's head and leapt up on the mahogany table. He plucked a leather-bound book from a shelf and hurled it, striking his adversary in the chest; he stumbled and nearly fell, but quickly straightened and charged again. Diego avoided two thrusts and shot off several more books, then jumped to the floor and crawled beneath the table.

"Truce, truce! I do not want to die like a chicken," he whined in a tone of frank burlesque, huddled beneath the table with another book held like a shield to defend against the maddened Moncada's blind attacks.

Beside a library chair was the ivory-handled cane Tomás de Romeu had used during his attacks of gout. Diego used it to hook Moncada's ankle. He pulled sharply, and Moncada sat down on the floor, but he was in good shape and he jumped up and renewed his attacks. By then Isabel and Nuria had come in answer to Juliana's screams. Isabel needed only one look to take in the situation; believing that Diego was soon for the cemetery, she picked up his sword, which had gone flying into the far corner of the room, and without hesitation confronted Moncada. It was her first opportunity to put into practice the skills she had acquired in four years of fencing in front of a mirror.

"En garde," she called out, euphoric.

Instinctively, Rafael Moncada's blade clashed against Isabel's; he was certain that his first move would disarm her, but he encountered a determined resistance. Then, despite his brutalizing rage, he reacted, realizing the madness of dueling with a girl, particularly the sister of the woman he hoped to conquer. He dropped his weapon, which fell noiselessly to the carpet.

"Do you plan to murder me in cold blood, my girl?" he asked sarcastically.

"Pick up your sword, coward!"

His only answer was to cross his arms over his chest, smiling scornfully.

"Isabel! What are you doing?" Juliana interceded.

Her sister ignored her. She placed the tip of her sword beneath Rafael Moncada's chin, but then did not know what to do. The absurdity of the scene was revealed in all its magnitude.

"Slitting the gentleman's craw, as he doubtlessly deserves, will cause some legal problems, Isabel. You can't go around killing people. But we must do something with him," Diego interjected, taking his handkerchief from his sleeve and flicking it in the air before wiping his brow with an affected gesture.

That distraction gave Moncada opportunity to grab Isabel's arm and twist it, forcing her to drop the sword. He pushed the girl with such force that she sailed across the carpet and banged her head on the table. She dropped to the floor, slightly stunned, as Moncada whirled to confront Diego with her weapon in his hand. Diego immediately retreated and dodged several thrusts from his enemy, looking for a way to disarm him and engage in hand-to-hand combat. Isabel's head had cleared; she picked Moncada's sword up off the floor and with a cry of warning tossed it to Diego, who caught it in the air. With a weapon he felt secure, and he recovered the bantering tone that had sent his adversary into such a frenzy a few moments before. With a swift lunge he drew blood on Moncada's left arm, barely a scratch but in exactly the same spot he himself had been wounded during their duel. Moncada grunted with surprise and pain.

"Now we are even," Diego said, as he executed an attack that flicked Moncada's sword from his hand.

His enemy was at his mercy. With his right hand he clasped the wounded arm just at the tear in his jacket, now stained with a thread of blood. He was beside himself, with rage more than fear. Diego touched the tip of his sword to Moncada's chest, as if to run him through, but instead smiled amiably.

"For the second time, I have the pleasure of sparing your life, Señor Moncada. I hope this will not become a habit," he said, lowering his sword.

There was no need for discussion. Both Diego and the de Romeu girls knew that Moncada's threat was real, and that the king's minions could appear at the door at any moment. It was time to travel. They had prepared for that eventuality ever since Eulalia bought the family properties and Tomás de Romeu was executed, but they had thought they would walk out the front door, rather than flee like criminals. They gave themselves half an hour to get away, leaving with what they had on plus the gold and precious stones that, following the banker's suggestion, they had sewn into pouches tied around their waists beneath their clothing. Nuria surprised them with a plan to lock Moncada in the hidden chamber in the library. She took a book from its place, pulled a lever, and the wall of shelves slowly turned upon itself, revealing the entrance to a room whose existence Juliana and Isabel had never known about.

"Your father had a few secrets, but none that I didn't know," Nuria told them.

The secret room was tiny and windowless, with no exit other than the door disguised by the shelving. When they lighted a lantern, they found cases of cognac and the favorite cigars of the master of the house, shelves with more books, and some disturbing paintings on the walls. On closer view they could see a group of six ink drawings representing the cruelest episodes of the war, quarterings, rapes, even cannibalism, which Tomás de Romeu had not wanted his daughters ever to see.

"How horrible!" Juliana exclaimed.

"These are by the maestro Goya! They are very valuable, we can sell them," said Isabel.

"They do not belong to us. Everything in this house belongs to Doña Eulalia de Callís now," her sister reminded her.

The books, in several languages, were on the blacklists of either the church or the government, all banned. Diego picked up a volume at random, and it turned out to be an illustrated history of the Inquisition, with extremely realistic drawings of their methods of torture. He slammed it shut before Isabel, who was peering over his shoulder, could see. There was also a shelf devoted to erotica, but they had no time to examine it. The tightly sealed chamber was the perfect place to leave Rafael Moncada locked up.

"Have you lost your minds? I will die here of starvation or suffocate from lack of air!" the culprit protested when he realized what they intended to do.

"His Excellency is right, Nuria. A gentleman as distinguished as he cannot survive on liquor and tobacco alone. Please bring him a ham from the kitchen, so he will not go hungry, and a towel for his arm," said Diego, pushing his rival into the chamber.

"How will I get out?" the captive whimpered, terrified.

"There must be a hidden mechanism in the chamber for opening the door from inside. You will have more than enough time to discover it, most esteemed señor." Diego smiled. "With persistence and luck you will be free in less time than the crow of the cock."

"We will leave you a lamp, Moncada, but I advise you not to light it; it will consume all the air. Let's see, Diego, how long do you calculate that a person can live in here?" Isabel queried, enthusiastic about their plan.

"Several days. Enough to meditate at length on the wise proverb that the ends do not justify the means," Diego replied.

After Nuria cleaned and bandaged the cut on Moncada's arm, they left him with a store of water, bread, and ham. It was unfortunate that he would not bleed to death from that insignificant scratch, was Isabel's judgment. They recommended that he not waste air and strength shouting, as no one would hear him; the few servants who remained were never in this part of the house. Moncada's last words before the shelves turned to close the entrance to the chamber, sealing him in silence and darkness, were that they would learn who Rafael Moncada was. They would regret that they had not killed him; he would get out of that hole and find Juliana sooner or later, even if he had to pursue her to hell itself.

"Oh, you won't have to go that far, we are on our way to California," Diego said in farewell.

I regret to tell you that I can write no more, because I have run out of the goose-quill pens I always use. I have ordered more, and soon I will be able to finish this story. I do not use quills from ordinary birds; they stain the paper and rob elegance from the page. I have heard that some inventors dream of creating a mechanical device for writing, but I am sure that such a whimsical invention would never prosper. There are certain activities that cannot be mechanized, for they require fondness, and writing is one of them.

I fear that this is turning out to be a long narration, even though I have left a lot out. In the life of Zorro, as in all lives, there are brilliant moments and some that are dark; between the extremes are many neutral zones. You will have noted, for example, that in 1813 very little worthy of mention happened to our protagonist. He dedicated himself to his own activities with neither suffering nor glory, and made no progress in his conquest of Juliana. Rafael Moncada had to return from his chocolate odyssey for this story to acquire a little life. As I said before, villains, however unsympathetic in real life, are indispensable in a novel, which is what these pages are. At first I determined to write a chronicle or a biography, but I am unable to tell the legend of Zorro without straying into the widely scorned genre of the novel. Between each of his adventures are long uninteresting periods that I have omitted to prevent boring my potential readers to death. For the same reason, I have embellished the memorable episodes. I have made generous use of adjectives, and I have added suspense to Zorro's feats, though I have not exaggerated too greatly his praiseworthy virtues. This is called literary license and, as I understand it, it is more legitimate than all-out lies.

In any case, dear readers, there is in my inkwell more story to tell. In the next pages, to be no fewer than one hundred, I believe, I shall relate Zorro's voyage with the de Romeu girls and Nuria across half the world, as well as the dangers they met in fulfilling their destinies. I can skip ahead, without fear of ruining the end, to disclose that they survive unharmed, and at least some of them reach Alta California, where, unfortunately, not everything is milk and honey. In fact, it is actually there that the true epic of Zorro begins, the saga that has carried his fame throughout the world. So I beg of you, a little more patience, please.

# PART FOUR

Spain, late 1814–early 1815

now have new goose-quill pens to continue the story of Zorro's youth. It took a month for the pens to arrive from Mexico, and in the meantime I have lost the rhythm of my narration. We shall see whether I can recapture it. We left Diego de la Vega fleeing from Rafael Moncada with the de Romeu girls and Nuria, through a Spain convulsed by political repression, poverty, and violence. Our characters were in a difficult situation, but the gallant Zorro did not lose sleep over external dangers, only the jolts to his surrendered heart. Love is a condition that tends to cloud men's reason, but it is not fatal. Usually all the patient needs is to have his love returned, and he will snap out of it and begin to sniff the air in search of new prey. As chronicler of this story, I can see that I will have some problem with the classic ending of "and so they were married and lived happily ever after." In fact, I had best get back to the tale before I fall into a depression.

When the hidden door in the library shelves swung shut, Rafael Moncada was alone in the secret chamber. His cries for help were not heard because the thick walls, books, drapes, and carpets all deadened sound.

"We will leave as soon as it is dark," Diego de la Vega told Juliana, Isabel, and Nuria. "And we will take the bare essentials for the journey, as we agreed."

"Are you sure there is a mechanism to open the door of that chamber from inside?" asked Juliana.

"No."

"This joke has gone too far, Diego. We cannot bear the burden of Rafael Moncada's death, especially not a slow and horrible death in a sealed tomb."

"But look at the harm he's done to *us*!" exclaimed Isabel.

"We are not going to repay him in the same coin, because we are better persons than he is," was her sister's categorical reply.

Diego laughed. "Don't worry, Juliana, your suitor will not die of asphyxiation on this occasion."

"Why not?" Isabel interrupted, disappointed.

Diego jabbed her with his elbow and explained that before they left, he would give Jordi a letter to be delivered to Eulalia de Callís in person, within two days. With it she would find the keys to the house and instructions for finding and opening the chamber. In case Rafael had not been able to open the door, his aunt would rescue him. The mansion, like everything else the de Romeu family had owned, now belonged to that grand lady, who would rescue her favorite nephew before he drank all the cognac. To be sure that Jordi would carry out his mission, he would give him a few *maravedís,* and the hope that Doña Eulalia would give him more when the note was delivered.

At nightfall they left in one of the family coaches, driven by Diego. Juliana, Isabel, and Nuria took one last look at the large house where they had spent their lives. They were leaving behind memories of a safe and happy time; behind them, too, was everything that gave witness to Tomás de Romeu's passage through this world. His daughters had not been able to give him a decent burial; his remains came to rest in a common grave beside other prisoners executed in La Ciudadela. The only thing they kept was a miniature painted by a Catalan artist in which he appeared young, slim, and unrecognizable. The three women sensed that at that moment they were crossing a definitive threshold to begin a new stage in their lives. They were silent, fearful, and sad. Nuria began to recite the rosary in a quiet voice, and the sweet cadence of her prayers accompanied them for a good distance, until they fell asleep. Up on the coachman's box, Diego urged the horses along and thought about Bernardo, as he did almost every day. He missed him so much that he often found himself talking aloud, as he had always done with his brother. His silent presence, his unflagging protection, guarding his back and defending him from all danger, was just what he needed now. Diego asked himself whether he alone was capable of helping the de Romeu girls or whether, to the contrary, he was leading them into disaster. His plan to travel across Spain might be another of his hare-brained ideas, and he was tormented by doubt. And like his passengers, he was frightened. It was not the delicious fear that preceded the danger of combat, that cold fist in the pit of his stomach, that glacial tingle at the nape of his neck; this was the oppressive weight of a responsibility he was not prepared for. If something should happen to those women, especially Juliana . . . No, he would not even consider such a possibility. He cried out, calling Bernardo and his grandmother, White Owl, to come to his aid, but his voice was lost in the night, swallowed up in the sound of the wind and the horses' hooves. He knew that Rafael Moncada would look for them in Madrid and other important cities, that he would have the border with France watched and every boat that left Barcelona or any other Mediterranean port searched, but he hoped that it would not occur to him to pursue them to the other coast. He planned to outsmart Moncada by leaving for America from the Atlantic port of La Coruña, as no one in his right mind would travel *away* from Barcelona to take a ship. It would be very risky for a captain to shelter fugitives from justice, as Juliana pointed out, but he could think of no other solution. They would resolve the problem of getting across the ocean when they came to that; first they had to deal with the obstacles they might meet on dry land. Diego decided to go as far as they could in the next hours and then get rid of the coach. Someone might have seen them leave Barcelona.

After midnight the horses were showing signs of fatigue, and Diego thought that they were far enough away from the city that they could rest. By the light of the moon, he left the road and headed the vehicle into a wood, where he unhitched the horses and let them graze. The night was cold and clear. All four slept inside the coach, bundled in blankets, until Diego waked them a couple of hours later, when it was still dark, to share a meal of bread and sausage. Nuria then gave them the clothing they would wear for the rest of the journey; the pilgrims' habits that she had made in case Santiago de Compostela saved Tomás de Romeu's life: tunics that fell to mid-calf, wide-brimmed hats, long pilgrim's staffs with a curved end to hold a gourd for collecting water. The girls left on their layers of petticoats to combat the cold, and they all wound themselves in scarves and donned heavy wool leggings and gloves. Nuria had also brought a couple of bottles of a potent liquor that was extremely effective for forgetting one's troubles. The chaperone had never imagined that those rough robes would be used by the remnants of the family to escape, much less that she would end up keeping her vow to the saint when he had not fulfilled his part of the bargain. To her it seemed a deceit unworthy of a man as serious as the apostle James, but she supposed that he had some hidden design that would be revealed at the opportune moment. At first Diego's idea had seemed wise, but after looking at the map Nuria realized what it meant to cross the widest part of Spain on foot. It was not a journey, it was an epic. Ahead of them lay at least two months of walking through every kind of weather, eating what they could beg, and sleeping beneath the stars. In addition, it was already November, it was raining constantly, and soon they would wake to find the ground covered with ice. None of them was accustomed to walking long distances, and certainly not in a laborer's sandals. Nuria allowed herself to curse Santiago under her breath, and, in passing, to tell Diego what she thought about his preposterous pilgrimage.

Once they had put on their pilgrim's robes and eaten, Diego decided it was time to abandon the coach. They all took their own belongings, wrapped them in a blanket, and slung the bundle over their shoulders; the rest they loaded onto the horses. Isabel was carrying her father's pistol hidden among her petticoats. Diego carried

his Zorro disguise in his bundle, unable to part with it, and beneath
his pilgrim's robe he had hidden two double-edged Basque daggers a
hand's span long. His whip hung at his waist, as always. Though he
had never before been separated from the sword his father had given
him in California, he had to leave it behind because it was impossible to disguise. Pilgrims did not carry weapons. There were
scoundrels of every ilk along the roads, but usually no one troubled
travelers who were going to Compostela, since they took a vow of
poverty for the duration of the pilgrimage. No one could imagine
that that modest quartet had a small fortune in precious stones sewn
into their clothing. They were no different in appearance from the
usual penitents on their way to prostrate themselves before the
famous Santiago, to whom they attributed the miracle of having
saved Spain from the Muslim invaders. For centuries, the Arabs had
been victorious in battles, thanks to the invincible arm of Muham-
mad, their guide, until a shepherd made the timely discovery of the
bones of Saint James abandoned in a field in Galicia. How they got
there from the Holy Land was part of the miracle. Those relics had
the power to unify the small Christian kingdoms of the region, and
were so effective in directing the brave Spanish forces that they
drove out the Moors and recovered their land for Christianity. Santiago de Compostela became the most important site for pilgrims in
all of Europe. At least, that was Nuria's story, though hers was
slightly more embellished. The chaperone believed that the head of
the apostle remained intact and every Good Friday shed real tears.
The supposed remains lay in a silver coffin beneath the altar of the
cathedral, but in his desire to protect them from the raids of the
pirate Sir Francis Drake, a bishop had hidden them so well that it
was a long time before they were found again. For that reason—the
war and the lack of faith—the numbers of pilgrims had been greatly
reduced; previously they had come by the hundreds of thousands.
Those who traveled to the sanctuary from France followed the
northern route, crossing through Basque country, and that was the
one our friends chose. For centuries, churches, convents, hospitals,

even the poorest peasants, offered a roof and a meal to the penitents. That hospitable tradition worked in favor of the small group led by Diego; it allowed them to travel without having to carry foodstuffs. Although pilgrims were rare in that season—it was easier to travel in the spring and summer—they did not expect to attract special attention; religious fervor had increased since the French had been driven out, and the many Spaniards who had promised to visit the saint if they won the war were fulfilling their vows.

It was growing light when they took to the road. That first day they walked more than five leagues, until Juliana and Nuria gave up because their feet were bleeding and they were faint from hunger. About four in the afternoon they stopped at a hut whose owner turned out to be a tragic woman who had lost her husband in the war. As she informed them, the French had not killed him; he had been murdered by Spaniards, who had accused him of hiding food instead of giving it to the guerrilla fighters. She knew who the murderers were—she had seen their faces clearly, country people like herself who were using the bad times as an excuse to wreak havoc. They were not guerrillas, they were brutes, and they had raped her poor daughter, who had been mad from birth and never harmed anyone, and taken all her animals. Only a nanny goat that had been off wandering in the hills was spared, she said. One of the men's nose had been eaten away by syphilis, and the other had a long scar on his face. She remembered them very well, and not a day went by that she didn't curse them and cry out to heaven for revenge, she added. She had no one but her daughter, whom she tied to a chair to keep her from clawing herself. Her home was a stinking, windowless stone and mud cube that mother and daughter shared with a pack of dogs. This woman had very little to give, and she was weary of having beggars stop in, but she did not want to leave them without shelter. Because Saint Joseph and the Virgin Mary could not find a place in the inn, the child Jesus was born in a manger, she said. She believed that refusing a pilgrim was repaid with many centuries of suffering in purgatory. The travelers sat down on the earthen floor, surrounded by flea-bitten dogs, to recover from their exhaustion, while their host cooked a few potatoes on the coals and dug a couple of onions from her wretched garden.

"This is all I have. My daughter and I have eaten nothing else for months, but maybe tomorrow I will be able to milk the nanny goat," she said.

"May God repay you, señora," Diego murmured.

The only light in the hut entered through the door opening, which she closed at night with a stiff horse hide, and the glow from the small brazier in which she had roasted the potatoes. While they ate the frugal meal, the peasant observed them from the corner of her rheumy eyes. She drew the obvious conclusions as she took in their soft white hands, their noble features and slim bodies, and remembered that they were traveling with two horses. She did not want to know the details; the less she knew, she reasoned, the fewer problems she would have. These were no days to be asking questions. When her guests had eaten, she gave them half-tanned, smelly sheepskins and led them to a shed where she stored firewood and ears of corn. There they bedded down. Nuria found the shed considerably more welcoming than the hut, with its dog odors and the yowls of the pitiful girl. They chose spaces and skins and got ready for a long night. They were making themselves as comfortable as possible when the peasant woman reappeared carrying a small pot of fat, which she gave them with the recommendation that they rub it on their raw feet. She stood staring at the battered group with a mixture of distrust and curiosity.

"Pilgrims indeed. Anyone can see that you are genteel folk. I do not want to know what you are running from, but here is some free advice. There are wicked men on these roads. You cannot trust anyone. Best if the girls are not seen. Cover their faces, at least," she added before she left.

Diego did not know how to relieve the women's discomfort, particularly that of the one most important to him, Juliana. Tomás de Romeu had entrusted his daughters to him, and what would he think if he could see them now? Accustomed to feather mattresses and embroidered sheets, they were resting their bones on a pile of corn and scratching fleas with both hands. Juliana had been admirable: she had not complained once during that arduous day, and even ate the raw onion without comment. In fairness, he had to admit Nuria had not put a bad face on things, either. And as for Isabel, well, she seemed enchanted with the adventure. Diego's fondness for the women had grown as he saw them so vulnerable and brave. He felt an infinite tenderness for their aching bodies and a tremendous desire to erase their fatigue, to shelter them from the cold, to save them from danger. He was less worried about Isabel, who was frisky as a filly, and Nuria, who was coping by nipping at her restorative liquor. But Juliana . . . The laborer's sandals had worn blisters on her feet despite her wool stockings, and the scratchy habit had scoured her skin. And what was Juliana thinking? I cannot say, but I imagine that in the dying light of evening, she found Diego handsome. He hadn't shaved for a day or two, and the dark shadow of his beard lent a rough, virile air to his looks. He was not the clumsy, skinny boy who had come to their home four years before, all smile and ears. He was a man. In a few months' time he would celebrate twenty intensely lived years; he had grown tall, and had poise. No, Diego was not bad-looking, and besides, he loved her with the moony loyalty of a pup. Juliana would have had to be made of stone not to soften toward him. The healing lard gave Diego an excuse to rub his beloved's feet, and in the process forget his gloomy thoughts. Soon his optimistic nature prevailed, and he offered to extend the massage to Juliana's calves. "Don't be depraved, Diego," Isabel scolded, breaking the spell.

The sisters fell asleep while Diego went back to mulling over his various worries. He concluded that the only good part of this journey would be Juliana; everything else would be struggle and exhaustion. Rafael Moncada and other suitors had been eliminated; finally he had an open field to win the beauty: weeks and weeks in close company. There she was, an arm's length away, exhausted, dirty, in pain, fragile. He could reach out and touch her cheek, rosy with sleep, but he did not dare. They would sleep side by side every night, like chaste spouses, and share every moment of the day. He was the only protector Juliana had in this world, a situation that favored him enormously. He would never take advantage of that, of course—he was a caballero—but he could not help but notice that only a single day had worked a change in her. Juliana was seeing him in a different light. She had fallen asleep curled up in a corner of the shed, shivering beneath the sheepskins, but as she got warm and wriggled to find a comfortable spot on the corn, her head emerged. Bluish moonlight filtered through the chinks of the boards and fell on her perfect face, abandoned in sleep. Diego wished that the pilgrimage would never end. He moved so close to her that he could sense the warmth of her breath and the fragrance of her dark curls. The good countrywoman was right; they must hide her beauty and not attract bad luck. If a gang assaulted them, he alone could do little to defend her now that he did not have his sword. There were a hundred reasons to worry, but there was no sin in giving free rein to his fantasy, and he drifted off imagining Juliana exposed to terrible dangers and saved again and again by the invincible Zorro. "If she does not fall in love with me now, it is because I am a dolt," he muttered.

At the cock's crow Juliana and Isabel were shaken awake by Nuria, who had brought them a cup of warm goat's milk. She and Diego had not rested as peacefully as the girls. Nuria had prayed for hours, terrified of what lay ahead, and Diego had only half slept, aware of Juliana's closeness and keeping one eye open and a hand on his dagger to defend her, until the timid light of a winter morn put an end to that eternal night. The travelers prepared to begin another day's journey, but Juliana and Nuria's legs would scarcely obey them; after a few steps they had to lean on something to keep from falling down. Isabel, on the other hand, demonstrated her physical prowess with a few knee bends, congratulating herself on the endless hours she had spent practicing her fencing in front of the mirror. Diego's advice to Juliana and Nuria was that if they would start walking, their muscles would warm up and the cramping would pass, but that didn't happen; the pain only got worse. Finally those two had to ride on the horses while Diego and Isabel carried the bundles. It was an entire week before they could make the six leagues a day that had been their goal when they started. Before they left that day, they thanked the peasant woman for her hospitality and left her a few *maravedís*, which she stared at with amazement, as if she had never seen a coin before.

In stretches, the route was a mule path, in others, nothing but a narrow trail snaking through primeval growth. An unexpected transformation took place among the four false pilgrims. The peace and silence forced them to listen, to look at the trees and the mountains through new eyes, to open their hearts to the unique experience of following in the footsteps of the thousands of pilgrims who had walked that road for nine centuries. Some monks taught them to set their course by the stars, as travelers had done in the Middle Ages, and by the rocks and boundary stones marked with the symbol of Santiago, a scallop shell, left by previous journeyers. In some places they found words carved on pieces of wood or written on stained parchments, messages of hope and wishes for good fortune. That journey to the tomb of the apostle James became an exploration of their own souls. They walked in silence, in pain and weary, but content. They lost their initial fear and soon forgot that they were fleeing. They heard wolves at night and expected to meet highwaymen at every turn of the path, but they went forward with confidence, as if some superior force were protecting them. Nuria began to make her peace with Santiago, whom she had cursed when Tomás de Romeu was executed. They traversed forests, broad plains, lonely mountains, in a changing and always beautiful landscape. They never lacked for a welcome. Sometimes they slept in the houses of peasants, other times in monasteries and convents. And perfect strangers always shared their bread or soup with them. One night they slept in a church and awoke to the sound of Gregorian chants, enveloped in a dense blue mist as if in another world. On another occasion they took their rest in the ruins of a small chapel in which thousands of white doves were nesting, sent, according to Nuria, by the Holy Spirit. Following the counsel of the peasant woman who had sheltered them the first night, the girls covered their faces as they approached populated places. In villages and inns, the sisters lagged behind while Nuria and Diego went ahead to ask for charity, passing themselves off as mother and son. They always referred to Juliana and Isabel as if they were boys, and explained that they hid their faces because they had been disfigured by illness; in that way they did not pique the interest of the bandits, rustics, and army deserters who were wandering the land that no one had cultivated since before the war.

Diego calculated how far it was to the port at La Coruña by distance and time, and to that mathematical computation added his progress with Juliana; it had not been spectacular, but at least she seemed to feel safe in his company and was treating him more seriously and with less teasing: she took his arm for support, allowed him to caress her feet, let him prepare her bed, and even let him spoon soup into her mouth when she was too tired to eat. At night Diego waited for the other three to fall asleep before he crawled as close to her as decency allowed. He dreamed of her and waked in glory with his arm across her waist. She pretended not to notice their growing intimacy and during the day acted as if he had never touched her, but in the black of night she invited that contact, and he wondered if it was because she was cold, afraid, or moved by the same passions he felt. He awaited those moments with delirious eagerness, and made the most of what befell him. Isabel was aware of that nocturnal nestling and was not bashful about making jokes on the subject. How the girl found out was a puzzle, since she was always the first to fall asleep and the last to wake up.

One day they had walked for hours; they were tired and had also been slowed when one of the horses came up lame. The sun had set, and they still had a way to go before reaching the convent where they planned to spend the night. They saw smoke rising from a nearby house and decided they would try to stop there. Diego went ahead, confident that he would be welcomed because it looked like a rather prosperous place, at least compared with others. Before he knocked at the door, he reminded the girls to cover their faces, even though it was dark. Eyeholes allowed them to see through the cloths, which were so caked with dust that they looked like lepers. A man opened the door; against the light he looked as threatening as an orangutan. They could not see his features, but to judge by his attitude and rude tone he was displeased to see them. At first he refused them shelter, using the excuse that he had no obligation to help pilgrims, that was what monks and nuns—and all their wealth—were for. He added that if they were traveling with two horses, they must not have taken the vow of poverty and could pay for their own expenses. Diego did not give up, and finally the farmer agreed to give them something to eat and permission to sleep beneath his roof in exchange for a few coins, which he demanded in advance. He led them to a stable that housed a cow and two Percheron plow horses. He pointed to a pile of straw where they could bed down, and told them he would be back with something to eat. In half an hour, after they had begun to lose hope of eating that day, the man reappeared with a companion. The stable was dark as a cave, but they were carrying a lantern. They set down a loaf of black bread and half a dozen eggs, and some por-ringers containing a hearty country soup. As they bent down, Diego and the women could see in the lantern light that one of them had a scar running from his eye down his cheek, and that the other had no nose. They were short and strong, with bull necks and arms like logs, and their expressions were so formidable that Diego fingered his daggers and Isabel her pistol. The sinister men did not leave all the while his guests spooned their soup and broke bread, watching Juliana and Isabel with malicious curiosity as they tried to eat with-out removing the face cloths.

"What is the matter with those two?" one of them asked, point-ing to the girls.

"Yellow fever," said Nuria, who had heard Diego mention that plague, but had no idea what it was.

"It's a tropical disease that eats the skin like acid, and rots the tongue and eyes. They should have died, but the Apostle saved them. That's why we're on this pilgrimage to the sanctuary, to give thanks," Diego babbled, inventing on the fly.

"Is it catching?" the host wanted to know.

"Not from a distance, only by contact," Diego explained. "You don't want to touch them."

The men did not seem convinced; they could see the girls' healthy hands and young bodies, which the robes could not conceal. Furthermore, they suspected that these pilgrims carried more money than was usual, and they also had their eyes on the horses. One of them was a little lame, but they were good stock; they would be worth something. Finally they left, taking their lantern and leaving the group in darkness.

"We have to get out of here. Those men are terrifying," Isabel whispered.

"We can't travel at night, and we have to rest. I'll keep watch," Diego replied softly.

"Then," Isabel proposed, "I will sleep a couple of hours and take your place."

They still had the raw eggs; Nuria poked a hole in four for them to suck, and kept the other two. "Too bad I have no idea how to milk a cow, otherwise we would have some milk," the chaperone sighed. Then she asked Diego to leave for a few minutes so the girls could rinse off with a wet cloth. Finally they lay down on the straw, covered by their blankets, and slept. Three or four hours went by while Diego sat and nodded with his daggers within reach, dead tired, struggling to keep his eyes open. Suddenly he was jarred awake by the barking of a dog and realized that he had dozed off. For how long? He had no idea, but any sleep was a forbidden pleasure under the circumstances. To clear his head he went outside, taking deep breaths of the icy night air. Smoke was still coming from the chimney of the house, and light was shining through the one window in the solid stone wall; that indicated that he had not been asleep as long as he had feared. While he was outside, he walked a little farther away from the shed to relieve himself.

As he returned a few moments later, he saw two silhouettes moving toward the stable with suspicious stealth: their villainous hosts. They had something in their hands, perhaps guns or clubs. He knew that his daggers, which were good only in close combat, would be next to useless against those armed brutes. He uncoiled the whip at his waist and immediately felt the cold at the nape of his neck that always preceded a fight. He knew that Isabel had her pistol, but he had left her sleeping, and to add to that, the girl had never fired a weapon. He was counting on the advantage of surprise, but he could do nothing in that dark. Praying not to be betrayed by the dogs, he trailed the men to the stable. For a few minutes there was absolute quiet, as the evildoers checked to be sure that their unwary guests were sound asleep. Once satisfied, they lighted an oil lamp in order to locate the figures on the straw. They were not aware that one of the group was missing, confusing Diego's mantle for another body. One of the horses neighed and woke Isabel. For a few seconds she could not remember where she was; then she saw the men, understood the situation, and groped for the pistol that she had left beneath her cover. She did not reach it; a couple of roars from the attackers, who were waving thick sticks, froze her in mid-action. By then, Juliana and Nuria were awake.

"What do you want!" Juliana cried.

"You, you whores, and your money!" one of them replied, moving toward her with upraised bludgeon.

And then in the wavering light of the flame, the blackguards saw the faces of their victims. With a bellow of absolute terror they jumped back, turned to run, and found themselves facing Diego, whose arm was already upraised. Before they could recover, the whip fell with a crack upon the closer of the two, who cried out in pain and dropped his truncheon. The other man lunged toward Diego, who danced aside and kicked him in the stomach, doubling him over. But now the first had recovered from his shock and had leaped toward Diego with an agility unexpected in someone so heavy, falling on top of him like a sack of rocks. The whip was now useless, and the peasant had grabbed Diego by the wrist that held the dagger. He had him pressed flat to the ground, and was reaching for his throat with one hand as with the other he tried to shake loose the dagger. He had a strong grip and exceptional strength. His foul breath and saliva nauseated Diego, who fought back desperately, not understanding how this beast had managed in an instant to do what the expert, Julius Caesar, had not been able to do in La Justicia's test of courage. Out of the corner of his eye, Diego could see that the other man had struggled to his feet and was reaching for his stick. There was more light now because the oil lamp had rolled across the ground, setting fire to some straw. At that instant a shot sounded, and the man who was on his feet dropped to the ground, roaring like a lion. That distracted the man atop Diego sufficiently that he was able to push him off with a ferocious knee to the groin.

The recoil of the gun knocked Isabel off her feet. She had fired almost blindly, holding the weapon with both hands, and by pure luck she had shattered the attacker's knee. She could not believe it. The idea that the twitch of a finger on a trigger would have such consequences had never entered her head. A sharp command from Diego, who had her victim's partner immobilized with his whip, roused her from her trance. "Quick! The stable is on fire! We have to get the animals out!" The three women sprang up to save the cow and horses, which were bawling and whinnying with terror, while Diego pulled the two miscreants outside, one of whom was still bellowing with pain, his leg crushed to a pulp and slick with blood.

The stable went up like an enormous bonfire, lighting the night. Now Diego could see Juliana and Isabel's faces, which had so frightened their assailants. He, too, yelled with disgust. Their skin, yellow and lumpy like the hide of a crocodile, oozed pus in some places and in others had dried like a scab, tugging at their features. Their eyes were distorted, their lips had disappeared—the two girls were monsters.

"What happened to you!" Diego cried.

"Yellow fever." Isabel laughed.

It had been Nuria's idea. The chaperone had suspected that their depraved hosts would return to attack during the night. She knew how evil those men were from the story of the peasant woman whose husband had been killed. She remembered an old egg-based beauty formula that her ancestors had learned from Muslim women, and she had used the two yolks left from supper to paint the girls' faces. As the eggs dried, they turned into cracked, stinking masks. "It comes off with water, and it does a lot for the skin," Nuria explained, very proud of herself.

They bandaged the wound of the bully with the scar—who yelled and screamed as if he were being tortured—to at least prevent his bleeding to death, though there was little hope the leg could be saved. They left his friend tied to a chair, but did not gag him, so he could call for help. The house was close to the road, and more than one passerby would hear. "An eye for an eye, a tooth for a tooth; you pay for everything in this life, or in hell," were Nuria's words of farewell. They took a ham they found hanging from a beam in the house and the two ponderous, heavy-hoofed Percherons. They were not good as mounts, but they would always be better than walking; besides, they did not want to leave the pair of bandits a means of pursuit.

The incident with the noseless man and his cohort with the scar served to make the travelers more cautious. From that night on they had decided they would take shelter only in sites designated by pilgrims from time immemorial. After several weeks of following the northern route, all four had lost weight, and were tougher in body and soul. The sun burned their skin, the dry air and freezing weather cracked it. Nuria's face became a map of fine wrinkles, and she was suddenly old. That once stiff-backed, apparently ageless woman now dragged her feet and was slightly bowed, but far from making her ugly, it made her beautiful. Her grim expression relaxed, and a teasing, grandmotherly humor blossomed forth, something they had never seen before. She also looked better in the simple pilgrim's robe than she had in the severe black uniform and cap she had worn all her life. Juliana's curves disappeared; she looked smaller and younger with her enormous eyes and red, chapped cheeks. She rubbed her skin with lanolin as protection against the sun, but she could not escape the onslaught of the weather. Isabel, strong and slender, was the one who suffered least from the journey. Her features sharpened, and she acquired a long, sure stride that made her appear boyish. She had never been happier; she was born for freedom. "Curses! Why wasn't I born a man?" she exclaimed on one occasion. Nuria gave her a good hard pinch, with the warning that such blasphemy could lead straight to the cauldrons of hell, but then she laughed heartily. Had Isabel been born a male, she commented, she would have been another Napoleon, given the battles she was always waging. They all adapted to the routine imposed by the march.

Diego assumed command quite naturally; he made the decisions and dealt with strangers. He tried to arrange a bit of privacy for the women's most personal needs, but they were never out of his sight for more than a few minutes. They drank and washed in rivers; that was why they had brought the gourds, the symbol of a pilgrim. With each league they traveled, they forgot past comforts: a piece of bread tasted like heaven, a sip of wine was a blessing. In one monastery they were given cups of thick, sweet chocolate, which they savored slowly, sitting on a bench outdoors. For several days that was all they could think of; they could not remember a more perfect pleasure than that warm, fragrant drink beneath the stars. During the day they survived on the leftovers of food they were given where they lodged: bread, hard cheese, an onion, a slice of sausage. Diego still had some money for emergencies, but they tried not to use it; pilgrims lived off charity. If they had no choice but to pay for something, he bargained a long time, until what they needed was nearly a gift; that way he avoided raising suspicions.

They had traveled across half of the Basque country when winter set in without mercy. Sudden wintry blasts penetrated to the bone, and chill winds kept them shivering beneath wet mantles. The horses, also affected by the cold, seemed phlegmatic. Nights were longer, the fog denser, their progress slower, the frost heavier, and the journey more difficult, but the landscape was breathtakingly beautiful. Green and more green, hills of green velvet, enormous forests in every shade of green, rivers and waterfalls of crystalline, emerald green water. For great distances the track would disappear in the moist soil, only to reappear later as a faint path through the trees or the worn cobblestones of an ancient Roman road. Nuria convinced Diego that it was a good economy to spend money on liquor, the only thing that warmed them at night and made them forget the torment of the day. At times they had to stay two days in a shelter because of the pitiless rain and their need to collect their strength. They used that time to listen to the stories of the other travelers and the monks and nuns who had seen so many sinners on the road to Santiago de Compostela.

One day in the middle of December, when they were still a long way from the next village and had not seen a house for a long time, they saw flickering lights through the trees, something like dying bonfires. They approached with caution, thinking it might be army deserters, who were more dangerous than any felon. They tended to travel in groups, ragged and filthy, armed to the teeth and ready for anything. In the best of cases, those war-hardened men hired themselves out as mercenaries and fought for money, to settle arguments, to deliver revenge, and other livelihoods that might be dishonorable but were preferable to life as bandits. Their only skill lay in their swords, and manual labor was unthinkable to them. In Spain only peasants worked; on their backs they bore the enormous weight of the empire, from the king down to the last bailiff, pettifogger, priest, gambler, page, streetwalker, or beggar.

Diego left the women behind some shrubs, armed with the pistol, which Isabel had learned to use, to scout out those distant signs of life. At closer range he confirmed that, as he had thought, the light came from several campfires. He did not, nevertheless, think it was a gang of outlaws or deserters because he could hear the soft melody of a guitar. His heart leaped when he recognized the music, a passionate lament that Amalia used to dance to with whirling skirts and clicking castanets while the rest of her tribe kept time with tambourines and clapping hands. It was not unique; all Gypsies played similar songs. He slowly rode on until he reached the clearing with several tents and fires. "God help me," he muttered, ready to shout with relief. These were his friends. No doubt about it, it was the family of Amalia and Pelayo. Several men of the tribe came out to see who the intruder was, and in the gray light of evening they saw an unkempt and unshaven monk coming toward them on a large plow horse. They did not recognize him until he jumped to the ground and ran toward them—the last person they expected to see again was Diego de la Vega, and certainly never in a pilgrim's robe.

"What the devil has happened to you!" exclaimed Pelayo, clapping him affectionately on the back, and Diego couldn't tell whether it was tears running down his cheeks, or drops of rain.

The Gypsy went back with him to look for Nuria and the girls. Once they were all seated around the fire, the travelers, in broad strokes, painted a picture of their recent adventures, from the execution of Tomás de Romeu to their encounter with Rafael Moncada, omitting the minor twists and turns that added nothing to the story.

"As you see, we are fugitives, not pilgrims. We have to reach La Coruña to see if we can sail from there to America, but we have traveled only halfway, and winter is nipping at our heels. May we travel on with you?" Diego asked.

The Romany had never received a plea of that sort from a *gadje*. By tradition they distrusted non-Gypsies, especially when they showed good intentions—most likely they had a viper up their sleeves—but they had had good opportunity to know Diego well, and they respected him. They walked off to consult among themselves, then left the group of *gadjes* drying their clothes beside the fire while they went to one of the tents. Stitched together from several cloths, ragged and filled with holes, it nevertheless offered shelter against the caprices of the weather. The meeting of the tribe, called a *kris,* lasted a good part of the night. It was presided over by Rodolfo, the *rom baro,* the eldest of the men, the patriarch, counselor, and judge, who knew the laws of the Roma. Those laws had never been written or codified; they were passed down from generation to generation in the memory of the *rom baros* who interpreted them according to variables in time and place. Only males could participate in decisions, but enforcement of that custom had relaxed during those years of misery, and the women did not stay silent, especially Amalia, who reminded everyone that Diego had saved their necks in Barcelona, and then had given them a pouch of money that allowed them to escape and survive. Even so, some members of the clan voted against Diego's request; they believed that the prohibition against fraternizing with *gadjes* was stronger than any amount of gratitude. Only commercial dealings were allowed; anything else led to *marimé,* or bad luck. Finally they reached an agreement, and Rodolfo cut off discussion with an irrevocable verdict. They had seen much betrayal and evil in their lives, he said, and they should appreciate it when someone held out a hand to them. Let no one say that the Roma were ungrateful. Pelayo left to take the decision to Diego. He found him asleep on the ground beside the women, all of them huddled together because by then the fire had gone out. They looked like a pitiful litter of pups. "The assembly voted for you to travel with us to the sea," he notified them. "That is, as long as you live like the Roma and do not violate any of our taboos."

The Gypsies were poorer than ever. They did not have their wagons, which French soldiers had destroyed the year before in the circus fire, and their tents had been replaced by others even more ragged, but they did have horses, as well as forges, pots and pans, and a couple of carts for transporting their belongings. They had suffered want, but they were all together; not even a child had been lost. The only one who was looking bad was Rodolfo, who once had been able to lift a horse and now had symptoms of tuberculosis. Amalia had not changed at all, but Petrina had turned into a fine adolescent who no longer fit into the olive jar, however much she squeezed. She was promised to a distant cousin from another tribe, a youth she had never seen. The wedding would take place in summer, after the family of the groom paid the *darro,* money to compensate Petrina's tribe for her loss.

Juliana, Isabel, and Nuria were installed in the women's tent. At first the chaperone was terrified, convinced that the Gypsies would kidnap the de Romeu girls and sell them as concubines to the Moors in North Africa. A whole week went by before she let the girls out of her sight, and still another before she spoke to Amalia, who was in charge of teaching them their Roma customs to prevent offensive breaches of etiquette. She provided them with full skirts, peasant blouses, and fringed scarves from the women's shared wardrobe, all old and dirty but brightly colored, and in any case more comfortable, and warmer, than the pilgrim's robes. The Roma believed that women are impure from waist to feet, so that showing any leg was a grave offense; they had to wash downstream, far from the men, especially during days they were menstruating. They were held to be inferior to males, to whom they owed submission. Isabel's furious arguments had no effect; she, too, had to walk behind the men, never ahead, and she could not touch them because that would contaminate them. Amalia explained that they were always surrounded with spirits, whom they had to pacify with spells. Death was an unnatural event that infuriated the victim, which was why you had to watch out for the vengeance of the dead. Rodolfo clearly seemed to be ill, and that had the clan very worried, especially because recently he had heard the cry of several owls, an augury of death. They had sent messages to distant family members so they could come and say good-bye with the proper respect before he left for the world of spirits. If Rodolfo left unwillingly or with anger, he could be turned into a *muló*. Just in case, they had made preparations for the funeral ceremony, even though Rodolfo himself mocked them, convinced that he would live several years more. Amalia taught the women to read the future in palms, in tea leaves, and in crystal balls, but none of the three *gadjes* showed any signs of being a true *drabardi*. On the other hand, they did learn the use of certain medicinal herbs, and how to cook Roma style. Nuria added to the tribe's basic recipes—vegetable stew, rabbit, venison, wild boar, porcupine—her knowledge of Catalan food, with excellent results. The Roma decried cruelty to animals, killing only what they needed. There were a few dogs in the camp but no cats, for they too were thought to be impure.

In the meantime, Diego had to resign himself to observing Juliana from afar; it was considered very bad manners to approach women without a specific purpose. He used the time he had formerly spent contemplating his beloved in learning to ride like a true Roma. He had grown up galloping across the vast plains of Alta California, and he was proud of his horsemanship until he saw the acrobatics of Pelayo and other men of the clan. By comparison, he was almost inept. No one in the world knew more about horses than these people. They not only raised them, they trained them and healed them if they were ill; like Bernardo, they were also able to communicate with them. No Gypsy used a whip; hitting an animal was considered the worst form of cowardice. Within a few weeks, Diego could slide down and touch the ground at a full gallop, bounce, flip in the air, and come down sitting backward in the saddle; he could jump from one horse to another, and also gallop standing on two, with nothing to hold on to but the reins. He tried to perform these feats in front of the women, or, more accurately, where Juliana could see him; that compensated a little for the frustration of being separated from her. Pelayo outfitted him in his clothes: knee-length trousers, high boots, full-sleeved blouse, leather jerkin, kerchief tied around his head—which unfortunately revealed his ears—and a musket slung over his shoulder. He looked so manly in his new sideburns, with his tanned skin and caramel eyes, that even Juliana admired him from afar.

The tribe would camp for several days near a town, where the men offered their services in breaking horses or doing metalwork while the women read fortunes and sold their potions and curative herbs. Once that market was exhausted, they went on to the next town. At night they ate around the fire and then always told stories or had music and dance. When he wasn't busy, Pelayo fired up the forge and worked on shaping a sword that he had promised to Diego, a very special weapon, better than any Toledo saber, he said; it was made from an alloy of metals, the secret of which was fifteen hundred years old and came from India.

"In olden times the weapons of heroes were tempered by plunging the blade, red hot from the forge, into the body of a prisoner of war," said Pelayo.

"I will be content if we temper mine in the river," Diego replied. "It is the most precious gift I have ever received. I will call it Justine, because it will always serve just causes."

Diego and his friends lived and traveled with the Roma until February. They had two brief encounters with the military, who lost no opportunity to exert authority and harass the Gypsies, but they did not pick up that there were non-Gypsies among the tribe. Diego deduced that no one was looking for them as far away as Barcelona, and decided that his idea of fleeing in the direction of the Atlantic had not been as absurd as it had at first seemed. They spent the worst part of the winter protected from the weather and the dangers of the road in the sheltering arms of the tribe, which took them in as they had never done before for *gadjes*. Diego did not have to defend the girls from the men because the thought of betrothal to any woman other than a Gypsy never entered their heads. They did not seem impressed with Juliana's beauty, but they took notice when Isabel practiced fencing and strove to learn to ride like the men. During those weeks, our friends traveled across the remaining part of the Basque country and Galicia, and eventually found themselves at the gates of La Coruña. For sentimental reasons, Nuria asked to be allowed to go into Compostela to see the cathedral and kneel before the sanctuary. She had with time again become friends with the apostle, once she understood his twisted sense of humor. The entire tribe accompanied her. The city, with its narrow alleyways and passages, ancient houses, artisans' shops, inns, taverns, plazas, and churches, spread out in concentric circles from the sepulcher, one of the spiritual hubs of Christianity. It was a bright day with a cloudless sky, invigoratingly cool. The cathedral, with its arches and slender spires, rose before them in all its millenary splendor, dazzling and proud.

The Roma broke the calm hawking their trinkets, their various means of prognostication, and their potions to cure illness and revive the dead. In the meantime, Diego and his friends, like every traveler who reached Compostela, fell to their knees before the central portico of the basilica and placed their hands on the stone foundation. They had completed their pilgrimage; it was the end of a long road. They gave thanks to the apostle for having protected them, and asked him not to abandon them yet but help them cross the ocean safely. Before they had even finished, Diego noticed a man on his knees only a short distance away, praying with extravagant fervor. He knelt in profile, barely lighted by the many-colored reflections of the stained-glass windows, but even though it had been five years, Diego recognized him immediately. It was Galileo Tempesta. He waited until the sailor stopped beating his breast and crossing himself, and then went over to him. Tempesta turned, startled to see himself approached by a Gypsy with long sideburns and mustaches.

"It is I, Señor Tempesta, Diego de la Vega—"

"*Porca miseria!*" exclaimed the cook and, muscles bulging, lifted his old friend off the floor in an effusive embrace.

"Sssshhh! More respect, you are in a cathedral," a monk scolded them.

They went outside, ecstatic, clapping each other on the back, not believing they had been lucky enough to run into each other, although that happenstance was easily explained. Galileo Tempesta was still working as cook on the *Madre de Dios,* and the ship was anchored in La Coruña harbor, loading on weapons to take to Mexico. Tempesta had used his time on shore to visit the saint and ask him to cure him of an unspeakable illness. In whispers he confessed that he had contracted a shameful illness in the Caribbean, a divine punishment for his sins, especially for having hacked his poor wife with a hatchet years before, an unforgivable outburst, it is true . . . though she deserved it. Only a miracle could cure him, he added.

"I don't know whether the saint devotes himself to those kinds of miracles, Señor Tempesta, but it occurs to me that perhaps Amalia could help you."

"Who is Amalia?"

"She is a *drabardi.* She was born with the gift of seeing others' destinies, and of healing sickness. Her remedies are very effective."

"God bless Santiago, who put her in my path. You see how miracles happen, young de la Vega?"

"And speaking of Santiago, whatever happened to Captain Santiago de León?" Diego inquired.

"He is still captain of the *Madre de Dios,* and more eccentric than ever, but he will be very happy to have news of you."

"Perhaps not, because I am a fugitive—"

"Even more reason," the cook interrupted. "What are friends for if not to offer a hand when a person is down on his luck."

Diego led Tempesta to a corner of the plaza where several Gypsy women were selling fortunes and introduced him to Amalia, who listened to his confession and agreed to treat his malady for a steep price. Two days later, Galileo Tempesta arranged a meeting between Diego and Santiago de León in a tavern in La Coruña. As soon as the captain was convinced that this Gypsy was the lad who had been a passenger on his ship in 1810, he was eager to hear his story. Diego gave him a summary of his years in Barcelona and told him about Juliana and Isabel de Romeu.

"There is an order for the arrest of those poor girls. If they are captured, they will end up in prison or deported to the colonies."

"What offense could those young women have committed?"

"None. They are victims of a heartless villain. Before he died, the girl's father, Don Tomás de Romeu, asked me to take them to California and place them in the custody of my father, Don Alejandro de la Vega. Can you help us get to America, Captain?"

"I work for the government of Spain, young de la Vega. I cannot transport fugitives."

"I know that you have done it before, Captain—"

"What, señor, are you insinuating?"

As answer, Diego opened his shirt and showed him the medallion of La Justicia that he always wore around his neck. Santiago de León studied the talisman for a few seconds and then for the first time Diego saw him smile. His avian features changed completely, and his tone grew soft as he recognized a brother. Although the secret society was temporarily inactive, both were forever bound by their oath to protect the persecuted. De León explained that his ship was scheduled to leave within a few days. Winter was not the best season for crossing the Atlantic, but summer was worse, when the hurricanes raged. He had urgent orders to transport his cargo of weapons to combat insurrection in Mexico: thirty cannons, a thousand muskets, and lead and gunpowder for a million rounds of ammunition. De León regretted that his profession, and economic necessity, forced him to that task, because he considered the struggle for independence to be legitimate. Spain, determined to recover its colonies, had sent ten thousand men to America. The royalist forces had retaken Venezuela and Chile in a crushing campaign of blood and atrocities. The Mexican insurrection had similarly been snuffed out. "If it were not for my loyal crew, who have been with me for many years and need this employ, I would leave the sea and devote myself exclusively to my maps," the captain confided. They agreed that Diego and the women would steal aboard at night and stay hidden until the ship was on the high seas. No one other than the captain and Galileo Tempesta would know the identity of the passengers. Diego thanked him with all his heart, but the captain replied that he was merely fulfilling an obligation. Any member of La Justicia would do the same.

The week went by in preparations for the journey. The girls had to rip open their petticoats and take out the gold doubloons because they wanted to leave something to the Roma, who had treated them so well, and they also needed to buy clothing and other indispensables for the crossing. The handful of precious stones was again sewn into their petticoats. As the banker had told them, there was no better way to carry money in times of difficulty. The girls chose simple, practical clothes suitable for the life that awaited them, all black, because at last they could wear mourning for their father. There was not much to choose from in the modest port shops, but they bought a few articles of clothing and accessories on an English ship anchored there. For her part, Nuria had taken a liking to the Gypsies' gaily colored garments during her time with them, but she, too, wanted to wear black for at least a year, in memory of her deceased master.

Diego and his friends said their good-byes to the Roma tribe with heavy hearts, but without sentimentality, which would not have been welcomed among those people hardened by the habit of suffering. Pelayo gave Diego the sword he had forged for him, a perfect weapon, strong, flexible, and light, so well balanced that he could throw it up, watch it somersault in the air, and catch it by the hilt with no effort at all. At the last moment Amalia tried to give the pearl tiara back to Juliana, but she refused to take it, saying that she wanted Amalia to have it as a remembrance. "I don't need that to remember you and your friends," the Gypsy said with a nearly contemptuous gesture, but she kept it.

The four friends set sail one night in early March, a few hours after the port guards had come aboard to inspect the cargo and authorize the captain to weigh anchor. Galileo Tempesta and Santiago de

León showed their charges to their assigned cabins. The ship had been refitted two years before and was in better shape than it had been on Diego's first voyage; now on the poop deck there was space for four passengers in individual cabins on either side of the officers' mess room. Each minute cabin had a wooden bed strung from the overhead by lines, a table, chair, and trunk, and a small armoire for clothing. Those compartments were not commodious, but they offered privacy, the greatest luxury on a ship. The three women closed themselves in their cabins during the first twenty-four hours at sea without taking a bite, green with seasickness, sure that they would not survive the horror of rocking on the waves for weeks. As soon as they left the coast of Spain behind, the captain authorized the passengers to come out, but he ordered the girls to maintain a discreet distance from the sailors, to prevent any problems. He did not give any explanations to the crew, and they did not dare ask for them, but behind the captain's back they muttered that it was not a good idea to bring women aboard.

On the second morning the de Romeu girls and Nuria, their nausea passed, came to life to the muted sounds of the bare feet of the sailors changing watch, and the aroma of coffee. By then they were used to the bells ringing every half hour. They washed with salt water and wiped away the salt with a cloth dampened in fresh water, then dressed and staggered out of their cabins. In the officers' salon they found a rectangular table with eight chairs, where Galileo Tempesta had set out breakfast. Coffee sweetened with molasses and fortified with a dash of rum restored soul to body. Oats with the spicy scent of cinnamon and clove was served with an exotic American honey, courtesy of the captain. Through the half-open door they could see Santiago de León and his two young officers at the worktable, checking the lists of watches and the manifest of the provisions, wood, and water that would have to be distributed prudently until the next port of supply. On the wall were a compass indicating the ship's heading and a mercury barometer. On the table, in a beautiful mahogany box, was the chronometer, which Santiago de León cared for as if it were a religious relic. He greeted them with a brief good morning, showing no surprise at his guests' mortal pallor. Isabel asked about Diego, and the captain pointed vaguely in the direction of the deck. "If young de la Vega hasn't changed over the years, you will find him high up the mainmast or sitting on the fig-urehead. I don't think he will be bored, but for you three this journey will be very long." However, that was not the case; soon each woman found an occupation. Juliana devoted herself to embroidering and to reading the captain's books, one after the other. In the first pages she found them boring, but then heroes and heroines were introduced, and thus wars, revolutions, and philosophical treatises acquired their own romance. She was free to invent ardent, star-crossed love affairs and choose the ending. She preferred the tragic ones, which made her weep more. Isabel found distraction in helping the captain reproduce his fantasy maps; once she proved her skill at drawing, she asked permission to sketch portraits of the crew. The captain even-tually gave his consent, and she won over the sailors. She studied the mysteries of navigation, from the use of the sextant to the way to identify underwater currents by changes of color or the behavior of fish. She made drawings of the sailors' many duties: caulking the deck seams with fiber oakum and tar, pumping the water that col-lected in the bilges, mending sail, repairing frayed line, oiling the masts with rancid fat, painting, scraping, and scrubbing decks. The crew worked every minute; only on Sunday was the routine relaxed and approval given to fish, whittle carvings, sew, tattoo, or pick fleas off one another. They stank like wild beasts because they rarely changed clothing, and they considered bathing to be dangerous to the health. They could not understand why the captain bathed once a week, and even less the mania of the four passengers for washing every day. The *Madre de Dios* was not ruled by the cruel discipline of ships of war: Santiago de León demanded respect without resorting to brutal punishments. He allowed games of cards and dice, which were prohibited on other ships, as long as money was not bet; he doubled the rum ration on Sundays; he was never behind in paying his men; and when they anchored in a port, he organized shifts so everyone would have time ashore. Although he had a cat-o'-nine-tails in a red pouch hanging in a visible spot, he had never used it. At most he sentenced men who broke rules to a few days without grog.

Nuria made her presence felt in the kitchen; in her opinion Galileo Tempesta's dishes left much to be desired. Her culinary innovations, prepared with the usual limited ingredients, were celebrated by everyone from the captain down to the last ship's boy. The chaperone quickly adjusted to the sickening odor of the provisions, especially the cheeses and salt meat, to cooking with murky water, and to the dead fish Galileo Tempesta laid on the sacks of biscuits to combat weevils. When the fish were crawling with worms, he replaced them, and in that way kept the biscuits more or less weevil-free. Nuria learned to milk the two goats on board. They were not the only animals; there were also hens, ducks, and geese in cages, and a sow and her piglets in a pen, in addition to the sailors' pets—monkeys and parrots—and the irreplaceable cats, without which rats would be lords and masters of the ship. Nuria discovered new ways to combine milk and eggs, so there was dessert daily. Galileo was a grouch, and he resented Nuria's invasion of his territory, but she found the simplest way to resolve that problem. The first time Tempesta raised his voice to her, she popped him on the head with a cooking spoon and went back to stirring the stew. Six hours later, the crusty old Genoese proposed marriage. He confessed that Amalia's remedies were beginning to take effect and that he had saved nine hundred American dollars, enough to open a restaurant in Cuba and live like kings. He had been waiting eleven years to find the right woman, he said, and he didn't care that Nuria was a little older than he was. Nuria did not dignify this with a reply.

Several sailors who had been on the ship during Diego's first voyage did not recognize him until he won their handfuls of garbanzo beans playing cards. Time for sailors follows its own laws; the years pass by without leaving a trace on the smooth surfaces of sky and sea, which was why they were surprised that the boy who only yesterday had frightened them with stories of the living dead was today a man. Where had five years gone? It comforted them that even though he had grown and changed, he continued to enjoy their company. Diego spent a good part of the day working with them in duties around the ship, especially the sails, which fascinated him. Only at dusk did he disappear briefly into his stateroom to wash and dress like a caballero to join Juliana. The sailors realized from the first day that Diego was in love with the girl, and although they sometimes made jokes, they observed his devotion with a mixture of nostalgia for something they would never have and curiosity about the outcome. Juliana to them was as unreal as a mythological siren. That unblemished skin, those liquid eyes, that ethereal grace could not be of this world.

Running with ocean currents and the mandate of the wind, the *Madre de Dios* headed south along the coast of Africa, passed the Canary Islands without stopping in, and reached Cape Verde to take on water and fresh food before initiating the crossing, which, depending on the weather, might take more than three weeks. It was there they learned that Napoleon Bonaparte had escaped from his exile on Elba and returned in triumph to France. Troops sent to block his march toward Paris had defected to his side, and he had regained power without firing a single shot—while the court of Louis XVIII took refuge in Ghent—and prepared to conquer Europe for the second time. On Cape Verde the travelers were welcomed by the local authorities, who presented a ball in honor of the captain's daughters, which is how they introduced the de Romeu girls. Santiago de León thought that that would allay suspicions in case the arrest order had traveled that far. Many of the administrative officials were married to tall, proud, beautiful African women who appeared at the party dressed in spectacular finery. By comparison, Isabel looked like a wet dog, and even Juliana seemed nearly mousy. That first impression changed completely when, urged by Diego, she agreed to play the harp. A full orchestra was already providing music, but the moment she began to pluck the strings, a silence fell over the large salon. A couple of time-honored ballads were all it took to enchant everyone there. For the rest of the evening, Diego had to stand in line with the other caballeros to win a dance.

Soon after the *Madre de Dios* unfurled her sails, leaving the island behind, two sailors appeared with a canvas-wrapped bundle and set it down in the officers' salon: a gift from Captain Santiago de León for Juliana. "For you to calm the wind and waves," he told her, whipping off the cloth with a gallant flourish. It was an Italian harp fashioned in the shape of a swan. From then on, every afternoon they carried the harp out to the deck, and she made the men weep with her melodies. She had a good ear and could play any song they hummed. Soon guitars, harmonicas, flutes, and improvised drums appeared to accompany her. The captain, who kept a violin hidden in his stateroom to console himself in secret during the long nights when the laudanum could not dull the pain of his bad leg, joined the group, and the ship filled with music.

They were in the middle of one of those concerts when the sea breezes brought to their nostrils a stench so nauseating that it could not be ignored. Moments later they glimpsed the silhouette of a ship in the distance. The captain got his spyglass to confirm what he already knew: it was a slave ship. There were two methods of transport among the slave traders, *fardos prietos* and *fardos flojos*. In the former, the "tight packers," the captives were stacked like firewood, one atop another, bound with chains and covered in their own excrement and vomit, healthy mixed with sick, dying, and dead. Half of those Blacks died at sea, but when they arrived in port the traders "fattened" the survivors, and their sales compensated for losses; only the strongest reached their destiny or sold at a good price. The "loose packer" traders carried fewer slaves in more supportable conditions, so as not to lose too many during the crossing.

"That ship has to be *fardo prieto,* that's why you can smell it several leagues away," said the captain.

"We have to help those poor people, Captain!" Diego exclaimed, horrified.

"I fear that La Justicia can do nothing in this case, my friend."

"We are armed, we have a crew of forty. We can attack that ship and free the Blacks."

"The traffic is illegal, and that cargo is contraband. If we approach, they will throw the chained slaves overboard so they sink to the bottom. And even if we could free them, they have no place to go. They were captured in their own country by African traffickers. Blacks sell other Blacks, didn't you know that?"

During those weeks at sea, Diego regained some ground in the conquest of Juliana that he had lost during their time with the Gypsies, when they were required to be apart and never had a moment of privacy. It was that way on the ship as well, but there were always sunsets and other new sights when they went up on the quarterdeck to gaze at the sea, as lovers have done through the ages. At those moments Diego would slip his arm around the beauty's shoulders or waist, very delicately, so as not to startle her. He liked to read love poems aloud—not his, which were so mediocre that even he recognized it. He had had the foresight to buy some books in La Coruña before they sailed, which were very helpful. The sweet metaphors would mellow Juliana, preparing her for the moment he took her hand and held it in his. Nothing more than that, sadly. Kisses? Not to be considered. Not for any lack of initiative on our hero's part, but because Isabel, Nuria, the captain, and forty sailors never took their eyes off them. Besides, Juliana did not facilitate little meetings behind a door, partly because there were very few doors on the ship, and also because she was not sure of her sentiments, even though she had lived beside Diego for months and there were no other suitors on the horizon. She had confided that much to her sister in the private conversations they had at night. Isabel kept her opinion to herself, since anything she said might tip the scales of love in Diego's favor, which she did not want to encourage. In her way, Isabel had loved him since she was eleven, but that had no bearing on anything, since he had never suspected it. Diego continued to think of Isabel as a runny-nosed kid with four elbows and enough hair for two heads, even though her looks had improved over the years; she was fifteen now and looked slightly better than she had at eleven.

On several occasions, other ships could be seen in the distance, which the captain had the good sense to elude because there were many dangers on the high seas, from pirates to swift American brigantines searching for arms shipments. The United States needed every weapon they could get their hands on for the war against England. Santiago de León paid very little attention to the flag a ship was flying, as it was often changed to deceive the unwary; he determined her origin from other signs and prided himself on knowing all the ships that plied these routes.

Several winter storms shook the *Madre de Dios* during those weeks, but they were never a surprise; the captain could smell them before they were announced on the barometer. He would order his crew to shorten the sails, batten down anything loose, and lock up the animals. Within a few minutes the crew would be prepared, and when the wind came and the sea turned rough, everything on board was secured. The women had instructions to close themselves in their cabins to prevent a soaking or an accident. The seas swept over the decks, washing off anything in their path. It was easy to lose one's footing and end up at the bottom of the Atlantic. After its dunking the ship would be clean, fresh, and smelling of wood; the sea and sky would clear, and the horizon would gleam like pure silver. Different fish would be stranded on the deck, and more than one ended up fried in Galileo and Nuria's galley. The captain would take his readings and correct the course while the crew repaired minor damages and settled back into their daily routines. The rain collected in canvas awnings and drained into barrels allowed them the luxury of a good bath with soap, something impossible to do in salt water.

Finally they sailed into the waters of the Caribbean. They saw turtles, swordfish, translucent medusas with long tentacles, and gigantic squid. The weather seemed benign, but the captain was nervous. He could feel the change of pressure in his leg. The earlier brief storms had not prepared Diego and his friends for a true tempest. They were on course to Puerto Rico and from there to Jamaica when the captain told them that they were running into a major challenge. The sky was clear and the sea was smooth, but within thirty minutes heavy black clouds had blotted out the sun, the air became sticky, and the rain came down in torrents. Soon the first lightning flashes split the sky and foam-crested waves rose all around them. The ship creaked, and the masts seemed close to being torn from their fittings. The men barely had time to furl the sails. The captain and the helmsmen tried to control the ship with four hands. Among the steersmen was a husky black man from Santo Domingo, hardened by twenty years at sea, who calmly chewed his tobacco as he struggled with the wheels, indifferent to the buckets of water blinding him. The ship would teeter on the crest of a monstrous wave and seconds later careen to the bottom of a watery abyss. With the buffeting, a pen opened, and one of the goats flew out like a comet and was lost in the sky. The sailors tied themselves down any way they could as they fought the storm; one slip meant sure death. The three women trembled in their cabins, sick with fear and nausea. Even Diego, who prided himself on having a stomach of iron, vomited, but he was not the only one; several members of the crew followed suit. He thought how ludicrous humankind was to dare defy the elements. The *Madre de Dios* was like a nut that might crack open at any instant.

The captain gave the order to secure the cargo, its loss would mean economic ruin. They withstood the tempest for two full days, and when finally it began to lessen, lightning struck the mainmast. The impact shook the ship like a whiplash. The tall, heavy mast swung back and forth a few minutes—eternal for the terrified crew—and finally broke off, plummeting with its sail and tangle of line into the sea, dragging with it two sailors who could not be saved. The ship sat listing to one side, in danger of foundering. The captain lurched about, shouting orders. Several sailors immediately came running with hatchets to cut the lines that joined the broken mast to the ship, a task made difficult by the tilting, slippery deck; the wind was buffeting them, the rain blinding them, and waves were washing over the deck. It took a good while, but they were able to free the mast, which floated away as the ship righted herself, rolling from side to side. There was no hope of rescuing the men, who were swallowed up in the black waves.

Finally the wind diminished and the seas were not running as high, but the rain and lightning continued the rest of that night. At dawn, with the light, they could take an inventory of the damages. In addition to the drowned sailors, many had cuts and contusions. Galileo Tempesta seemed to have broken an arm in a fall; the bone had not come through the skin, so the captain did not think he would have to amputate it. He gave the cook a double ration of rum and with Nuria's help set the bones and stabilized the arm. The crew began pumping water from the bilge and redistributing the cargo while the captain went over the ship from stem to stern to evaluate their situation. The ship was so damaged that it was impossible to make repairs at sea. Since the storm had sent them off course, away from Puerto Rico and to the north, the captain decided that they could reach Cuba with their two masts and remaining sails.

The next days were spent making slow progress without the mainmast, taking on water through several breaches in the hull. Those seasoned sailors had gone through similar situations without losing heart, but when the word spread that it was the women that had brought on their trouble, murmurs began to circulate. The captain gave them a strong dressing down and was able to prevent a mutiny, but discontent was as strong as ever. None of the men thought of the harp concerts; they refused to eat Nuria's food, and looked the other way when the girls came out on the deck to take the air. At night the ship limped along, heading toward Cuba through dangerous waters. Soon they saw sharks, blue dolphins, giant turtles, gulls, pelicans, and flying fish that dropped like rocks onto the deck, ready to be grilled by Tempesta. The warm breeze and the distant scent of ripe fruit announced the proximity of land.

At dawn, Diego went on deck to get some air. The sky was beginning to show tones of orange, and a veil of fog blurred the world's outlines. The ship's lanterns were hazy in the misty air. The ship sailed softly between two low islets covered with mangrove, and except for the eternal creaking of the wood, everything was quiet. Diego stretched, breathed deeply to clear his head, and saluted the helmsman who was on his way to the bridge, then broke into a run as he did every morning to loosen his tight muscles. His bed was too short for him, and he slept with his knees drawn up; several turns around the deck at a trot served to stimulate his mind and loosen his stiff body. When he reached the bow he leaned over to pat the figurehead, a daily ritual he observed with superstitious punctuality. And that was when he saw something through the fog. It looked like a sailing ship, although he couldn't be sure. At any rate, as it was close, he needed to advise the captain. Moments later Santiago de León came out of his cabin buttoning his trousers, spyglass in hand. One glance, and he raised the alarm and rang the bell, calling all hands, but it was too late: pirates were swarming up the sides of the *Madre de Dios*.

Diego could see the grappling hooks they were using to climb aboard but had no time to try to cut the ropes. He raced to the cabins on the poop deck, yelling warnings to Juliana, Isabel, and Nuria not to come out for any reason. He grabbed the sword Pelayo had made for him and prepared to defend them. The first attackers, holding their daggers between their teeth, reached the deck. The crew of the *Madre de Dios* poured out like rats from everywhere, armed with anything they could find, while the captain barked useless orders, for in an instant a battle royal was under way, and no one heard him. Diego and the captain, side by side, fought off a half dozen attackers, terrifying, bald devils marred by horrible scars, with daggers even in their boots, two or three pistols at their waist, and short cutlasses.

They roared like tigers, but they fought with more noise and courage than technique. No one man could stand up to Diego, but several were able to trap him. He broke out of that circle and wounded two of them. He leaped up for the mizzen shrouds and climbed up the inside of the ratlines, then caught a running backstay and swung across the quarterdeck, all the while never losing sight of the women's staterooms. The doors were frail and could be opened with one kick. He could only hope that none of the girls would stick her nose outside. He pushed off the pole, swung across the deck, made a formidable leap, and landed in front of a man who was calmly awaiting him, cutlass in hand. Unlike the others, who were a scruffy crew, this man was dressed like a prince, entirely in black, with a yellow silk sash around his waist, fine lace collar and cuffs, high boots with gold buckles, a gold chain around his neck, and rings on several fingers. He was tall and smooth-shaven, with long, lustrous hair, expressive black eyes, and lips that lifted in a mocking smile that revealed snow-white teeth. Diego took one quick admiring look but did not pause to establish who he was; from his attire and attitude, he had to be the leader of the pirates. This elegant fellow saluted Diego in French— "En garde"—and made his first thrust, which Diego avoided by only a hair's breadth. They crossed swords and after three or four minutes realized that they were cut from the same cloth, made to challenge one another. Both were excellent swordsmen. Despite the circumstances, they felt a secret pleasure in combating a rival of that stature, and without reaching an accord, each decided his opponent deserved a clean fight, even if it were to the death. The duel was almost a demonstration of the art; it would have filled Maestro Manuel Escalante with pride.

On the *Madre de Dios*, each man was fighting for his life. Santiago de León looked around and in one second evaluated the situation. The pirates were two or three times more numerous than his crew; they were well armed, they knew how to fight, and they had caught them by surprise. His men were peaceable merchant seamen. Several of them were already combing gray hair and dreaming of retiring from the sea and starting a family; it wasn't fair for them to give their lives defending alien cargo. With a brutal effort the captain broke away from his attackers and in two leaps reached the bell to signal surrender. The crew obeyed and laid down their weapons in the midst of the triumphant yells of the pirates. Only Diego and his elegant adversary ignored the bell and fought on for a few minutes, until the former disarmed his competitor with a reverse stroke. Diego's victory was short-lived, however, because in an instant he found himself in the center of a circle of swords so tight that some scratched his skin.

"Release him, but do not lose sight of him! I want him alive!" his rival ordered, and then greeted Santiago de León in perfect Spanish. "Jean Lafitte, at your service, Captain."

"So I feared, señor. It could only be the pirate Lafitte," de León replied, wiping the sweat from his brow.

"Pirate, no, Captain. I have a privateer's license issued in Cartagena, Colombia."

"The same thing. What may we expect from you?"

"You may expect fair treatment. We do not kill, unless it cannot be helped, because we prefer a commercial arrangement. I propose that we deal with one another as caballeros. Your name, please."

"Santiago de León, merchant seaman."

"I am interested only in your cargo, Captain de León, which, if I am well informed, is weapons and ammunition."

"What will happen to my crew?"

"You may use your longboats. With fair winds, you will reach the Bahamas or Cuba in a couple of days; it is all a matter of luck. Is there anything on board that might interest me, aside from weapons?"

"Books and charts," replied Santiago de León.

That was the moment Isabel chose to come out of her cabin in her nightgown, barefoot, and with her father's pistol in her hand. She had stayed inside, obeying Diego's order, until the uproar on the deck and the sound of cannons quieted, then she could stem her anxiety no longer and had come out to see how the battle ended.

"*Mortdieu!* A beautiful lady," Lafitte exclaimed when he saw her.

Isabel started with surprise and lowered her pistol; that was the first time anyone had ever used that adjective to describe her. Lafitte walked to within a step of her, bowed deeply, held out his hand, and she tamely handed him the gun.

"This complicates matters a little. . . . How many passengers do you have on board?" Lafitte asked the captain.

"Two señoritas and their chaperone, all of whom are traveling with Don Diego de la Vega."

"Very interesting."

The two captains went to de León's cabin to discuss the surrender, while on the deck two pirates detained Diego, with their pistols pointed at him, and the rest took possession of the ship. They ordered the vanquished sailors to lie facedown with their hands behind their heads, then searched the ship for booty. They consoled the wounded with rum and threw the dead overboard. They took no prisoners, it was too great a nuisance. Their own wounded were carefully loaded onto their boarding crafts and from there to the corsair. Meanwhile, Diego was planning how he might rescue the de Romeu girls. Even if he reached them, he could not imagine a way to escape. His enemies were a brutal lot; the idea that any of those men might touch the girls drove him mad. He must think coolly, because getting out of this predicament would require cunning and luck; his fencing skills would be of very little help.

Santiago de León, his officers, and the surviving crew bought their freedom with a quarter of their year's pay, the usual fee in these cases. The sailors, as an alternative, were offered the opportunity to join Lafitte's band, and some did. The privateer knew that the debt of the captain and his men would be paid. It was the honorable thing to do. If they did not, they would be scorned even by close friends. It was a clean and simple transaction. Santiago de León had to turn over his four passengers to Jean Lafitte, who planned to demand a ransom for them. The captain explained that the two girls were orphans and had no money, but the pirate decided to take them anyway because there was a great demand for white women in the prestigious bawdyhouses of New Orleans. De León pleaded with him to respect the virtue of those girls who had suffered so much and did not deserve that horrible fate, but Lafitte explained that such considerations interfered with business, something he could not allow, and that anyway, being a courtesan was a very pleasant fate for most women. The captain was demoralized as he left the meeting. He didn't care that he was losing the weapons—on the contrary, one of the reasons he had surrendered so quickly had been the desire to rid himself of that cargo—but he was horrified at the thought that the de Romeu girls, whom he had become truly fond of, would end up in a brothel. He had to inform his passengers of the fate that awaited them, clarifying that the only one with any hope of emerging unharmed was Diego de la Vega, because surely his father would do whatever necessary to save him.

"My father will also pay the ransom for Juliana, Isabel, and Nuria—as long as no one lays a finger on them! We will immediately send a letter to California," Diego assured Lafitte, but the minute he said it he felt a strange pressure in his chest, like a bad presentiment.

"The mail is very slow, so you will be my guests for some weeks, perhaps months, until we receive the ransom. In the meantime, the girls will be respected. For the good of all, I hope that your father does not have to be begged to answer," the pirate replied, never taking his eyes off Juliana.

The women, who barely had time to dress, nearly swooned when they saw all the blood on the bridge, the wounded, and especially the horrible band of cutthroats. Juliana, however, was not only shivering with horror, as one might have thought, but also from the effect of Jean Lafitte's gaze.

The pirates maneuvered their schooner alongside, placed planks between the bridges, and formed a human chain to transport the light bounty between ships, including animals, barrels of beer, and hams. They were not in a hurry; the *Madre de Dios* now belonged to

Lafitte. Captain de León impassively witnessed the operation, but his heart was racing; he loved his ship as he would love a bride. Fluttering on the enemy mainmast, beside the flag of Colombia, was another, red, called the *jolie rouge*; it indicated that the ship freed captives for a price. That calmed the captain a little; he knew the corsair would allow him to save his crew after all. A black pennant, which sometimes carried a skull and crossbones, would have signaled the intention to fight to the last man, and to massacre adversaries.

Once the cargo had been transferred, Lafitte kept his word and authorized Santiago de León to supply the longboats with fresh water and provisions, to take his instruments, without which he would not have been able to navigate, and to load on his crew. At that moment, Galileo Tempesta, who using the pretext of his broken arm had managed to remain hidden during the battle, emerged and was one of the first to get into the boats. The captain told Diego good-bye with a firm handshake and kissed the women's hands with the promise that they would see each other again. He wished them luck and got into one of the boats without a backward look. He did not want to see the spectacle of the *Madre de Dios*, which had been his only home for three decades, taken away by the pirates.

On the pirate ship, which was loaded to the gunnels, it was difficult to move about. Lafitte was never at sea for more than a couple of days, and for that reason he could pack a crew of a hundred and fifty into a space that normally accommodated no more than thirty. His headquarters were on Grand Island near New Orleans, in the swampy region of Barataria. He sat there until his spies reported the proximity of a possible prey, then sprang to life. He used the cover of fog or darkness of night, when ships trimmed their sails or anchored, and attacked with speed and stealth. Surprise was always his greatest advantage. He used his cannons to intimidate more than to sink an enemy ship; if the ship stayed afloat, he could incorporate her into his fleet, which was composed of thirteen brigantines and assorted schooners, pinnaces, and feluccas.

Jean and his brother Pierre were the most feared corsairs on the seas, but on dry land they could pass for businessmen. The governor of New Orleans, weary of the Lafittes' smuggling, slave trafficking, and other illegal activities, had put a price of five hundred dollars on their heads. Jean responded by offering fifteen hundred for the head of the governor. That was the culmination of a long hostility. Jean had escaped, but Pierre was held prisoner for months. Grand Island was attacked and all its contraband requisitioned. However, the situation had changed when the Lafittes became allies of the American troops. General Andrew Jackson had come to New Orleans at the head of a ragtag, malaria-riddled contingent of men with the assignment to defend the vast Louisiana territory against the English. He could not allow himself the luxury of rejecting the aid offered by the pirates. Those bandits, a mixture of black, brown, and white men, became essential to the battle. Jackson confronted the enemy on January 8, 1815—three months before our friends, against their will, came to that region. The war between England and the United States had ended two weeks before, but neither side was aware of that. With a handful of men of various origins, who did not even share a common language, Jackson routed an organized and well-armed English army of twenty thousand. While the men were killing each other in Chalmette, a few leagues from New Orleans, women and children were praying in the Convent of the Ursulines. At the end of the battle, when the bodies were counted, it was found that England had lost two thousand men, while Jackson left only thirteen soldiers on the field. The bravest and most ferocious fighters had been the Creoles, or free men of color, and the pirates. Some days later they celebrated the triumph with arches of flowers and white-gowned damsels from every state of the Union, who crowned General Jackson with a laurel wreath. In the crowd were the Lafitte brothers with their pirates, who had been promoted from outlaws to heroes.

During the forty hours Lafitte's boat had taken to reach Grand Island, Diego de la Vega was kept in bonds on the deck, and the three women confined to a small cabin beside the captain's. Pierre

Lafitte, who had not taken part in the attack upon the *Madre de Dios* because he had been left in charge of the pirate ship, turned out to be a very different man from his brother, rougher, more robust, more brutal; unlike his brother, he had light hair, and one side of his face had been paralyzed by a stroke. He liked to eat and drink to excess, and when he saw a young woman, he had to have her. He refrained from molesting Juliana and Isabel, however, because his brother reminded him that business is more important than pleasure. Those girls would bring a good sum of money. Jean veiled his early years in mystery—no one knew where he had come from—but he confessed to being thirty-five. He was smooth in his dealings and had exquisite manners; he spoke several languages, among them French, Spanish, and English, and he loved music and gave great sums of money to the New Orleans opera. Despite his success with women, he did not just take what he wanted, like Pierre; he preferred to court them with patience. He was gallant, jovial, a fine dancer and teller of tales, most of them invented as he went along. His sympathy for the American cause was legendary; his captains knew that "anyone who attacks an American ship dies." Under his command he had three thousand men who called him boss, and he moved millions in merchandise on barges and pirogues along the intricate channels of the Mississippi Delta. No one knew that region as well as he and his men; authorities could not control them or capture them. They sold the gains of their piracy only a few leagues from New Orleans, at an ancient sacred site of the Indians called the Temple. Plantation owners, rich and not so rich Creoles, even relatives of the governor, bought anything they saw at a reasonable price and in a festive atmosphere, and without paying taxes. That was also the place where they auctioned slaves bought on the cheap in Cuba and sold for high prices in the United States, where traffic in Blacks was illegal though slavery was not. Lafitte advertised his sales in posters on every street corner: "Come One, Come All, to Jean Lafitte's Slave Auction at the Temple! Clothing, Jewels, Furniture, and Other Articles from the Seven Seas!"

On the ship, Jean had invited his three female hostages to share a small meal on the deck, but they refused to leave their cabin. He sent them a tray of cheeses, cold meats, and a good bottle of Spanish wine from the *Madre de Dios,* with his respectful greetings. Juliana could not get the man out of her head and was dying with curiosity to know him, but thought it more prudent to stay inside.

Diego spent those forty hours in the open, tied up like a sausage, without food. The pirates took his La Justicia medallion and what few coins he had in his pocket; they gave him a little water from time to time and a kick or two if he seemed too active. Jean Lafitte approached him a couple of times to assure him that once they were on his island he would be more comfortable, and to beg him to forgive his men's rough manners. They were not used to dealing with refined people, he said. Diego had to swallow the sarcasm, muttering to himself that sooner or later he would cut that reprobate down to size. The important thing now was to stay alive. Without him the two de Romeu girls would be lost. He had heard of the orgies of alcohol, sex, and blood the pirates threw in their lairs when they returned triumphant from their villainy, of how unfortunate women prisoners suffered terrible abuse, of the raped and mutilated bodies buried in the sand during those bacchanals. He tried not to think of those things, only of how to escape, but he was tormented by those images. Besides, he could not lose that uncomfortable presentiment he had felt earlier. It had something to do with his father, of that he was certain. It had been weeks since he had communicated with Bernardo, and he decided to use those tedious hours to attempt it. He concentrated on calling his brother, but telepathy was not something they could summon at will; messages came and went following no fixed pattern and without the control of either of them. That long silence between Bernardo and him, so rare, seemed a very bad omen. He wondered what was going on in Alta California and what could have happened to Bernardo and his parents.

Grand Island in Barataria, where the Lafittes had their empire, was large, humid, flat, and, like the rest of the region, distinguished by an aura of mystery and decadence. That capricious and hot climate, which swung between bucolic calm and devastating hurricanes, invited grand passions. Everything decayed rapidly, from vegetation to human souls. In moments of good weather, like that that welcomed Diego and his friends, a warm breeze carried the heavy, sweet scent of orange blossoms, but as soon as the breeze ceased, a sweltering heat descended. The pirates put their prisoners ashore and escorted them to Jean Lafitte's residence on a promontory surrounded with a forest of palm trees and twisted live oaks, with leaves burned by salt spray. The pirates' town, protected from the wind by a thicket of shrubs, could barely be seen through the leaves. Oleanders provided notes of color. Lafitte's home was two stories high, Spanish style, with latticework at the windows and a broad terrace facing the sea. The house was constructed of brick covered with a mixture of plaster and ground oyster shells. The farthest thing from a cave, as the prisoners had expected, it was clean, organized, even luxurious. The rooms were large and cool, and the views from its balconies were spectacular; the light wooden floors shone, the walls had been freshly painted, and on every table were vases of flowers, trays of fruit, and carafes of wine. A pair of black slave girls took the women to their rooms. For Diego they produced a pitcher of water for washing up; they gave him coffee, then led him to a veranda where Jean Lafitte, accompanied by two brightly colored parrots, was resting in a red hammock, strumming a stringed instrument with his gaze lost on the horizon. Diego judged that the contrast between the man's evil reputation and his refined behavior could not be more startling.

"You may choose between being my prisoner and being my guest, Señor de la Vega. As my prisoner you have the right to try to escape, and I have the right to prevent you in any way I can. As my guest you will be treated well until we receive your father's ransom, but you will be obliged by the laws of hospitality to respect my house and my instructions. Do we understand one another?"

"Before I answer, señor, I must know your plans regarding the de Romeu sisters, who are in my charge," Diego replied.

"They *were*, señor; they no longer are. Now they are in *my* charge. Their fate depends on your father's response."

"If I agree to be your guest, how will you know that I will not try to escape anyway?"

"Because you would not do that without the de Romeu girls, and because you will give me your word of honor," the pirate replied.

"You have it, Captain Lafitte," said Diego, resigned.

"Very well. Please, join me within the hour to dine with your friends. I believe that you will not be disappointed with my cook."

In the meantime, Juliana, Isabel, and Nuria were going through some upsetting experiences. Several men had brought tubs to their room and filled them with water; then three young slave girls appeared, equipped with soap and brushes; they were under the direction of a tall, beautiful woman with sculpted features and long neck, a large turban gave her another handspan of height. She introduced herself in French as Madame Odilia and clarified that she was the person who ran the house of Lafitte. She told the prisoners to take off their clothes, that they were going to be bathed. None of the three had ever bathed naked in their lives; they had always washed with great modesty beneath a light cotton tunic. The fuss Nuria kicked up provoked an attack of the giggles in the slave girls, and the madame of the turban dryly commented that no one dies from taking a bath. That sounded reasonable to Isabel, so she took off everything she was wearing. Juliana imitated her, covering her private parts with both hands. This brought on new giggles from the Africans, who compared their own mahogany color with that of this girl who was white as the dining room china. Nuria was another matter. To get her clothes off, she had to be held down, and her screams shook the walls. The young slaves put the women in the tubs and lathered them from head to toe. After the first shock, what they had thought would be an ordeal proved to be not really so bad, and soon Juliana and Isabel began to enjoy it. The slaves took away their clothes without explanation and brought back rich brocade gowns, badly suited for the warm climate. They were in good condition, but it was evident that they had been worn; one had bloodstains on the hem. What had happened to the former wearer? Was she, too, a prisoner? Better not to think of her fate, or the fate that awaited them. Isabel deduced that the haste to get them out of their clothes was in response to specific instructions from Lafitte, who wanted to be sure that they had nothing hidden beneath their skirts. They had prepared for that eventuality.

Diego decided to take advantage of the conditional freedom he had been granted by the corsair, and went out to reconnoiter the grounds in the hour before dinner. The pirate town was made up of vagabonds from every corner of the globe. Some were living with their women and children in palm-thatched huts, though bachelors moved about without a place of their own. Good French and Creole food was available, along with bars, brothels, and artisan's shops. Those men of many races, languages, creeds, and customs had in common a fierce love of liberty, but they accepted the laws of Grand Island because they seemed reasonable and the system was democratic. Everything was decided by vote; they even had the right to elect and remove their captains. The rules were clear: anyone who molested another man's woman ended up marooned on a waterless island with one flagon of water and a loaded pistol; theft was disciplined with a lashing, and murder with hanging. There was no blind submission to a leader, except on shipboard during action, but everyone had to obey the rules or pay the consequences. At one time they had been criminals, adventurers, or deserters from warships; they had always been outsiders, and now they were proud to belong to a community. Only the most capable went to sea; the others worked in smithies, cooked, cared for the stock, repaired ships and small boats, built houses, fished. Diego saw women and children as well as men who were ill or had amputated limbs, and realized that veterans of battles, orphans, and widows were given protection. If a sailor lost a leg or arm at sea, he was compensated in gold. Booty was shared equally among the men, and some was given to widows; the rest of the women mattered very little. They were prostitutes, slaves, captives from assaults, and a few courageous free women—not many— who had come there of their own will.

On the beach, Diego came across a score of drunks who were punching each other for the pure joy of fighting and chasing after women in the light of bonfires. He recognized several of the crew who had boarded the *Madre de Dios,* and decided that this was not his opportunity to get back the La Justicia medallion that one of them had taken from him.

"Señores! Listen up!" he yelled.

He gained the attention of the least intoxicated, and they formed a circle around him while the women used the distraction to pick up their clothes and run. Diego looked around at the puffy faces, the bloodshot eyes, the toothless mouths cursing him, the claws reaching for daggers. He did not give them time to organize.

"I want to have a little fun. Do any of you dare fight me?" he asked.

An enthusiastic chorus answered him, and the circle around Diego tightened; he could smell their sweat and the alcohol, tobacco, and garlic on their breaths.

"One at a time, please. I will begin with the hero who has my medallion; then I will whip each of you, one by one. How does that sound?"

Several pirates fell on their backs in the sand, weak with laughter. The others consulted among themselves, and finally one opened his filthy shirt and showed Diego the medallion, more than ready to fight this sissified man with woman's hands who still smelled of his mother's milk, as he put it. Diego said he wanted to be sure that it was in fact his medallion. The man took it from his neck and dangled it before Diego's nose.

"Don't take your eyes off that medallion, friend, because if you are careless for an instant, I will have it."

The pirate immediately pulled a curved dagger from his waistband and shook off the alcohol fumes, while the others stood back to give them room. The villain threw himself toward Diego, who was waiting with his feet planted firmly in the sand. It was not for nothing that he had learned La Justicia's secrets. As his opponent rushed him, he made three simultaneous moves: he blocked the hand with the dagger, stepped to one side and crouched, and, using the other man's momentum, pushed up and flipped the pirate over his back. As soon as he hit the ground, Diego stepped on his wrist and wrested the dagger from his hand. Then he turned toward the spectators with a small bow. "Where is my medallion?" he asked, looking at the pirates one by one. He approached the tallest of them, who was standing a few steps away, and accused him of having hidden it. The man unsheathed his knife, but Diego stopped him with a gesture and told him to take off his cap, because that was where he would find it. Nonplussed, the man obeyed. Diego reached into the cap and pulled out his jewel. Surprise paralyzed the others, who didn't know whether to laugh or attack, until they opted for the behavior most appropriate to their temperaments: to give this upstart a good lesson.

"All of you against one? Doesn't that seem a bit cowardly?" Diego challenged, whirling with knife in hand, ready to leap.

"This caballero is right; that would be cowardice unworthy of you," came a voice from behind him.

It was Jean Lafitte, amiable and smiling, with the look of a man out for a walk but with his hand on his pistol. He took Diego by one arm and calmly walked away. No one tried to stop them.

"That medallion must be very valuable if you are willing to risk your life for it," Lafitte commented.

"My grandmother gave it to me on her deathbed," Diego joked. "With this I can buy my freedom and that of my friends, Captain."

"I'm afraid it isn't worth that much."

"Our ransom may come, and it may not. California is a long way away, and something could happen to our message. If you will allow me, I will go to New Orleans to gamble. I will bet the medallion and win enough to pay for our ransom."

"And if you lose?"

"In that case, I would have to wait for my father's money, but I never lose in cards."

The pirate laughed. "You are an original, all right. I think we have a lot of things in common."

That night Justine, the beautiful sword Pelayo had made for Diego, was returned to him, along with the trunk containing his clothing, saved from going down with the ship by the greed of a pirate who could not open it but had brought it with him, thinking it contained something of value. The three hostages dined with Lafitte, who looked very elegant, all in black, cleanly shaved and hair recently curled. Diego thought that by comparison his Zorro cape and mask were rather sad-looking; he needed to copy some ideas from the corsair, like the sash and the full sleeves of the shirt. Their meal was a parade of dishes influenced by Africa, the Caribbean, and the Cajuns, the latter being what the immigrants from Canada were called: crab gumbo, red beans and rice, fried oysters, turkey roasted with nuts and raisins, fish with various spices, and the best wines stolen from French galleons, which the host barely tasted. A young black boy was pulling the rope of a cloth fan above the table, meant to stir the air and keep away flies, and on a balcony three musicians were playing an irresistible blend of Caribbean rhythms and slave songs. Silent as a shadow, Madame Odilia stood in the doorway, directing the slave serving girls with her eyes.

For the first time Juliana saw Jean Lafitte at close quarters. When the pirate bent to kiss her hand, she knew that the long journey of recent months that had led her here was at last over. She discovered why she had not wanted to marry any of her suitors; she had rejected Rafael Moncada so many times that he was crazed, and had not responded to Diego's advances in five years. She had waited her entire lifetime for what her romantic novels described as "Cupid's arrow." How else could she describe this sudden love? It was an arrow in her breast, a sharp pain, a wound. (Forgive me, dear readers, for this ridiculous euphemism, but clichés contain great truths.) Lafitte's dark gaze sank into the green water of her eyes, and his long-fingered hand took hers. Juliana stumbled as if she were going to fall, nothing new—she tended to lose her balance with strong emotion. Isabel and Nuria believed it was fear at meeting the corsair—the symptoms were similar—but Diego understood immediately that something irrevocable had changed his destiny. Compared to Lafitte, Rafael Moncada and all Juliana's other suitors were pesky insects. Madame Odilia, too, noted the corsair's effect on Juliana, and like Diego, she intuited the gravity of what had happened.

Lafitte led them to the table, and sat at its head to conduct polite conversation. Juliana stared at him, hypnotized, but he purposely ignored her, so much so that Isabel wondered if their host had a problem. Perhaps he had lost his manhood in a battle; these things happened—a stray musket ball or a blow and the most interesting part of a man could be reduced to a dried fig. There was no other explanation for his indifference toward her sister.

"We appreciate your hospitality, Señor Lafitte," Diego said, figuring that he had to get Juliana out of there as quickly as possible. "Even if it is forced upon us. However, it does not seem to me that this community of pirates is an appropriate place for these señoritas."

"What other solution do you suggest, Señor de la Vega?"

"I have heard of an Ursuline convent in New Orleans. The señoritas can wait there until we receive news from my father—"

"I would rather die than live with those nuns," Juliana interrupted, with a vehemence they had never known. "I am not leaving here!"

Every eye turned toward her. She was red, feverish, sweating beneath the heavy brocade dress. Her expression left no room for doubt: she was prepared to kill anyone who tried to separate her from her pirate. Diego opened his mouth, but he did not know what to say, so he closed it, defeated. Jean Lafitte interpreted Juliana's outburst as the message he desired and feared, almost as a caress. He had tried to stay aloof from the girl, repeating to himself what he always said to his brother Pierre—business before pleasure—but apparently she was as taken as he was. That devastating attraction confused him, as he prided himself on thinking coolly. He was not an impulsive man, and beautiful women were not new to him. He preferred quadroons, famous for their grace and beauty and trained to satisfy a man's most secret whims. White women to him had always seemed arrogant and complicated; they were often ill, they didn't know how to dance, and they were rather useless when it came to making love—they did not even like to take their hair down. However, this young Spanish woman with the cat eyes was different. She could hold her own in beauty when compared to the most celebrated Creoles in New Orleans, and it seemed that her limpid innocence did not interfere with a passionate heart. He veiled a sigh, trying not to lose himself in the traps of his imagination.

The rest of the evening went by as if they were all sitting on beds of nails. Conversation was painful. Diego was watching Juliana, she was watching Lafitte, and the rest of the guests were staring at their plates with great attention. The heat inside the house was suffocating, and at the end of the meal the corsair invited them to have a cool drink on the terrace. There a palm fan hung from the ceiling, moved fitfully by a young black slave. Lafitte picked up his guitar and began to sing in a musical, agreeable voice, until Diego announced that they were all exhausted and needed to retire. Juliana sent him a lethal glance but did not dare argue.

No one in the house slept. The night, with its concert of frogs and distant sound of drums, dragged on at a sluggish pace. Unable to contain herself any longer, Juliana confessed her secret to Nuria and Isabel in Catalan, so the slave girl attending them would not understand.

"Now I know what love is. I want to marry Jean Lafitte," she said.

"Blessed Virgin, save us from such misfortune," Nuria whispered, crossing herself.

"You are his prisoner, not his sweetheart. How do you plan to resolve that small dilemma?" Isabel asked, rather jealous; she too was quite impressed by the corsair.

"I will do anything. I cannot live without him," her sister replied, her eyes as wild as a madwoman's.

"Diego is not going to like that."

"What does Diego have to do with it? My father must be whirling in his grave, but I don't care!" Juliana exclaimed.

Helpless, Diego witnessed the transformation of his beloved. Juliana appeared on the second day of captivity on Barataria smelling of soap, with her hair down her back; she was wearing a filmy dress, obtained from the slaves, that revealed her every charm. That was how she presented herself the next day at noon, where Madame Odilia had set out a bountiful lunch. Jean Lafitte was waiting for her, and judging by the gleam in his eyes, there was no doubt that he preferred that informal style to the European mode so ill suited to the climate. Again he kissed her hand, but much more intensely than the night before. The servants brought fruit juices cooled with ice that had been brought downriver in boxes filled with sawdust from distant mountains on the mainland, a luxury only the rich could afford. An excited and talkative Juliana, who was usually a light eater, drank two glasses of the iced beverage and tried everything she saw on the table. Diego's and Isabel's hearts were heavy as Juliana and Lafitte chatted almost in whispers. They could capture something of the conversation, and realized that Juliana was exploring the terrain, testing weapons of seduction she had never had occasion to use. She was telling the pirate, with smiles and fluttering eyelashes, that she and her sister would not find certain amenities unwelcome. To begin with, a piano and music scores, some books, preferably novels and poetry, and also summer clothing. Her belongings were all lost, and whose fault was that? she asked with a little pout. She also wanted to be free to take a stroll and to enjoy a little privacy: the constant vigilance of the slave girls bothered her. "And, by the way, Señor Lafitte, I must tell you that I abominate slavery; it is an inhuman practice." He answered that if they walked around the island alone, they would run into vulgar people who did not know how to treat damsels as delicate as she and her sister. He added that the role of the slaves was not to watch them, but to wait on them and frighten away the mosquitoes, rats, and snakes that made their way into the rooms.

"Give me a broom and I will take care of those problems myself," she replied with an irresistible smile that Diego had never seen.

"In respect to your other requests, señorita, perhaps we will find what you need in my bazaar. After siesta, when it is a little cooler, we will all go to the Temple."

"We have no money, but I suppose that you will pay, since you have brought us here against our will," she replied coquettishly.

"It will be an honor, señorita."

"You may call me Juliana."

From a corner of the room, Madame Odilia had followed this flirtatious exchange as attentively as Diego and Isabel. Her presence suddenly reminded Jean Lafitte that he could not continue down that dangerous road, he had inescapable obligations. Drawing strength from he knew not where, he determined to be frank with Juliana. He waved over the beautiful woman in the turban and whispered something in her ear. She disappeared for a few minutes and returned carrying a small bundle.

"Juliana, Madame Odilia is my mother-in-law, and this is my son Pierre," Lafitte explained, pale as death.

Diego uttered a cry of joy and Juliana one of horror. Isabel stood, and Madame Odilia showed her what she held. Unlike most women, who tend to melt at the sight of a baby, Isabel did not like children; she preferred dogs, but she had to admit that this little one was attractive. He had his father's eyes and turned-up nose.

"I did not know that you were married, Señor Pirate," Isabel commented.

"Privateer," Lafitte corrected.

"Señor Privateer, then. May we meet your wife?"

"I am afraid not. I myself have not been able to visit her for several weeks. She is weak and can see no one."

"What is her name?"

"Catherine Villars."

"Forgive me, I feel very tired," whispered Juliana, near fainting.

Diego pulled back her chair and led her out with an air of sympathy, though he was jubilant at the turn of events. What fabulous luck! Now Juliana had no choice but to reevaluate her feelings. Not only was Lafitte an old man of thirty-five, a womanizer, a criminal, a smuggler, and slave trafficker, all of which a girl like Juliana might easily excuse, but he had a wife and a child. "Thank you, God!" He could not ask for more.

Nuria spent all the afternoon applying cool cloths to Juliana's fevered brow, while Diego and Isabel accompanied Lafitte to the Temple. Four men rowed them through a labyrinth of foul-smelling swamps, where they saw dozens of alligators and drowsy water snakes sunning themselves on the banks. With the heat, Isabel's hair went in every direction, kinky and thick as mattress stuffing. The channels all looked the same; the land was flat, with not even a hillock to serve as reference in the high grass. The trees sank roots into the water and had wigs of moss hanging from their branches. The pirates knew every turn, every tree, every rock in that nightmarish landscape, and rowed without a moment's hesitation. When they reached the Temple, they saw the barges the pirates used to transport merchandise, along with the pirogues and rowboats of clients, although most had come by land on horseback or in shiny carriages. The cream of society had arranged to meet there, from aristocrats to dusky-skinned courtesans. The slaves had set up tents so their masters could rest and eat and drink while the ladies wandered through the bazaar examining the merchandise. The pirates called out their wares: China silk, Peruvian silver pitchers, Viennese furniture, jewels from every part of the world, sweets, articles for the toilette—that fair had everything, and bargaining was part of the entertainment. Pierre Lafitte was already there, holding a teardrop lamp in his hand and proclaiming at the top of his lungs that all prices were reduced:

"Take it away, messieurs, mesdames, you won't have another opportunity like this." With the arrival of Jean and his companions, murmurs of curiosity spread through the crowd. Several women came up to the attractive privateer, mysterious beneath their gay parasols, among them the wife of the governor. The caballeros focused their attention on Isabel, amused by her wild mane, reminiscent of the Spanish moss on the trees. Among the whites there were two men for every woman, and any new face was welcome, even one as unusual as Isabel's. Jean made the introductions, without a word about how he had obtained these new "friends," and immediately set off to look for the things Juliana had listed, even though he knew that no gift could console her for the blow she had received when he broke the news about Catherine so brutally. He'd had no other choice; he had to nip that mutual attraction in the bud before it destroyed both of them.

On Barataria, Juliana lay on her bed, sunk in a morass of humiliation and wild love. Lafitte had wakened a diabolical flame in her, and now she had to fight with all her will against the temptation to woo him away from Catherine Villars. The only solution that occurred to her was to enter the Convent of the Ursulines and end her days tending smallpox patients in New Orleans; at least that way she could breathe the same air her man breathed. She could never face anyone again. She was confused, embarrassed, restless, as if a million ants were crawling under her skin; she sat down, she paced, she lay on the bed, she twisted and turned beneath the sheets. She thought of the baby, little Pierre, and wept some more. "There's nothing so bad it lasts a hundred years, my child; this madness will have to pass. No one in her right mind falls in love with a pirate," Nuria consoled her. Madame Odilia arrived to ask about the señorita, with a tray of sherry and cookies. Juliana welcomed this as her one opportunity to get details, and so, swallowing her pride and her tears, she asked her first question.

"Can you tell me, madame, is Catherine a slave?"

"My daughter is free, as I am. My mother was a queen in Senegal, and there I would have been a queen also. My father, and the father of my children, were white, owners of sugar plantations in Santo Domingo. We had to escape during the revolt of the slaves," Madame Odilia replied proudly.

"I understand that whites cannot marry people of color," Juliana insisted.

"White men marry white women, but we are their real wives. We do not need the blessing of a priest; love is enough. Jean and Catherine love one another."

Juliana burst into tears again. Nuria pinched her to signal that she should control herself, but that only added to the girl's misery. She asked Madame Odilia if she could see Catherine, thinking that if she did, she would have reason to resist the assault of love.

"That is not possible. Drink your sherry, señorita, it will do you good." And with that she turned and left.

Juliana, burning with thirst, drank down the sherry in four gulps. Moments later she fell onto the bed and slept thirty-six hours without moving. The drugged wine did not cure her passion, but as Madame Odilia had expected, it gave her courage to face the future. She awoke with aching bones, but her mind was clear, and she was resolved to renounce Lafitte.

The privateer had similarly decided to tear Juliana from his heart, and to look for somewhere other than his home for the sisters to stay, somewhere her nearness could not torment him. Juliana avoided him; she did not come to meals but he could sense her through the walls. He thought he saw her silhouette in a corridor, heard her voice on the terrace, smelled her scent, but it was only a shadow, a bird, an aroma on the sea breeze. Like a caged animal, his senses were always raw, seeking her. The Convent of the Ursulines, which Diego had suggested, was a bad idea. It would be the same as condemning her to prison. He knew several Creole women in New Orleans who could put her up, but there was always the danger that her situation as a hostage would come out. If that reached the ears of the American authorities, he would be in serious trouble. He could bribe a judge, but not the governor; a slip on his part and there would be a price on his head again. He contemplated the possibility of forgetting the ransom and shipping his captives to California immediately; that would get him out of the mess he was in, but to do that he needed his brother Pierre's consent, as well as that of other captains and all the pirates; that was the drawback of a democracy. He thought of Juliana, comparing her to the sweet and submissive Catherine, the girl who had been his wife since she was fourteen, and now was the mother of his son. Catherine deserved his unconditional love. He missed her. Only their prolonged separation could explain his enchantment with Juliana; if he were sleeping in his wife's arms this would never have happened. After the birth of the boy, Catherine had wasted away. Madame Odilia had left her in the care of some African healers in New Orleans. Lafitte had not opposed it because her physicians had given her up for lost. A week after the birth, when Catherine was burning with fever, Madame Odilia insisted that her daughter was under the spell of the evil eye cast by a jealous rival, and that the only remedy was magic. Madame and Jean had taken Catherine, who was not strong enough to stand, to consult Marie Laveau, a high priestess of voodoo. They traveled deep into the woods, far from the sugar plantations of the whites, threading between small islands and through swamps, to the place where drums conjured up the spirits. By the light of bonfires and torches, officiants danced wearing animal and demon masks, their bodies painted with the blood of roosters. The powerful drums throbbed, stirring the forest and heating the blood of the slaves. A prodigious energy connected humans with the gods and with nature; the participants fused into a single being; no one escaped the bewitchment. In the center of a circle, upon a box containing a sacred serpent, danced Marie Laveau, proud, beautiful, covered with sweat, nearly naked and nine months pregnant, about to give birth. When she fell into a trance her limbs jerked uncontrollably, she twisted, her belly swinging from side to side, and she uttered a stream of words in languages no one remembered. The chant rose and fell like gigantic waves, while vessels containing the blood of sacrificed animals passed from hand to hand, so everyone could drink. The drums picked up tempo; men and women, convulsing, fell to the ground transformed into animals; they ate grass, they bit and clawed, and some fell unconscious, while others ran off in pairs toward the forest. Madame Odilia explained that in the voodoo religion, which came to the New World in the heart of slaves from Dahomey and Yoruba, there were three connected zones: the living, the dead, and the unborn. The ceremonies honored the ancestors, summoned the gods, cried out for freedom. Priestesses like Marie Laveau cast spells, stuck pins in dolls to bring on sickness, and used *gris-gris,* magic powders, to cure many ills. But nothing worked with Catherine.

Even though he was a prisoner and Lafitte's rival for Juliana, Diego could not help but admire the man. As a privateer he was unscrupulous and without mercy, but when he posed as a caballero no one could surpass him in good manners, culture, and charm. That double personality fascinated Diego; it echoed his own relationship with Zorro. And besides, Lafitte was one of the finest swordsmen he had ever known. Only Manuel Escalante was on the same level. Diego felt honored when his captor invited him to practice with him. In recent weeks the young man had seen democracy in action, something that until then had been only an abstract concept. In the United States, democracy was controlled by white men; on Barataria it worked for everyone—except women, of course. Lafitte's peculiar ideas seemed worthy of consideration. He maintained that the powerful invented laws to preserve their privileges and to control the poor and discontented; therefore it would be stupid to obey them. For example, taxes, which in the end the poor paid while the rich found ways to avoid it. He believed that no one, least of all the government, could claim a slice of what was his. Diego pointed out certain contradictions to him. Lafitte punished theft among his men with a lashing, but his financial empire rested on piracy, a higher form of theft. The privateer replied that he never took from the poor, only the powerful. To strip the imperial ships of what they had stolen by blood and whip in the colonies was not a sin but a virtue. He had appropriated the weapons that Captain Santiago de León was carrying to royalist troops in Mexico in order to sell them at a reasonable price to the insurgents of the same country.

Lafitte took Diego to New Orleans, a city made to the privateer's measure, proud of its decadent, adventurous, pleasure-loving, capricious, and tempestuous character. It had survived wars with the English and the Indians, hurricanes, floods, fires, and epidemics, but nothing could squelch its courtly arrogance. It was one of the principal ports of the United States, through which tobacco, indigo, and sugar were exported and every manner of merchandise imported. The cosmopolitan population coexisted with no concern for the heat, mosquitoes, swamps, or especially the law. Music, alcohol, brothels, gambling houses . . . there was a little of everything in those streets where life began with the setting sun. Diego found a bench in the Plaza de Armas where he could observe the crowd: blacks with baskets of oranges and bananas, women telling fortunes and selling voodoo fetishes, puppet shows, dancers, musicians. Candy vendors wearing turbans and blue aprons carried trays of ginger, honey, and nut sweets. At food stands one could buy beer, fresh oysters, and plates of shrimp. There was always some drunk raising a ruckus, side by side with well-dressed caballeros, plantation owners, merchants, and officials. Nuns and priests crossed paths with prostitutes, soldiers, bandits, and slaves. The celebrated quadroons strolled about the plaza, receiving compliments from the caballeros and hostile glances from their rivals. They did not wear jewels or hats—those adornments had been forbidden to satisfy the white women who could not compete with them—but they had no need of them. They had the reputation of being the most beautiful women in the world: golden skin, fine features, large liquid eyes, wavy hair. They were always accompanied by mothers or chaperones, who never took their eyes off them. Catherine Villars was one of these Creole beauties. Lafitte met her at one of the balls the mothers offered to present their daughters to wealthy men, another of the many ways to get around absurd laws, as the corsair explained to Diego. There were few white women and many women of color; it did not take a mathematician to see the solution to the dilemma. However, mixed marriages were forbidden by law. In that way the social order was preserved, the power of the whites guaranteed, and people of color kept subjugated, none of which prevented whites from having Creole concubines. The quadroons found a convenient solution for everyone. They trained their daughters in domestic skills and arts of seduction that no white woman even suspected existed, to create the rare combination of mistress of the house and courtesan. The mothers dressed their daughters opulently but also taught them to make their gowns. They were elegant and hardworking. The mothers used the balls, which only wealthy white men attended, to place their daughters with a man capable of providing well for them. To maintain one of those beautiful girls was considered a mark of distinction for a caballero; celibacy and abstinence were not virtues except among the Puritans, but there were few of those in New Orleans. The quadroons lived in modest houses, but in comfort and style; they had slaves, educated their children in the best schools, and dressed like queens in private, although they were discreet in public. Those arrangements were carried out in accord with unspoken rules, with decorum and etiquette.

"To sum it up, mothers offer their daughters to men," Diego protested, scandalized.

"Is that not always so? Marriage is an arrangement by which a woman lends her services and gives sons to the man who supports her. Here a white woman has less freedom to choose than a Creole," Lafitte replied.

"But the Creole loses her protection when her lover decides to marry or replace her with another concubine."

"The man leaves her with a house and a pension, and also pays the expenses of his children. The woman sometimes forms another family with a Creole man. Many of those Creoles, children of other quadroons, are professionals educated in France."

"And you, Captain Lafitte, would you have two families?" Diego asked, thinking of Juliana and Catherine.

"Life is complicated—anything can happen," the pirate rejoined.

Lafitte took Diego to the best restaurants, the theater, the opera, and introduced him among his acquaintances as his "friend from California." Most were people of color: artisans, merchants, artists, and professionals. He knew a few Americans, who lived apart from the Creole and French population, separated by an imaginary line that divided the city. Lafitte preferred not to cross that boundary, because on the other side there was a moralistic atmosphere that did not sit well with him. He took Diego to several gaming houses, as the latter had requested. It seemed suspicious to him that the youth had such certainty about winning, and he warned him to be careful; in New Orleans cheating was punished with a knife between the ribs.

Diego paid no attention to Lafitte's counsel; the bad feeling he had had for several days had only grown worse. He needed money. He could not hear Bernardo with the usual clarity, but he felt his milk brother was calling him. He had to go back to California, not only to save Juliana from falling into Lafitte's hands, but also because he was sure that something had happened there that required his presence. Using the medallion as his initial capital, he gambled in several different houses so as not to raise suspicions with his exceptional winnings. It was very easy for him, trained in tricks of illusion, to replace one card for another, or to make one disappear. In addition, he had a good memory and a talent for numbers; minutes into a game, he could guess his opponents' cards. As a result, he did not lose the medallion but was filling his money pouch; at that rate he would soon have the eight thousand American dollars of the ransom. He knew how to pace his game. He began to lose, to give the other players confidence, then set a time to end the game and began winning. He never went too far. As soon as other players got uneasy, he went on to the next place. One day, however, his luck was so good that he didn't want to quit, and he continued betting. His fellow players had drunk a lot and could barely focus on the cards, but they were still sharp enough to realize that Diego had to be cheating. The game erupted into a squabble that ended in the street, after Diego was pushed and shoved outside with the justifiable intention of beating him up. Diego could barely make himself heard above the shouting, but he challenged his attackers with an original proposition. "One moment, señores! I am prepared to return his money, which I have won honestly, to the man who can split open that door by butting it with his head," he announced, pointing to the thick wood, metal-studded door of the Presbytery, a colonial building that stood beside the cathedral.

That idea immediately captured the drunks' attention. They were discussing the terms of the competition when a sergeant appeared and instead of breaking up the wrangle stood aside to watch the action. Asked to act as judge, he happily accepted. Musicians came out of several locales and began playing lively tunes; in a few minutes the plaza was filled with curious onlookers. It was beginning to get dark, and the sergeant lighted several lamps. Other men who were just passing by and wanted to participate in this new sport gathered around the card players; the idea of splitting open a door with your cranium seemed highly entertaining. Diego decided that the hardheads should pay five dollars each to enter. The sergeant collected forty-five dollars from the contestants in a flash and then made them get in line. The musicians improvised a drum roll, and the first subject rushed toward the door of the Presbytery with a sash wrapped around his head. The impact cold-cocked him. A burst of applause, whistles, and laughter greeted his performance. Two beautiful Creoles ran up to comfort the fallen man with a glass of barley water, while the second seized his opportunity to crack his head open, with no better results than the first. Some participants repented at the last moment but did not get their five dollars back. In the end, no one was able to put even a crack in the door, and

Diego was left with the money he had won at the gaming table, plus thirty-five dollars from the contest. The sergeant received ten for his trouble, and everyone was happy.

The slaves came to Lafitte's property by night. The traders beached their boats silently and unloaded, then locked the Blacks in a wood-shed: five young men and two older ones, as well as two young girls and a woman with a six-year-old child clinging to her legs and one in her arms. Isabel had gone outside to get a breath of air on the ter-race, and in the light of torches saw silhouettes moving through the night. Unable to contain her curiosity, she walked toward the line of pathetic humans in rags. The girls were crying but the mother walked in silence, her eyes straight ahead, like a zombie; all of them dragged their feet, bone-weary and hungry. They were guarded by several pirates under the command of Pierre Lafitte, who left the "merchandise" in the shed and then went to report to his brother Jean, while Isabel ran to tell Diego, Juliana, and Nuria what she had seen. Diego had seen posters in the town, so he knew that a slave auction was scheduled at the Temple within a couple of days.

On Barataria the friends had more than enough time to learn about slavery. Bringing slaves from Africa was illegal, but neverthe-less they were sold and "raised" in America. Diego's first impulse was to try to set them free, but the girls pointed out that even if they could get into the shed, break the chains, and convince the Blacks to run, they had nowhere to go. They would be hunted down with dogs. Their one hope would be to get to Canada, but they could never do it alone. Diego decided to at least see for himself the con-ditions in which the prisoners were held. Without saying what he meant to do, he told the girls he would be back, put on his Zorro disguise, and, taking advantage of the darkness, went out. The Lafitte brothers were on the terrace. Pierre had a drink in his hand and Jean was smoking, but Diego could not get close enough to hear them without running the risk of being discovered, so he continued on to the shed. A single torch illuminated a pirate standing guard with his musket over his shoulder. Zorro approached with the idea of taking him by surprise, but he was the one surprised when another man suddenly spoke at his shoulder.

"Good evening, boss," he said.

Diego half turned to face him, ready to fight, but the man was relaxed and friendly. He realized that in the shadow the man had taken him for Jean Lafitte, who always dressed in black. The first pirate came over, too.

"We fed them, and they're resting, boss. Tomorrow we will clean them up and get them clothes. They're in good shape, except for the baby. It has a fever, and I don't think it will last long."

"Open the door," said Diego in French, imitating the corsair's tone. "I want to see them."

He kept his face in the shadow as they pulled back the bolt on the door, an unnecessary precaution because the pirates suspected nothing. He ordered them to wait outside, and went in. A lantern hanging in one corner shed a faint light, just enough to allow him to see each of the faces staring at him with terror. Everyone except the child and the baby wore iron rings around the neck attached to chains that fastened to posts. Diego went toward them making calming gestures, but when the slaves saw his mask they believed he was a demon, and shrank back as far as their chains permitted. It was futile to try to communicate with them. He realized they had just arrived from Africa; this was "fresh merchandise," as the traders called them, and they had not had time to learn their captors' language. Possibly they had been taken to Cuba, where the Lafitte brothers had bought them to resell in New Orleans. They had survived the sea voyage in horrible conditions and suffered mistreatment ashore. Were they from the same village? the same family? In the sale they would be separated and never see one another again. Their suffering had broken their spirit; they seemed on the verge of madness. Diego left them with unbearable sorrow in his heart. Once before, in California, he had felt that same crushing weight in his chest, when he and Bernardo witnessed soldiers attacking an Indian village. He recalled the feeling of impotence he had felt then, identical to what was oppressing him at this moment.

He returned to Lafitte's house, changed clothes, and went to the de Romeu girls and Nuria to tell them what he had seen. He was desperate.

"How much do slaves cost, Diego?" Juliana asked.

"I don't know exactly, but I have seen the lists of sales in New Orleans, and as an estimate, I would say that the Lafittes will get a thousand dollars for each young man, eight hundred for the other two, six hundred for each of the girls, and a thousand, more or less, for the mother and her children. I don't know if they can sell the children separately, since they are less than seven years old."

"How much would that be altogether?"

"Let's say about eighty-eight hundred."

"That is more or less what they want for our ransom."

"I don't see the connection," said Diego.

"We have money. Isabel, Nuria, and I have decided to use it to buy those slaves," said Juliana.

"You have money?" Diego asked, surprised.

"The precious stones, don't you remember?"

"I thought the pirates had taken them!"

Juliana and Isabel explained how they had saved their modest fortune. While they were being taken to the corsairs' ship, Nuria had a brilliant idea for hiding the stones. She knew that if the pirates suspected they had them, they would lose them forever, so they had swallowed them, one by one, with sips of wine. Sooner than they expected, the diamonds, rubies, and emeralds were eliminated from their digestive systems; all they had to do was inspect their chamber pots and recover them. It was not a pleasant procedure, but it had worked, and now the stones—carefully cleaned—were again sewed into their petticoats."

"But with that much you can buy your ransom!" Diego exclaimed.

"We know, but we would rather set the slaves free. Even if your father's money never arrives, we know that you can win it with your 'skill' at cards," Isabel replied.

Jean Lafitte was sitting on the terrace before a cup of coffee and a plate of *beignets*, entering figures in his account book, when Juliana presented herself and set a handkerchief tied by its four corners upon the table. The corsair looked up, and once again his heart turned over at the sight of that young woman who had been in his dreams every night. He untied the packet and could not hold back a grunt of surprise.

"How much do you think these are worth?" she asked, blushing, and proceeded to propose the business deal she had in mind.

The corsair's first surprise was that the girls had been able to hide the stones; the second, that they wanted to buy the slaves instead of their own freedom. What would Pierre and the other captains say to all this? The one thing he wanted was to erase the bad impression that piracy, and now the slaves, had made on Juliana. For the first time he felt unworthy, ashamed of his past. He had no plan to win this girl's love, because he was not free to offer his, but he at least needed her respect. He didn't care a fig about the money; he could get that back, and besides, he had more than enough to seal the mouths of his colleagues.

"These are very valuable, Juliana. There is enough here to buy the slaves, pay for your ransom and that of your friends, and pay your passage to California as well. There is also enough for your and your sister's dowries," he said.

Juliana had never imagined that those colored pebbles would do so much. She divided them into two piles, one big and another smaller, wrapped the former in the handkerchief, put it into the low neck of her dress, and left the rest on the table. She started to leave but Jean, agitated, stood and took her arm.

"What will you do with the slaves?"

"Take off their chains, first of all. Then I will see how we can help them."

"All right. You are free, Juliana. I will find a way for you to leave as soon as possible. Forgive me for all the unpleasantness I have caused you. You cannot know how much I wish that we had met under different circumstances. Please, accept these as my gift," said the pirate, and handed her the stones she had left on the table.

It had required all Juliana's strength to confront the man, and now this gesture completely disarmed her. She was not sure what it meant, but her instinct told her that the emotion that had undone her was fully returned by Lafitte: the gift was his declaration of love. The corsair saw her waver, and without thinking took her in his arms and kissed her. It was Juliana's first kiss, and surely the longest and most intense she would receive in her lifetime. In any case, it was the most memorable, as the first always is. The pirate's nearness, his arms around her, his breath, his warmth, his manly scent, his tongue in her mouth, stirred her to her bones. She had anticipated this moment after reading hundreds of romantic novels, with years of imagining the gallant predestined for her. She desired Lafitte with a passion she had never known, but also with an ancient and absolute certainty. She would never love another; this forbidden obsession would be the only love she would have in this world. She clung to him, both hands grasping his shirt, and returned the kiss with equal intensity, as her heart shattered inside her because she knew that his caress was a farewell. When at last they broke apart, she leaned her head on the pirate's chest, dizzy, trying to catch her breath and calm her heart, as he repeated her name—Juliana, Juliana—in a long murmur.

"I must go," she said, pushing away.

"I love you with all my soul, Juliana, but I love Catherine, too. I will never abandon her. Can you possibly understand?"

"Yes, Jean. My misfortune is to have fallen in love with you and to know that we can never be together. But I love you even more for your loyalty to Catherine. May God bless her, and may she soon recover and the two of you be happy. . . ."

Jean Lafitte tried to kiss her again, but she turned and ran away.

Absorbed as they were, neither of them saw Madame Odilia, who had witnessed the scene from a short distance away.

Juliana had no doubt that her life was over. It was not worth the effort to live in this world without Jean. She would rather die, like the heroines in tragic novels, but she had no idea how to contract tuberculosis or any other refined illness; to die of typhus seemed somehow undignified. She eliminated doing away with herself; no matter how deeply she was suffering, she could not condemn herself to hell. Not even Lafitte was worth that sacrifice. Besides, if she committed suicide, Isabel and Nuria would never forgive her. Entering a convent loomed as her only option, however unalluring the thought of wearing a habit in the New Orleans heat might be. She imagined what her father—who with God's favor had always been an atheist—would say if he knew what she was thinking. Tomás de Romeu would rather have seen her married to a pirate than become a nun. Her best choice would be to leave as soon as they could get a passage and end her days caring for Indians under the directions of Padre Mendoza, who according to Diego was a good man. She would treasure the clear and pure memory of that kiss and of Jean Lafitte's image: impassioned face, jet-black eyes, dark hair combed back from his face, gold chain against his chest at the open collar of his black silk shirt, strong hands embracing her. She did not have the comfort of tears. She was cried out; over the last few days she had spent her complete reserve of tears and believed she would never weep again.

She was thinking these things, staring through the window at the beach and silently suffering the pain of her broken heart, when she felt someone behind her. It was Madame Odilia, more spectacular than ever, all in white linen, with a turban of the same color, several amber necklaces, bracelets on her wrists, and gold rings in her ears. A queen of Senegal, like her mother.

"You have fallen in love with Jean," she said in a neutral, but for the first time personal, tone.

"Have no fear, madame. I would never stand between your daughter and son-in-law. I will go away, and he will forget me," Juliana replied.

"Why did you buy the slaves?"

"To set them free. Can you help them? I have heard that the Quakers protect slaves and take them to Canada, but I do not know how to contact them."

"There are many free Negroes in New Orleans. They can find work and live here; I will find them a place," said the queen. She stood without speaking for a long time, fingering the amber beads of her necklaces, her hazel eyes studying Juliana, calculating. Finally her hard gaze seemed to soften slightly.

"Do you want to see Catherine?" she asked point-blank.

"Oh, yes, madame. And I would also like to see the child. I want to carry an image of them with me; that way it will be easier for me to visualize Jean's happiness when I am in California."

Madame Odilia led Juliana to another wing of the house, as clean and well decorated as the rest, where she had set up a nursery for her grandson. It looked like the bedchamber of a small European prince, except for the voodoo fetishes that protected him from the evil eye. Pierre was sleeping in a brass cradle with lace ruffles; in the room with him were his wet nurse, a young black woman with large breasts and languid eyes, and a very young girl in charge of keeping the fans moving. The grandmother pulled back the mosquito netting, and Juliana leaned in to see the baby of the man she adored. She found him precious. She had not seen many infants with whom to compare him, but she would have sworn that there was no child more beautiful in all the world. Clad only in a diaper, he lay on his back, arms and legs outspread, deep in sleep. With a nod, Madame Odilia authorized Juliana to pick him up. She held him in her arms, and as she nuzzled his nearly bald head, saw his gummy smile, and touched fingers plump as little worms, the enormous black stone in her breast seemed to grow smaller, crumble, disappear. She kissed him all over—the bare feet, the belly with the protruding navel, the neck wet with sweat—and then a trickle of warm tears bathed her face and fell onto the baby. She was not weeping out of jealousy for something she would never have, but from a well of tenderness. The grandmother put Pierre back in the cradle and without a word motioned for Juliana to follow her.

They crossed through the garden of orange trees and oleanders, away from the house to the beach, where a rowboat was waiting to take them to New Orleans. There they hurried through the streets of the city center and cut through the cemetery. Floods prevented burial beneath the ground, so the cemetery was a small city of mausoleums, some decorated with marble statues, others with wrought iron, cupolas, and bell towers. They walked a little farther to a street with tall, narrow houses, all identical, with a door in the center and a window on either side. These were called shotgun houses, because a gun fired at the front door passed through the house and out the back door without encountering any walls. Madame Odilia went in without knocking. An indescribable chaos of small children of various ages met their eyes, cared for by two women dressed in calico aprons. The house was crammed with fetishes, bottles of potions, dried herbs hanging from the ceiling, wooden statues studded with nails, masks, and countless articles of the voodoo religion. There was a sweet, clinging odor like molasses. Madame Odilia greeted the women and went right on to one of the small rooms. Juliana followed and found herself facing a dark mulatto woman with long bones and the yellow eyes of a panther, her skin shiny with sweat, her hair pulled into fifty braids decorated with ribbons and colored beads, nursing a newborn child. This was the famous Marie Laveau, the pythoness who on Sunday danced with the slaves in Congo Square and in the sacred ceremonies in the forest fell into a trance and called forth the gods.

"I brought her to you for you to tell me if this is the one," said Madame Odilia.

Marie Laveau stood and walked over to Juliana, the babe still at her breast. She was determined to have a child every year as long as her youth lasted, and she now had five. She put three fingers on Juliana's forehead and looked deep into her eyes. Juliana felt a formidable energy, a surge that shook her from head to foot. A minute went by.

"She is the one," said Marie Laveau.

"But she is white," objected Madame Odilia.

"I tell you she is the one," the priestess repeated, and with that the interview was ended.

The queen of Senegal took Juliana back to the dock—once again through the cemetery and the Plaza de Armas—where they rejoined the boatman, who had waited patiently, smoking his tobacco. He took a different route toward the bayou. Soon they were in the labyrinth of the swamp, with its channels, ponds, lakes, and islets. The absolute solitude of the countryside, the miasma rising from the mud, the sudden slashings of caimans, the cries of the birds, all contributed to an air of mystery and danger. Juliana remembered that she had not told anyone that she was leaving. Her sister and Nuria must be looking for her by now. It occurred to her that this woman might have evil intentions—after all, she was Catherine's mother—but she immediately discarded that thought. The journey seemed very long to her, and the heat began to make her sleepy; she was thirsty, it was late afternoon, and the air was filled with mosquitoes. She did not dare ask where they were going. After a long time, as it began to grow dark, they pulled up on a bank. The boatman stayed with the boat, and Madame Odilia lighted a lantern, took Juliana's hand, and led her through tall grass where not even a track marked a direction. "Take care not to step on a snake," was all she said. They walked a long way, and finally the queen found what she was looking for: a small clearing identifiable by two tall trees streaming moss and marked with crosses. These were voodoo, not Christian, crosses that symbolized the intersection of two worlds, that of the living and that of the dead. Several masks and carved wood figures of African gods guarded the site. In the light of the lantern and the moon, the scene was terrifying.

"There lies my daughter," said Madame Odilia, pointing to the ground.

Catherine Villars had died of puerperal fever five weeks before. Nothing had been able to save her—the resources of medical science, Christian prayers, or the spells and herbs of African magic. Her mother and other women had wrapped her body, consumed by infection and hemorrhaging, and transported it to this sacred place in the swamp, where the dead girl would be temporarily buried until she was able to indicate the person destined to replace her. Catherine could not allow her son to fall into the hands of just any woman Jean Lafitte might choose, the queen of Senegal explained. Her own duty as Catherine's mother was to help her in that task, and that was why she had concealed her death. Catherine was now in an intermediate region; she came and went between two worlds. Had Juliana not heard her footsteps in Lafitte's house? Had she not seen her standing beside her bed at night? That odor of orange blossoms that floated on the island air was Catherine's scent, who in her spiritual form was watching over little Pierre and searching for the right stepmother. Madame Odilia was surprised that Catherine had gone to the other side of the world to find Juliana, and she did not like the idea that she had chosen a white woman, but who was she to oppose her? From the region of the spirits, Catherine, better than anyone, could determine what was best, Marie Laveau had assured her. "When the right woman appears, I will know how to recognize her," the priestess had promised. Madame Odilia had her first suspicion that it might be Juliana when she saw that she loved Jean Lafitte but was ready to give him up out of respect for Catherine. The second indication came when the girl felt pity for the fate of the slaves. Now she was satisfied, Madame Odilia said; her poor daughter could rest easy in heaven and be buried in the cemetery where the floodwaters would not carry her body out to sea.

Madame had to repeat several details, because Juliana could not get the story into her head. She could not believe that this woman had hidden the truth from Jean for five weeks. How would she explain that now? Madame Odilia said that there was no reason her son-in-law had to know the truth. The exact date didn't matter; she would tell him that Catherine had died the day before.

"But Jean will demand to see the body!" Juliana contended.

"That is not possible. Only we women may see the bodies of the dead. It is our mission to bring children into the world and to send the dead off to theirs. Jean will have to accept that. After Catherine's funeral, he will belong to you," the queen replied.

"Belong to m-me . . . ," Juliana stammered, confused.

"All that matters is my grandson Pierre. Lafitte is only the means Catherine used to lead you to her son. She and I will keep watch to see that you meet your obligation. To do that, you must stay close to the child's father and keep him happy and tranquil."

"Jean is not the kind of man who can be satisfied and tranquil; he is a corsair, an adventurer—"

"I will give you magic potions and secrets to keep him happy in bed, as I gave them to Catherine when she was twelve."

"I am not that kind of . . . ," Juliana defended herself, blushing.

"Have no worry, you will be, though never as skillful as Catherine. You are a little old to learn, and you have many silly ideas in your head, but Jean will not notice the difference. Men are stupid; desire blinds them, they know very little about pleasure."

"I cannot use courtesans' tricks or magic potions, madame!"

"Do you love Jean or not, girl?"

"Yes," Juliana admitted.

"Then you will have to work at it. Leave everything in my hands. You will make him happy, and it is possible that you will be as well, but I warn you that you must think of Pierre as your own son, or you will have to deal with me. Is that clear?"

I do not, dear readers, know how to convey the true magnitude of the unhappy Diego de la Vega's reaction when he learned what had happened. The next boat to Cuba sailed from New Orleans in two days; he had bought the passages and had everything ready to fly out of Jean Lafitte's hunting preserve, dragging Juliana with him. He was going to save his beloved after all. His soul had been reunited with his body, but then the whole apple cart turned over with the news that his rival was a widower. Diego threw himself at Juliana's feet to convince her of the stupidity of what she was about to do. Well, that is a manner of speaking. He was on his feet, pacing with long strides, gesticulating, pulling his hair, yelling, while she watched him with a silly smile on her siren's face. How can you convince a woman in love! Diego believed that in California, far from her pirate, the girl would come to her senses, and he would gain back the ground he had lost. Juliana would have to be a true simpleton to keep loving a man who trafficked in slaves. He was confident that in the end she would learn to appreciate a man like himself, as handsome and brave as Lafitte but much younger, honest, with a good heart and pure intentions, and he could offer her a very comfortable life without murdering innocents to steal their belongings. Diego was nearly perfect, and he adored her. Good God! What more could Juliana want? Nothing was enough for her. She was a bottomless sack. A few weeks in the heat of Barataria had been enough to wipe out at one stroke the advances he had achieved over five years of courting her. A wiser man than he would have come to realize that his darling had a fickle heart, but not Diego. Vanity clouded his eyes, as tends to be the case with ladies' men like him.

Isabel observed the events with awe. In the last forty-eight hours so many things had happened that she was incapable of remembering them in order. Let us say that it was more or less like this: after removing the chains from the slaves, feeding them, providing clothing, and explaining with great difficulty that they were free, they had witnessed a heartrending scene when the baby that had been so ill on arrival died. It took three strong men to pull the lifeless body from its mother's arms, and there was no way to calm her; they still could hear her howls, chorused by the island dogs. The wretched slaves did not understand what difference it made whether they were free or not if they had to stay in this detestable country. The only thing they wanted was to go back to Africa. How were they going to survive in such a hostile and barbaric land? The black man acting as interpreter tried to soothe them with the promise that they would not lack for a livelihood, that more pirates were always needed on the island, that with a little luck the girls would find a husband and the poor mother could work for a family that would teach her to cook, and she would not have to be separated from her surviving child. It was useless; the miserable group repeated like a litany that they wanted to be sent back to Africa.

Juliana returned from her long excursion with Madame Odilia transformed by happiness and telling a story that would curl the hair of any rational being. She made Diego, Isabel, and Nuria swear that they would not repeat a single word and then stunned them with the news that Catherine Villars was not ill but instead a kind of zombie, and more important, she had chosen her, Juliana, to be the step-mother of the tiny Pierre. She would marry Jean Lafitte—except he didn't know that yet; she would tell him after Catherine's funeral. As a wedding gift she intended to ask him to give up the slave traffic forever, the one thing she could not tolerate; the other skullduggery was not as bad. She also confessed, a little shamefacedly, that Madame Odilia was going to teach her to make love the way the pirate liked. At that point, Diego lost control. Juliana was mad, who could doubt it? There was a fly that transmitted that illness, it must have bitten her. Did she think that he would leave her in the hands of that criminal? Hadn't he promised Don Tomás de Romeu, may he rest in peace, that he would bring her back safe and sound to California? He would keep his promise if he had to knock her in the head to get her there.

Jean Lafitte was suffering an assortment of emotions during that time. The kiss had left him addled. Giving up Juliana was the most difficult thing he had done in his life; he needed all his courage, which was more than a little, to conquer his dejection and frustration. He met with his brother and the other captains to give them their share from the sale of the slaves and the hostages' ransoms, which they in turn would divide fairly among the rest of the men. The money came from his own funds, was the only explanation he offered. The amazed captains pointed out that from a business point of view, that made no sense at all; why the devil did he transport slaves and hostages, with all the expense and bother, if he meant to let them go free? Pierre Lafitte waited until the others had left before expressing his opinion to Jean. He thought that his brother had lost the ability to conduct business; his brain had gone soft. Perhaps the time had come for him to step down.

"Fine, Pierre. We will put it to a vote among the men—that is the usual way. Do you want to take my place?" Jean challenged.

As if it were a small thing, a few hours later his mother-in-law came to give him the news that Catherine had died. No, he couldn't see her. The funeral would take place in two days in New Orleans, with the aid of the Creole community. There would be a brief Christian rite, to appease the priest, and then an African ceremony with feasting, music, and dancing, as was fitting. Madame Odilia was sad, but serene, and she had enough fortitude to console Lafitte when he burst out crying like a baby. He adored Catherine, she had been his companion, his only love, he sobbed. Madame Odilia gave him a drink of rum and a few pats on the back. She did not feel any greater than usual compassion for the widower, knowing that very soon he would forget Catherine in the arms of another. Out of decency, Jean Lafitte could not go running to ask Juliana to marry him—he would have to wait a prudent amount of time—but the idea had already taken shape in his mind and in his heart, though he had not dared put it in words. The loss of his wife was a terrible blow, but it offered him unexpected liberty. Even in her grave, his sweet Catherine was seeing to his most hidden desires. He was willing to mend his ways for Juliana's sake. The years were racing by, and he was tired of living like an outlaw, with a pistol at his waist and the possibility that at any moment there would be a price on his head. Over the years he had amassed a fortune; Juliana and he could take little Pierre to Texas, where bandits traditionally ended up, and he would devote himself to less dangerous, though naturally still illegal, activities. No trafficking in slaves, of course, since apparently that irritated Juliana's sensibility. Lafitte had never allowed a woman to stick her nose in his business, and his new love was not going to be the first, but neither would he ruin his marriage fighting over that matter. Yes, they would go to Texas, he had already decided. The West offered many possibilities for a man of flexible morals and adventurous spirit. He was prepared to give up piracy, although that did not mean he would turn into a respectable citizen. No need to go to extremes.

# PART FIVE

# Alta California, 1815

*D*iego, Isabel, and Nuria set sail on a schooner from the Port of New Orleans in the spring of 1815. Juliana stayed behind. I regret that it happened that way, because every good-hearted reader hopes for a romantic denouement that favors the hero. I realize that Juliana's decision is frustrating, but it could be no other way, since in her place most women would have done the same. To steer a sinner down a good path is an irresistible project, and Juliana set her goal with religious zeal. Isabel asked why she had never attempted to do that with Rafael Moncada, and Juliana explained that the task was not worth the effort, since Moncada was not a man of breathtaking vices, like Lafitte, only mean-spirited and petty ones. "And those, everyone knows, cannot be cured," the beauty added. In those days Zorro still was a long way from being bad enough for a woman to take the trouble to reform him.

We have come to the fifth and last part of this book. We shall soon be saying good-bye, dear readers, since the story ends when the hero returns to where he began, transformed by his adventures and by obstacles overcome. This is the norm in epic narratives from the Odyssey to fairy tales, and I shall not be the one to attempt innovation.

The tremendous fit Diego threw when he learned of Juliana's decision to remain behind with Lafitte in New Orleans had no effect at all; she brushed him away as she would a mosquito. Who was Diego to give her orders? They were not even related by blood, she declared. Besides, she was plenty old enough to know what was good for her. As a last try, Diego challenged the pirate to a duel to the death, "to defend the honor of Señorita de Romeu," as he said, but Lafitte informed him that that very morning they had been married in a Creole church in strictest privacy, their only witnesses his brother Pierre and Madame Odilia. They had done it that way to avoid the talk that would inevitably circulate among those who did not understand the urgency of love. There was nothing Diego could do, the marriage was legal. And so he lost his beloved forever and, a prisoner of immeasurable anguish, swore to remain celibate for the rest of his days. No one believed him. Isabel pointed out that Lafitte would not live forever, given his dangerous way of life, and that as soon as Juliana became a widow he could pursue her until he dropped, but that argument was little consolation to Diego.

Nuria and Isabel told Juliana good-bye with copious tears, despite Lafitte's promise that they would soon come to visit them in California. Nuria, who thought of the de Romeu girls as her own children, hesitated between staying with Juliana to protect her from voodoo, pirates, and other unpleasantness that destiny undoubtedly had in store for her and going on to California with Isabel, who even though she was several years younger, needed her less. Juliana resolved the dilemma by begging her to go; Isabel's reputation would be forever soiled if she traveled alone with Diego de la Vega. As a farewell gift, Lafitte gave the chaperone a gold chain and a length of the finest silk. Nuria chose black, for her mourning.

The schooner left port in the midst of a warm downpour, a daily occurrence during that season, and Juliana stood bathed in tears and drenched with rain, with little Pierre in her arms and escorted by her ineffable corsair and the queen of Senegal, now her instructress and guardian. Juliana was simply dressed, according to her husband's taste, and was so obviously happy that Diego burst into tears. Juliana had never seemed as beautiful as she was at the moment he was losing her. She and Lafitte made a splendid couple, he all in black, with a parrot on his shoulder, she in fine white dimity, both partly protected from the rain by umbrellas held by two African girls, once slaves and now free. Nuria locked herself in her cabin so no one would see her wildly sobbing, while Diego and Isabel, disconsolate, waved good-bye until the figures on the dock were out of sight. Diego was gulping tears for the reasons we know, and Isabel because she was being parted from her sister. Besides, it must be said, she had her own dreams in regard to Lafitte, who was the first man ever to call her beautiful. Life is like that, pure irony. Let us get back to our story.

The ship carried our characters to Cuba. The historic city of Havana, with its colonial houses and long seawall washed by a crystalline sea and the impossible light of the Caribbean, offered decadent pleasures that Diego did not take advantage of because he was too depressed, Nuria, because she felt too old, and Isabel, because she was not allowed. Under the watchful eye of the other two, the girl could not visit the casinos or join in the parades of merry street musicians. Poor and rich, black and white, ate in the taverns and street cafés, drank quantities of rum, and danced till dawn. Given the opportunity, Isabel would have renounced her Spanish virtue, which had done her very little good till then, to investigate Caribbean sensuality, which seemed much more interesting, but her wishes were left unsatisfied. Through the owner of the hotel they heard news of Santiago de León. The captain had managed to reach Cuba safely with the other survivors, and as soon as he recovered from sunstroke and fright he had sailed for England. He planned to collect his insurance and retire to a cottage in the country, where he would continue to draw fantasy maps for collectors of antiquities.

The three friends stayed in Havana several days, which Diego used to order two complete sets of attire for Zorro, on the model of Jean Lafitte. When he saw himself in the mirror of the tailor shop, Diego had to admit that his rival was unquestionably elegant. He looked at himself full-length and in profile; he put one hand on his hip and the other on the hilt of his weapon, lifted his chin, and smiled contentedly—he had perfect teeth and liked to display them. He thought he looked magnificent. For the first time he lamented the necessity for his dual personality; he would like to dress like this all the time. "Oh, well, one cannot have everything in life," he sighed. All he needed now was the mask to cover his ears and the false mustache to throw his enemies off the track and Zorro would be ready to appear wherever his sword was required. "By the way, handsome, you need a second sword," he told his image in the mirror. He would never part from his cherished Justine, but one sword was not enough. He had his new clothing sent to the hotel, and went to the port armorers' shops looking for a sword like the one Pelayo had given him. He found exactly what he wanted, and also bought a pair of Moorish daggers, slim and flexible but very strong. The money he had won dishonestly in New Orleans flew out of his hands, and a few days later, when they caught a ship for Portobelo, he was as poor as when he'd been kidnapped by Jean Lafitte.

For Diego, who had crossed the isthmus of Panama in the opposite direction, that part of the journey was not as interesting as it was for Nuria and Isabel, who had never seen poisonous toads, much less naked Indians. Horrified, Nuria fixed her eyes on the Chagres River, convinced that her worst fears about the savagery of the Americas were being confirmed. Isabel, on the other hand, took advantage of that display of nudity to try to satisfy an ancient curiosity. For years she had asked herself how men and women might be different. She was in for a disappointment, however, because that difference was small; it could be tucked comfortably into her reticule, as she commented to her chaperone. In any case, thanks to Nuria's rosaries, they escaped contracting malaria or being bitten by vipers and reached the port of Panama without difficulties. There they took a ship to Alta California.

The ship dropped anchor in the small harbor of San Pedro, near Los Angeles, and the travelers were transported to the beach in a dinghy. It was not easy to get Nuria down the rope ladder, but a sailor with goodwill and strong muscles took her by the waist, without asking her permission, threw her over his shoulder, and carried her down like a sack of sugar. As they neared the beach, they saw the figure of an Indian waving to them. Minutes later, Diego and Isabel began to shout with joy; it was Bernardo.

"How did that boy know that we were coming today?" Nuria asked, amazed.

"I told him," Diego replied, without explaining how he had done it.

Bernardo had been waiting on that spot for more than a week, after he'd had the clear revelation that his brother was about to arrive. He did not doubt the telepathic message, and had been watching the horizon with his infinite patience, certain that sooner or later a ship would appear. He did not know that Diego had anyone with him, but he had reasoned that he would have a lot of luggage, so he had taken the precaution of bringing several horses. He had changed so much that it was difficult for Nuria to recognize in this well-built Indian the quiet servant she had known in Barcelona. Bernardo was wearing nothing but linen pants held at the waist with a cowhide sash. He was deeply tanned, his skin nearly black; and he wore his black hair in long braids. He carried a knife in his sash and a musket strapped over his shoulder.

"How are my parents?" was Diego's first question. "And Light-in-the-Night and your son?"

Bernardo signed that he had bad news, and that they must go directly to the San Gabriel mission, where Padre Mendoza would tell them all about it. He himself had been living with the Indians for several months, and was not up-to-date on the details. They lashed part of the luggage onto one of the horses, buried the rest in the sand, and marked the site with rocks, to be recovered later, then swung up onto the remaining horses and set off for the mission. Diego realized that Bernardo was taking them on a detour, avoiding the Camino Real and the de la Vega hacienda. After riding for several leagues, they saw the grounds of the mission. Diego uttered a cry of surprise when he saw that the fields Padre Mendoza had planted with such dedication had been overtaken with weeds; half the roof tiles were missing on the main building, and the neophytes' cabins seemed abandoned. An air of desolation hung over what once had been a prosperous operation. At the sound of horses' hooves a few Indian women came outside with their little ones trailing behind, and a few moments later Padre Mendoza appeared in the courtyard. The missionary had failed a lot in those five years; he looked thin and fragile, and the few hairs on his head no longer hid the scar of the lopped-off ear. He knew that Bernardo was expecting his brother and had no doubt about his presentiment, so seeing Diego was no surprise. He opened his arms wide, and the young man leaped from his horse and ran to greet him. Diego, who now was half a head taller than the priest, had the sensation that he was embracing a pile of bones, and his heart shrank with this proof of the passage of time.

"This is Isabel, daughter of Don Tomás de Romeu—may God hold him in His right hand—and this lady is Nuria, her chaperone," Diego said as introduction.

"Welcome to the mission, daughters. I can imagine that the voyage has been difficult. You may wash and rest while Diego and I catch up. I will send for you when we are ready to eat," said Padre Mendoza.

The news was worse than Diego had imagined. His parents had been living apart for five years; the very same day that he left to study in Spain, Regina, too, went away, taking nothing but the clothes she had on. Since that time she had been living with White Owl's tribe, and no one had seen her in town or at the mission; it was said that she had renounced her ways as a Spanish lady and had turned back into the wild Indian she had been in her youth. Bernardo, who lived with the same tribe, confirmed the priest's words. Diego's mother was using her native name, Toypurnia, and was readying herself to someday take White Owl's place as healer and shaman. The two women's reputations as visionaries had spread beyond the mountains, and Indians from other tribes traveled from afar to consult them. In the meantime, Alejandro de la Vega forbade even the mention of his wife's name, but he never got used to her absence and had aged in his sorrow. To avoid having to explain to the petty white society of the colony, he had given up his post as mayor and devoted himself completely to the hacienda and his business interests, multiplying his fortune. All his work had been for naught, because a few months ago, just about the time when Diego met up with the Gypsies in Spain, Rafael Moncada had arrived in California as envoy plenipotentiary of King Ferdinand VII, with the official mission of writing a report on the political and economic state of the colony. His authority was superior to that of the governor and the military chief. Diego had no doubt that Moncada had obtained his post through the influence of his aunt, Eulalia de Callís, and that his only reason for leaving the Spanish court was his hope of winning Juliana. That was what he told Padre Mendoza.

"Moncada must have had a terrible shock when he learned that Señorita de Romeu wasn't here," said Diego.

"He anticipated that you were on your way here, so he stayed. In the meantime, he has not been wasting time; it is rumored that he is making a fortune," the missionary replied.

"That man despises me for many reasons, the first being that I helped Juliana escape his attentions," Diego explained.

"I understand better, now, Diego. Greed is not Moncada's sole motivation." Padre Mendoza sighed. "He also wants revenge on you."

Rafael Moncada's first official act in California had been to confiscate the de la Vega hacienda, after ordering the arrest of its owner, whom he accused of leading an insurrection to make California independent of the kingdom of Spain. There was no such movement, Padre Mendoza assured Diego—the idea had not as yet crossed the minds of the colonists, even though the germ of rebellion had exploded like gunpowder in some countries of South America, and was spreading to the rest of the continent. With the unfounded charge of treason, Alejandro de la Vega had been thrown into the dreaded El Diablo prison. Moncada settled in with his entourage at the hacienda, which was now his residence and troop headquarters. The missionary added that the man had done a great deal of harm in very little time. He, too, was on Moncada's list, because he defended the Indians and had dared to tell the envoy certain truths, but it had cost him dearly: the mission was in ruins.

Moncada cut off the traditional resources and in addition had taken his men; there were no hands to work the land, only women, children, and the aged. The Indian families were split apart, the people demoralized. There were rumors about a trade in pearls headed by Rafael Moncada, for which he needed the forced labor of the Indians. California pearls, more valuable than the gold and silver of other colonies, had poured into the coffers of Spain for two centuries, but a moment had come when they had been overharvested, the missionary explained. No one thought of pearls again for fifty years, which had given the oysters time to recover. The authorities, occupied with other matters and tangled in bureaucracy, lacked the initiative to revive the trade. It was assumed that the new banks of oysters were farther north, near Los Angeles, but no one had taken the trouble to confirm that until Moncada appeared with his maritime charts. Padre Mendoza believed that he intended to take the pearls without sending word back to Spain, though in principle they belonged to the crown. To get them, he needed Carlos Alcázar, the commander of El Diablo prison, who provided him with slaves for diving. Both of them were getting rich quickly and quietly. In the past the divers had been Yaqui Indians from Mexico, robust men who for generations had lived along the sea and could stay submerged for almost two minutes, but it would have attracted attention to bring them to Alta California. As an alternative, the partners were using the Indians of the region, who were not expert swimmers and would never have performed the task willingly. That was no problem for Moncada; he had them arrested on any excuse at all and worked them until their lungs burst. He got them drunk or beat them and soaked their clothing with alcohol, then dragged them before the judge, who cast a blind eye on the entire proceedings. The poor devils ended up in El Diablo despite the desperate objections of the missionary. Diego asked if that was where his father was, and Padre Mendoza confirmed that it was. Don Alejandro was ill and weak; he would not survive much longer in that place, he added. He was the oldest, and the only white, among the prisoners; all the others were Indians or mestizos. Whoever entered that hell did not come out alive; several had died in recent months. No one dared speak of what happened inside those walls, neither guards nor prisoners; the silence of the tomb enveloped El Diablo.

"I cannot even take spiritual consolation to those poor souls. I used to go rather often to say mass, but I had words with Carlos Alcázar, and he forbade me to come. A priest from Baja California will be coming soon to take my place."

"Is Carlos Alcázar the bully we were so afraid of when we were boys?" Diego asked.

"The same, my son. His character has gone from bad to worse; he is a despot and a coward. His cousin Lolita, on the other hand, is a saint. The girl used to go with me to the prison to take medicine, food, and blankets to the prisoners, but unfortunately she has no influence over Carlos."

"I remember Lolita. The Pulido family is noble and virtuous. Francisco, Lolita's brother, studied in Madrid. We corresponded a few times when I was in Barcelona," said Diego.

"Well, the fact is that Don Alejandro's situation is very grave. You are his only hope, you must do something quickly," concluded Father Mendoza.

For a long time Diego had been pacing around the room, trying to control his indignation. From his chair, Bernardo followed the conversation with his eyes fixed on his brother, sending him mental messages. Diego's first impulse had been to seek Moncada out and challenge him to a duel, but a look from Bernardo made him understand that these circumstances demanded more cleverness than valor; this was a mission for Zorro, and he would have to carry it out with a cool head. Diego pulled out a lace handkerchief, sighed, and wiped his forehead with an affected gesture.

"I will go to Monterey to speak with the governor. He is a friend of my father," he proposed.

"I already did that, Diego. When Don Alejandro was arrested, I spoke personally with the governor, but he told me that he had no authority over Moncada. And he didn't listen to me when I suggested he find out why so many prisoners die in El Diablo," the missionary added.

"Then I will have to go to Mexico to see the viceroy."

"But that will take months!" Padre Mendoza objected.

It was difficult for the priest to believe that the bold young boy, whom he had brought into the world with his own hands and had watched grow up, had turned out to be a dandy. Spain had softened his brain and his muscles; it was embarrassing. He had prayed that Diego would return in time to save his father, and the answer to his prayers was this fop with a lace handkerchief. He could barely hide his scorn.

Isabel and Nuria were advised that dinner was ready, and the four of them sat down at the table. An Indian woman brought a large clay bowl of maize soup and a few pieces of boiled beef as hard and tasteless as shoe leather. There was no bread, no wine, no vegetables, not even any coffee, the one vice Padre Mendoza allowed himself. They were eating in silence when they heard horses and voices in the courtyard, and moments later a group of uniformed men burst into the room, led by Rafael Moncada.

"Excellency! What a surprise," Diego exclaimed, not rising.

"I have just been informed of your arrival," Moncada replied, looking around for Juliana.

"We are here, as we promised in Barcelona, Señor Moncada. May we know how you escaped from the secret chamber?" Isabel asked sarcastically.

"Where is your sister?" Moncada interrupted.

"Oh, she is in New Orleans. I have the pleasure of informing you that Juliana is happily married."

"Married! That cannot be! To whom?" the dashed suitor cried.

"To a wealthy and handsome man of business who bewitched her at first sight," Isabel explained with the most innocent expression in the world.

Rafael Moncada pounded the table and clamped his lips

together to hold back a string of curses. He could not believe that Juliana had slipped out of his hands yet again. He had crossed half the world, left his post at court, and put his career on hold for her. He was so furious at that instant that he could have strangled her with his own hands. Diego took advantage of the pause to approach a fat and sweating sergeant who was looking at him with the eyes of a pet hound.

"García?" he asked.

"Don Diego de la Vega—you recognize me—what an honor!" the fat sergeant murmured with pleasure.

"Why would I not? The unmistakable García!" Diego exclaimed, embracing him.

That inappropriate demonstration of affection between Diego and his own sergeant briefly distracted Moncada.

"I would like to use this opportunity to inquire about my father, Excellency," said Diego.

"He is a traitor and will be punished as such," Moncada replied, spitting out each word.

"Traitor? No one can say that about Señor de la Vega, Excellency!" An anguished García stepped in. "You are new to this land, you do not know people. But I was born here and I can tell you that the de la Vega family is the most honorable and distinguished in all California."

"Silence, García! No one asked your opinion!" Moncada interrupted, shooting him an icy glance.

Immediately he barked an order, and the sweating sergeant had no choice but to salute, clicking his heels, and lead his men outside. At the door he hesitated and, turning toward Diego, made a gesture of ineffectiveness, which his old friend responded to with a wink of complicity.

"May I remind you that my father, Don Alejandro de la Vega, is a Spanish hidalgo, the hero of many battles in the service of the king. Only a Spanish tribunal is authorized to judge him."

"His case will be reviewed by the pertinent authorities in Mexico City. In the meantime, your father is well guarded in a place where he cannot continue to conspire against Spain."

"The trial will take years, and Don Alejandro is an old man," Padre Mendoza interceded. "He cannot stay in El Diablo."

"Before he violated the law, de la Vega must have thought about the fact that he was risking the loss of his liberty and his wealth. By his imprudent actions, the old man condemned his family to poverty," Moncada replied in an insulting tone.

Diego's right hand grasped his sword, but Bernardo caught his arm and held him back, to remind him of the need to be patient. Moncada suggested that Diego find a way to earn a living, now that he did not have his father's fortune, and with that turned and went out after his men. Padre Mendoza gave Diego a comradely pat on the back and repeated his offer of hospitality. Life was austere and difficult at the mission, he said, they lacked the comforts to which they were accustomed, but at least they would have a roof over their heads.

Isabel smiled. "Thank you, Padre. One day I will tell you all the things that have happened to us following the death of my poor father. You will learn that we walked across Spain, lived with Gypsies, and were kidnapped by pirates. More than once our lives were saved by a miracle. As for lack of comforts, I assure you, we are well used to that."

"And beginning tomorrow morning, Padre, I shall take charge of the kitchen, because you eat worse than if we were at war," Nuria added in a critical tone.

"The mission is very poor," Padre Mendoza apologized.

"With the same ingredients and a little more invention, we will eat like normal people," Nuria replied.

That night when everyone else was sleeping, Diego and Bernardo crept out of their rooms, took a pair of horses, and without stopping to saddle up, galloped off in the direction of the Indian caves where they had so often played in their childhood. They had decided that the first thing they should do would be to get Alejandro de la Vega out of prison and take him to a safe place where Moncada and Alcázar could not find him; then would come the difficult task of clearing his name of the charge of treason. This was the week of both of their birthdays: they had been born exactly twenty years ago. It seemed to Diego that this was a very important moment in their lives, and he wanted to celebrate it in some special way, so he had proposed to his milk brother that they go to the caves. It was also true that if the tunnel that joined them to the de la Vega hacienda had not been blocked by earthquakes, they might be able to spy on Rafael Moncada.

Diego scarcely recognized the terrain, but Bernardo led him unhesitatingly to the entrance hidden by thick brush. Once inside, they lighted a candle and made their way through the labyrinth of passageways to the main cavern, breathing mouthfuls of the indescribable underground smell that they had liked so much as boys. Diego remembered the fateful day his house was attacked by pirates and he had hidden here with his wounded mother. The smells of that moment came rushing back: a combination of blood, sweat, fear, and the dark fragrance of the earth. Everything was just as they had left it, from the bows and arrows, candles, and pots of honey they had stored there five years before—even the medicine wheel that they had laid out with stones when they aspired to *okahué*. Diego lighted the circular altar with a pair of torches and in the center placed the packet he had brought, wrapped in dark cloth and tied with string.

"Brother, I have waited for this moment a long time. We are twenty years old, and we both are prepared for what I am going to propose," he announced to Bernardo with unusual solemnity. "Do you remember the virtues of *okahué*? Honor, justice, respect, dignity, and courage. I have tried to live my life by those virtues, and I know they have guided yours."

In the red splendor of the torches, Diego untied the packet, which contained a complete array of Zorro's identifying pants, shirt, cape, boots, hat, and mask, and handed it to Bernardo.

"I want Zorro to be the foundation of my life, Bernardo. I will dedicate myself to fighting for justice, and I invite you to come with me. Together we will multiply into a thousand, confusing our enemies. There will be two Zorros, you and I, but we will never be seen together."

Diego's tone was so serious that for once Bernardo was not tempted to answer with a jest. He realized that his milk brother had thought about this long and hard. It was not an impulse born of his father's misfortune; the black disguise that he had brought back from his journey proved that. The young Indian removed his trousers and, as solemn as Diego, put on the pieces of the disguise, one by one, until he was a replica of Zorro. Then Diego pulled the sword he had bought in Cuba from its sheath and offered it to Bernardo with both hands.

"I swear to defend the weak and to fight for justice!" Diego exclaimed. Bernardo took the sword and in an inaudible whisper repeated his brother's words.

The two young men cautiously opened the secret door of the fireplace in the grand salon, finding that in spite of the years it still slid noiselessly on its track. They had kept the metal oiled, and apparently five years later it was still smooth. The huge logs were the same as always, though now covered with a thick layer of dust. No one had lighted that fire since Diego left. And the rest of the room had not changed: the furniture Alejandro de la Vega had bought in Mexico to please his wife, the huge chandelier with its hundred and fifty candles, the wood table and upholstered chairs, the same pretentious paintings. Everything was the same, but to them it seemed that the house was smaller and more dismal than they remembered. A patina of neglect had taken the shine off everything; a funereal silence hung in the air, and a stale and unpleasant smell had seeped into the walls. The brothers slipped like cats down corridors badly lighted by a few lanterns. Once there had been an aged servant whose only task was to see that there was light; he slept by day and

spent the night keeping an eye on the candles and oil lamps. They
wondered if that old man and the other elderly servants were still on
the hacienda staff, or if Moncada had replaced them with his own
men. At that hour even the dogs were resting and only one man was
standing guard in the main patio; his weapon was slung over his
shoulder, and he was fighting to keep his eyes open. The intruders
located the soldiers' quarters, where they counted twelve hammocks
hung at differing heights, some above others, although only eight
were occupied. Another room contained an arsenal of firearms, gunpowder, and swords. They dared not explore any more for fear of
being caught, but through a half-open door they glimpsed Rafael
Moncada writing or entering accounts in the library. Diego choked
back a cry of rage when he saw his enemy sitting in his father's chair,
using his paper and his ink. Bernardo elbowed him and motioned
they should go, that their exploration was getting dangerous. They
silently slipped out the way they had come in, after blowing thick
dust from the fireplace to cover their tracks. They were back at the
mission by dawn, an hour when Diego felt for the first time the
fatigue that had accumulated since they disembarked the day before.
He fell into bed and slept until late the next morning, when
Bernardo waked him to say that the horses were ready. It had been
his idea to go see Toypurnia and ask for her help in rescuing Alejandro de la Vega. They did not see Padre Mendoza, whom he had left
early to go to Los Angeles, but Nuria served them a hearty breakfast
of beans, rice, and fried eggs. Isabel came to the table with her hair
pulled back into a braid, wearing a riding skirt and a blue linen
blouse like the ones the neophytes wore in the mission, and
announced that she was going with them; she wanted to meet
Diego's mother and see what an Indian village was like.

"In that case, I will have to come, too," grumbled Nuria, to
whom the idea of a long ride on horseback in this land of barbarians
was less than enticing.

"No. Padre Mendoza needs you here," Isabel replied, giving her
a consoling kiss. "We will be back soon."

The three young people rode off on the best palomino horses in the mission, leading another loaded with supplies. They would have to ride all day, camp at night beneath the stars, and start up into the mountains the next morning. To elude soldiers, the tribe had moved as far away as possible, and often shifted their camp, but Bernardo knew where it was. Isabel, who had learned to ride astride long ago, followed her two friends without complaint. At their first stop, which they made to cool off in a creek and to share the lunch Nuria had prepared, she realized how saddle-sore she was. Diego made fun of her because she was walking like a duck, but Bernardo gave her one of White Owl's herbal pomades to rub on her aching thighs. The next day at noon Bernardo pointed to some markings on the trees that indicated the tribe was near; that was how they advised other Indians when they changed location. Instants later they were met by two nearly naked men with war paint and ready bows, who lowered their weapons when they recognized Bernardo and came forward to greet him. After Bernardo had introduced his companions, the Indians led them through the trees to the village, a cluster of wretched straw huts animated by a few roving dogs. The Indians whistled, and within minutes the inhabitants of that phantasmal village materialized from out of nowhere; they were a pathetic group, some naked and others in rags. With horror Diego recognized his grandmother, White Owl, and his mother. It took him a few seconds to recover from his anguish at seeing them so impoverished and to leap from his horse and run to embrace them. He had forgotten how poor the Indians were, but he had not forgotten his grandmother's scent of smoke and herbs. It went straight to his heart, as did the new aroma of his mother. Regina had smelled of milk soap and flower cologne. Toypurnia smelled of sage and sweat.

"Diego, how you have grown," his mother murmured.

Toypurnia spoke to him in the Indian tongue, the first sounds Diego had heard in his infancy, and which he had not forgotten. In that language they could be affectionate; in Spanish they would have spoken formally, without touching. The first language was for sentiments, the second for ideas. Toypurnia's callused hands patted her son, his arms, chest, and neck, recognizing him, measuring him, frightened by the changes. Then it was his grandmother's turn to welcome him. White Owl lifted his hair to study his ears, as if that were the one way she could be sure it was he. Diego laughed happily and, taking her by the waist, lifted her high off the ground. She weighed almost nothing—it was like picking up a child—but beneath the rags and rabbit skins, Diego could feel her hard, sinewy body: pure wood. She was not as old or as fragile as she had at first seemed. Bernardo had eyes only for Light-in-the-Night and his son, little Diego, a boy of five, the color and hardness of a brick, with dark, dark eyes and his mother's laugh; he was naked, and carried a miniature bow and arrows. Diego, who had known Light-in-the-Night as a child when he visited his grandmother, through Bernardo's telepathic references, and from a letter from Padre Mendoza, was struck by her beauty. Beside her and his son, Bernardo seemed a different man; he grew taller, and his face glowed.

After the first euphoria of the meeting, Diego remembered to introduce Isabel, who had watched from a short distance. From the stories Diego had told her about his mother and grandmother, she had imagined figures of epic proportions, paintings in which the conquistadors are portrayed in gleaming armor and the indigenous Americans are represented as demigods wearing feathers. These skinny, uncombed, dirty women did not remotely resemble the paintings in the museums, but they had the same dignity. She could not communicate with the grandmother, but within a few minutes she felt comfortable with Toypurnia. She intended to visit her often, as she knew she could learn a great deal from that strange and wise woman. I want to be that indomitable, she thought. And Toypurnia liked the young Spanish girl with the wandering eye. She thought it must indicate an ability to see what others cannot see.

Of the tribe, a large group of children, women, and old men remained, but there were only five hunters, who had to go farther and farther for game because the whites had divided up the land and defended it with guns. Sometimes hunger forced them to steal cattle, but if they were caught, they paid with lashings or the gallows. Most Indian men were now to be found working on the ranches. The clan of White Owl and Toypurnia had chosen freedom, with all its risks. They had no problem with warrior tribes, thanks to the two women's reputation as shamans and healers. If any stranger came to the camp, it was to ask for counsel and medicines, which they paid for with food and skins. They had survived, but ever since Rafael Moncada and Carlos Alcázar had begun to arrest their young men, they had not been able to stay in one place. The nomadic life had brought an end to their fields of maize and other grains; they had to be content with mushrooms and wild fruit, fish, and meat when they could get it.

Bernardo and Light-in-the-Night brought the gift they had for Diego: a black steed with large, intelligent eyes. It was Tornado, the motherless colt that Bernardo had encountered during his initiation rite seven years before and that Light-in-the-Night had tamed and taught to obey to whistles. He was of noble breed, a splendid companion. Diego stroked the animal's nose and burrowed his head into his long mane, repeating, "Tornado . . . Tornado . . . Tornado . . ."

"We will have to hide you, Tornado. Zorro alone will ride you," he said, and the horse responded with a neigh and a flick of his tail.

The rest of the afternoon went by in roasting some raccoons and birds they had been fortunate enough to catch, and in passing on bad news. As night fell, Isabel, exhausted, wrapped herself in a blanket and fell asleep by the fire. Toypurnia heard from her son's lips the tragedy that had befallen Alejandro de la Vega. She confessed that she missed him; he was the only man she had ever loved, but she had not been able to stay with him as his wife. She preferred the miserable nomadic life of her tribe to the luxury of the hacienda, where she felt like a prisoner. She had spent her childhood and youth in the outdoors; she could not bear the oppression of adobe walls and a roof over her head, the arrogance of the customs, the discomfort of Spanish clothes, the weight of Christianity. With age, Alejandro had become more severe in judging his neighbor. In the end they had little in common, and after their son went to Spain and the passion of youth had cooled, there was nothing left. Nevertheless, she was moved to hear of her husband's fate and offered her help in rescuing him from the dungeon and hiding him in some remote part of the territory. California was vast, and she knew almost all the trails. She confirmed that Padre Mendoza's suspicions were real.

"For a couple of months there has been a barge anchored near the oyster banks, and they transport prisoners there in small boats," said Toypurnia.

She explained to him that they had taken away several youths from the tribe and forced them to dive from dawn to sunset. They lowered them with a rope, with a large stone as weight and a basket to put the oysters in. When the divers tugged on the rope, they pulled them back up to the boat. The day's harvest was emptied onto the barge, where other prisoners opened the oysters, looking for pearls, a chore that cut their hands raw. Toypurnia assumed that Alejandro was among that group, as he was too old to dive. She added that the captives slept on the beach, chained together on the sand, and went hungry because no one can live on oysters as their only nourishment..

"I do not see how you can rescue your father from that hell," she said.

It would be impossible as long as he was on the barge, but Diego knew through Padre Mendoza that a priest was going to visit the prison. Moncada and Alcázar, who had to keep the matter of the pearls a secret, had suspended operation for a few days so the prisoners would be in El Diablo when the priest came. That was his one opportunity, Diego explained. He realized that it would be impossible to hide Zorro's identity from his mother and grandmother, and he needed their help. When he told them about Zorro, and about his plans, he was aware that his words sounded like pure lunacy; for that reason he was surprised that the two women did not change expression, as if the idea of putting on a mask and assaulting El Diablo were absolutely normal. They promised to protect his secret. And they agreed that in a few days Bernardo, along with three men of the tribe, the most athletic and brave, would be at La Cruz de Las Calaveras with horses. This was a crossroads where two bandits had been hanged; their skulls, the *calaveras*, bleached by rain and sun, were mounted on a wooden cross. They would not tell Bernardo's companions the details; the fewer people who knew, the better in case they were captured.

Diego imparted the broad outlines of his plan to rescue his father, and if possible the other prisoners as well. Most were native peoples; they knew the terrain very well and, given the chance, would slip away and fade into the landscape. White Owl told Diego that many Indians had helped construct El Diablo, among them her own brother, whom the whites called Arsenio, though his true name was Eyes-That-See-in-the-Dark. He was blind, and the Indians believed that those who are born without sight can see in the dark, like bats. Arsenio was a good example. He was so skillful with his hands that he could forge tools and repair any mechanism. He knew the prison like no one else; he moved through it confidently because it had been his only world for forty years. He had worked there long before Carlos Alcázar arrived, and carried in his prodigious memory the names of all the prisoners who had passed through El Diablo. Diego's grandmother handed him some owl feathers.

"Perhaps my brother can help you. If you see him, tell him you are my grandson and give him the feathers; that way he will know you are not lying," she said.

The next morning very early Diego and Isabel, after planning with Bernardo the time and place they would meet at El Diablo, started back to the mission. Bernardo stayed with the tribe to put together his part of the things they would require, using items he had taken from the mission a few days before without Padre Mendoza's knowledge. "This is one of those rare cases in which the end justifies the means," he had assured his brother as they foraged through the missionary's cellar in search of a long rope, potassium nitrate, powdered zinc, and wicks. Before they left the Indian camp, Diego had asked his mother why she had chosen Diego for his name.

"That was my father's name, your Spanish grandfather, Diego Salazar. He was a good and brave man who understood the Indian soul. He deserted from a Spanish ship because he wanted to be free; he never accepted the blind obedience demanded on board. He respected my mother and adapted to the customs of our tribe. He taught me many things—among others, the Spanish language. Why do you ask?" Toypurnia replied.

"I have always been curious. Did you know that Diego means supplanter?"

"No. What is that?"

"Someone who takes another's place," Diego answered.

Diego told his friends at the mission good-bye, saying he was going to Monterey. He would insist that the governor do the just thing in his father's case. He did not want anyone to come with him. He could make the journey easily, he said, stopping at missions along the Camino Real. Padre Mendoza watched him ride away on a palomino, with another horse behind, carrying his gear. He was sure that it was a futile trip, a waste of time that might cost Don Alejandro his life—every day the old man awoke in El Diablo could be his last. His arguments had no effect on Diego.

As soon as Diego was out of sight of the mission, he left the road and, making a half turn, headed toward the open country to the south. He was confident that Bernardo had done his part and would be waiting for him at La Cruz de las Calaveras. Hours later, when he was near the meeting place, he stopped to change his clothing. He put on the mended priest's habit "borrowed" from the good Padre Mendoza, glued on a beard he had improvised from strands of White Owl's hair, and completed the disguise with Nuria's glasses—

the chaperone would be looking for them everywhere. Reaching the place where the skulls of the bandits were nailed to the arms of the cross, he did not have to wait long. Soon Bernardo and three young Indians appeared out of nowhere, dressed only in breechclouts, armed with bows and arrows, and wearing war paint. Bernardo did not reveal the traveler's identity to his companions; neither did he offer them an explanation when he handed the priest the sacks containing bombs and rope. The brothers exchanged a wink: everything was ready. Diego noticed that Tornado was among the six horses the Indians had brought with them, and he could not resist the temptation to go over and pat his neck before he said good-bye.

Diego started off down the road to the prison on foot; it seemed to him that that way he would look inoffensive, a pathetic blot in the shimmering white sunlight. One of the horses was loaded with his gear, and another with the things Bernardo had put together, including a large wooden cross about waist high. As he reached the crest of a small hill, he could see the ocean in the distance and identify the outlines of the somber prison of El Diablo rising from the rocks. He was thirsty, and his habit was wet with sweat, but he stepped up his pace because he was eager to see his father and set his scheme in motion. He had walked about twenty minutes when he heard the sound of hoof beats and turned to see the dust of a carriage. He could not hold back a curse; this was going to complicate things. No one traveled this road unless they were going to El Diablo. He lowered his head, adjusted his hood, and made sure his beard was in place. His sweat might have loosened it, even though he had used a heavy glue made from the best resin. The coach stopped beside him, and to his immense surprise he saw a very attractive young woman at the small window.

"You must be the priest who is coming to the prison, yes? We were expecting you, Padre," she greeted him.

The girl's smile was enchanting, and Diego's capricious heart gave a leap. He was beginning to recover from his dejection over Juliana and was able to admire other women, especially one as charming as this. He had to make an effort to remember his new role.

"That is true, daughter. I am Padre Aguilar," Diego replied in the quavery voice of an old man.

"Climb up here in my coach, Padre; that way you can rest a little," she offered. "I too am going to El Diablo, to see my cousin."

"God will repay you, daughter."

So this was the beautiful Lolita Pulido! The same skinny little girl who used to send him love notes when he was fifteen. What a stroke of luck. When Lolita's coach arrived at the prison with the false priest and his two horses tied behind, Diego did not have to give explanations. As soon as the coachman announced the girl and Padre Aguilar, the guards were happy to open the gates and let them through. Lolita was known here; the soldiers greeted her by name, and even a couple of prisoners in the stocks smiled at her. "Give those poor men water, they're cooking in the sun," she said to a guard, who flew to do her bidding. In the meantime Diego was looking the building over and quietly counting the uniformed men. He would be able to slide down the wall with his rope, but he had no idea how he would get his father out; the prison looked escape-proof, and there were far too many guards.

The visitors were immediately shown to the office of Carlos Alcázar, a room furnished only with a table, chairs, and the shelves holding the prison files. Everything was entered in those large, worn books, from feed for the horses to the deaths of prisoners—everything except the pearls, which traveled from the oyster directly into the coffers of Moncada and Alcázar, leaving no visible trail. In one corner stood a painted plaster statue of the Virgin Mary crushing the devil with one foot.

"Welcome, Father," said Carlos, after kissing his cousin, whom he still loved as he had in his childhood, on both cheeks. "We were not expecting you until tomorrow."

Diego, head bowed, eyes lowered, voice servile, answered by reciting the first thing that came to his mind in Latin and topped it off with an emphatic *sursum corda,* which had no bearing on anything but sounded impressive. It went right over Alcázar's head; he had never been a good student of dead tongues. Though he was young—he couldn't have been more than twenty-three or twenty-four years old—his cynical expression made him look much older. He had cruel lips and the eyes of a rat. Diego wondered how Lolita could be from the same family; that girl deserved better than to be Carlos's cousin.

The impostor accepted a glass of water and announced that he would say mass the next day; he would confess and give communion to any who asked for the sacraments. He was weary, he added, but that same afternoon he wanted to see the sick prisoners and those being punished, including the pair in the stocks. Lolita volunteered to help; among other things, she had brought a box of medicines, which she put at Padre Aguilar's disposal.

"My cousin has a very soft heart, Padre. I have told her that El Diablo is not a suitable place for señoritas, but she pays no attention. She does not understand that most of those men are beasts with no morals or feelings, likely to bite the hand that feeds them."

"No one has bitten me yet, Carlos," Lolita replied.

"We will dine shortly, Padre. Do not expect a feast, we live very modestly here," said Alcázar.

"Do not worry, my son, I eat very little, and this week I am fasting. Bread and water will be sufficient. I would be grateful to have that in my room, because after I visit the sick I must pray."

"Arsenio!" Alcázar called.

An Indian stepped out of the shadows. He had been in the corner all the time, so silent and motionless that Diego had not been aware of his presence. He recognized him by White Owl's description. A white film covered his pupils, but he moved with precision.

"Take the padre to his room so he can pray. Do whatever he requests, do you hear me?" Alcázar ordered.

"Sí, señor."

"Then you may take him to see the sick."

"Sebastian, too, señor?"

"No, not him, that miserable—"

"Why not?" Diego intervened.

"He isn't sick. We had to give him a little lashing, nothing much, nothing to be concerned about, Padre."

Lolita broke into tears; her cousin had promised her that there would be no further punishments of that nature. Diego left them arguing and followed Arsenio to the room he had been assigned, where his bundles were waiting, including the large cross.

"You are not a man of the church," Arsenio said when they reached the locked door of the room for guests.

Diego flinched, frightened; if a blind man could divine that he was disguised, he had no chance to deceive people who could see.

"You don't smell like a priest," added Arsenio, by way of explanation.

"No? What do I smell like?" Diego asked, amazed, because he was wearing Padre Mendoza's habit.

"Like Indian hair and glue to bind wood," Arsenio replied.

The young man touched his false beard and could not help but laugh. He decided to seize the moment, for surely he would not have another, and confessed to Arsenio that he had come on a specific mission and needed his help. He placed his grandmother's feathers in Arsenio's hand. The blind man stroked them with his all-seeing fingers, and his face revealed his emotion when he recognized they came from his sister. Diego clarified that he was White Owl's grandson, and with that knowledge Arsenio was eager to talk. He had had no news of his sister for many years, he said. He confirmed that El Diablo had been a fortress before it was a prison, and that he had helped build it. He had stayed on to serve the soldiers, and now the jailers. Life had always been hard within those walls, but since Carlos Alcázar took charge it had been a hell; the man's greed and cruelty were beyond description. He imposed forced labor and brutal punishments upon the prisoners, he held back money intended for food, and he fed the prisoners what was left from the soldiers' mess. At that moment, one man was dying, others had high fevers from being stung by poisonous jellyfish, and several had collapsed lungs and were bleeding from the nose and ears.

"And Alejandro de la Vega?" Diego asked with his heart in his mouth.

"He won't last long; he has lost his will to live, he scarcely moves. The other prisoners do his work so he won't be punished, and they spoon food into his mouth," said Arsenio.

"Please, Eyes-That-See-in-the-Dark, take me to him."

Outside there was still sunlight, but inside the prison it was dark. The thick walls and narrow windows admitted very little light. Arsenio, who did not need a lamp to find his way, took Diego by one sleeve and unhesitatingly led him through shadowy corridors and down narrow stairs to the dungeons that had been added to the fortress when they decided to use it as a prison. Those cells were below sea level, and when the tide came in, humidity seeped through the wall, producing a nauseating odor and a greenish patina on the stones. The guard on duty, a mestizo with a pocked face and a seal's mustache, opened an iron-barred door and handed Arsenio a large ring of keys. Diego was surprised by the silence. He supposed there were several prisoners, but apparently they were so exhausted and weak that they were not making a sound. Arsenio went to one of the cells, felt the keys, chose the right one, and opened the cell door. It took Diego's eyes several seconds to adjust to the darkness and make out a few dark figures sitting against the wall, and one bundle on the ground. Arsenio lighted a candle, and Diego knelt beside his father, so moved that he could not speak. Carefully he lifted Alejandro de la Vega's head and laid it in his lap, brushing back tangled locks from his forehead. In the light of the trembling flame he could see better, but he did not recognize his father. There was no trace of the well-built and proud hidalgo, the hero of ancient battles, mayor of Pueblo de los Angeles, and prosperous hacienda owner. He was weathered, filthy, nothing but skin and bones. He was trembling with fever, his eyelids were stuck together, and a thread of saliva trickled down his chin. Only fifty-five years old, he looked like an old man.

"Don Alejandro, can you hear me? This is Padre Aguilar," said Arsenio.

"I have come to help you, señor. We are going to get you out of here," Diego murmured.

The three other men in the cell showed a spark of interest but then turned back to the wall. They were beyond hope.

"Give me the last sacraments, Padre. It is too late for me," said the old man in a wisp of a voice.

"It is not too late. Come, señor, sit up," Diego pled.

He managed to sit his father up and give him water. Then he cleaned his eyes with the wetted hem of his habit.

"Try to stand, señor, because you have to walk if we are going to get you out," Diego insisted.

"Leave me alone, Padre; I will not get out of here alive."

"Yes, you will. I promise you that you will see your son again, and I do not mean in heaven, I mean in this world."

"My son? You said my son?"

"It is I, Diego, sir. Do you not recognize me?" the priest whispered, trying not to let the others hear.

Alejandro de la Vega studied him for a few seconds, trying to focus his clouded eyes, but he did not find the familiar image in this hooded and bearded priest. Still in a whisper, the young man explained that he was wearing a habit and a false beard so no one would know that he was in El Diablo.

"Diego, Diego . . . God has heard my prayer. I have prayed so often that I would see you again before I die, my son!"

"You have always been a brave and strong man, sir. Do not give up, I beg you. You have to live. I must go now, but be prepared, because in a short while a friend of mine will come to rescue you."

"Tell your friend that it is not I that he should free, Diego, but my companions. I owe them a great deal; they have taken bread from their own mouths to feed me."

Diego turned to look at the other prisoners, three Indians as dirty and thin as his father, with the same expression of absolute surrender, but young and still healthy. Apparently in a few weeks' time those men had succeeded in dissolving the sense of superiority the Spanish hidalgo had displayed all his life long. Diego thought about the twists and turns of fate. Captain Santiago de León had once told him when they were observing the stars over the ocean that if a man lives long enough, he will come to revise his convictions and mend some of his ways.

"They will leave with you, sir, I promise," Diego assured him as he said good-bye.

Arsenio left the supposed priest in his room and shortly after returned with a simple supper of stale bread, watery soup, and ordinary wine. Diego realized that he was hungry as a coyote and regretted that he had told Carlos Alcázar that he was fasting. No reason to have carried his imposture that far. He thought of Nuria, at that hour cooking oxtail stew at the San Gabriel mission.

"I have come only to get the lay of the land, Arsenio. A different person will try to free the prisoners and take Don Alejandro de la Vega to a safe place. That man's name is Zorro. He is a courageous masked caballero dressed in black; he will always appear when there are wrongs to be righted." Arsenio thought it was all empty talk. He had never heard of such a person; he had lived fifty years, witnessing injustice on all sides, and no one had mentioned a masked man. Diego assured him that things were going to change in California. They would see who Zorro was! The weak would receive protection, and the evil would feel the edge of his sword and the crack of his whip. Arsenio burst out laughing, now completely convinced that the man was soft in the head.

"Do you think that White Owl would have sent me to talk to you if this were a joke?" Diego cried, annoyed.

That argument seemed to make an impression on the Indian, who asked how Zorro planned to free the prisoners, considering that no one had ever escaped from El Diablo. It was not just a matter of calmly walking out the main door. Diego explained that even though the masked man was magnificent, he could not do it alone; he needed help. Arsenio stood thinking a long while and finally told Diego that there was another way out, but he did not know whether it was in good repair. When the fortress was built, a tunnel had been dug as a way of escape in case of a siege. In those days pirates often attacked, and there had been talk that the Russians were planning to take over California. The tunnel, which had never been used and now no one remembered, came out in some thick woods to the west, in an old Indian sacred site.

"Blessed Mary! That is exactly what I need . . . I mean, that Zorro needs. Where is the entrance to the tunnel?"

"If this Zorro comes, I will show it to him," Arsenio replied sarcastically.

Once he was alone, Diego opened his bundles, which contained his black clothes, his whip, and a pistol. In the bags Bernardo had brought, he found the rope, a small metal anchor, and several clay pots. These were the smoke bombs Bernardo had made with the nitrate and zinc powders following the instructions Diego had copied, among other curiosities, from Captain Santiago de León's books. At the time, he had planned to make one of those bombs to frighten Bernardo; he had never imagined it would be to save his own father. Diego removed the beard with some difficulty, gritting his teeth not to cry out with pain every time he pulled. It left his face irritated as if he had been burned, and he decided it was not worth the trouble to glue on the mustache; the mask would be enough. Sooner or later he would have to grow a mustache, he thought. He washed with the water Arsenio had left in a basin and dressed as Zorro. Then he took apart the large wooden cross and pulled out his sword. He put on his leather gloves and practiced a few patterns with his sword, testing the flexibility of the steel and the strength of his muscles. He smiled with satisfaction.

When he looked out the window, he saw that it was already dark, and speculated that Carlos and Lolita had dined and by now would be in their rooms. The prison was tranquil and silent; the moment for action had come. He strapped on his whip and pistol, sheathed the sword, and was ready to leave. "May God be with us!" he murmured, and crossed his fingers for good luck. He had memorized the plan of the building and counted the steps on the stairways, so he would not need a light. In his dark clothing he was invisible in the shadows, and he was counting on there not being many guards.

Silently he made his way to one of the terraces, where he looked for a place to hide the bombs, which he brought out two at a time: they were heavy, and he could not run the risk of dropping one. On the last trip he threw the rope and small anchor over his shoulder. After making sure that the bombs were well hidden, he leaped from the terrace to the stone and mortar wall that encircled the prison; it was lighted by torches every fifty steps and was wide enough for sentinels to walk on. From his hiding place, Diego watched one guard go by and counted the minutes until the second also passed him. When he was sure that there were only two men making the rounds, he figured that he would have just enough time to carry out the next step in the plan. He ran in a crouch toward the south wing of the prison to the place he and Bernardo had arranged to meet. Diego would wait, they had agreed, where an outcropping of rock facilitated the climb. As boys they had explored the prison's surroundings more than once, and that familiarity now served them well. Once he had located the precise site, he let the sentinel pass, then took one of the torches and swung it several times above his head; that was the signal for Bernardo. He secured the iron anchor onto the wall and threw down the rope, praying it would reach the ground and that his brother would see it. He had to hide again because of the approach of the second sentinel, who stopped less than an arm's length from the anchor to gaze at the sky. Zorro's heart leaped in his chest and he felt his mask grow damp with sweat when he saw that the guard's feet were so close to the anchor that if he took a step he would trip on it. If that happened, he would have to give him a push and throw him over the wall, although he detested that kind of violence. As he had often explained to Bernardo, Zorro's greatest challenge was to do justice without staining his hands with blood. Bernardo, whose feet were always solidly on the ground, had argued that that was not always going to be possible.

The guard renewed his round at the moment Bernardo pulled the rope down, slightly shifting the anchor. To Zorro the noise sounded deafening, but the sentinel merely hesitated a second, then lifted his weapon to his shoulder and wandered on. With a sigh of relief the masked man peered over the wall. Although he could not see his companions, the tension on the rope indicated that they had begun their climb. As he had foreseen, all four arrived in time to hide before the next guard approached. Zorro described the location of the tunnel exit in the woods, which they knew as sacred ground, and ordered two of the Indians to descend to the courtyard of the prison and be ready to run off the soldiers' horses so they could not follow them. Then everyone left to carry out his part of the mission.

Zorro went back to the terrace where he had hidden the bombs and, after exchanging coyote barks with Bernardo, tossed them one by one down to the wall. He kept two to use inside the building. Bernardo lighted the wicks of his and handed them to the Indian with him, who ran along the wall, as silent and swift as if he were on the hunt. They took up positions, and at the moment the flame burned down the wick to the contents of the clay pots, they threw them toward their targets: the stables, the arsenal, the soldiers' quarters, and the courtyard. While the thick white smoke of the bombs enveloped the outside of the central building, Zorro's exploded on the first and second floors inside. Panic broke loose within minutes. At the cry of "Fire!" and the sound of the alarm bell, soldiers came rushing out, pulling on their trousers and boots. Everyone ran to save what he could; some passed buckets of water from hand to hand and poured them out blindly, choking, while others opened the stable doors. The courtyard filled with terrified horses, contributing to the pandemonium. Toypurnia's Indians, who had climbed down and were hidden in the courtyard, used this confusion to open the main gate of the fortress and stampede the horses, which galloped off, though they were domesticated and did not go far. They slowed enough a short distance away that the Indians caught up with them; superior horsemen, they jumped onto two and herded the others toward the place Zorro had told them to meet, close to the tunnel exit.

Carlos Alcázar, waked by the bell, went out to see what the devil was going on. He tried to calm his men, reminding them that stone walls would not burn, but no one paid the least attention; the Indians had shot flaming arrows into the straw of the stables, and flames were visible through the white clouds from the bombs. By then the smoke inside the building was intolerable and Alcázar ran to find his beloved cousin but did not get as far as her room before bumping into her in the corridor. "The prisoners! We have to save the prisoners!" Lolita cried desperately, but Carlos had other priorities. He could not allow the fire to destroy his precious pearls.

In two months' time the prisoners had harvested thousands of oysters, and Moncada and Alcázar had collected several handfuls of pearls. Their agreement was that two-thirds went to Moncada, who had provided the financing, and one-third to Alcázar, who oversaw the operation. Since the business was illegal, they kept no records, but they had designed an accounting system. Pearls were dropped through a hole in a sealed coffer that was bolted to the floor and only could be opened with two keys. Each partner kept one key in his possession, and at the end of the season they planned to meet, open the coffer, and divide the contents. Moncada had assigned a man he trusted to watch over the process on the barge, and demanded that Arsenio be the one to drop them one by one into the box. The blind man, with his extraordinary tactile memory, was the only one capable of remembering the exact number of pearls; were it necessary, he might even be able to describe the size and shape of each of them. Carlos Alcázar detested him because he carried those figures in his mind, and had proved to be incorruptible. He was careful not to mistreat Arsenio because Moncada protected him, but he lost no opportunity to humiliate him. He had, however, bribed the man who was supposed to keep an eye on the boat, who for a reasonable fee allowed Alcázar to take the roundest, largest, and most lustrous, which did not pass through Arsenio's hands or reach the small chest. Rafael Moncada would never know anything about them.

While the three Indians from Toypurnia's tribe sowed chaos and stole horses, Bernardo had slipped into the building where Zorro was waiting to lead him to the dungeons. They had run a short way down the passage, covering their faces with damp kerchiefs in order to breathe, when a hand seized Zorro's arm.

"Padre Aguilar! Follow me, it is shorter this way."

It was Arsenio, who could not perceive the transformation of the supposed missionary into the grand and great Zorro, but had recognized his voice. It seemed unnecessary to point out his error. The brothers hurried to follow him, but the figure of Carlos Alcázar suddenly appeared in the corridor before them, blocking their way. When he saw that pair of strangers, one of them dressed in very striking attire, the prison chief drew his pistol and shot. A scream of pain echoed down the hall, and a bullet lodged in a ceiling beam. With his whip, Zorro had jerked Alcázar's gun from his hand at the instant he was pulling the trigger. Bernardo and Arsenio continued toward the cells, but Diego, sword in hand, chased Alcázar up the steps. An idea had flashed through his mind that would solve Padre Mendoza's problems and, in the process, give Moncada a bad turn. It is true, I *am* a genius, he concluded as he ran.

Alcázar was up the stairs and into his office in four leaps, and was able to close and lock the door before Zorro caught up to him. The smoke had not yet filtered into that room. Zorro shot open the lock and pushed, but it did not yield, it was bolted from inside. He had used his only shot, and he did not have time to reload the weapon; each minute counted. He knew, because he had been there, that the windows opened onto a balcony. It was obvious, when he first looked, that he could not jump to it as he had hoped without the risk of cracking his skull on the paving stones of the courtyard, but on the floor above the balcony there was a carved stone gargoyle. He wrapped the end of his whip around the figure, tugged to test it, and, praying that it would hold his weight, swung cleanly to the balcony. In his office, Carlos Alcázar was busily loading his pistol to blow the locks off the coffer and did not see the shadow at the window. Zorro waited until he had shot one of the locks, shattering it, then burst in through the open window. He stepped on his cape and stumbled a second, enough time for Alcázar to throw down his now useless pistol and pick up his sword. That man, so cruel with the weak, was a coward when he met an opponent his own size, and in addition he had had little experience fencing: in fewer than three minutes his blade went flying through the air, and he found himself with his arms raised and the pressure of a sword tip digging into his chest.

"I could kill you, but I do not want to stain myself with the blood of a dog. I am Zorro, and I have come for your pearls."

"The pearls belong to Señor Moncada!"

"Belonged. They are mine now. Open the coffer."

"It takes two keys, and I have only one."

"Use your pistol. And be careful. At the least suspicious move I will slit your throat without a moment's thought. Zorro is generous; he will grant you your life, as long as you obey," the masked man threatened.

Trembling, Alcázar reloaded the pistol and shot off the other lock. He lifted the wooden lid, and there was the treasure, so white and gleaming that he could not resist the temptation to thrust his hand into them and let the marvelous pearls trickle through his fingers. As for Zorro, he had never seen anything so valuable. Compared to these, the gems they had obtained in Barcelona in exchange for Tomás de Romeu's properties seemed modest. There was a fortune in that box. He indicated to his vanquished adversary that he should pour the pearls into a bag.

"The fire will reach the powder magazine at any moment, and El Diablo will go up. I keep my word; I give you your life, make something of it," he said. Carlos Alcázar did not answer. Instead of running out the door, as Zorro expected, he stayed in the office. Zorro had noticed that he was casting furtive glances toward the other end of the room, where the statue of the Virgin Mary stood on her stone pedestal. Apparently it meant more to him than his own life. Zorro picked up the bag with the pearls, unbolted the door, and disappeared into the corridor, but he did not go far. He waited, counting the seconds, and when Alcázar did not come out, Zorro returned to the office and found him shattering the statue's head with the butt of his pistol.

"What an irreverent way to treat the Madonna!" he exclaimed.

Carlos Alcázar turned, his face contorted with fury, and threw his pistol at the masked man's face, missing by a good margin, at the same time he bent to pick up the sword lying two steps away in a corner. As he stood up, Zorro was upon him, as billowing smoke from the corridor poured into the room. The two men crossed swords for several minutes, coughing and blinded by smoke. Alcázar kept backing up toward his desk, and when he lost his sword for the second time, he pulled a loaded pistol from a drawer. Before he had time to aim, Zorro kicked his weapon from his hand, then marked his cheek with three dizzying slashes, forming the letter Z. Alcázar screamed, fell to his knees, and clutched his cheek.

"It is not a mortal wound, swine, it is the mark of Zorro, so you will not forget me," the masked man said.

On the floor, among the pieces of the statue, was a small chamois pouch that Zorro swept up as he ran from the room. Only later, when he examined the contents, would he find that it contained a hundred and three magnificent pearls, more valuable than all the pearls in the coffer.

Zorro had memorized the plan of the prison, and he quickly made his way to the cells. The dungeon was the only part of El Diablo that the smoke and the uproarious noise of bells, aimless running, and yells had not reached. The poor wretches there had ignored what was going on above them until Lolita appeared to warn them, running down barefoot and in her nightgown to tell the guards to rescue the prisoners. Given the possibility of fire, the guards grabbed the torch from the wall and ran out, without a thought to the prisoners, and Lolita found herself feeling her way in the dark, looking for the keys. When they heard the word *fire,* the terrified captives began to yell and shake the bars, trying to get out. That was when Arsenio and Bernardo appeared. The former went calmly to the small cabinet where the supplies were kept along with the keys to open the cells, which he recognized by touch, while the latter lighted candles and tried to calm Lolita.

A moment later Zorro made his entrance. Lolita cried out when she saw the mourning-clad man brandishing a bloody sword, but her fright turned into curiosity when he sheathed the weapon and bent to kiss her hand. Bernardo interrupted his brother by tapping his shoulder: this was no time for gallantry.

"Be calm! It is only smoke! Follow Arsenio, he knows another way out," Zorro directed the prisoners as they stumbled from the cells.

He threw his cape on the ground, and they laid Alejandro de la Vega upon it. Four Indians took the corners, making a kind of hammock to carry the sick man in. Others helped the poor man who had been lashed, and all of them, including Lolita, followed Arsenio toward the tunnel, with Bernardo and Zorro in the rear as protection. The entrance lay behind a pile of barrels and discarded tools, not with the intention of hiding it but because it had never been used, and things had accumulated there. It was obvious that no one had noticed it. They cleared the small door and one by one entered the dark opening. Zorro explained to Lolita that there was no danger of fire, that the smoke was a distraction to help them rescue these men, most of them innocent of any crime. She barely heard his words, but she nodded as if hypnotized. Who was this magnetic man? Perhaps he was an outlaw, and that was why he hid his face, but instead of disconcerting her, she found the possibility fascinating. She was prepared to follow him to the ends of the earth, but he did not ask; instead he instructed her to pile the barrels and tools back in front of the little door once they were all in the tunnel. And one thing more: he wanted her to set fire to the straw in the cells, which would give them more time to escape. Lolita, whose will was no longer her own, nodded with a foolish smile but with burning eyes.

"Gracias, señorita," he said.

"Who are you?"

"My name is Zorro."

"What nonsense is that, señor?"

"No nonsense, I assure you, Lolita. I cannot explain everything now, for time is precious, but we shall see each other again," he replied.

"When?"

"Soon. Leave the window of your balcony open, and one of these nights I will come to visit you."

That proposition should have been taken as an insult, but the stranger's tone was gallant and his teeth very white. Lolita did not know what to answer, and when she felt his strong arm around her waist she did nothing to dislodge it—just the opposite; she closed her eyes and offered him her lips. Zorro, a little taken aback at the speed at which things were progressing, kissed her, with no trace of the shyness he felt with Juliana. Hidden behind the mask of Zorro, he dared be as dashing as he wished. Considering the circumstances, it was a rather good kiss. In reality, it would have been perfect if they both had not been coughing from the smoke. Zorro reluctantly released her and ducked into the tunnel, following the others. It took Lolita three whole minutes to recover the use of her reason and to breathe normally, but then she carried out the instructions of the fascinating masked man, whom she planned to marry someday in the not-too-distant future. She had made up her mind. She was a quick-witted girl.

A half hour after the smoke bombs had exploded, the smoke began to dissipate. By then the soldiers had put out the fire in the stables and fought the flames Lolita had started in the cells, and

Carlos Alcázar, stanching the blood on his cheek with a cloth, was back in control. He still could not grasp what had happened. His men had found the arrows that started the fire, but no one had seen those responsible. He did not think it was an Indian raid—that hadn't happened for twenty-five years; it had to be a distraction of that Zorro person to steal the pearls. He did not know until considerably later that the prisoners had disappeared without a trace.

The tunnel, reinforced with boards to prevent cave-ins, was narrow, but it offered no difficulty to the escapees. The air was stale because the ventilation conduits had been filled in with the passing of time, and Zorro decided that they should not burn up the sparse amount of oxygen by lighting candles; they would have to go forward in the dark. Arsenio, who did not need light, went in the lead, carrying the one candle permitted as a signal for the others. The sensation of being buried alive and the idea that a collapse of the walls would trap them forever were terrifying. Bernardo rarely lost his composure, but he was accustomed to wide-open spaces, and here he felt like a mole; panic was overtaking him. He could not go faster or turn back; there wasn't enough air, he was choking, he thought he was stepping on rats and snakes, and he was sure that the tunnel was growing narrower with every step and he would never get out. When he froze with terror, his brother's strong hand on his back and his soothing voice gave him courage. Zorro was the only one of the group who was not affected by confinement—he was too busy thinking about Lolita. Just as White Owl had told him during his initiation, caves and night were the fox's elements. The tunnel seemed very long to all of them, although the exit was not far from the prison. By day the guards would have seen them, but in the middle of the night the fugitives emerged into the protection of the trees without danger. They were covered with dirt, thirsty, eager to breathe fresh air. The Indian prisoners took off their rags, brushed off the dirt, and, naked, raised their faces and arms to the heavens to celebrate that first moment of freedom. When they realized that they were at a sacred site, they took it as a good omen and felt comforted. Bernardo's whistles were quickly returned, and soon Toypurnia's Indians appeared, leading the stolen horses and the ones they had brought with them, among them Tornado. The fugitives, riding double, scattered toward the hills. They knew the region and would rejoin their tribes before the soldiers were organized enough to come after them. They planned to stay as far away from the whites as possible, until normality returned to California.

Zorro brushed the dirt off his own clothes, lamenting that the garments he had just bought in Cuba were already filthy, but he congratulated himself that things had turned out even better than planned. The prisoner who had been lashed was hoisted up behind Arsenio; Bernardo seated Alejandro de la Vega on his horse and rode behind him to steady him. The mountain road was steep, and it would take the greater part of the night. Cold air had stirred the old man from his lethargy, and the joy of seeing his son had given him hope. Bernardo assured him that Toypurnia and White Owl would take care of him until the time came when he could return to his hacienda.

In the meantime, Zorro, riding Tornado, was galloping toward the San Gabriel mission.

Padre Mendoza had spent several nights tossing and turning on his cot, unable to sleep or find peace for his soul. He had read and prayed ever since he discovered that his spare habit and several items from the storeroom were missing. He had only two robes, which he rotated and washed every three weeks, and they were so worn and ragged that he could not imagine who had been tempted to take one. He had wanted to give the thief the opportunity to return what he had stolen, but that had not happened, and now he could no longer put off his decision to act. The thought of calling the neophytes together, giving them a sermon on the third commandment, and finding who was guilty was keeping him awake. He knew that his people had many needs, and this was not a time to punish them, but he could not let the matter go by. He simply could not understand why instead of sneaking food they had taken rope, nitrate, zinc, and his habit; none of it made sense. He was weary of so much struggle and work and loneliness; his bones and his heart ached. Times had changed so much that he no longer recognized the world; greed reigned; no one remembered the teachings of Christ, no one respected him, and he could not protect his neophytes from the abuse of the whites. Sometimes he wondered if the Indians had not been better off before, when they were the lords of California and followed their own ways, with their customs and their gods, but the priest immediately crossed himself and asked God's forgiveness for such heresy. "Where will we be if I myself doubt Christianity?" He sighed, feeling repentant.

The situation had grown much worse with Rafael Moncada's arrival. He represented the negative elements of colonization; he had come to make a quick fortune and then leave. To him the Indians were beasts of burden. In the twenty-some years Padre Mendoza had been at San Gabriel, he had lived through many crises—earthquakes, epidemics, droughts, and even Indian raids—but he had never lost heart, sure that he was following a divine mandate. Now he felt abandoned by God.

Night was drawing near, and they had lighted the torches in the courtyard. After a long day of hard labor, Padre Mendoza, sweating and with his sleeves rolled up, was cutting wood for the kitchen. He groaned as he lifted the axe; every day it seemed heavier, and every day the wood was harder. He heard a galloping horse. He paused and squinted; his eyes were not as good as they had been, and he wondered who could be in such a hurry at this late hour. As the horseman approached, he could see it was a man in dark clothing, his face covered by a mask; no doubt a bandit. He yelled to the women and children to take cover, then turned to meet the man with the axe in his hands and a prayer on his lips; there was no time to run to get his old musket. The stranger jumped to the ground even before his horse had stopped and called the missionary by name.

"Have no fear, Padre Mendoza, I am a friend!"

"Then you do not need that mask. Your name, son," the priest replied.

"Zorro. I know this seems strange, but stranger still is what I am going to tell you, Padre. Please come inside."

The missionary led the mysterious horseman to the chapel, thinking that there he would find divine protection and could convince him that there was little of value in the mission. The man was frightening; he had a sword, a pistol, and a whip. He was outfitted for war, but there was something vaguely familiar about him. Where had he heard that voice? Zorro began by assuring him that he was not a ruffian, and then confirmed the priest's suspicions about Moncada and Alcázar's having harvested the pearls. Legally their share was only ten percent; the rest of the treasure belonged to Spain. They were working the Indians like slaves, sure that no one except Padre Mendoza would intercede for them.

"I have no one to go to, son. The new governor is a weak man, and he is afraid of Moncada," the missionary stated.

"Then you must go to the authorities in Mexico and Spain, Padre."

"With what proof? No one will believe me; I have a reputation for being an old fanatic, obsessed with the Indians' well-being."

"Here is proof," said Zorro, placing a heavy bag in his hands.

The missionary looked inside and cried out with surprise when he saw so many pearls.

"God in heaven, son! How did you get this!"

"How is unimportant."

Zorro suggested that Padre Mendoza take the bag to the bishop in Mexico City and report what had happened, the only way to prevent the neophytes from being enslaved. If Spain decided to exploit the oyster banks, they could pay Yaqui Indians, as they had before. Then he asked the missionary to tell Diego de la Vega that his father was free and safe. The priest commented that the young man had been a disappointment; he lacked grit, and did not seem like a son of Alejandro and

Regina. Again he asked the visitor to show his face. Otherwise he could not trust his word; all this could be a trap. The masked man told him that his identity had to remain a secret, but he promised the priest that he would not be alone in his work to defend the poor. From now on Zorro would stand for justice. Padre Mendoza laughed nervously; possibly the fellow was an escaped madman.

"One last thing, Padre. This chamois pouch contains one hundred and three pearls finer than all the others; they are worth a fortune. They are yours. You do not need to mention them to anyone; I assure you that the one person who knows of their existence would not dare ask about them."

"I suppose they are stolen."

"Yes, they are, but in all fairness they belong to the ones who ripped them from the sea with their last breaths. You will know how to use them wisely."

"If they were unfairly taken, I do not want to see them, my son."

"You do not have to see them, Padre, but take good care of them," Zorro replied with a wink of complicity.

The missionary hid the pouch among the folds of his habit and walked with the visitor to the courtyard where the lustrous black horse was waiting, surrounded by the children of the mission. The masked man mounted his steed. To thrill the children, he whistled, and his mount whirled and reared; then he pulled out his sword and flashed it, making it glint in the lantern light, and sang a verse that he himself had composed during the idle months in New Orleans: something about a valiant horseman who rides out on moonlit nights to defend justice, punish evildoers, and slash a *Z* with his sword. The song beguiled the children but increased Padre Mendoza's fear that the man was out of his mind. Isabel and Nuria, who had spent most of the day in their room sewing, came out onto the courtyard just in time to glimpse the gallant figure making pirouettes on his black mount before riding off. They asked who the dashing horseman was, and Padre Mendoza replied that if he wasn't a devil, he must be an angel sent by God to reinforce his faith.

†

That same night Diego de la Vega returned to the mission covered with dust and full of the story of how he had nearly perished at the hands of bandits and so had cut his trip short. He had seen a couple of suspicious characters in the distance and to avoid them had left the Camino Real and galloped into the woods, but he got lost. He spent the night curled up beneath the trees, safe from the brigands but at the mercy of bears and wolves. At dawn he realized where he was and decided to return to San Gabriel; it would have been imprudent to go on alone. He had ridden all day without a bite to eat; he was completely fatigued, and he had a headache. He would leave for Monterey in a day or two, but this time he would go armed and with an escort. Padre Mendoza informed him that his visit to the governor was no longer necessary because an unknown hero had rescued Don Alejandro de la Vega from prison. All that was left for Diego was to recover the family fortune. He kept to himself his doubts about whether this sickly dandy was capable of doing it.

"Who rescued my father?" Diego asked.

"He called himself Zorro, and he wore a mask," the missionary said.

"Mask? Was he an outlaw, then?" was Diego's question.

"I saw him, too, Diego, and for an outlaw he was not at all bad. I cannot tell you how handsome and elegant he was! Furthermore, he was riding a horse that must have cost an eye from his head," Isabel intervened enthusiastically.

"You always have had more imagination than is good for you," he replied.

Nuria interrupted to announce dinner. That night Diego ate voraciously, despite the heralded migraine, and when he finished he congratulated the chaperone, who had greatly improved the mission fare, as he had known she would. Isabel questioned him mercilessly: she wanted to know why his horses were not worn out, what the purported highwaymen he saw on the road looked like, how long it took him to go from one point to another, and the reason why he had not stayed in another mission only a day's ride away. Padre Mendoza was so immersed in his own musings that he did not notice the vagueness of Diego's answers. He ate with his right hand and with his left kept feeling the chamois pouch, thinking how its contents could restore the mission to its former condition. Had he sinned by accepting those pearls stained with suffering and greed? No. Not sinned, certainly, but they might bring bad luck. . . . He smiled at how superstitious he had become over the years.

A day or two later, after Padre Mendoza had sent a letter about the pearls to Mexico City and was packing for the trip with Diego, Rafael Moncada and Carlos Alcázar came riding up at the head of a number of soldiers, among them the chubby Sergeant García. Carlos had a disfiguring scar on his cheek, and he was nervous because he had not been able to convince his partner how the pearls had disappeared. The truth was little help in this case, as it only highlighted his sorry role in defending the prison and the treasure. He had chosen to tell Moncada that fifty Indians had burned down El Diablo while a gang of outlaws under the leadership of a black-clad, masked man who identified himself as Zorro ransacked the prison. After a bloody struggle, in which he was wounded, the attackers had overcome the soldiers and ridden away with the pearls. The prisoners had escaped in the confusion. Alcázar knew that Moncada would not be happy until he knew the whole truth and found the pearls. The escaped fugitives were of the least importance; there were plenty of Indians to take their places.

The curious shape of the cut on Alcázar's face—a perfect Z—had reminded Moncada of a masked man whose description corresponded to Zorro's, and who had traced a similar letter at the residence of Le Chevalier's residence and in a barracks in Barcelona. On both occasions the pretext had been to set some prisoners free, as had been the case in El Diablo. Worse, however, on the second occasion he had had the audacity to use his, Moncada's, name and that of his aunt Eulalia. He had sworn to repay that insult, but he had not as yet laid a glove on him. He was, however, quickly reaching the only possible conclusion: Diego de la Vega was in Barcelona when someone had left a Z on a wall, and as soon as he landed in California someone had made the same mark on Alcázar's cheek. It was not mere coincidence. This Zorro could be no one but Diego. It was difficult to believe, but it was reason enough to make de la Vega pay for the trouble he had caused. Moncada had ridden at top speed to the mission, fearing that his prey might have escaped, but here was Diego, sitting beneath a grape arbor, drinking lemonade and reading poetry. Moncada ordered Sergeant García to arrest him, and the poor tubby sergeant, who had never lost his unconditional boyhood admiration for Diego, unwillingly started to do his bidding. He was stopped by Padre Mendoza, who declared that the masked man was not even remotely like Diego de la Vega. Isabel backed him up; not even an idiot could confuse those two men, she said. She knew Diego like a brother, she had lived at his side for five years; he was a good young man, inoffensive, sentimental, often ill. There was no touch of bandit, much less hero, in him.

"Well, thank you," Diego cut her off, offended, but he noticed that his friend's wandering eye was whirling like a top.

"Zorro helped the Indians because they are innocent," said the missionary. "You know that as well as I, Señor Moncada. He did not steal the pearls; he took them as proof of what is going on in El Diablo."

"What pearls are you talking about?" Carlos Alcázar interjected. He was extremely uneasy; until that moment no one had mentioned them, and he had no idea how much the priest knew about their trickery.

Padre Mendoza admitted that Zorro had given him the bag with the charge of taking it to the authorities in Mexico City. Rafael Moncada tried to hide a sigh of relief; it would be easier to recover his treasure than he had imagined. This ridiculous old man would be no problem, he could erase him from the map with one breath; terrible accidents happened all the time. With a preoccupied expression, he thanked Padre Mendoza for his cleverness in getting the pearls and his zeal in caring for them. Then he demanded that the priest hand them over; he would assume responsibility. If Carlos Alcázar, as administrator of the prison, had committed irregularities, he would take the necessary measures. There was no reason to bother anyone in Mexico City. The priest had no choice but to obey. He did not dare accuse Moncada of complicity with Alcázar because one false step would have cost him the most important thing in this world: his mission. He brought the bag and laid it on the table.

"This belongs to Spain. I have sent a letter to my superiors, and there will be an investigation of the matter," he said.

"A letter? But the ship hasn't come," Alcázar protested.

"I have other means, quicker and more secure than the ship."

"Are all the pearls here?" Moncada asked with annoyance.

"How can I know that? I was not present when they were taken, and I do not know how many there were originally. Only Carlos can answer that question," the missionary replied.

Those words added to suspicions Moncada already had of his partner. He took the missionary by one arm and dragged him to a crucifix hanging above a ledge on the wall.

"Swear before the cross of Our Lord that you have not seen other pearls. If you lie, your soul will be condemned to hell," he ordered.

An ominous silence fell over the room; everyone held his breath, and even the air grew still. Furious, Padre Mendoza jerked away from the hand that was paralyzing him.

"How dare you!" he muttered.

"Swear!" Moncada repeated.

Diego and Isabel stepped forward to intervene, but Padre Mendoza, stopping them with a gesture, put one knee on the floor, his right hand on his chest, and his eyes on the Christ an Indian had carved from wood. He was trembling with shock and rage at the violence to which he had been subjected, but he had no fear of going to hell, at least not for that reason.

"I swear before the Cross that I have seen no other pearls. May my soul be condemned if I am lying," he said in a firm voice.

For a long moment no one spoke; the only sound was Carlos Alcázar's sigh of relief. His life would not be worth a centavo if Rafael Moncada learned that he had been keeping back the greater part of the treasure. He assumed that the small chamois pouch was in the hands of the masked man, but he did not understand why he had given the other pearls to the priest when he could have kept them all. Diego followed the course of his thoughts and smiled, defiant. Moncada had to accept Padre Mendoza's oath, but he reminded everyone that he would not consider the matter finished until the guilty party was swinging from the gallows. "García! Arrest de la Vega!" Moncada repeated. The fat sergeant dried his forehead with the sleeve of his uniform and reluctantly prepared to carry out his orders. "I'm sorry," he blubbered, motioning to two soldiers to lead Diego away. Isabel ran to stand before Moncada, arguing that there was no proof against her friend, but he pushed her aside.

Diego de la Vega spent the night in one of the former servants' quarters of the hacienda in which he had been born. He even remembered whose room it had been when he was living there with his parents: a Mexican Indian woman named Roberta, whose face had been badly burned in an accident involving boiling chocolate. What had become of her? He had not remembered, on the other hand, that the rooms were so wretched: windowless cubicles with dirt floors and unpainted adobe walls, furnished with a straw mat, one chair, and a wooden chest. He lay there thinking, This is how Bernardo spent his childhood, while a short distance away he, Diego, slept in a brass bed with a tulle net to protect him from spiders, in a room crammed with toys. Why hadn't he noticed it then? The house was divided by an invisible line that separated the family quarters from the complex universe of the servants. The former, generous and luxurious, decorated in ornate colonial style, was a marvel of order, calm, and cleanliness; it smelled of bouquets of flowers and his father's tobacco. Life seethed in the servants' area: incessant chatter, domestic animals, quarrels, work. That part of the house smelled of ground chili, baked bread, clothes soaking in lye, garbage. The family's terraces, with their ornamental tiles, bougainvillea, and fountains, were a paradise of coolness, while the patios of the servants were dusty in summer and muddy in winter.

Diego spent countless hours on the straw mat, sweating in the heat of May, with no natural light. He was gasping for air, and his chest burned. He had no way to measure time, but he felt that he had been there several days. His mouth was dry, and he feared that Moncada's plan was to wear him down with thirst and hunger. At times he closed his eyes and tried to sleep, but he was too uncomfortable. There was no room to take more than a couple of steps, and his muscles were cramping. He examined the room minutely, searching for a way to get out, but found nothing. The door was bolted from outside; not even Galileo Tempesta could have opened it. Diego tried to loosen the boards of the ceiling, but they were reinforced: it was obvious that the place was used as a cell. Much later the door of his tomb opened, and the ruddy face of Sergeant García appeared in the threshold. Despite his weakness, Diego speculated that he could stun the good sergeant with a minimum of violence by pressing the place on the neck that Maestro Escalante had taught him when he was being trained in the combat skills of La Justicia. He did not want to get his old friend in trouble with Moncada. He might get out of his cell, but he could not escape from the hacienda; it would be better to wait. The rotund sergeant placed a jug of water and a bowl of beans and rice on the ground.

"What time is it, my friend?" Diego asked, simulating a cheerful manner he was far from feeling.

García twisted up his face and counted on his fingers.

"Nine o'clock Tuesday morning, you say? That means I have been here two nights and a day. How well I've slept! Do you know what Moncada intends to do?"

García shook his head.

"What is the matter? Do you have orders not to talk to me? Very well, but no one told you not to listen, isn't that right?"

"Ummm," the other nodded.

Diego stretched, yawned, drank the water, and slowly ate the food, which tasted delicious, he told García, all the time chatting about old times: the wonderful adventures of childhood, the courage García had shown when he confronted Alcázar and trapped a live bear. It was with good reason that he was admired by the boys at school, he concluded. That was not exactly how the sergeant remembered those days, but Diego's words fell like a healing balm on his bruised spirit.

"In the name of our friendship, García, you have to help me get out of here," Diego concluded.

"I would like to, but I am a soldier, and my duty comes before anything else," García replied in a whisper, looking over his shoulder to be sure no one was listening.

"I would never ask you to fail in your duty or do anything illegal, García, but no one could blame you if the door was not tightly bolted—"

There was no time to continue the conversation because a soldier came to tell the sergeant that Don Rafael Moncada wanted to see the prisoner. García straightened his jacket, stuck out his chest, and clicked his heels with a martial air, but he also winked at Diego. He pulled his childhood friend up by his arms and led him to the main salon, almost carrying him until Diego could stand on legs that had fallen asleep from lack of use. Sadly, Diego noted the changes once again; his home looked like a barracks. He was put in one of the salon chairs, arms and chest roped to the chair back and ankles tied to its legs. He realized that the sergeant was only half carrying out his obligation; the bonds were not tight, and with a little manipulating Diego might get free, but there were soldiers everywhere. "I need a sword," he whispered to García at a moment when the other guard moved a few steps away. García nearly choked with fright at such a request. Diego was asking too much; how could he give him a weapon under such circumstances? It would cost him several days in the stocks, say nothing of his military career. He patted Diego fondly on the shoulder and left the room, head lowered and feet dragging, as the guard took up his post in a corner to watch the captive.

Diego sat in that chair for more than two hours, which he used to loose his hands from the rope, but he could not untie his ankles without attracting the attention of the soldier, an emotionless mestizo who looked like an Aztec statue. He tried to draw him over by pretending to choke, then later begged him for a cigar, a glass of water, a handkerchief, but nothing succeeded. The guard's answer was to clutch his weapon tighter and observe him through eyes of stone barely visible above his prominent cheekbones. Diego concluded that if this was Moncada's strategy to take the wind out of his sails and bend his will, it was working very well.

Finally, about mid-afternoon, Rafael Moncada made his entrance, apologizing for having to inconvenience a person as refined as Diego. Nothing farther from his mind than to make him uncomfortable, he said, but given the circumstances, he'd had no choice. Did Diego know how long he had been in the servant's room? Exactly the number of hours he had been locked in Tomás de Romeu's secret chamber before his aunt came to get him out. A curious coincidence. Although he, Moncada, had a good sense of humor, that joke had grown a little stale. At any rate, he was grateful to Diego for having taken Juliana off his hands; to marry a woman of inferior station would have ruined his career, just as his aunt had warned him so often. But . . . he wasn't there to talk about Juliana, that was a closed chapter. He supposed that Diego—or should he call him Zorro?—would like to know what lay in store for him. He was a criminal of the same caliber as Alejandro de la Vega: a chip off the old block. They would capture his aged father, there was no doubt about that, and he would wither away in a cell. Nothing would give him more pleasure than to hang Zorro with his own hands, but that was not his role. He would send him back to Spain in chains and under heavy guard, to be tried where he had begun his criminal career and where he had left enough evidence to be sentenced. In the government of Ferdinand VII the law was applied with proper firmness, not as it was in the colonies, where authority was a travesty. In addition to the crimes committed in Spain were those in California: Zorro had attacked El Diablo prison, caused a fire, destroyed royal property, wounded a soldier, and conspired in the escape of prisoners.

"It is my understanding that an individual called Zorro is the author of those offenses," Diego replied. "And I believe that he also has some of the pearls in his possession. Or would you, Excellency, prefer not to discuss that matter?"

"*You* are Zorro, de la Vega!"

"I wish I were, the man seems fascinating, but my delicate health does not allow me such adventures. I suffer from asthma, headaches, and heart palpitations."

Rafael Moncada thrust a document in Diego's face—for lack of a secretary written in his own hand—and demanded that he sign it. The prisoner argued that it would be unwise to sign something when he did not know what it said. At the present time, he could not read it, he said; he had forgotten his glasses and he was near-sighted, unlike Zorro, who, he had heard, had deadly aim with a whip and a lightning-fast sword. No half-blind man could do such things, he added.

"Enough!" Moncada exclaimed, slapping Diego.

Diego was awaiting a violent reaction, but nevertheless had to exert great effort to control himself and not attack Moncada. This was not yet his opportunity. He kept his arms behind him, holding the rope, as blood from his nose and mouth dripped onto his shirt. Sergeant García erupted into the room and stopped short when he saw his old friend bleeding, not knowing which side to take. Moncada's voice shook him from his stupor.

"I did not call you García!"

"Excellency . . . D-Diego de la Vega is innocent. I told you he could not be Zorro. We j-just saw the real Zorro outside," the sergeant stammered.

"What the devil are you saying!"

"It's true, Excellency, we all saw him."

Moncada shot out of the room, followed by the sergeant, but the guard stayed where he was, pointing his weapon at Diego. At the entrance to the garden, clearly outlined against the violet sky of evening, Moncada saw the theatrical figure of Zorro for the first time, and for a moment he was paralyzed with surprise.

"Follow him, imbeciles!" he shouted, pulling out his pistol and firing without taking aim.

A few of the soldiers flew to get their horses, and others fired their weapons, but the horseman had already galloped away. The sergeant, more interested than anyone in discovering Zorro's identity, leaped on his mount with unexpected agility, dug in his spurs, and set off in pursuit, followed by half a dozen of his men. They disappeared toward the south, over hills and through woods. The masked man had a good start and knew the countryside, but even so, the distance between him and the soldiers was closing. After a half hour, when the horses were beginning to foam with sweat, the sun had disappeared, and the soldiers were close to catching up, they came to the cliffs: Zorro was trapped between them and the sea.

Meanwhile, still under guard in the house, Diego thought he saw the secret door in the fireplace opening. It could only be Bernardo, who somehow had managed to get back to the hacienda. Diego did not know the details of what had happened outside, but from Moncada's curses, the shouts, shots, and whinnying of horses, he assumed that his brother had confused the enemy. To distract the guard, he feigned another loud attack of coughing, gave a push, overturned the chair, and hit the floor. The man ran over to him and ordered him to lie still or he would blow his brains out, but Diego noted that his tone was hesitant; perhaps the Aztec statue's instructions had not included killing him. Out of the corner of his eye he caught sight of a shadow moving toward them from the fireplace. He began coughing again, struggling as if he were choking, while the guard poked him with the barrel of his weapon, not sure of what to do. Diego let loose of the rope and beat his fists hard on the guard's legs, but he must have been made of granite; he did not budge. But at that instant the guard felt a pistol pressed to his temples and saw a masked man smiling at him wordlessly.

"Surrender, my friend, before a bullet gets away from Zorro," Diego advised from the floor, as he quickly untied the rope around his ankles.

The new Zorro took the soldier's pistol, threw it to Diego, who caught it, then quickly retreated toward the dark fireplace, winking. Diego gave the guard no opportunity to see what was happening behind him, he dropped him with a sharp blow to the nape of the neck dealt by the hard edge of his palm. The man lay unconscious for a few minutes, time Diego used to tie him up with the same rope that had been used on him; then he kicked out the window, taking care not to leave any sharp pieces around the frame—he planned to return that way—and disappeared through the secret door toward the caves.

When Rafael Moncada returned to the room, he found that de la Vega had vanished, and the man entrusted with watching him occupied his place in the chair. The window was broken, and the only thing the dazed guard remembered was a dark form and the glacial cold of a pistol against his temple. "Imbeciles, hopeless imbeciles, all of you!" was Moncada's only comment. At that moment half his men were chasing a ghost, while his prisoner had slipped away right under his nose. Despite the evidence, Moncada was still convinced that Zorro and Diego de la Vega were one and the same person.

Diego did not find Bernardo in the cave, as he had expected, but his brother had left several lighted candles, his disguise, his sword, and Diego's horse. Tornado was snorting impatiently, shaking his luxuriant mane and pawing the ground. "You will get used to this place, my friend," Diego told him, stroking the animal's sleek neck. He also found a wineskin, bread, cheese, and honey to help him recover from his recent bad treatment—apparently his brother did not overlook even the small details. He also had to admire his skill in having tricked the soldiers and appeared magically to rescue him at just the right moment. How elegantly and silently he had performed! Bernardo was as good a Zorro as he was; together they would be invincible, he concluded. There was no hurry about the next step; he would have to wait until late at night, when the excitement at the house calmed down. After he ate, he exercised briefly to relax his stiff muscles, and lay down a few steps away from Tornado to sleep the sleep of the just.

Hours later, he awakened rested and happy. He washed and changed his clothes, donned his mask, and even had energy to paste on the mustache. "Without a mirror it isn't easy to paste on hair from memory. It's a fact. I will have to grow a mustache. I look good with it. This cave needs a few comforts to facilitate our adventures, don't you think, Tornado?" He rubbed his hands, delighted at the boundless possibilities of the future; as long as he had good health and strength he would never be bored. He thought about Lolita and felt a tingle in the pit of his stomach not unlike the one he used to feel when he saw Juliana, though he did not connect them. Lolita's attraction was as fresh as if it were the first and only love of his life. Careful! He must not forget that she was Carlos Alcázar's cousin; for that reason alone, she could not be his bride. Bride? He laughed aloud. He would never marry—foxes are solitary animals.

Diego confirmed that his sword, Justine, slid easily in its sheath, put on his hat, and was ready for action. He led Tornado to the exit from the caves, which Bernardo had carefully camouflaged with rocks and brush, mounted his horse, and rode off toward the hacienda. He did not want to run the risk that someone would discover the secret passageway in the fireplace. He speculated that he had slept several hours; it must be after midnight, and possibly everyone except the guards would be asleep. He left Tornado beneath some nearby trees, reins trailing on the ground, sure that he would not move until he was called; the magnificent animal had absorbed Light-in-the-Night's teaching very well. Although the guard had been doubled, Zorro had no difficulty approaching the house; he looked through the window of the grand salon, the only room with light. A candelabrum lighted part of the room, but the rest was in shadow. Cautiously, he put his legs through the broken-out window, eased himself down, and, using the furniture lined up against the walls as cover, moved toward the fireplace, where he crouched behind the huge logs. At the far end of the room, Rafael Moncada was pacing back and forth, smoking a cigar, and Sergeant García, standing at attention and staring straight ahead, was trying to explain what happened. He had followed Zorro at full tilt toward the cliffs, he said, but just as he had him cornered, our subject had jumped into the sea rather than surrender. By then it was getting dark, and it was impossible to go too near the edge without falling on the loose rocks. Though they couldn't see the bottom of the precipice, they had emptied their guns. In conclusion, Zorro had broken his neck on the rocks and in addition was shot full of holes.

"Imbecile!" Moncada repeated for the hundredth time. "That person led you on a wild goose chase, and in the meantime de la Vega escaped."

An innocent expression of relief danced across García's ruddy face, but it disappeared instantly, wiped off by the knife-edge stare of his superior.

"Tomorrow you will go to the mission with a detachment of eight armed men. If de la Vega is there, arrest him immediately; if he resists, kill him. In case he is not there, bring me Padre Mendoza and Isabel de Romeu. They will be my hostages until that renegade surrenders. Is that understood?"

"But how can we do that to the Padre! I think—"

"Do not think, García. Your brain is not made for thinking. Obey and keep your mouth closed."

"Yes, Excellency."

From his refuge in the dark hollow of the hearth, Diego asked himself how Bernardo had managed to be in two places at the same time.

Moncada barked one last insult at García and dismissed him,

then poured himself a glass of Alejandro de la Vega's cognac and sat down to think, tilting back in the chair with his feet on the table. Things had gotten more complicated; there were too many loose ends. He would have to eliminate several people, otherwise he could not keep the pearls a secret. He sipped his liquor, examined the document he had written for Diego to sign, then went over to a sturdy cabinet and took out the bag. One of the candles had burned down and the wax dripped onto the table before he finished counting the pearls once more. Zorro waited a prudent time and then crept from his refuge with the stealth of a cat. He had taken several steps, clinging to the wall, when Moncada, feeling he was observed, turned. His eyes passed over the man who was a shadow among shadows, but instinct warned him of danger. He took up the ornate sword with the silver hilt and red silk tassels hanging over a corner of the chair.

"Who goes there?" he called.

"Zorro. I believe we have some unfinished business," the masked man said, stepping forward.

Moncada sprang up with a cry of hatred, determined to impale him on his sword. Zorro dodged the blade like a torero, with a graceful swirl of his cape, then moved to one side, again with elegance: his right, gloved hand on his sword, the left on his hip, eyes alert, and a broad smile beneath his mustache, by now slightly askew. As Moncada thrust a second time, Zorro unsheathed his sword, in no hurry, as if the other's insistence on killing him was a bore.

"It is a bad idea to fight in anger," he challenged.

He parried three two-handed slashes and a reverse, scarcely raising his own weapon, then retreated to build the confidence of his adversary, who attacked anew, without a pause. Zorro leaped onto the table and from there defended himself, almost as if dancing, from Moncada's frenzied attacks. Sometimes the sword passed between his legs; other sweeps he avoided with fancy footwork or parried with such force that the blades struck sparks. He jumped down from the table and hopped from chair to chair, closely pursued by Moncada, who was more and more maddened. "Do not tire yourself, it is not good for the heart," Zorro goaded him. At times Zorro faded into the shadows in the corners, where the weak light of the candles did not reach, but instead of using that advantage for a treacherous attack, he would reemerge on the opposite side of the room, summoning his opponent with a whistle. Moncada had very good command of his sword, and in a sporting situation he would have tested any adversary, but he was blinded with maniacal rage. He could not stomach this upstart who defied authority, disregarded order, made fun of the law. He had to kill him before he destroyed the thing Moncada valued most: the privileges that were his by birth.

The duel continued in the same vein, one desperately attacking and the other escaping with mocking ease. When Moncada was ready to nail Zorro to the wall, he would tumble to the floor and jump up with an acrobat's flourish two sword lengths away. Moncada at last realized that he was not gaining ground but losing it, and he began to yell for his men. At that point Zorro ended the game. With three long strides he reached the door and locked and bolted it with one hand, holding his enemy at bay with the other. He shifted his sword to the left hand, a trick that always disconcerted his opponent, at least for a few seconds. Again he jumped onto the desk and from there leaped to the great iron chandelier and swung above Moncada, landing behind him in a rain of one hundred and fifty dusty candles that had been there since the house was built. Before Moncada could realize what happened, he was disarmed and the tip of another sword was at his throat. The maneuver had lasted only a few seconds, but already soldiers were thumping and kicking the doors open and bursting into the salon with muskets at the ready. At least that is how Zorro told it on several occasions, and since no one has contested it, I must believe him, although he tends to exaggerate his feats. (Forgive this brief digression; let us get back to the salon.) He said that the soldiers trooped in behind Sergeant García, who was just out of bed and in his underdrawers, though his uniform cap sat squarely on his greasy locks. The men stumbled around on the candles, and several of them fell. One of their guns went off, and the bullet grazed Rafael Moncada's head and lodged in the painting above the fireplace, perforating the eye of Queen Isabel La Catolica.

"Careful, imbeciles!" bawled Moncada.

"Heed your chief, my friends," Zorro recommended amiably.

Sergeant García could not believe what he was seeing. He would have wagered his soul that Zorro was lying on the rocks at the bottom of the cliffs; instead, here he was, revived like Lazarus, with his sword pricking the neck of His Excellency. The situation was grave. Why then did he feel a pleasant fluttering of butterflies in his glutton's belly? He directed his men to leave—not an easy task because they were tripping over the candles, but once they left, he closed the door and stayed inside.

"Your musket and your sword, Sergeant, please," Zorro requested in the same friendly tone.

García lay down his weapons with suspicious promptness and then planted himself before the door, legs wide apart and arms crossed, imposing despite the underdrawers. It would be difficult to decide whether he was concerned about his superior's physical safety or preparing to enjoy the spectacle.

Zorro motioned Rafael Moncada to sit at the table and read the document aloud. It was a confession to having incited the colonies to rebel against the king and declare California an independent state. The punishment for such blatant treason was death; in addition the family of the accused lost its holdings and its honor. The paper was unsigned, and all that was lacking was the name of the guilty party. Apparently Alejandro de la Vega had refused to put his signature to it, and that was why Moncada was so insistent that his son sign.

"Very clever, Moncada. As you see, there is still space at the bottom of the page. Pick up the pen and write what I dictate," Zorro commanded.

Rafael Moncada was forced to add to the document the matter of the pearls, in addition to the crime of enslaving Indians.

"Sign it."

"I will never sign this!"

"And why not? It is written in your hand, and it is God's truth. Sign it!" the masked man ordered.

Rafael Moncada put his pen on the table and started to get up, but in three rapid moves Zorro's sword traced a Z on his throat, beneath his left ear. A roar of pain and wrath escaped Moncada. He put his hand to the wound and saw blood when he took it away. The tip of the sword was now pressing against his jugular and the firm voice of his enemy was saying that he would count to three, and if Moncada had not put his name and his seal on the paper, it would give him the greatest pleasure to kill him. One . . . Two . . . and Moncada signed the paper, then melted sealing wax in the candle flame, dribbled a few drops on the paper, and stamped it with the ring bearing his family crest. Zorro waited for the ink to dry and the wax to harden, then called García to sign as a witness. The sergeant wrote his name with painful concentration, then rolled up the document and, unable to disguise a satisfied smile, handed it to the masked man, who stuffed it into his shirt.

"Very well, Moncada. You will take the ship that is sailing within the next few days and leave here forever. I will keep this confession in a safe place, and if you ever return I will date it and present it to the courts; otherwise, no one will see it. Only the sergeant and I know of its existence."

"Keep me out of this, please, Señor Zorro," babbled García, terrified.

"As for the pearls, you have no worry, because I will take care of the problem. When the authorities ask about them, Sergeant García will tell the truth, that Zorro took them."

He picked up the bag, went to the window, and whistled. Moments later, he heard Tornado's hooves in the courtyard; he bowed and exited through the window he had prepared. Rafael Moncada and Sergeant García ran after him, yelling for the soldiers. Dark against the full moon, they saw the black silhouette of the mysterious masked man astride his magnificent steed.

"Hasta la vista, señores!" called Zorro, ignoring the bullets whizzing around him.

†

Two days later Rafael Moncada sailed on the *Santa Lucía* with his numerous pieces of luggage and the servants he had brought from Spain for his personal service. Diego, Isabel, and Padre Mendoza accompanied him to the beach, partly to make sure that he left and partly for the pleasure of seeing the fury on his face. Diego asked in an innocent tone why he was leaving so suddenly and why his throat was bandaged. To Moncada, the image of that foppishly dressed young man who sucked anise pills for his headaches and carried a lace handkerchief did not fit the image of Zorro, but he clung to the suspicion that they were one and the same person. The last thing he said to them as he stepped into the boat that would take him to the ship was that he would not rest a single day until he unmasked Zorro and had his revenge.

That same night Diego and Bernardo met in the caves. They had not seen each other since Bernardo's timely appearance at the hacienda to save Zorro. They went by way of the small door in the fireplace of the house, which Diego had reclaimed and was beginning to repair following the abuse of the soldiers, with the idea that as soon as it was ready he would bring Alejandro de la Vega back to live there. For the moment, his elderly father was convalescing, looked after by Toypurnia and White Owl, while his son cleared up his legal situation. With Rafael Moncada out of the picture, it would not be difficult to persuade the governor to lift the charges. The two young men were ready to begin the task of converting the caves into Zorro's den. Diego asked how Bernardo had been able to show up at the hacienda, gallop a long distance pursued by García's men, leap from the cliff, and simultaneously appear at the door in the fireplace. He had to repeat the question because Bernardo seemed not to fully understand what he was talking about. He had never been at the house, he gestured; Diego must have dreamed that episode. He had jumped his horse into the sea because he knew the terrain and knew exactly where to make the leap. It had been a black night, he explained, but the moon came out, lighting the water, and he was able to get a bearing on the shore. Once he reached land, he realized that he could not demand any more of his exhausted horse, and he turned him loose. He had to walk several hours in order to reach the San Gabriel mission by dawn. He had left Tornado in the cave much earlier for Diego to find; he was sure his brother would manage to escape once he distracted his captors.

"I tell you, Zorro came to the hacienda to help me. If not you, who was it? I saw him with my own eyes."

Bernardo whistled, and Zorro emerged from the shadows in all his splendor: black clothes, hat, mask, and mustache, with his cape over one shoulder and his right hand on the grip of his sword. Everything that distinguished the impeccable hero was there, down to the whip coiled at the waist. There he stood, flesh and blood, lighted by several dozen wax candles and two torches, proud, elegant, unmistakable. Diego was speechless, while Bernardo and Zorro smothered their laughter, savoring the moment. The mystery lasted for less time than they would have wished, because behind the mask Diego had recognized a pair of crossed eyes.

"Isabel." He laughed. "It can only be you!"

The girl had followed him when he went to the cave with Bernardo the first night they landed in California. She had spied on them when Diego gave his brother the black outfit and planned for there to be two Zorros in place of one. She had decided that three would be even better. It was not difficult to gain Bernardo's cooperation; she always got her way with him. Helped by Nuria, she cut the black silk that had been a gift from Lafitte and sewed her disguise. Diego argued that Zorro's task was man's work, but she reminded him that she had rescued him from Moncada's hands.

"More than one defender of justice is needed because there is so much evil in this world, Diego. You will be Zorro, and Bernardo and I will help you," Isabel concluded.

There was no choice but to do as she asked, because as her final argument she threatened to reveal Zorro's identity if they excluded her.

The brothers put on their disguises, and the three Zorros formed a circle inside the old Indian medicine wheel the brothers had laid out in their youth. With Bernardo's knife they each made a cut on their left hands. "For justice!" Diego and Isabel exclaimed in unison, and Bernardo signed the appropriate words. At that moment, when the mixed blood of the three friends dripped onto the center of the circle, they thought they saw a brilliant light surge from the depths of the earth and dance in the air for a few seconds. It was the *okahué* that grandmother White Owl had promised.

# Alta California, 1840

*U*nless you are very inattentive readers, you have undoubtedly divined that the chronicler of this story is I, Isabel de Romeu. I am writing this thirty years after I met Diego de la Vega in my father's house, in 1810, and many things have happened since then. Despite the passing of time, I am not afraid that I will set down serious inaccuracies because all through my life I have taken notes, and if I have memory lapses, I consult Bernardo. In the episodes in which he was present, I have been obliged to write with a certain rigor; he does not allow me to interpret events in my own manner. I have more freedom in other places. Sometimes my friend drives me out of my mind. They say that the years make people more flexible, but that is not true in his case. He is forty-five years old and is as rigid as ever. I have explained in vain that there is no such thing as absolute truth, that everything passes through the filter of the observer. Memory is fragile and capricious; each of us remembers and forgets according to what is convenient. The past is a notebook with many leaves on which we jot down our lives with ink that changes according to our state of mind. In my case, the notebook resembles the fantasy maps of Captain Santiago de León and deserves to be included in the *Encyclopedia of Desires, Complete Version*. In Bernardo's case, the book is as exciting as a brick. In the end, that exactitude has at least served him in bringing up several children and wisely overseeing the de la Vega hacienda. He has multiplied his fortune, and Diego's, who is still obsessed with dispensing justice, in part because he has a good heart, but more than anything because he so enjoys dressing up as Zorro and stirring up his cloak-and-dagger adventures.

I have not mentioned pistols, because early on Diego discarded them. He believes that in addition to being inaccurate, firearms are not worthy of a courageous man. All he needs in a battle is Justine, the sword he loves as he would a bride. He is a little too old for such childish behavior, but apparently he will never settle down.

I imagine that you are curious about the other characters in this story; no one likes to be left wondering after having read so many pages. Isn't that true? There is nothing as unsatisfactory as a book that does not tie up the loose ends, that new tendency to leave books half finished. Well, Nuria has white hair; she has shrunk to the size of a dwarf, and her breathing is noisy, like a sea lion's, but she is healthy. She does not plan to die; she says that we will have to kill her with a stick. Not long ago we buried Toypurnia, with whom I had an excellent friendship. She never came back to live among whites; she stayed with her tribe, but from time to time she visited her husband at the hacienda. They were fine friends. Nine years before, we had buried Alejandro de la Vega and Padre Mendoza, both of whom died during the influenza epidemic. Don Alejandro's health was never completely the same following his experience in El Diablo, but he rode his horse over the hacienda up till the last day of his life. He was a true patriarch; they do not make men like him anymore.

The Indian mail spread the news that Padre Mendoza was dying, and whole tribes came to bid him farewell. They came from Alta and Baja California, Arizona, and Colorado: Chumash, Shoshone, and many others. For days and nights at a time they danced, chanting funeral songs, and before they left they placed gifts of shells, feathers, and bones on his tomb. The most ancient repeated the legend of the pearls, about how the missionary found them one day on the beach, brought there by dolphins from the depths of the sea to aid the Indians.

As for Juliana and Lafitte, you can learn about them elsewhere, since I have no more room in these pages. Much has been written in the newspapers about the corsair, although his actual fate is a mystery. He disappeared after the Americans, whom he had defended in more than one battle, wiped out his empire on Grand Island. All I can tell you is that Juliana, who grew into a robust matron, had the originality to remain enamored of her husband. Jean Lafitte changed his name, bought a ranch in Texas, and is posing as a respectable man, though deep down he will always be a bandit, please God. The couple has eight children, and I have lost count of the grandchildren.

I would rather not mention Rafael Moncada. That wicked man will never leave us alone, but Carlos Alcázar was shot to death in a tavern in San Diego, shortly after Zorro's first intervention. They did not find the assassins, but it is said that they were paid killers. Who hired them? I would like to tell you it was Moncada when he learned that his partner had deceived him in the business of the pearls, but that would be a literary trick to round out the story, because Moncada was back in Spain when Alcázar was shot down. His death, well deserved, of course, left the field open for Diego de la Vega to court Lolita, to whom he had to confess his identity as Zorro before she would accept him. They were married only a couple of years before she broke her neck in a fall from a horse. Bad luck. Years later, Diego married a young woman named Esperanza, who also had a tragic death. But that story has no place in these pages.

If you would see me, dear friends, I believe you would recognize me, since I have not changed much. Beautiful women lose their beauty with age, whereas women like myself just grow old, and some even look better. I myself have softened with the years. My hair is specked with gray, and none has fallen out, as Zorro's has; I still have enough for two heads. I have a few wrinkles, which give me character, and I have almost all my teeth. I am still strong, bony, and cross-eyed. I do not look too bad for the life I have lived. Yes, I bear several proud scars from swords and bullets, suffered while helping Zorro on his missions of justice.

You will ask me, I have no doubt, whether I am still in love with him, and I will have to confess that I am, but I do not suffer because of it. I remember when I saw him for the first time; he was fifteen and I was eleven, we were mere children. I was wearing a yellow dress that made me look like a wet canary. I fell in love with him right then, and he has been my only love, except for a very brief period when I took a fancy to the pirate Jean Lafitte, but my sister won him away from me, as you know. That does not mean that I remained a virgin, certainly not; I have not lacked for willing lovers, some better than others, but none was memorable. Fortunately, I did not fall madly in love with Zorro, as most women do when they meet him; I always have kept a cool head in regard to him. I realized in time that our hero is capable of loving only women who do not love him back, and I decided to be one of them. He has tried to marry me every time he has lost one of his sweethearts or been made a widower—that has happened twice—and I have refused. Perhaps for that reason, he dreams of me after he eats a heavy meal. If I accepted him as a husband, he would soon feel trapped, and I would have to die to set him free, as his two wives did. I would rather await our old age with the patience of a Bedouin. I know that we will be together when he is an old man with feeble legs and a soft brain, when other, younger foxes have replaced him and, in the remote possibility that some lady opened her balcony to him, he would be unable to climb to it. *Then* I will avenge myself of the troubles Zorro has put me through!

And with that, dear readers, I conclude my narrative. I promised to tell you the origins of the legend, and I have done that; now I can devote myself to my own interests. I have had my fill of Zorro. The moment has come to put the final period to his tale.

P.S.

Insights,
Interviews
& More...

## About the author

## About the book

## Read on

# Life at a Glance

William Gordon

ISABEL ALLENDE was born in Lima, Peru, in 1942, and raised in Chile. She fled Chile after the 1974 assassination of her uncle, President Salvador Allende. She worked in Venezuela from 1975 to 1984 and then moved to America. She now lives in California with her husband, Willie Gordon.

She has worked as a television presenter, journalist, playwright, and children's author. Her first book for adults, the acclaimed *House of the Spirits,* was published in Spanish in 1982 and was later translated into twenty-seven languages.

Isabel holds to a very methodical, some would say menacing, literary routine. She writes using a computer, working Monday through Saturday, 9:00 A.M. to 7:00 P.M. She sits in what she refers to as a "small cabin off my garden." Her routine shuns music in favor of silence and includes at least one superstition: "I always start on January 8." Asked how she begins a book, she replies, "With a first sentence that comes from the womb, not the mind."

Her favorite reads include *One Hundred Years of Solitude* by Gabriel García Márquez,

**"** Asked how she begins a book, she replies, 'With a first sentence that comes from the womb, not the mind.' **"**

2

*The Female Eunuch* by Germaine Greer, *La Lumière des Justes* by Henri Troyat, *The Aleph* by Jorge Luis Borges, *Aunt Julia and the Scriptwriter* by Mario Vargas Llosa, and the poetry of Neruda.

She has written seven novels, among them *Portrait in Sepia* and *Daughter of Fortune*. She has also published a celebration of the senses entitled *Aphrodite*. *My Invented Country* is an account of her life in Chile. Her adventure trilogy for children—*City of the Beasts, Kingdom of the Golden Dragon,* and *Forest of the Pygmies*—takes as its themes the environment and ecology. ∾

# Isabel Allende on Destiny, Personal Tragedy, and Writing

*"Life is nothing but noise between two unfathomable silences." Can you describe that noise, what it is, and what it means to you?*

We have very busy lives—or we make them very busy. There is noise and activity everywhere. Few people know how to be still and find a quiet place inside themselves. From that place of silence and stillness the creative forces emerge. There we find faith, hope, strength, and wisdom. Since childhood, however, we are taught to *do* things. Our heads are full of noise. Silence and solitude scare most of us.

*You often talk and write about destiny. What is destiny for you?*

We are born with a set of cards and we have the freedom to play them the best we can, but we cannot change them. I was born female in the forties into a conservative Catholic family in Chile. I was born healthy. I had my shots as a child. I received love and a proper education. All that determines who I am. The really important events in my life happenedin spite of me. I had no control over them: the fact that my father left the family when I was three; the 1973 military coup in Chile that forced me into exile; meeting my husband Willie; the success of my books; the death of my daughter; and so forth. That is destiny.

66 The really important events in my life happened in spite of me. I had no control over them. 99

*Just before your daughter Paula went into a coma she said, "I look everywhere for God but can't find him." Do you, can you, have faith in God after such a tragedy?*

Faith has nothing to do with being happy or not. Faith is a gift. Some people receive it and some don't. I imagine that a tragedy like losing a child is more bearable if you believe in God because you can imagine that your child is in heaven.

*There is a lot of autobiographical writing in your books, but no actual autobiography. Do you imagine ever writing an autobiography?*

Yes, I suppose that one day I will write another memoir. I think that my book *Paula* has a lot about me. It is a kind of personal memoir, is it not?

*After finishing the Jaguar and Eagle trilogy you returned to writing adult fiction. Do you think you will write for children again? Do you have a favorite genre of writing as a reader or writer?*

I don't know if I will write for kids again. It is not an easy genre. I feel more comfortable writing for adults. I love to write novels with strong plots and characters. I am not a minimalist writer! But as a reader I like many kinds of books, mainly literary fiction. I don't read romance novels or thrillers. They bore me.

*Do you think that fiction has a moral purpose? Or can it simply be entertainment?*

It can be just entertainment, but when fiction makes you think it is much more exciting. However, beware of authors who pound their "moral messages" into you.

*You have written letters all your life, most notably a daily letter to your mother. You've also worked as a journalist. Which form or experience of writing helped you most when you started writing books?*

The training of writing daily is very useful. As a journalist I learned to research, to be disciplined, to meet deadlines, to be precise and direct, and to keep in mind the reader and try to grab his or her attention from the very beginning. ▶

**Isabel Allende on Destiny, Personal Tragedy, and Writing** *(continued)*

*Does writing each book change you?*

Writing is a process, a journey into memory and the soul. Why do I write only about certain themes and certain characters? Because they are part of my life, part of myself, they are aspects of me that I need to explore and understand.

*You loved science fiction as an adolescent. Do you think it inspired your love of creating other worlds?*

Science fiction reinforced the idea—planted by my grandmother—that the universe is very strange and complex. Everything is possible and we know very little. My mind and my heart are open to the mystery.

*You always start writing on January 8, but when do you finish? How long does it take you to write your books?*

I write approximately a book per year. It takes me three or four months to write the first draft, then I have to correct and edit. I write in Spanish, so I also have to work closely with my English translator Margaret Sayers Peden. And then I have to spend time on book tours, interviews, traveling, etc.

*Do you have a favorite among your books?*

I don't read my own books. As soon as I finish one I am already thinking of the next. I can hardly remember each book. I don't have a favorite but I am grateful to my first novel *The House of the Spirits,* which paved the way for all the others, and to *Paula,* because it saved me from depression.

*You grew up in Chile but now live in the United States. Which country has had the most influence on your writing and why?*

It is very easy for me to write about Chile. I don't have to think about it. The stories just flow. My roots are in Chile and most of my books have a Latin American flavor. However, I have lived in the United States for many years, I read mainly English fiction, I live in English, and certainly that influences my writing.

*The United States was, to a Chilean, an enemy country in the seventies. How did you overcome that and learn to love it?*

I know that most Americans are not responsible for the evil that their government has done or does today abroad. Most people in this country have good intentions. They think of themselves as decent citizens and moral human beings. They want to do good. But there is great ignorance and indifference. The United States has supported in other countries the kind of brutal tyranny that it would never tolerate in its own territory. If Americans were better aware of the atrocities that have been committed in their name and with their tax money they would be horrified.

*Emigrants "lose their crutches" and their past is "erased." Is that both positive and negative?*

When one moves to another country as an immigrant one loses everything that is familiar. To survive one needs to draw strength from within and make double the effort of the locals to get half the results. I think that it is important to remember the past and be proud of one's roots. ໑

# Loving Zorro, Writing *Zorro*
## A Conversation with Isabel Allende

*How were you approached to write a novel about Zorro? What was your first reaction?*

When the owners of the character's copyright—Zorro Productions—came to my house in August 2003 and asked me to write a novel about the masked avenger I felt a little offended. "I am a serious writer, I don't write on commission," was my first reaction. But then I thought it over and . . . well, the rest is history.

*What won you over to writing a novel about Zorro?*

As a young woman I was in love with Zorro. My stepfather, a diplomat, would leave important meetings to hide in his room and watch the daily *Zorro* TV series. My children dressed like Zorro every Halloween. I had seen the movie *The Mask of Zorro* three times with my grandchildren. So it was only natural that I would be tempted to write the novel. Also, the historical period in which the story happens is fascinating. In the nineteenth century the Western world was changing. The ideas of the French Revolution were spreading the concepts of democracy and freedom. It was the time of the Napoleonic Wars in Europe, the wars of independence in America, the pirates of the Caribbean, the secret societies, new discoveries in science, and the exploration of the world.

> " As a young woman I was in love with Zorro. "

*What kind of research was necessary to evoke the many settings of the novel?*

I researched for several months and went to all the places mentioned in the book, including Panama, New Orleans, and Barcelona. I believe that if the setting is historical and geographically accurate, the story is believable.

*This is a character with a lot of baggage. He's appeared in television, movies, pulp fiction, and comic books. How much reading and watching did you do before starting to write? To what degree were you influenced by the character's previous incarnations?*

I didn't even think of Zorro's previous incarnations. I wrote about his youth, before he became Zorro. This had not been done before. I felt free to invent whatever I wanted, as long as the final product would be a young man in a black outfit, with a cape, a mask, a hat, a whip, and a sword, who fights for justice.

*What drew you to the character's early years as the subject of your novel?*

For several decades we had seen Zorro in many different incarnations. It was hard to come up with something new. The creative team of Zorro Productions suggested that the youth of the character could be a good idea and I developed the story.

*What is your earliest memory of Zorro? Were you or your childhood friends animated by this legend?*

When I was growing up in Chile there was no television. Zorro came to my life a little later, when I was in my twenties and I watched the TV series with my young kids. Zorro is known all over the world, including remote villages in Asia and Africa. Where there is access to television Zorro has a presence.

*Douglas Fairbanks, star of the 1920 production* The Mark of Zorro, *was (according to* Encyclopedia Britannica*) "the first to ask a fencing master to advise on a production." As a novelist, how did you research the fencing scenes?*

The fencing scenes were the most difficult for me. Today readers are used to seeing action scenes on the screen filmed by four cameras with all ▶

kinds of special effects. Very few people are familiar with fencing terms, so I had to come up with a way of describing the fights without those terms. I took a couple of fencing classes and I read books on the subject, including a couple of books about how to choreograph sword fights for the movies.

*Speaking of cinematic treatments, have you a preference for any particular Zorro films?*

I loved the first silent movie done by Douglas Fairbanks. I also loved *The Mask of Zorro* and *The Legend of Zorro,* both with Antonio Banderas and Catherine Zeta-Jones. In these three movies I liked the humor, the athletics, and (of course) the stories.

*Johnston McCulley, the creator of Zorro, first introduced his character to the world in a novel published in 1919. Why is it that people are still captivated by Zorro?*

Zorro is not a magical character. He is not like Superman, Spiderman, or so many other fantastic action heroes. He is a human being, a man who loves life, who is willing to take risks to defend the underdog, and who is brave, funny, and romantic. Maybe his appeal is that we can all become Zorro given the right circumstances. We can all have courage and live life to its fullest. Just give us a mask, a cape, and a sword!

# Have You Read?
## More by Isabel Allende

*The following books are also available in Spanish from Rayo, and can be found at www.harpercollins.com.*

### DAUGHTER OF FORTUNE

Orphan Eliza Sommers goes on a search for love, but ends up on a journey of self-discovery. Brought up in the British colony of Valparaíso in Chile by the well-intentioned spinster Miss Rose (and her stuffier brother Jeremy), Eliza falls unsuitably in love with the humble but handsome clerk Joaquín. When he heads to California to take part in the 1849 Gold Rush Eliza follows him. But in the rough-and-tumble life of San Francisco our unconventional heroine finds that personal freedom might be a more rewarding choice than a traditional gold band on the wedding finger. *Daughter of Fortune* is now available in trade paperback from Harper Perennial.

"Brilliant."—*New York Times* Book Review

"Like a slow, seductive lover, Allende teases, tempts, and titillates with mesmerizing stories." —*Washington Post*

**PORTRAIT IN SEPIA**

As a young girl Aurora del Valle suffered a brutal trauma that shaped her character and erased from her mind all recollection of the first five years of her life. Raised by her ambitious grandmother, the regal and commanding Paulina del Valle, she grows up in a privileged environment. Aurora is free of the limitations that circumscribed the lives of women at that time, but is tormented by terrible nightmares. When she finds herself alone at the end of an unhappy love affair, she decides to explore the mystery of her past and to discover exactly what it was all those years ago that had such a devastating effect on her young life. Richly detailed and epic in scope, this engrossing story of the dark power of hidden secrets is intimate in its probing of human character and thrilling in the way it illuminates the complexity of family ties. *Portrait in Sepia* is now available in trade paperback from Harper Perennial.

"[R]ich with color and emotion and packed with intriguing characters."
—*San Francisco Chronicle*

## APHRODITE: A MEMOIR OF THE SENSES

Under the aegis of the Goddess of Love, Isabel Allende uses her storytelling skills brilliantly in *Aphrodite* to evoke the delights of food and sex. After considerable research and study she has become an authority on aphrodisiacs, which include everything from food and drink to stories and, of course, love. Readers will find here recipes from Allende's mother, poems, stories from ancient and foreign literature, paintings, personal anecdotes, fascinating tidbits on the sensual art of food and its effect on amorous performance, tips on how to attract your mate and revive flagging virility, passages on the effect of smell on libido, a history of alcoholic beverages, and much more.

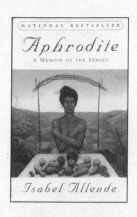

"Allende turns the joyous preparation and consumption of fine food into an erotic catalyst."           —*New York Times Book Review*

## THE INFINITE PLAN

Selling more than 65,000 copies and topping bestseller lists around the world, *The Infinite Plan* tells the engrossing story of one man's quest for love and for his soul. Gregory Reeves is the son of Charles, an itinerant preacher. As a boy Gregory accepts the endless journeying and poverty which is his family's lot, never questioning the validity of his father's homespun philosophy of life—the infinite plan. But as manhood approaches he finds himself possessed by a yearning to escape. Hankering after worldly wealth, he longs to break away from the teeming Hispanic barrio of downtown Los Angeles where his family

has finally settled. Gregory's quest, so different from his father's, takes him first to law school at Berkeley, next to the killing fields of Vietnam, and then into a headlong (and hedonistic) pursuit of the American Dream.

"Spellbinding. . . . Allende has caught the mood of our spiritually troubled times with uncanny precision and insight."

—*Miami Herald*

### MY INVENTED COUNTRY: A MEMOIR

Isabel Allende evokes the magnificent landscapes of her country, a charming, idiosyncratic Chilean people with a violent history and an indomitable spirit, and the politics, religion, myth, and magic of a homeland that she carries with her even today. The book circles around two life-changing moments. The assassination of her uncle Salvador Allende Gossens on September 11, 1973, sent her into exile and transformed her into a literary writer. And the terrorist attacks against her adopted homeland the United States on September 11, 2001, brought forth an overdue acknowledgment that Allende had indeed left home. *My Invented Country,* mimicking the workings of memory itself, ranges back and forth across that distance between past and present lives. It speaks compellingly to immigrants and to all of us who try to retain a coherent inner life in a world full of contradictions.

"[T]he book gets my undivided attention when it expounds on the relationship of the author to that country of hers, invented, imaginary, fictional, to the story of her family, which is itself invented memory, and to her vocation as a narrator." —*Los Angeles Times*

## PAULA: A MEMOIR

With an enchanting blend of magic realism, politics, and romance reminiscent of her classic bestseller *The House of the Spirits,* Isabel Allende presents a soul-baring memoir that seizes the reader like a novel of suspense.

Written for her daughter Paula when she became ill and slipped into a coma, *Paula* is the colorful story of Allende's life—from her early years in her native Chile, through the turbulent military coup of 1973, to the subsequent dictatorship and her family's years of exile. In the telling, bizarre ancestors reveal themselves, delightful and bitter childhood memories surface, enthralling anecdotes of youthful years are narrated, and intimate secrets are softly whispered.

In an exorcism of death and a celebration of life, Isabel Allende explores the past and questions the gods. She creates a magical book that carries the reader from tears to laughter, and from terror through sensuality to wisdom. In *Paula,* readers will come to understand that the miraculous world of her novels is the world Isabel Allende inhabits— it is her enchanted reality.

"Spellbinding. . . . In flawlessly rich prose, [Allende] shares with us her most intimate feelings."          —*Washington Post Book World*

## The Jaguar and Eagle Trilogy (for children)

### CITY OF THE BEASTS

*City of the Beasts* is Isabel Allende's first novel for children. It's an ecothriller in which fifteen-year-old Alexander Cold has the chance to take the trip of a lifetime. Parting from his family and ill mother, Alexander joins his fearless grandmother, a magazine reporter for *International Geographic,* on an expedition to the remote and dangerous world of the Amazon. Their mission, along with the others on their team—including a celebrated anthropologist, a local guide and his young daughter Nadia, and a doctor—is to document the legendary Yeti of the Amazon known as the Beast.

Alexander is amazed to discover under the dense jungle canopy much more than he could have imagined about the hidden worlds of the rain forest. Drawing on the strength of the jaguar, the totemic animal Alexander finds within himself, and the eagle, Nadia's spirit guide, both young people are led by the invisible People of the Mist on a thrilling and unforgettable journey to the ultimate discovery.

"Allende's writing is so vivid we hear the sounds, see the bright birds, smell, and even taste the soft fruit."      —*The Times* (London)

## KINGDOM OF THE GOLDEN DRAGON

Not many months have passed since teenager Alexander Cold followed his bold grandmother into the heart of the Amazon to uncover its legendary Beast. This time reporter Kate Cold escorts her grandson and his closest friend Nadia, along with the photographers from *International Geographic*, on a journey to another remote niche of the world in the Himalayas. The team's task is to locate its fabled golden dragon, a sacred statue and priceless oracle that can foretell the future of the kingdom.

In their scramble to reach the statue before it is destroyed by the greed of an outsider, Alexander and Nadia must use the transcendent power of their totemic animal spirits—Jaguar and Eagle. With the aid of a sage Buddhist monk, his young royal disciple, and a fierce tribe of Yeti warriors, Alexander and Nadia fight to protect the holy rule of the golden dragon.

"Imagining this utopian land and animating Buddhist beliefs is clearly fun for Allende, and her joy translates onto the page."
　　　　　　　　　　　—*San Francisco Chronicle*

### FOREST OF THE PYGMIES

Alexander Cold knows all too well his grandmother Kate is never far from an adventure. When *International Geographic* commissions her to write an article about the first elephant-led safaris in Africa, they head—with Nadia Santos and the magazine's photography crew—to the blazing red plains of Kenya. Days into the tour a Catholic missionary approaches their camp in search of his companions, who have mysteriously disappeared. Kate, Alexander, Nadia, and their team, agreeing to aid in the rescue, enlist the help of a local pilot to lead them to the swampy forests of Ngoubé. There they discover a clan of Pygmies who unveil a harsh and surprising world of corruption, slavery, and poaching. Alexander and Nadia, utilizing the magical strengths of their totemic animal spirits Jaguar and Eagle, launch a spectacular and precarious struggle to restore freedom and return leadership to its rightful hands.

"[C]aptures the romance of exotic travel. . . . [H]as at least two things Allende's adult fiction is known for: passion and politics." —*Philadelphia Inquirer*

Don't miss the next book by your favorite author. Sign up now for AuthorTracker by visiting www.AuthorTracker.com.

*Three Allende titles are available from Rayo in Spanish only:* Cuentos de Eva Luna, De Amor y de Sombra, *and* La Casa de Los Espiritus.